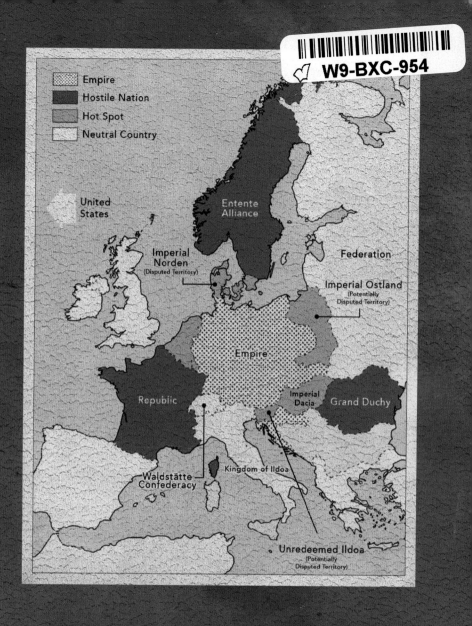

Empire

Hostile Nation

Hot Spot

Neutral Country

United
States

Entente
Alliance

Federation

Imperial
Norden
(Disputed Territory)

Imperial Ostland
(Potentially
Disputed Territory)

Empire

Republic

Imperial
Dacia

Grand Duchy

Waldstätte
Confederacy

Kingdom of Ildoa

Unredeemed Ildoa
(Potentially
Disputed Territory)

Deus lo Vult

THE SAGA OF TANYA THE EVIL

Deus lo Vult

〔1〕

Carlo Zen

Illustration by Shinobu Shinotsuki

YEN
ON

New York

The Saga of Tanya the Evil, Vol. 1

Carlo Zen

Translation by Emily Balistrieri, Kevin Steinbach
Cover art by Shinobu Shinotsuki

YOJO SENKI Vol. 1 Deus lo Vult
© 2013 Carlo Zen
All rights reserved.
First published in Japan in 2013 by KADOKAWA CORPORATION ENTERBRAIN
English translation rights arranged with KADOKAWA CORPORATION ENTERBRAIN
through TUTTLE-MORI AGENCY, INC., Tokyo.

English translation © 2017 by Yen Press, LLC

Yen On
1290 Avenue of the Americas
New York, NY 10104

Visit us at yenpress.com
facebook.com/yenpress
twitter.com/yenpress
yenpress.tumblr.com
instagram.com/yenpress

First Yen On Edition: December 2017

Yen On is an imprint of Yen Press, LLC.
The Yen On name and logo are trademarks of Yen Press, LLC.

The publisher is not responsible for websites (or their content) that are not owned by the publisher.

Library of Congress Cataloging-in-Publication Data
Names: Zen, Carlo, author. | Shinotsuki, Shinobu, illustrator. | Balistrieri, Emily,
translator. | Steinbach, Kevin, translator.
Title: Saga of Tanya the evil / Carlo Zen ; illustration by Shinobu Shinotsuki ; translation by
Emily Balistrieri, Kevin Steinbach.
Other titles: Yōjo Senki. English
Description: First Yen On edition. | New York : Yen ON, 2017-
Identifiers: LCCN 2017044721 | ISBN 9780316512442 (v. 1 : pbk.)
Classification: LCC PL878.E6 Y6513 2017 | DDC 895.63/6—dc23
LC record available at https://lccn.loc.gov/2017044721

ISBNs: 978-0-316-51244-2 (paperback)
978-0-316-51245-9 (ebook)

10 9 8 7 6

LSC-C

Printed in the United States of America

THE SAGA OF TANYA THE EVIL

Deus lo Vult

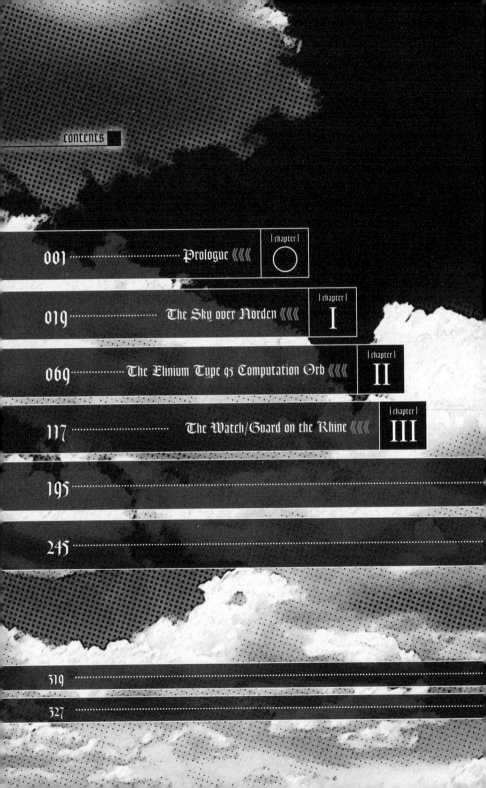

contents

Prologue

In the beginning, there was only light. Then came a gentle sensation of floating, a brief repose. There was warmth and a vague restlessness, provoking a desire to lose oneself. *Lose oneself? Yes, I've forgotten something. But what could it be? What could I have possibly forgotten?*

Before a chance to face such questions came along, *it* suddenly began shivering. A moment later, *its* mind registered the cold. A chill that pierced the skin. Such was the nature of a newborn babe's first brush with the crisp, raw air outside the womb. Not that there was time to realize.

But the sudden onslaught of alien yet once familiar sensations caused a panic. At the same time, *it* began writhing in distress, caught up in a violent struggle to breathe. The pain was nearly unbearable as the lungs—the entire body, each and every cell—cried out for oxygen. Unable to remain calm enough for rational thought, all *it* could do was thrash about.

The overwhelmed, unresponsive senses ravaged by agony left no option other than flailing in pain. Strangled by these things, *it* easily lost consciousness. Fully free of the emotions of a human who hadn't wept in ages, the body sobbed instinctively.

Awareness faded, and the concept of self grew muddled. Upon awakening, *it* saw the ashen sky. The world was blurry... Or perhaps that was due to hazy vision? Everything seemed distorted, as if seen through glasses with the wrong prescription.

Despite having been out of touch with human emotions for so long, even *it* was unsettled by such clouded eyesight. It was impossible to discern even rough shapes.

Chapter 0

After nearly three years of objective time, having finally begun to regain a sense of self, *it* was struck with utter confusion.

What is this? What happened to me? This vessel couldn't maintain awareness for very long, and the memory of being placed in it had yet to surface. So when *its* fading consciousness just barely registered an infant's wails, *it* found the cries shameful yet failed to understand why.

Perhaps mature adults didn't cry, but babies certainly did. Infants were supposed to be protected and given equal opportunities, not despised. Thus, with a deep sense of relief, *it* relegated the vague shame to a dark corner of *its* mind, blaming it on the lack of a clear consciousness.

The next time a hazy sense of comprehension dawned, *it* was absolutely bewildered, not surprisingly. If memory served correctly, *it* should have been on a Yamanote train platform. Yet after coming to, *it* was somehow inside a massive Western-style stone building, getting *its* mouth wiped by a nun who seemed to be a nursemaid. If this was a hospital, then a safe assumption could be made that there had been some sort of accident. Blurry vision could be explained by injury as well.

Yet now that *its* eyes could see clearly in the poor lighting, *it* could make out nuns in old-fashioned dress. And the inadequate illumination…apparently came from anachronistic gas lamps, unless things were not what they seemed.

"Tanya, dear, say 'ahh.'"

At the same time, *it* noticed a bizarre lack of electrical appliances nearby. In the civilized society of 2013, here was a room devoid of electronics yet riddled with items long considered antiques. *Are they Mennonites or Amish? But…why? What am I doing here with them?*

"Tanya, dear. Tanya!"

The situation was a difficult one to grasp. The confusion only deepened.

"Come now. Won't you open your mouth for me, dear? Tanya?"

I don't understand. That was precisely the problem. That was why *it* hadn't noticed the spoon the nun held out. But of course. Even if *it* had, never in a million years would *it* have dreamed of eating the proffered food. Surely the spoon was meant for this "Tanya, dear."

But while all these thoughts were swirling around, the nun finally lost her patience. With a sweet yet stern smile that brooked no argument, she stuffed the spoon into *its* mouth.

"You mustn't be picky, dear. Open up!"

It was a scoop of vegetables that had been stewed into mush. But that single spoonful also thrust the truth at hitherto uncomprehending "Tanya."

Stewed vegetables. That's all the nun had stuffed into *its* mouth. But for the person in question, the action only made things more bewildering. *In other words,* it—*I*—*am Tanya.*

Thus, a cry arose from the depths of *its* soul: *Why?*

⟫⟫⟫   **AUGUST 14, AD 1971, UNITED STATES OF AMERICA**   ⟪⟪⟪

On August 14, 1971, a team of researchers led by Dr. Philip Zimbardo commenced an experiment under a grant received from the United States Department of the Navy's research institute, the Office of Naval Research (ONR). The planned duration was a mere two weeks. Its objective was to collect rudimentary data on an issue with Marine Corps prisons that the navy was also facing.

The participants recruited for this experiment were normal college students of sound mind and body. On the second day, however, the team ran into a serious ethical problem.

Not only did those who had been assigned to be guards verbally abuse and degrade the ones in the prisoner role, despite the prohibition of such behavior, but also acts of physical violence had become increasingly prevalent. As a result, the team was forced to discontinue the trial only six days after it began.

This later became known as the Stanford Prison Experiment. Ironically enough, notwithstanding the pitfalls of the project's dubious morality, the results were replete with implications for the field of psychology. Along with its predecessor, the Milgram Experiment, the Stanford Prison Experiment demonstrated something fundamental about human nature.

Chapter 0

In an isolated space, individuals would submit to power and authority, while those in dominant positions would wield it without restriction. Analysis of this phenomenon, known as "obedience to authority," yielded shocking results. Surprisingly, this deference had nothing to do with a person's rationality, sensibility, or personality but was instead the product of remarkable deindividuation triggered by the assignment of roles.

In other words, the two experiments demonstrated that human behavior was dependent on environment. To put it in extreme terms, the results indicated that anyone could have worked as a guard at Auschwitz, regardless of their individual disposition or moral character.

In the end, environment played a larger role defining an individual than personal traits. When he learned in university that humans were that sort of creature, it felt right rather than wrong.

Surely everyone learns as part of compulsory education in elementary school that all people are born equal. Children are taught that they are all equally unique and irreplaceable. But it isn't hard to find disparities that contradict those familiar maxims.

Why is the kid sitting in front taller than me?
Why are some of my classmates good at dodgeball and others aren't?
Why can't the kid next to me solve such a simple problem?
Why can't the kids in the back be quiet when the teacher's talking?

But in an elementary school environment, children are expected to be "good." They are told that everyone is different yet special. They are terrified that if they don't follow etiquette, they will be "bad." And so the "good kids" strive to avoid becoming "bad."

By the time they begin attending cram schools to prepare for entrance exams, the good kids secretly look down on the bad kids and make a point of avoiding them. They will enter a good junior high, followed by a respectable high school, and then a prestigious university. These people are on the fastest track, doing their best within the rules and regulations presented to them.

In order to remain good in that environment, students have to do exactly as they are told and always meet everyone's expectations. Just as they are told, they spend day after day hunched over textbooks and reference books, competing with classmates for grades. As they lead such a life, those engaged in the fierce battle of college entrance exams come to view idlers as losers. Within an environment where grades determine everything, it's only natural for high achievers to hold poor students in contempt. On the other hand, the majority of those successful students don't consider themselves especially bright. After all, it has long been the case that whenever a regular student shows even a little pride, the truly gifted in their grade put them in their place.

One student might be having a hard time while the kid next to him is nonchalantly entering the International Physics or International Mathematical Olympiads. It takes more than a little effort to sit shoulder to shoulder in a classroom with geniuses for whom comprehending all the material is a given. Despite the warped perspective, they have a strong enough grasp on reality to diligently pursue their studies.

Whether they like it or not, all college-bound students know the truth. If they want an income comparable to what their parents possess, they have to attend a good university and get a decent job, at the very least. This group is driven by a strong, youthful desire to succeed. But along with that desire comes the fatal fear of failure. As such, they have no choice but to chain themselves to their desks.

After struggling in that harsh world, the best students pass the entrance exams for universities worthy of being called "prestigious." Then the game changes. Many are forced to realize that they have entered a world where people are no longer evaluated by grades but the question *What have you achieved?*

Those who can adapt to the sudden paradigm shift and new environment do. *Obey the rules. Search for the loopholes. Sneer at the guidelines despite being bound by them.* In the end, everyone learns that rules are necessary to make the system run smoothly.

Freedom without laws means anarchy; laws without freedom means tyranny. So as much as they hate restrictions, they fear unlimited freedom.

He failed to understand people who came late to class. He couldn't see the value of people who drank themselves into oblivion. He couldn't comprehend the sporty types who droned on about the power of the human spirit.

But when he encountered the Chicago school[1] and saw how these works applied rationality to the relationship between rules and freedom, he was ecstatic. After all, it meant that he could stay on track as long as he played by the rules. He managed to exude the appearance of a diligent university student while hiding the fact that he was a nerd. In essence, that's what it meant to be free within the confines of the rules.

As far as friends were concerned, he enjoyed hanging around with his high school buddies as well as a bunch of kindred spirits he met in college. This was his moratorium until he went out into the world, although he still made sure to improve himself and develop connections. Naturally, he invested in his human capital by acquiring language skills and culture to a point. That plus his educational background, according to the theory of signaling, would project society's ideal of a "good college student."

Surprisingly, what people like him needed wasn't actually talent; the most important thing was looking good on paper. In other words, recruiters preferred someone who passed the company's exam with flying colors, came from a prestigious school, and was a familiar face to the interviewers. It was for precisely that reason that the headwind of the recession's employment slump didn't particularly blow against him.

After all, he was on his mark at a different starting line compared to everyone else. In truth, he had the advantage—this contest was completely rigged. From the get-go, it was only natural to visit alumni who came from the same alma mater. In fact, he'd gone so far as to accept invitations to grab a few drinks with the recruiters from human resources.

Now just imagine if someone on the employment side attended the same junior and senior high or was a graduate of his college. They would offer guidance about what qualities recruiters looked for at such and such company and how to present himself in the interviews.

---

[1] **Chicago school**   The Chicago school (of economics) is, in brief, a delightful school of economic thought hailing the market mechanism. Some extremists even use economic values to analyze social issues across the board—drugs, families, education, immigrants, and so on. You can learn more from the slightly dated book *The Economics of Life: From Baseball to Affirmative Action to Immigration, How Real-World Issues Affect Our Everyday Life* or by checking out the latest on this blog: http://www .becker-posner-blog.com.

As long as he combined his various connections and did decently in the interviews, he would have nothing to worry about. If he wasn't too picky, he could get a job that put food on the table for sure. By obediently doing whatever he was told, he became a societal gear that performed well at a steady pace. Somewhere along the line, he began to view himself as a mature adult in that work setting.

Job satisfaction? Individuality? Creativity? He was a cog in society, and he could assert that the content of his work didn't matter as long as he received fair compensation. From the company's perspective, the ideal employee was required to complete assignments promptly while maintaining a level of quality appropriate to their salary. Adhering to the company's philosophy in all things, the ideal employee would take initiative and search for ways to turn a profit. It wasn't terribly difficult for him to adapt to life as a slave to corporate logic.

Heartless? Robotic? Callous? Impersonal? Concerns of that nature only troubled him in the very beginning. He was terrified of people who howled ingloriously or resorted to violence; it wasn't possible for him to comprehend such disgraceful behavior. But with time, he acclimated. It was just like school.

Humans are creatures designed to adapt to change. When it comes down to it, conforming to the environment means assuming one's assigned role—a guard acts like a guard, and a prisoner acts like a prisoner. The days passed uneventfully, alternating between work and hobbies. Naturally, work progressed efficiently. Following company directives and avoiding mistakes as much as possible were important to not let work cut into precious free time.

Consequently, by the time he entered his thirties, he not only was close to matching his parents' income, but also had most definitely gotten on the promotion track. He was highly regarded for his devotion to the company and loyalty to the executives, and he climbed the advancement ladder in the human resources department. He even received a touchstone award as a section manager.

Yes, that's right. I had an important job. There is absolutely no reason—none whatsoever—for a nun to stuff a spoonful of boiled vegetables down my throat. I'm being quite the gentleman, not even screaming at the top of my lungs to demand what right you have to call me "Tanya, dear."

Growing impatient, he attempted to stand in order to launch his "why me" tirade. That was when it hit him. His head throbbed as unpleasant memories suddenly surfaced.

>>> **FEBRUARY 22, AD 2013, TOKYO, JAPAN** <<<

"Why? Why me?!"

Why? It's obviously because your cost performance is abysmal! On top of that, you've been absent quite a lot. And as another nail in the coffin, I have a report from your direct supervisor claiming that you've taken out multiple cash advance loans of who knows how much. Plus, you adamantly refuse to see the occupational physician at every turn. In conclusion, it's clear that you're becoming a costly employee. More importantly, we can't have you causing some sort of scandal and marring the company's good name.

I'd love to ask you, *Is there any reason we should keep you on board?* But due to certain laws, I must conceal such sentiments deep within my heart and respond with as much tact as possible.

"You've already failed to complete your PIP twice. The company gave you a perfectly reasonable order to attend PIP completion training, but you refused. And you have numerous unexcused absences." False courtesy? That's just fine. It's not prohibited by law. This is a for-profit corporation, not a charity for the societally inept. "That said, as you've contributed to our company for such a long time, I believe a voluntary resignation, rather than a disciplinary dismissal, would better serve both our interests."

While this may be a huge waste of time, it's still part of the job description.

"I've never had to go on client visits before! How the hell does that count as training?!"

"It combats deteriorating work results by helping supervisors under-stand sales representatives and find ways to improve their managerial practices. With that in mind, we felt it was necessary for you to undergo this training."

Even if it's all in a day's work, this is still tiring. It's an utter pain to deal with this endless parade of weeping and wailing employees who try to cling to us. If you think crying will change things, go for it. In some parts of the business world, that's a valid tactic, but if you think it'll work after calling me things like a "heartless monster," "boss's pet," or "cyborg," you've got another think coming.

I've always known that I wasn't the best. Unable to compete with the geniuses and unable to match the gifted through hard work and dedication, my personality has grown utterly warped. I'm a mess of convoluted complexes.

Truly benevolent people are awe-inspiring. As far as hypocrisy is concerned, I have what society as a whole deems to be a healthy level, but knowing I'm insincere makes me scoff all the more.

Despite being self-aware about this—how ghastly I am—I still harbor the arrogant belief that I'm superior to the inept fool wailing before me. At least as far as cost performance is concerned, I've maintained superior results. So even though restructuring departments assigned for consolidation through layoffs is a pain, I take it seriously. From here, I should shoot straight up the ladder and land in the chair for director of human resources.

My life should have been fairly smooth sailing.

...*Should have been.*

After reflecting to that point, a rather unpleasant event resurfaces.

It's said that humans are political animals by nature, but apparently the type of humans who get pink slips are animals who prioritize primal emotions over logic or commonly accepted taboos. When you get down to it, aren't there more people who, unlike the "good" academic elite, act out their impulses? The director specifically warned me to watch my back at the station, but I couldn't see what he was getting at.

Wham! Something slams into me. I fall from the platform in bizarre slow motion. The moment I see the train, my consciousness cuts off.

When I wake up, I encounter an unspeakable injustice.

"Are you really living creatures of flesh and blood?"

"Sorry, who are you?"

An elderly man taken straight out of a cookie-cutter novel heaves a heavy sigh as he observes me. It has to be one of three possible explanations:

1. I miraculously survived, and a doctor is examining me, but I'm unable to perceive it correctly. In other words, it's possible either my eyes or my brain have suffered serious trauma.

2. I'm dying, and this is either a delusion or a hallucination. Maybe my life is flashing before my eyes.

3. I've woken up in the real world after mistaking a dream for reality. I could still be half-asleep.

"…The whole lot of you have the most twisted personalities. What a bunch of nonsense in that head of yours!"

Did he just read my mind? If he did, that's an extremely indecent and unwelcome violation of my privacy, as well as an intrusion on confidential matters.

"I certainly did. But it's disgusting, reading the minds of uncompassionate disbelievers."

"Well, what do you know…? I never dreamed the devil was real."

"You come up with the craziest ideas!"

Only God or the devil is capable of defying universal laws. If God existed, he wouldn't ignore all the injustice in the world. Thus, this world lacks a God. Therefore, Being X before me is the devil. I rest my case.

"…Are you disbelievers trying to work your Creator to death?"

"You disbelievers"? In the plural. Which means he's referring to others along with me. Should I take comfort in the fact that I'm not alone? Hard to say. While I don't specifically hate myself, I don't particularly love me, either.

"I mean deranged souls like yours! They're everywhere these days. Why aren't you attaining enlightenment as humanity advances? Don't you want deliverance from your earthly bondage?"

"I suspect this is simply the result of that social progress."

Rawls's theory of justice[2] is absolutely wonderful, but actually applying it is unrealistic. Humans have already been divided into the haves and the have-nots. It might be interesting as a hypothetical proposal, but in reality, people can't give up what they have for the sake of others. Isn't it natural to pursue material gain in this life rather than worry about the future? Even so, what does it matter?

If I'm dead, what's going to happen to my soul? Let's discuss this constructively. What really matters is what comes next.

"I'll just throw you back into the cycle of life and death—you're getting reborn," replies the self-proclaimed God, Being X. The answer the stranger gives is quite simple. Ah, I bet he's fulfilling his duty to explain. Yes, work is not something to be taken lightly. I can appreciate the importance of assuming responsibility and acting in compliance with the law. Like it or not, as a member of society—of an organization—I should probably indicate that I understand how we're to proceed.

"Very well. In that case, go ahead and do your thing."

For starters, I plan on doing a better job of watching my back in my next life. I've learned that there are two types of people, rational and irrational, so I'll undoubtedly need to revisit behavioral economics.

"…Ugh! I've had it."

But the words he whispers under his breath leave me perplexed.

"Huh?"

"Can't you guys get your acts together? Far be it from any of you to attain enlightenment and break free from the cycle when you lack so much as a shred of faith!" he complains, making this awkward for me.

Quite honestly, I have no idea what this Being X (self-proclaimed

---

[2] **Rawls's theory of justice**   A theory that greatly influenced political philosophy. What would happen if we had to create rules to live by starting from scratch, when we don't know our place in society? After that discussion, Rawls explores what fair laws might look like. His conclusions are broadly split into two principles. The first guarantees individual equality and freedom, while the second permits inequality for the purpose of special consideration and equal opportunity for the weaker members of society. It's important to note that while he considers everyone equal, he takes the stance that the wealthy should pay progressive taxes to care for the weak and provide support for the needy. Also known as the Liberty Principle, the Difference Principle, and the Fair Equality of Opportunity principle.

God) is so mad about. I realize elderly folks can be quick-tempered, but when someone who appears to hold a fairly senior position flies into a blind rage, they can be hard to read. If this were an anime, you could write it off as a gag, but in the real world, you rarely get that luxury.

"Humans these days have strayed too far from the universal laws! They can't tell right from wrong!"

Geez! Being X can preach all he wants about universal laws, but I don't know what the hell he's talking about. And if these laws really do exist, it's annoying that he didn't give notice beforehand. He's asking for too much if he expects people to adhere to laws they've never seen, let alone consented to. I can't comprehend something that hasn't been put into words. To my knowledge, I've yet to develop telepathic powers.

"I gave you the Ten Commandments, you know!!"

1. Thou shalt have no other gods before me.
2. Thou shalt not take the name of the Lord thy God in vain.
3. Remember the Sabbath day, to keep it holy.
4. Honor thy father and thy mother.
5. Thou shalt not kill.
6. Thou shalt not commit adultery.
7. Thou shalt not steal.
8. Thou shalt not bear false witness against thy neighbor.
9. Thou shalt not covet thy neighbor's wife.
10. Thou shalt not covet thy neighbor's property.

The commandments suddenly flow into my mind via telepathy or something, but...uh...well...damn. See, I was born in a polytheistic region of the world, where we're used to letting things slide as "religious tolerance." So I'm honestly not sure how to react to someone bringing up the commandments. For the record, I happen to honor my parents, and I've never killed anyone. But I am biologically male. Certain sexual instincts are programmed into me. I can't do anything about those. It'd be another story if I had handled the programming, but I didn't.

"I'll regret that as long as I live!"

Just how long does God live? I'm mildly intrigued, if only from a purely academic perspective. Unsurprising, given my inquisitiveness and curiosity.

I've never fought the desire or impulse to murder someone. Sure, it's refreshing whenever I nail a head shot in an FPS, but that doesn't make me any more bloodthirsty than the next guy. I'm pro–animal rights; I'm pretty sure that at the very least, I've taken posters to support a movement trying to decrease the catch-and-kill programs of various shelters.

"So you didn't dirty your hands, but you still derived pleasure from the act of killing, didn't you?!"

I've never stolen anything, borne false witness against another, or had the joy of winning a married woman's heart. Above all else, I've gone through life as an upright, honest person. I fulfilled my duties at work and adhered to the law, and I can't recall ever actively defying the prescribed conduct for a human being. If I had been sent to war, maybe I would have received a revelation from God while parachuting that I should dedicate my life to farming shrimp. Unfortunately, my experience serving in the military was limited to online games.

"Have it your way! If you won't repent, I'll have no choice but to impose a fitting punishment on you!"

I'd like to think these false accusations can only go so far. And why me? But as a rule of thumb, I know it's never wise to let things pan out on their own.

"Wait a moment if you will."

"Stuff it!"

…I wish you wouldn't lose your temper. If you're claiming to be the Supreme Being (even if you're not doing a very good job at it), I wish you were a bit more mentally mature. I suppose you could even keep the disguise. This one lawyer acquaintance of mine comes across as two completely different people depending on whether he's in court or online. The man even has a full social life! While I don't expect you to reach his level of perfection, you could try a bit harder…

"I'm already overworked managing seven billion souls!"

The Bible says, "Be fruitful, and multiply, and fill the earth." Admittedly, my knowledge of the matter is limited, but I'm fairly certain mankind has been faithfully obeying this doctrine. I can just see Malthus turning in his grave. You might say that mankind has "multiplied" too much. If you're going to work in administration, I wish you'd keep track of the orders you issue. Hopefully you won't get fired after losing the respect of all your subordinates.

At any rate, seeing as you're the administrator, you should take full responsibility for what you said.

"A-all I ever get are you skeptics without a speck of faith! You're putting me in the red!"

Honestly, isn't that a flaw in the business model?

"I won't take this from someone who broke his contract! Aren't you guys the ones who wanted a shot at enlightenment in the first place?"

You can't expect me to know unless you notify me. That's what I really think. It's common sense to send important documents through certified mail, and really, a contract should be handed over in person. It would have been nice if you had left the contract on a permanent medium, too.

"You bowed before the laws of God, you know!"

Uh, the scientific advances these days are almost magical. Overdeveloped science is practically magic. Hooray for natural science! All is right in the world. In our society of abundance, neither a sense of crisis nor devotion will spread without an impending threat. That's why we desperately cling to things. Unless driven into a corner, people won't cling to religion.

"...So in other words, it's like...that...uh...you know?"

You say I know, but I'm afraid I won't until you tell me.

There's nothing to be done for the increasingly flippant way I am treating Being X. But not being able to have a conversation is truly frustrating. What can we do about that? At this point, if there were some sort of interpreter service, I'd hire them without too much concern for the fee.

"You're driven by lust, you lack faith, and you don't fear your Creator. Furthermore, you can't find a moral fiber in your entire body."

Objection! I want to shout. I'm not that bad. Based on moral and social norms, I'm not nearly as horrible as you make me out to be!

"Spare me! You're all the same, or we wouldn't turn around and repeat this song and dance every time one of you is reborn!"

Uh, like I said before, the real problem here is overpopulation. Or, at the very least, it has to do with our lengthening life spans… There's this thing called average life expectancy. Yes, of course there's also Malthus's "An Essay on the Principle of Population."[3] You haven't read it? The way we multiply like rats, you must have your hands full. It's not as though we're doing anything in particular; I believe a simple analysis will show that your business model is flawed.

"If the number of believers increased along with the population, things would be fine!"

Yeah, so there's the flaw in your business model. All I can say is that you did a sloppy job psychoanalyzing your consumer base. That's a structural mistake from back in the planning stages.

"So in your case, you don't believe it's because you were a male, living in a world of science, ignorant of war, and unthreatened?"

…Huh? What? I, uh, think I might have screwed up.

Okay, let's calm down. Right now, Being X is as dangerous as the director of human resources was during that mess when another company poached a bunch of our veteran engineers. I understand the situation. And I've already considered how to deal with it.

"So if I remedied that, even the likes of you would awaken to faith?"

Uh, aren't you jumping to conclusions? Why don't you calm down? I'll admit, I said that overdeveloped science has clouded faith. But, God, please calm down! That's right, relax. If we could feel the grace of the Lord, that would solve everything. Oh, but of course, I understand. I know all too well how graciously you watch over us, as you are guiding me right now. Yes, I fully understand, so would you be so kind as to lower your hand? And might I add, I'm afraid the part about how I'm ignorant of war was a misunderstanding.

"Groveling won't get you anywhere now!"

Wait, my Lord! Please remember that neither magic nor miracles have

---

[3] **"An Essay on the Principle of Population"** Mr. Thomas Robert Malthus's classic masterpiece on demography. According to his theory, population grows geometrically, but the food supply (resources to sustain life) only grows arithmetically. In other words, it's a brutal and blunt theory stating that mankind will quickly expand until all usable resources are stretched to the limit. Even without God's decree to multiply, our population would always increase to barely sustainable levels. It's a terrifying concept, yet surprisingly, it cannot be ignored.

been proven real in our world. Anyone who claims to have seen a miracle smells fishier than a fish market. Same with your existence! And for another thing, it doesn't matter whether you're male or female. It's obvious that both genders have sexual desire!

"Enough already. You've made your case. Anyway, I'm gonna try this out."

"Excuse me?"

"I'm going to test this on you!!!!"

So, yeah… That about sums up the memory. I wish I could forget it.

The Sky over Norden

Why am I out here fighting in a war? My conscious self, assigned the identity of Magic Second Lieutenant Tanya Degurechaff, poses the question again as I clasp an orb in tiny hands, leave the rifle that's serving as my scepter on the ground, and soar into the sky.

How did I end up like this?

"Fairy 08 to Norden Control. Fairy 08 to Norden Control. Acknowledge."

A single dot stands out over the gloomy, overcast skies of Norden. This miniscule speck blending into the clouds is none other than one of the Empire's mighty aerial magic officers. Due to a sick twist of fate, if I take a look at myself, I'm cursed to see a little girl participating in a war. The uniform and computation orb are proof that I'm a soldier. Through scientific means, the sphere I carry controls the supernatural phenomenon known as "formulas," which allow mages to influence the world with their will. As implied by the modern name of the ancient orbs, courtesy of science and magic, this fruit of magic engineering has unraveled the numeric values of the world.

My mission is to act as an artillery observer from a predesignated airspace while maintaining a comfortable ground speed at an altitude of six thousand feet.

"Fairy 08, this is Norden Control. We read you loud and clear. No problems tracking you."

Talk about a piece of cake. This is just an air support mission at the border between the Empire and the Entente Alliance. But this vigilant spotter magician, maintaining her flight formula with the computation orb around her neck, must look surprisingly small.

And I *am* pint sized. It makes people wonder if my age has hit double digits yet. Moreover, I have a petite frame, even for a girl. Comparing Tanya's height to the physically blessed body of my previous life is absolutely mortifying. It was miserable to hear that Tanya's neck was too narrow to properly wear the aviation throat mic headset.

"Fairy 08, roger. I've reached the mission airspace. Reading you loud and clear," I say. I'm already resigned to the voice spewing from my mouth, though the high-pitched tone makes me feel like something's haunting me. No matter how accustomed to hearing it I become, I can't stand it. Whenever my tongue can't keep up with my mind and I end up nearly biting it or stuttering, I feel utterly humiliated.

"Norden Control, roger. Proceed to your assigned mission."

Of course, the army is seriously something else for having no qualms even after hearing that girlish partial lisp. Perhaps it's simply a matter of being pragmatic, but the military has adopted the position that a person's aptitude for the magic arts can be a sufficient condition for military enlistment, since aerial mages focus on air combat. In the Empire, where that has been taken to its logical conclusion, age limits for mages are a thing of the past. Hence why the army has no problem deploying someone who looks young enough that they should still be with their guardian, if only as an artillery observer.

"Fairy 08, roger. The area is all clear. I say again, area is all clear."

"Norden Control, roger. There is an infantry battalion assigned to your observation area. Call sign Goliath 07. Barring new orders from airspace control, continue to perform your observation duties until the area is pacified. Out."

The demands of the Empire's geopolitical position have played a large role in this method of procuring human resources. Surrounded by world powers due to historical circumstance, the state has been forced to face potential enemies in every direction. Securing the military strength needed for their large territory's national defense is a perpetually pressing issue. In order to resolve the problem, the General Staff's frenzied efforts have reached the point where they'll exploit anyone within reach.

"Fairy 08, this is the Provisional Corps Artillery Battalion, call sign Goliath 07. How copy?"

This being the case, the army apparently thinks nothing of tossing a young girl out to the border on air patrol if it can use her. I am quite literally a child soldier.

"Goliath 07, this is Fairy 08. Reading you loud and clear. I've confirmed the enemy infantry advance. Sending data now. Acknowledge."
I bet the sight of a young girl flying through the air, her adorable voice confined to a matter-of-fact register, must seem terribly surreal. When you get down to it, a proper army is supposed to be composed of proper adult soldiers. That's only common sense.

But it isn't just static in the signal—hearing women's and children's voices on the mic has become commonplace among mages. The armed forces have a practical exception in place for just about everything. More than anything, the harsh days in service exhaust decent people, so any initial discomfort over allowing a girl to participate in combat has long since worn off.

"Goliath 07, roger... Base piece starting calibration fire."
That's why the aerial mage enlisted as Second Lieutenant Tanya Degurechaff is serving as an artillery observer during this battle in the northern reaches of Norden, calmly and skillfully delivering periodic reports via the radio set on her back that's nearly as big as she is. But actually, it isn't as though I don't question or doubt what I'm doing flying out here.

"Impact confirmed... Looks like a close hit. Looks to be within the allowable error margin of ten meters. Fire for effect."

"Goliath 07, roger. Commencing fire mission now."
While my blue eyes attentively look below, there's no denying they hold a glint of frustration. Why was I reborn into this world, made the opposite gender, and now stuck fighting a war?

The most annoying things are the physical changes. A child's body is horribly inconvenient. At first, even though girls develop quicker than boys, the size difference was simply too great to maneuver my body with the same equilibrium I had trusted for years. On top of that, I've keenly felt how much I've become a helpless child on multiple occasions since joining the army.

I couldn't hold a gun. It was too big. In the end, I couldn't aim worth a damn, and the recoil ended up bruising my shoulder. When I sparred, there was a streak of pity on my partner's face whenever he threw me.

Until I could see the world as three numeric vectors with the computation orb and get the hang of superposing the realm of numbers with magical interference formulas, I had to crawl on my belly with arms and legs that refused to obey me. Because they depended on brains, not brawn, the magic arts were the only area where I succeeded, if only barely. The constraints of my body couldn't trouble me, and I could soar across the sky as long as I superposed the world with my formulas.

Perhaps I was able to overcome any reservations I might've had about magic due to its usefulness as a tool. But why must I use a tool simply because I have it?

Oh, I get it. It's essential that we're able to use an ICBM[4] when the time calls for one. That's why it's necessary to make provisions for their maintenance, drills, and operations. That said, is there any reason we need to have ICBMs in the first place? In that same vein, gossip about seemingly strained relations with neighboring nations is hardly new.

The Empire and Entente Alliance have been struggling for quite some time with unofficial border conflicts. But in the international politics arena, at least, there's nominally no dispute over this territory.

The problem isn't acknowledged because the Empire is such an incredible powerhouse. As far as Tanya is concerned, it's a simple matter, comparable to how nations surrounding the Soviet Union independently avoid border disputes with it.

…Well, was. The only regrettable part of discussing the Empire's strength is that it has to be described in the past tense.

Multiple isolated accidents have occurred along the border. There has been "unintentional" fire on both sides, which led to firefights due to misunderstanding. All such incidents were resolved at the level of

---

[4] **ICBM**   Abbreviation for intercontinental ballistic missile. Dr. von Braun said, "The rocket worked perfectly, except for landing on the wrong planet." Then they went and came up with the most extreme use possible for it.

the local commanding officers, but there's no denying the continually mounting tension.

Under normal circumstances, if the Empire entered a state of "semi-war" at this point, Tanya's position would allow her to fall back to the rear echelon and serve in noncombat roles. After all, Warrant Officer Tanya Degurechaff had been a cadet attending the military academy up until the outbreak of hostilities. A greenhorn would only get in the way on the front lines, so it would be normal for her to serve somewhere in the rear, such as in the Technical Arsenal or Logistical Command, once the Empire began making preparations in anticipation of war.

Yet despite the unsettling state of world affairs, Tanya's optimistic superiors decided this was all merely brinkmanship diplomacy. Thanks to them, she was stuck completing her training out in the field. The flight patrols she took part of in coordination with the army were only intended to serve as an extension of the education she was receiving at the academy. Having lost her opportunity to withdraw to the rear, Tanya was officially commissioned as a second lieutenant and deployed upon completing her training. She was also assigned the call sign Fairy 08. Clearly, people were obnoxiously comparing her to a fairy. Based on outward appearances alone, she was a puny kid—really—an incredibly *young* child. On top of that, she had blue eyes that seemed to reflect a strong will and short blond hair tied back to make it easier to manage. And considering her pale, clear skin complexion as well, her call sign did start to seem appropriate.

The trouble began right after Tanya officially assumed her new post in the field with the border army. The administrative unit was composed of direct promotes from the magic officer training school and local relocations. As a new transfer, Tanya was forced to accept orders to stand by for forty-eight hours. Assuming it was a traditional training exercise conceived by the brass to test their capacity for coping and maintaining alertness, Tanya had reluctantly suited up and gone on duty twenty-four hours ago.

Then the emergency warnings came flying in from security outpost positions scattered along the border with such impeccable timing that it surely made the devil smile. Apparently there had been signs that the

Entente Alliance was planning to conduct a large-scale cross-border operation.

The Entente Alliance's new policy direction had already been a cause for concern. The reshuffling of executives, resulting from a change in administration, and the ensuing rise in nationalism had required a dramatic shift in doctrine. Honestly, the Entente Alliance's operation was carried out with such ridiculously poor planning that not only Tanya but also everyone in the Imperial Army was left wondering, *Why now of all times?* Before they knew it, the Entente Alliance was scattering notices demanding imperials to withdraw—a declaration of war.

In other words, the Entente Alliance had insisted, *Imperial soldiers are to withdraw from our nation's territory within twenty-four hours.* Perhaps a lowly company officer was incapable of understanding the Entente Alliance's reasons, but maybe the assumption was that the Empire would avoid full-blown military engagement since regional conflicts were extremely politically sensitive.

If the Entente Alliance couldn't face reality, it's possible it would go down in history for all the wrong reasons. *Are they stupid?* Or so people wondered. *Perhaps they devised some great plan that will lead them to victory?*

Despite being unable to comprehend the Entente Alliance's agenda or objective, the Empire nevertheless maneuvered its finely tuned bureaucracy and military organizations according to protocol. They played it by the book and made preparations to intercept enemy forces. As a cog for her country, Tanya had no choice but to put in work commensurate with her pay. Admittedly, at this point she rather optimistically predicted that all this was mostly for internal propaganda.

After all, there was no way the nearby Federation would want two neighboring nations fighting on its doorstep. Everyone expected this to hold the Entente Alliance in check, whether through mediation or intimidation. Moreover, the Commonwealth and Republic were propping up the Entente Alliance. Surely they would put the brakes on this suicidal advance for fear that all the aid they had provided would be wasted. Yes, the vast majority of officers and soldiers were certain of the future. Military folk were realists by nature, after all.

It goes without saying, but the Entente Alliance didn't stand a chance facing the Empire head-on. Everyone was certain one nation or another would step in to arbitrate, and then the politicians and diplomats from the two opposing nations would hash something out.

But the scenario that had been inconceivable to all—except for the Entente Alliance, apparently—became reality and astonished every human alive in this day and age.

"Disarm and surrender to the advancing Entente Alliance Army or leave immediately."

From a commonsense perspective, the Entente Alliance's demands could only be described as "shocking"; yet even then, the Empire continued to monitor the situation, incredulous. While reports that the Entente Alliance had crossed the border were not entirely unexpected, it was difficult for the Empire to see how such a thing could have actually come to pass.

It seemed so preposterous that Lergen, an officer in the Imperial Army General Staff, would much later voice his suspicion: "...We were so unable to determine what the Entente Alliance was hoping to achieve that it made more sense to suspect our own military leaders of scheming and acting behind closed doors."

Doubts and ambiguities aside, the pragmatic Imperial Army responded soberly by ordering an immediate response to the Entente Alliance's major cross-border operation. While there was hesitation and confusion over the Entente Alliance's agenda, once signs indicated that a potential conflict was brewing, the military began amassing supplies in preparation. All of the Great Army divisions that formed the core of the Empire's military power then assembled by rail from Central. The Imperial Army was so efficient that it pulled all this off without incident. In fact, everything went so smoothly that it was internally regarded as an "organizational victory."

But although the Empire had procured an abundance of supplies and even gone so far as to mobilize troops, it was continually troubled by partial skepticism. *Really? They'd never!*

The Empire was known for its superior armaments, even among the great world powers. During times of peace, it would deploy a corps-sized garrison to the border under the pretext of routine patrolling. The additional corps mustered to meet the minimum number of reserves, just in case, included Tanya's unit. With information warfare in mind, the Empire even extended invitations to mass media from various countries. So as usual, the military was completely prepared, but the "usual" was precisely what made everyone wonder, *Is the Entente Alliance really going to invade?*

Tanya never dreamed the Entente Alliance would, without any semblance of justification, launch their inferior forces across the border in an offensive against a military titan, right in front of the media.

But truth is stranger than fiction. Tanya naturally found the turn of events utterly bewildering. If she could have spoken freely, she probably would have described it as witnessing the moment a death wish took concrete form.

"It's war! Everyone, I repeat, it's war! A war has just begun! The Empire has declared war on the Regadonia Entente Alliance for violating the border! Moments ago, the Entente Alliance Army began crossing over at multiple locations! Imperial Army troops are rushing to the border one after the next to respond! We've received reports that fighting has already broken out in some areas!"

But there was no denying the sight of friendly armored forces and other troops rapidly deploying below her. At the same time, the war correspondents raised their voices to transmit the latest news to the whole world over the airwaves.

...Surely the Empire would only pull this publicity stunt with complete confidence in victory. Well, given its vastly superior national might, level of technology, and armaments, it was an obvious choice to make the next move with an eye on victory.

If journalists were reporting the developments at the border right up to the declaration of war, it meant the brass was relaxed enough about the situation to think about publicity; spreading propaganda about the fair, mighty Empire couldn't hurt the political situation, either. Furthermore, the Entente Alliance crossing the border first provided legitimate justification. And by admitting the mass media, they were essentially announcing this was a war they would win. Even in this alternate world, national leaders who would consider allowing journalists to freely cover losing battles only existed in fantasy. The fact that imperial officials had nothing to hide, or at least very little, was proof that everything was going smoothly.

All of these factors help ease Tanya's nerves. Honestly, when she first heard that she was getting sent to the north for field training, she wanted to yell, "I hope you rot!" to the military state that was planning to work a young girl to the bone out in the borderlands. She wanted to curse Being X for getting a good, decent person mixed up with this world to begin with.

But Tanya is completely fine with the Empire presenting her with an opportunity to climb the ranks in a one-sided conflict like the Gulf War. This war is winnable, and the soldiers are the winners. Her mission is simply to take out enemies from the safety of the sky and get promoted. While extraordinarily unexpected, it isn't a bad deal. In fact, it's better than "not bad"—Tanya's been presented with a one-in-a-million chance. Border patrol missions are simple but dangerous, and even if you get results, there is a tendency for the brass to claim your achievements don't officially exist thanks to some "political consideration" ridiculousness. As a result, patrol duty in the disputed Norden Territory has a reputation within the Imperial Army as an "all pain and no gain" endeavor.

It isn't easy to rack up achievements there, and to make unfavorable conditions worse, like it or not, Tanya Degurechaff has the physique of a fair-skinned, blue-eyed, blond-haired little girl. On top of that, a glance at her records shows that she's a military academy graduate on track to become an elite mage. If she's selected for an assignment and fails, there would be no way around the bad PR saying the army had ruined a young person with a promising future. Setting her capabilities aside and going strictly by outward appearance, even Tanya feels put off by her doll-like face. If I weren't Tanya, I wouldn't want anything to do with her outside of the call of duty.

This objective perspective has been consistent since she was commissioned in the Imperial Army. Before, Tanya didn't have a bad reputation among the instructors, but the fact that her work contributions matched her pay grade simply couldn't wipe out the stains of rumors about the "little girl mage." The only way around it was to produce even greater results, but as much as she wanted to do just that, the opportunity had never arisen—until now.

In other words, even though Tanya is a mage, no one recognizes her as one. She's treated like a baby getting in everyone's way. In a sense, they're claiming that she's defective. It's insulting how they barely pay attention to her career. Ironically, the Empire wound up giving her active combat duty in a situation where its army handily dominated the battlefield—an unexpected stroke of good fortune for her first battle.

It seems the war will continue for a while under favorable conditions. If Tanya hopes to keep surviving, she needs to use that time to gain status and influence. I also want her to secure some connections. To that end, it's imperative for her to play a proper role in this predictable war and rack up honors and commendations.

Having thought that far, Tanya unconsciously curls her rosy lips into a grin as she reassesses the situation. *This might not be so bad after all.*

"Actually, couldn't this work out wonderfully for my career...? I should consider this a pretty sweet deal." No one is around to overhear her egocentric whisper. Even if someone were flying nearby, the howling of the imperial artillery gunnery below would have drowned out her voice, not to mention the endless echo of shells making landfall and exploding. If I think of the cacophony as a VIP view of the Fuji Firepower Review[5] but with several times the roaring artillery, it isn't so bad.

"Fairy 08, this is Goliath 07. Requesting firing results."

"Goliath 07, this is Fairy 08. Good effect on target. I say again, good effect."

Tanya's job is simple. She only needs to calmly observe and report to the artillery batteries. Flying around with the radio set weighing her down while maintaining the flight formula isn't easy, but the Imperial

---

[5] **Fuji Firepower Review**   The biggest military exercises viewable in Japan. They're open to the general public to help civilians better understand the Japanese Self-Defense Forces, but people observe the large-scale maneuvers with the same attitude as watching a fireworks show. Thank you for all your hard work on the drills.

Army's computation orb is up to the task. Due to the disputed nature of the Norden Territory, many of the troops spread across the north are temporary transfers from Central Command. On paper, Tanya is only on loan from Central after she completed her field-training program.

If she takes her duties to heart, she could definitely return to the garrison in Central eventually. A position in the rear echelon isn't just a pipe dream. Once she's chosen as an officer magician in the rear, there's a distinct possibility Tanya could spend the rest of the war on standby under orders to defend the capital. Depending on how she looks at it, Personnel might have actually given her a golden ticket for developing a promising career in the long run.

Tanya was bitter when she first learned of the decision for her to train in the boring yet perilous north, but it just goes to show that there's no telling in life what could be a blessing in disguise. It's a bit late, but I should probably mail thank-you letters to my instructors with my latest updates as soon as possible. I have to build up my connections.

I can already foresee a rosy career. Even in the midst of battle, Tanya is in visibly high spirits as she spots for artillery on the battlefield.

"Fairy 08 to Norden Control. Please respond."

"This is Norden Control. Loud and clear."

The exploding shells below are satisfactorily laying waste to the Entente Alliance infantry who have crossed the national boundary. No matter how rugged the mountainous Norden terrain, once artillery is fully deployed, the soldiers casually advancing on the border become nothing more than targets. All the more so if the lay of the land leaves them exposed.

"Fairy 08, roger. Enemy currently under suppressive fire. I believe we've neutralized them. Enemy infantry is breaking ranks."

Maintaining a suitable distance, the exceptional artillery batteries fire at unarmored targets under the guidance of an observer in an area where ballistics data was precalculated beforehand. It's impossible that the barrage can fail to wipe them out. Down below, the swarms of once orderly infantry fall prey to the howitzers all too easily once they begin fleeing in all directions. As Tanya confirms the situation through a pair of binoculars, it becomes clear that any more will just be a waste of ammo.

"Norden Control, roger. Advance to patrol line two and guide suppressive fire against the enemy's primary infantry."

"Fairy 08, roger. Will advance and continue observation mission."

Her dispassionate exchange with Control is so free of noise that Tanya quietly thinks to herself, *I didn't expect radios to work so well in actual combat conditions.* The sky is overcast as far as her blue eyes can see, so it isn't as though weather will hinder enemy signal jamming. Yet the noise level can be termed the barely perceptible "clear." The signal is so clean it's almost ridiculous that she's carrying the massive airman radio set, which she was issued in anticipation of poor reception due to magnetic abnormalities caused by Norden mineral deposits. Tanya passes over the Entente Alliance's scrambling troops and feels genuinely puzzled as she advances in order to set her sights on the persevering remnants of the enemy army.

Seriously, what is the Entente Alliance trying to do? If they want to be targets for live-ammunition exercises, they should have said so. I would have volunteered to strafe instead of observe if I knew we were going to be hunting for dodoes instead of turkeys. The ones on bombing duty in this fight have escorts and control of the air, and if that isn't enough, they get dibs on the juiciest targets. I'm so jealous, I can hardly stand it.

"Fairy 08 to Norden Control. I've advanced to the designated position."

"Norden Control, roger. We see that. Relaying the situation to the artillery now. Continue to observe points of impact."

"Fairy 08, roger. Remaining on artillery observation until ordered otherwise. Over."

"Norden Control, roger."

〉〉〉〉   **THE SAME DAY, ENTENTE ALLIANCE, OVER NORDLAND**   〈〈〈〈

Dear God, why? How can this be happening? Lieutenant Colonel Anson Sue found himself asking the heavens, his rugged snow-tanned face contorted in distress. The volleys of Imperial Army heavy artillery resounded across the sky he had flown so many times as an Entente Alliance aerial mage. The battle unfolding below was completely one-sided. No, any sane soldier would describe it as a massacre, not a battle. It wasn't even an advance in soft-skinned vehicles—spongy infantry had marched in formation as if on parade through the wide-open hillocks toward a carefully arranged artillery position.

"This isn't what we were told! The bastards are opening fire!"

"Help! Medic! Hurry! Get over here!"

"Pull back! Retreat! Put down a smoke screen!"

"My arm! I lost my arm!"

"We still don't have air support…!"

"Command! Command, what's going on?! What's the situation?!"

The "border," according to the Empire, or the "provisional demilitarized zone," according to the Entente Alliance, was a type of pseudo-border established under the Treaty of Londinium.[6] If the Entente Alliance forces were simply going to waltz over the national boundary and strike the ever-diligent Imperial Army positions head-on, they should have known this would happen. No matter what was going on in the politicians' heads, the signals coming in over the radio proved that soldiers all across the battlefield were paying for an irredeemable political mistake with their lives—that's the *soldiers* paying with their lives.

"…Damn those bureaucrats to hell!"

The economy was in a slump, the gap between classes was widening, and the unemployment rate wasn't improving at all. Domestic problems that the Entente Alliance constantly faced threatened to throw it into a grave crisis due to destabilizing centripetal forces. The government was paying a horrifyingly high price for encouraging nationalism and exclusionism as a solution to those problems. No, the true horrors were yet to come.

---

[6] **Treaty of Londinium**   Some of it is completely original, while a good half is influenced by a real treaty. The reference was the 1852 London Protocol, which was signed as a diplomatic compromise in order to end a war. Since it wasn't a peace treaty, the nations involved violated it out of opposing interests. It's a sad fact of life that inconvenient international laws and treaties are broken with remarkable ease. But if a nation ignores them too much, they will face humanitarian intervention (especially if they have oil).

This spelled war—worse yet, a war the Entente Alliance had no hope of winning.

As such, Lieutenant Colonel Sue slung vulgar curses at the officials as he flew. He condemned them for their mistake in continuing to fan the flames of nationalism, refusing to face reality.

The Treaty of Londinium was an agreement regarding the border dispute between the Empire and the Entente Alliance with terms that were just barely tolerable, decided with the Commonwealth as a mediator. The provisional demilitarized zone that divided the disputed territory was in reality a national border, with administrative rights over the region serving as collateral to hold them to the agreement. All the treaty did was make a provisional show of respect for the assertions of both parties out of consideration for the Entente Alliance's claim of dominion.

"What part of this is 'just hiking under pressure'?!"

In short, the Entente Alliance was free to proclaim its actions as justified on the domestic front, but the treaty showed that in reality, the international community practically universally sided with the Empire. No matter how vehemently the domestic dreamers shouted that the territory was officially under dispute and fell within the Entente Alliance's sovereignty, others saw it as nothing more than the wailing of sore losers. Of course no one would take them seriously.

"Hiking?! This is their idea of hiking?!"

The Entente Alliance sent its military to parade around so it could patrol its own domain? Arbitrarily? That made no sense. Apparently all those politicians had started falling for their own publicity somewhere along the line. Sue wished someone would say it was all just a bad joke.

Some government spokesperson, or perhaps a salary thief only capable of spewing useless propaganda, actually had the balls to describe this invasion as a "highly organized hiking exercise under pressure" at a press conference. It was appallingly thoughtless.

"Cunningham! What's the status of our remaining forces?!"

"Sorry, sir. The signal is unstable and only getting worse. I can't get a grasp on the situation…"

The troops were in utter chaos. Of course they were. There was no way anyone could remain calm after mindlessly crossing the border

Chapter **I**

under the misconception that war wasn't a possibility—only to find the Imperial Army waiting in full formation to intercept and butcher them. No doubt this folly would go down in history.

"What about the command centers? Airspace Control or the Combat Direction Center is fine. Can you reach anybody?"

"The lines are a mess…and I can't call them, anyway; we weren't even assigned the right frequency."

First Lieutenant Cunningham, who was considered a veteran even in Sue's outfit, scowled as he fiddled with the long-range radio over his shoulders. The signals were tangled enough to stump a skilled veteran of the skies—proof that the Entente Alliance had kicked this operation off carelessly. If it weren't Sue's own country, no doubt he would have been flabbergasted.

"They would never violate the border without properly transitioning to a war footing first. Clearly, the Entente Alliance government is merely practicing brinkmanship diplomacy. At least, the Empire wouldn't play such a dangerous game if we weren't ready to risk war." A quote from an Imperial Army General Staff spokesman that Sue had read two days ago in a newspaper article. That comment said it all.

At most, the Entente Alliance's brinkmanship should have extended only to showing signs of increased military activity to discern how the Empire would react. The spokesman had offered a reasonable opinion, his face pulled into the scowl of a man who had bitten into something extremely unpleasant. Who would have thought the Entente Alliance would undertake military actions that risked the fate of the nation without preparing first?

"I don't care if you use short-range communications. At this point, you can hook up directly with the ground forces. We're gonna help the remaining troops retreat."

"Roger."

For better or for worse, Sue's battalion had been in a position at the rear when the border violation incident started. They were reorganizing after suffering heavy casualties in repeated irregular skirmishes near the national boundary. For units the size of a company or larger, it was possible to return to the capital to reorganize. Sue misread the situation precisely because he was often involved in operations that couldn't be written down in official records... If he and his men could fall back, then surely it meant the country had no intention of going to war; it meant the government was up to its usual propaganda.

Sue and his men—who were worthy of being called the best, even among the Entente Alliance's frontline troops—had no shortage of profanity to describe the sheer idiocy of the politicians and military statesmen. They were fully aware that their government was a cesspool of imbeciles. They just didn't realize the administration would pull a move so stupid it was beyond repair.

"Darton, sorry, but could you get in contact with the other troops? I want to get a solid idea about where we stand."

Due to their starting position, they had been too late to react and were now faced with the impossible task of helping troops retreat from hopelessly superior enemy forces while essentially blind. To make matters worse, not only were they unable to reach the designated forward controller, but things were so chaotic that they weren't even receiving support from the Combat Direction Center, which existed to guarantee at least the minimum necessary coordination between the mage troops, air corps, and ground forces.

"If necessary, we'll rendezvous with reinforcements. Platoons, in the event you get split up and can't regroup, you have the option of gathering into groups under whatever authority you can find."

"Commander, I got through!"

Sue snatched the proffered transceiver. From a brief exchange, he learned that the situation on the ground was completely unmanageable. The Entente Alliance was paying for its mistake of charging into wartime with the same chain of command they used during peacetime by losing any semblance of control. It was plain for anyone to see.

"Understood. In any event, we can't fight a war without some leadership. We need to do something about the bombardment causing all this turmoil. Agreed?"

The situation was so awful that instead of putting up a unified resistance, it was every unit for themselves. Even among their fellow soldiers on the battlefield with whom they could communicate, albeit barely, it was impossible to find a unit that saw the whole picture and possessed enough leadership to take the necessary measures.

"I fully agree. The artillery positions are certain to be fortified...but what about the observers?"

Sue had to agree that the most realistic and practical support he could offer, given the forces currently at his disposal, was to interfere with the enemy's indirect fire by eliminating their observers.

"Commander Sue! This just in from Ground Division Six. We can still observe and signal!"

"Great! See if they can find enemy artillery spotters."

As luck would have it, regaining communications with this division, which was maintaining discipline by a thread as it retreated, offered just the opportunity they needed.

"...Bingo! They're sending the numbers!"

Several observer mages were flying solo, not even bothering to conceal their locations. Based on the frequency of the encoded messages being sent at regular intervals, they were definitely encoded wavelengths unique to artillery spotters transmitting intel.

"Alone as expected, eh? They're taking us too lightly."

"Maybe, but aren't they behind a massive warning line?"[7]

Sue was aware of that. He wanted to groan, watching the way the imperial air corps and mage troops took the sure and easy route in the battle for air supremacy with a coordinated interception network. Clearly, they must have set up an air defense line adequate enough to allow support elements to fly solo.

"I swear, we're nuts to go to war with a military powerhouse. I should've taken my family and run."

"Commander Sue, I bet those imperial dogs are over there scratching their heads, wondering if war is supposed to be this easy."

"Good point. Let's hope they've let their guard down."

---

[7] **warning line**   While one can be used in a variety of ways, in this book, the word refers to an interception line or patrol line. Though an enemy breach means trouble, it's surprisingly easy to accomplish.

As he thought about how horrible everything had gotten, all Sue could do was turn to God.

...Honestly, God, where in the world did we go wrong?

The mission assigned to Tanya is important, but it's a monotonous job. All there is to do is keep an eye on impacting rounds with a radio and a set of observer gear. The task of processing the data in real time falls on the crew of the artillery arm that receives it. An operator at Norden Control provides the tactical commands.

The fact that we're winning probably has something to do with it, but my duty entails nothing more than watching the imperial artillery employ air bursts and time on target missions with praiseworthy expertise. Indeed, the Empire is a rising military force among the major world powers. And the army buoying that reputation is supplied with relatively new equipment, so much so that they've gone beyond believing in firepower supremacy and more in obeying it as accepted doctrine.

The Empire believes "bayonets never lie, but neither do resources." Accordingly, artillery is the Imperial Army's "gods of war." For someone like Tanya as well, these are deities much more absolute than some sketchy being who arbitrarily proclaims itself the supreme God.

After all, everyone on our side has been on alert for signs of war despite initial doubts. In other words, we were fully prepared to maintain air supremacy with an anti–air mage surveillance network in place. If I report any sporadic resistance or a glimmer of anti–air fire to the gods of war, they'll flatten the area with a single call.

This is a safe and sound job that's nonetheless well respected. I hope it stays like this. After all, I get to enjoy a prime view of the army's victory with a leading role in the firing of so much iron that it makes the Fuji Firepower Review seem cute.

It is by no means unpleasant to gaze out over our army effortlessly crushing the enemy from the secured safety of the sky. Artillery churns things up, then the infantry and armored vehicles advance in its wake. Us mages are in charge of air-ground support and combat air patrol. Soaring above the battlefield, the mixed fighter-bomber squadron go ahead as the vanguard for deep penetration. It's hard to say if things would go this smoothly even in a drill. Cheers to the General Staff for pulling this off so magnificently. I can't thank them enough for giving me such a safe and easy way to climb up the ranks.

I know it's a bit irreverent, but I'm afraid I have a hard time agreeing with General Lee's quote, "It is well that war is so terrible, otherwise we would grow too fond of it." For me, war is such a blast that I don't know what to do with myself.

"Norden Control to Fairy 08. Artillery commencing observed fire. Send your data."

"This is Fairy 08. Initial points of impact confirmed. Sending now. No need to adjust fire. I say again, no need to adjust fire. Initiate fire for effect."

First and foremost, our artillery is incredible for how it adheres to provided data with such astounding accuracy. The crews have to be awfully skilled to pull off everything from initial fire to consistent near hits with artillery integrated at the field corps level. Indeed, their performance is proof that the Empire isn't regarded as a military powerhouse for nothing. As a result, my workload is extremely light. Everything's great.

"Norden Control, roger. Watch out for stray shots. We plan to begin concentrated fire in two hundred. Over."

"Fairy 08, roger. Out."

I move west to distance myself somewhat from the battlefield as I ascend to a slightly higher altitude. I doubt the artillery's aim would slip that easily, but it would be outrageous if an ally inadvertently struck me down with shrapnel. And seeing as this is going to be concentrated fire, there'll be a whole slew of shells coming. The artillery guys will have a blast firing their hearts out, and I'll be looking on in envy. I need to stay out of their way so we can all enjoy doing our jobs.

Before long, the artillery begins launching such a relentless hail of iron that it flushes every war movie scene from my memory. As far as I can see from my spot in the sky, black specks are raining down all over toward the earth, and immediately after their explosive flames dissipate, chunks of what used to be humans fly in every direction before vanishing.

"Fairy 08 to Norden Control. Fire mission impact confirmed. Repeat."

"This is Norden Control with theater intelligence. Area α, blo— Bzzt…zzz."

"Norden Control, this is Fairy 08. Reception is poor. The interference is awful. Over."

Either there's electromagnetic interference or my equipment is simply acting up. Why couldn't it have happened at any time other than this crucial moment? Just to play it safe, Tanya starts checking if the problem has to do with the equipment strapped to her back by trying to radio Control again when it picks up an unexpected signal.

"Cherubim Leader issuing a theater warning! I say again, theater warning! Large number of incoming bogeys confirmed!"

It's not a regular message or an express message but an unknown warning. It's strange for the airborne controller to declare a theater warning when he's supposed to be patrolling on the first line. And since theater warnings generally aren't issued during intercept combat unless the warning line in front of patrol line one gets breached, a great deal can be read into that transmission.

Perhaps a fresh group of highly formidable soldiers has entered the fray. Well, this is war. It looks like the enemy won't go down so easily after all.

"...Norden Control to all airborne interceptors on standby. Transition ROE[8] from border patrol to mobile air defense. I say again, transition ROE from border patrol to mobile air defense."

Upon successfully regaining the connection, orders to intercept rushed in. Obviously, if bogeys have been spotted, the only option is to intercept them. That's why the Empire not only established massive formations on the front but also has reserves standing by in the air.

"Tally multiple bogey signals! Detecting formula interference! Consider them bandits! These are enemy signals! Take them out immediately!"

The tone of the incoming transmission hints at rough times ahead, even if the enemy is fighting in vain.

"Norden Control to all military forces. Norden Control to all military

---

[8] **ROE** Not "return on equity" but "rules of engagement." According to Professor Sumio Adachi's definition, the rules were established out of "a need, when it comes to combat operations, to make careful provisions for different contingencies, be able to apply legal evaluations of those scenarios to concrete problems, and especially determine if the situation calls for war, as well as the details of how it should be waged." In a nutshell, it describes fighting etiquette.

forces!" Although barely perceptible, a mixture of panic and confusion has slipped into the controller's voice. These people would probably sound as dry as an announcer reading the newspaper even if allies were getting shot down. Their distress is a good indication of how bad the situation must be. "A battalion of Entente Alliance mages has been confirmed violating the border. I say again, a battalion of Entente Alliance mages has been confirmed violating the border."

Well, the status report is undeniably surprising as the combat controller reads it with a tinge of confusion. Normally it would be taboo to employ piecemeal commitment in military operations. How to position reinforcements so they can best function as a relief force is crucial to planning military operations, but at the same time, command needs to keep a certain amount of strategic reserves available at all times. It's a classic dilemma but also the most difficult to overcome.

It's ludicrous for the Entente Alliance to make the infantry cross the border alone and then sortie their air assets afterward. I never dreamed the Entente Alliance would send out reserves when the imperial forces had already reached the point of transitioning from defense to pursuit. Strategically speaking, it would have made more sense for the Alliance to send in air support sooner, but then, that's precisely why the Empire was taken by surprise.

"Intercept them immediately according to the anticipated scenario! I say again, intercept immediately!"

The artillery did a half-baked job of crushing the enemy, and right after all their units began changing positions and making minor adjustments, more than a battalion's worth of enemy mages appeared to put up resistance on a massive scale. It isn't as though no one speculated something like this might happen, but the Imperial Army was under the impression they had completely crushed the enemy's main forces on the field.

Generally speaking, if the Entente Alliance had been aiming to cover the troop withdrawal, it should have acted a bit earlier. No doubt, the unexpected enemy reinforcements have thrown the front lines into chaos. Although I was fretting only moments ago that my lackluster position might harm my chances of a promotion, I'm genuinely grateful to be closer toward the rear. If I were with the airborne forces on standby, I would probably be flying into vicious aerial combat right about now, but luckily the observers don't have to go.

"...Bzzt...zzz...zzt..."

Just as I'm admiring my good fortune, noise completely drowns out the communications from Norden Control, even though they had informed me about the drastic change in the situation just seconds ago. This is a critical juncture for the battle, and all my radio can do is put out static.

Considering how it acted up earlier, there's a good chance the radio set itself is malfunctioning. It's undeniably regrettable, seeing as how the radio is vital for me to continue spotting for the artillery and receive troop intel. But according to Tanya's memory, the radio took more than its fair share of abuse during various drills. Prized for its durability, combat communication equipment isn't supposed to be this fragile.

It's odd, but maybe the breakdown happened because I'm using it in actual combat conditions. But not only does this prevent me from reporting on where incoming rounds are landing, it also worryingly renders me unable to carry out my duties as an artillery observer, even if it's due to technical difficulties. But in the end, I don't need to bemoan my wireless set's failure for long.

...Radar emissions?! It's pure coincidence that I catch it. Nonetheless, I listen to Tanya's instincts and quickly veer off course, narrowly avoiding the attack. Countless magic formulas explode along the flight path I had been following just moments ago. The enemy has arrived.

"Mayday! Mayday! Fairy 08 to Norden Control! Fairy 08 to Norden Control! Theater warning! Requesting immediate assistance!" Tanya shouts into the radio, the waves set at maximum amplitude; the static wasn't due to a defect but enemy jamming.

Without a doubt, these mages are the greatest threat among the surviving enemy forces along the border. The Entente Alliance is considered a developing country in the magician department, so their numbers are few, but to compensate for the short supply, the ones they do have are powerhouses. This has been made possible mostly due to support from nations who are aligned against the Empire. Essentially, it's a classic case of "the enemy of my enemy is my friend."

But the assumption that the Entente Alliance's mages were lacking led Imperial Army's mages, including me, to drop our guard even after receiving a situation report about enemy mage forces reorganizing behind enemy lines. According to intelligence obtained prior to the battle, the most elite enemy mages deployed to Norden were still hastily mustering in the Alliance a ways to the north. That's why no one expected any particularly dangerous enemy mage forces in the vicinity.

I suppose you could say this allowed the enemy to capitalize on our carelessness. In any event, the appearance of enemy forces will be reported immediately to the command post (CP). Not only is there tactical value in doing so, but there's also infinitely vast political implications to consider. Naturally, I follow procedure and report them, too. Still, I have no desire to go all out as a hero and single-handedly draw in the enemy. Anyone with a death wish is welcome to go die. My top priority is to survive. The problem is whether or not I can get away.

"I've detected a group of enemy mages, company sized, approaching rapidly," I call into the radio as I prepare for air combat after sighting a rather large group of flying bodies swiftly closing in. It's almost sickening how many there are. "Coordinates: Theater α, block eight. Altitude: 4,300!"

Whatever the other side's conflict or political agenda, they're certainly displaying a fierce will to fight. Honestly, it's an absolute pain the way they remain undaunted by the losing battle, charging forward even as they exude despair. Nevertheless, my foes are hardworking soldiers overflowing with fighting spirit. No way they give a damn about all the trouble this is making for me.

On the other hand, the Empire's forces are still winning across the board. It's only natural this battle will end with our victory—which is exactly why the situation can't be any worse. If the enemy only broke through the area under my supervision when imperial forces were dominating most of the field, it would literally go down as the Empire's one and only black mark for the whole battle.

"My incompetence would be recorded as the sole failure among everyone else's successes." I'm terrified that my actions might be remembered so poorly that I won't even be able to defend myself from censure. It's a dreadful thought that people might scorn my inability to do something as simple as fulfilling my assigned duties. Things being the way they are, that possibility alone is enough to rouse fear. And once the superiors give orders to intercept, grunts like me don't have the right to refuse.

I initiate erratic evasive maneuvers with everything I have. With my petite frame, I would normally be able to expect a slight reduction in the g-force. In actuality, narrowly evading the fusillade of magic formula warheads brings the strain to a whole new level.

Going by the size of the group hurtling toward me, there are enough of them to at least be a platoon. No, this could be an elite squad. They're going by the book, raining shells on the target they have under their thumb while using their superior firepower to dictate enemy movement. As they close in, their objective becomes indisputably clear.

Without so much as a single person providing air cover, the Empire's artillery batteries make superb tactical targets. Since the hostile company's main forces have already broken through, their plan to neutralize fire support is worth the risk from a strategic perspective. In any event, the situation is dire.

It might not be so bad if the corps used self-propelled artillery, but the lion's share consists of towed pieces. Even for the Empire, it's too much to ask to mechanize the artillery crews while also properly maintaining the armored divisions, mage troops, and air corps. Of course, the artillery lacks the time it needs to limber up the ungainly howitzers and run or hide.

Consequently, the fate of the weapons on the ground rests on how well the combat air patrol performs. But it's going to take a great deal of strength to halt the advance of a company-sized group of mages. In short, it's essential to keep them busy until allied air units can be organized.

"Engaging!"

"Norden Control to Fairy 08! Provide a status update!" Fortunately, our electronic counter-countermeasures must be up—the latest transmission is coming in clear. Agh, this is it. I predict a 100 percent chance of trouble. They say a woman's intuition is often right. But despite looking like a young girl on the outside, I don't particularly think of myself as a lady on the inside. So what is it? Why do I have such a bad feeling?

"This is Fairy 08. I've made contact. I say again, I've made contact. A hostile mage company is penetrating our airspace."

"Norden Control, roger. Maintain contact and delay the enemy. Also, if at all possible, gather intel."

Ah, that would explain it. I swear, it can't get any worse than this. Engage the enemy and gather intel? No, no, trying to slow them down comes first, right? But single-handedly trying to disrupt a whole company? Up in the open sky with no cover? If they're ordering me to die, I wish they would say it outright.

"There's a substantial gap in fighting power. Requesting reinforcements."

"Norden Control, roger. We're already scrambling an allied mage platoon. Additional company already in the air on standby should also arrive in six hundred."

Oh, really? Apparently reinforcements will arrive in ten minutes. That's more than enough time to whip up some instant ramen, eat it, and finish cleaning to boot. Honestly, there's no way I can pull off delaying actions for ten minutes against an entire company.

If I take into account preserving my own life, which I give the utmost importance, my wisest course of action is to beat a hasty retreat. It should be obvious, but I'm simply not patriotic enough to fight a grand battle out here alone. That said, I need a pretext to ensure I don't become immortalized in military history for the horrible disgrace of running from the enemy. If, at the very least, I could get an order from high command to move from this strategically worthless airspace...

"Fairy 08 to Norden Control. Requesting permission for immediate withdrawal. I say again, requesting permission for immediate withdrawal."

"Norden Control to Fairy 08. I'm afraid I can't approve that. Do your best to delay them until the allied response team arrives."

Arghh, damn you. Curse this elitist controller! You could take a life with a single order from the rear! I seriously want to scream, asking if they want to try switching places with me. They should come out to the front and give things a go before they start ordering the impossible.

"Fairy 08 to Norden Control. How is our artillery?"

That said, I'm an adult. I know that if I let Tanya's physical age get the best of me, act on these emotions, and raise hell, it'll just lead to problems down the line. I can always get my revenge after I make it big someday. And it's precisely because I hope to make everyone pay later that I need to do my best in the current situation.

My efforts will allow the mage known as Tanya Degurechaff to dodge criticism once everyone learns about how she gave her all to fulfill her duty even under the worst conditions. And just in case they eventually court-martial me as a scapegoat, I can take initiative to show that I'm acting with the knowledge of the danger facing the artillery in the rear. I can claim later that I did everything within my power to deal with the problem. It's always wise to have some insurance.

"The mage platoon is on their way to reinforce you. They should reach artillery airspace in approximately three hundred. And at the same time, the Seventh Mobile Mage Company is en route to intercept. As I said before, we expect them to reach you in six hundred."

Aghh, the worst-case scenario has been set in stone. Damn the law of causation that brought about this shitty situation!!

Why do the enemy mage troops have to rush straight at the artillery positioned right behind airspace under *my* jurisdiction? What the hell are the troops in charge of the early warning line doing?

How does a mage company make it this far before anyone notices? It'll be unbearable if I get blamed for this due to someone's complacency after our victory was virtually assured. And if these guys want to take out artillery, wouldn't it all be the same to them if they go to the next sector? Why do they have to come here of all places?!

Damn you, devil. Are you still cursing me?! Okay, fine. If that's how you're going to be, screw it. All these guys are out to get me, right? In that case, I won't go down alone. I've made up my mind. If I'm gonna die, we're all going together. I won't be satisfied unless I take a whole bunch of these bandits with me.

"Fairy 08, roger. Norden Control, I'll struggle with all my might!"

"Norden Control, roger. Good luck."

…I'll admit that I yelled in desperation. But "good luck"? Really? I mean, what's up with that unnecessary comment at the end? I can't help but furrow my brow as an ominous feeling flutters in my chest.

This situation reminds me of how, in a weird twist of fate, the Tokugawa soldiers who were dominating the Battle of Sekigahara encountered the peculiar Shimazu forces. In other words, what I want to say is *Don't come over here. Go away. Shoo.*

Biting my lower lip, I can't help but curse my rotten luck. Well, I am being toyed with by entities like Being X. I've braced myself, I really have…but I never dreamed I'd end up committing to a defensive delaying action in enemy-dominated airspace.

Are there no child welfare services? I dunno if I'm cute as a button, but at least I look the part. And not just any kid but one small enough that people regularly refer to me as "young" or "little." I wish the enemy would hesitate to shoot when they see me, but you can't expect humanitarianism on a battlefield.

Anyone who knows what happened in the Holocaust, and then in Sarajevo and Rwanda, should have realized by now how truly dangerous it is to blindly believe in the ideals of humanism. It's all too easy for humans to transform into demons capable of performing monstrous atrocities. That might not be taught in ethics class, but it's our nature.

Admittedly, the sensible Western comment that "a virtuous God must exist" precisely because of those demons committing such evils is intriguing. Unfortunately, since Being X doesn't come across as particularly virtuous to me, I have to disagree.

"'God is dead,' was it?"

While nevertheless controversial, Nietzsche's conclusion is probably right. It's impossible for God to exist. People have to save themselves. In this situation, that means a defensive delaying action.

The equipment on hand includes a light bulletproof uniform, observer gear, and a Type 13 Standard Computation Orb from the Volcker Arms Factory. Because I'm on observation duty, I don't have my magic ammunition rifle, which allows the shooter's will to cast at greater ranges by loading formulas. And besides, it's too heavy for me, anyway.

How am I supposed to slow the enemy down like this? Of course, I know my only option is to find a weak point. Naturally, I have absolutely no intention of dying quietly. If worse comes to worst, I intend to self-destruct or whatever it takes to bring them down. If it's that or get slaughtered, I won't be satisfied unless I take them out with me. Still, if at all possible, I'd prefer to survive.

In fact, survival is my highest priority. Really, I want to just make a break for it. If I dump my artillery support equipment, it'll make me lighter. The enemy troops trying to break through are targeting the artillery, so I can definitely take refuge in a safe zone if I focus on retreat and immediately put some distance between us. But even if I manage to escape, I don't stand a chance afterward. It goes without saying that the army punishes desertion in the face of the enemy—execution by firing squad. From the day I desert, I'll be trapped playing an epic game of tag with the military police that never ends. There's no choice but to fight, despite being completely isolated, without so much as a single wingman.

"...I guess that makes this my own personal war."

On a battlefield where my side's triumph is already assured, I'm currently preparing to die in mortal combat. Well, technically, the enemy's goal is to provide support for their withdrawing troops by striking at our artillery, not to eliminate me. In other words, shooting me down is probably something along the lines of swatting a pesky fly for the enemy mages.

It's truly insulting that my life and career are being endangered while I'm treated as nothing more than a side note. It's my right to look down on others; no one should be allowed to do that to me. Without a thought about what's going to come after, I start doping up with one interference formula after the next. Improved reaction time, increased instantaneous strength. Before my brain registers the shooting pain of forcing open the magic circuits, I alleviate it with intracerebral narcotics. Ahhh, I'm getting pumped. My body's running hot with excitement.

I wonder if this is how it feels to get high. Now, if the worst case happens and the enemy shoots me down, I'll be able to escape without collapsing from the pain.

"What an honor. This is great. Such a wonderful moment. Ahh, this is so, so much fun. I can barely contain myself."

"Fairy 08?"

I've been talking to myself intending to be heard, so I'm relieved that the CP seems to pick it up. This way, I have a witness who can testify how eager I am to fight. I'm bursting at the seams with excitement. Even when the world is delightfully spinning, a mage's brain manages to sustain clear thought. It's a truly wonderful thing.

It effectively protects my thought processes from being clouded by drugs or insanity. I'm so lucky to be a mage...though it's not like I want to be a soldier.

"I was afraid this job would be boring, but now I'm the star of the battlefield, getting to take on a whole army by myself."

There's absolutely no way I should die out here. The world isn't fair—far from it—but that's merely a matter of market failure. The market's shortcomings have to be corrected.

As the problem ultimately boils down to cost, I have to raise mine as high as possible. And a marketing strategy is always imperative. I need to put myself out there. Giving it my all, never letting a prime chance to self-promote pass me by. In other words, making the most of every opportunity. If I can manage that, life will become rather enjoyable.

"I was afraid I'd get lost among our friends and foes in the mayhem of battle, but instead I get to stand in the limelight."

It doesn't make me the least bit happy, and I'm the only one in this airspace. The fact that I can't even sneak away makes this situation all the worse. Circumstances on the field have left me with painfully few options. That being the case, all I can do is consider how best to please the audience (aka my superior officers) with my performance. Surprisingly, humans can put on quite a show when cornered.

"So this is what it's like to feel deeply touched. 'It's a good day to die...' Damn, it really is."

I chuck the observer gear. These heavily armed enemy mages are envisioning sluggish ground combat, but we're going to be dancing instead. Beginning basic fighter maneuvers, I pump myself up with the exhilarating thought. This is nothing more than the accursed best choice out of all the awful options, and as disinclined as I am to take it, the only thing that matters is carrying out my duty and surviving.

The appearance of fulfilling my mission will suffice. After a respectable dogfight, I can pretend the enemy either got away or shot me down.

Then someone else can deal with them. By my calculations, even a group willing to brave the impossible to take out our artillery won't bother coming after me if I fly off somewhere else.

Rather than desert in the face of the enemy, my efforts will merely fall short, rendering me unable to continue fighting. It'd be ideal if I could crash-land as close as possible to friendly troops. And it'd be even better if I could slow down those Entente Alliance maggots. After all, time is far more valuable than gold, and the jerks trying to break through are pillaging it. While only a minor consolation, it would also be nice to get some payback. Ergo, I won't allow anyone to come out the victor in this skirmish. And if anyone did, it would be me.

I don't enjoy pain in the slightest, and I have absolutely no desire to get all muddy, but I don't want to die. There is absolutely no reason I should die anyway. I'll lap up muddy water if that's what it takes to survive. Life is a battle in and of itself.

"...Commander Sue! Enemy reinforcements! A company is coming up fast! And I'm picking up a mage platoon behind them. I suspect they're reinforcements!"

God, Oh, God, why? Why does this have to happen?

"The enemy has breached the Sixteenth Holelstein Division's defenses!"

How in the world did it come to this?

"Colonel Lacamp's battalion is issuing a distress signal to the strike team! They're jumping into a fight with a battalion of imperial mages. They say they won't be able to hold the escape route for long."

Where did we go wrong?

"I know! We don't have time for this. Can't we take out the observer mage already?!"

From his view in the sky, Lieutenant Colonel Sue was forced to acknowledge that the situation of his fatherland's army, engulfed in flames and collapsing, was only growing worse with each passing second. His face contorted with anger and impatience, but even if he screamed to stop the indirect fire until his voice went hoarse, it wouldn't improve the situation whatsoever.

"Our shots are grazing!"

If his glare could start fires, Lieutenant Colonel Sue would have seared the enemy mage nimbly soaring through the sky until they were burned so badly not even a crisp remained. *Agh, how could this happen when we're flying over Nordland airspace that we know so well? Today everything is putting a sour taste in my mouth, even these familiar skies.*

"Bastard's got us in a fine position. Fighting over allies is a pain in the ass."

The majority of his men were pursuing a single enemy. Sue couldn't call that mage a coward for doing their best to survive. If he wasn't personally involved, he would have deeply admired and respected the display of valor and indomitable fighting spirit. As it was, though, they didn't have time to appreciate the enemy's bravery.

Anson Sue's ears heard only the incessant firing of artillery, and his eyes saw naught but allies blasted to smithereens in the bombardment.

"...Damn politicians!"

If asked who was to blame, the reply was indisputable. The lone curse that slipped out of his mouth said it all. Sue wanted to take the fools—those who mocked the Treaty of Londinium, casually ignored it, and then made it part of their election campaign—and stand them up out here. The ones the politicians were throwing into harm's way were the fatherland's citizens.

"Get in close! Prepare to charge!"

"Commander Sue! Let's go with the alternative plan and strike the enemy artillery! If you have one squad stay, no matter how fast the mage might be, they should be more than enough to deal with them!"

"Forget it, Lagarde. Enemy reinforcements are already on their way. We'd get wiped out!"

For better or for worse, Lieutenant Colonel Sue's troops had penetrated too deeply into enemy lines. Perhaps if they had come prepared with a few more men, they could have taken the enemy battery by assault. But when they initially broke through, he had to leave several units to hold the breach open. That left him with a group the size of a reinforced platoon.

"Cunningham, how long until enemy reinforcements arrive?!"

"The closest formation will be here in 480 seconds! If we don't hurry, they'll be on our tail!"

With imperial units coming to intercept one after the next, even if they risked annihilation to carry out the assault, he couldn't see how they would survive. Still, he would do what he could with the manpower available to him.

That was Lieutenant Colonel Anson Sue's sound decision as an Entente Alliance soldier, as well as the limit of what he could accomplish given the limited information he had. He was indifferent to military romanticism, so when he figured the enemy batteries would be heavily guarded, he quickly gave up on attacking them.

But the truth was cruel. The airspace above the batteries was wide open.

"I know. If we... Damn it! Lagarde?!"

"Captain?! Captain Lagarde?!"

"Cunningham, cover him! Lagarde, can you pull up? Lagarde?!"

Right before his eyes, Captain Lagarde had blindly rushed the enemy mage. His support, unsure how to react, fell out of sync, and the moment they stopped firing for fear of accidentally hitting the captain, the enemy cast a formula. Lagarde had charged under the assumption that support fire would stifle enemy mobility, and now he was too near to veer away.

"Oh no, you don't! Cover me."

Lagarde was caught by much more than just a shock wave—he took a direct hit from the blast itself. Slightly altering his course wouldn't have helped. In an instant, his protective film peeled off, and his defensive shell shattered. He made a split-second decision to shield his face with his arms, but it was still only through God's good grace that he survived.

"...Break! The bastard was aiming for that! Thor!"

Sue's side had superior numbers; they were concentrated on the firing line. But the price they paid for letting go of an enemy after pinning them down was too high.

"Casualty report!"

"Two downed, and Captain Lagarde is severely injured."

With both arms burned, Lagarde was falling, only dimly conscious through the blood loss and pain. First Lieutenant Thor had been hit by the explosive formula at close range as well when he darted into the line of fire, hoping to cover for his comrade, so practically speaking, he was also no longer combat capable.

"Grah, they won't get away with this. Commander, I'll make a rush at the enemy. Back me up!"

"Agh, damn it! Cover him!"

"Hit! Come on, hit!"

"You're mine!"

Amid all of that, Sue was certain he heard, "*Gotcha*."

The voice sounded almost happy—like the laugh of a lunatic.

"Stop, Baldr! Pull back. That mage is going to...," Sue began to cry out, but in the very next moment, the imperial mage cast a spell that engulfed everyone around them.

"A...suicide bombing...?"

He didn't want to comprehend such a sight, but he had witnessed it himself.

"Commander, time's up! They're almost on top of us!"

"...We took out the observer! Pull out!"

>>>> UNIFIED YEAR 1923, IMPERIAL CAPITAL BERUN, IMPERIAL ARMY GENERAL <<<<
STAFF OFFICE, PERSONNEL DIVISION, SECTION CHIEF OFFICE

Major von Lergen, part of the team who handled the Imperial Army's Personnel Division, was smoking as he relaxed a head weary from overwork. His well-defined features, reminiscent of the Junker aristocracy, gave an impression of masculine vitality and intelligence. At the moment, however, they were drawn into a grimace, and he emitted a groan in spite of himself.

The General Staff's Achievement Assessment Department of the Personnel Division investigated frontline achievements and suggested the appropriate decorations and bonuses to the top brass. It was a keystone of the Imperial Army's personnel affairs. The General Staff's mid-level officers were posted there to build experience as candidates to become the Empire's future generals. Naturally, the tradition was to choose the best.

As expected, these individuals were highly regarded for their ability. Lergen proved that the superior officer who designated him chief of decorations had a good eye by successfully processing all the award nominations in a timely manner despite the fierce battles to the north and the ensuing flood of recommendations.

Lergen unconsciously stopped his pen hand mid-scrawl as he stared at documents from the north regarding recommendations for distinctions and applications for medals and suddenly groaned. It was only natural for his subordinates in the department to send him worried looks that asked, *Is something the matter?*

"…I had no idea she was in Norden," Lergen whispered as he exhaled a puff of smoke, displaying irrefutable unease and disgust in response to the documents.

The name of the recommended officer printed there was "Magic Second Lieutenant Tanya Degurechaff." She had graduated from the Imperial Army Military Academy second in her class and encountered a disturbance in Norden after her unit training in the north. She then put up a valiant fight with the Northern Army Group, where her brilliant feat and valuable contribution to the army led the commanding officers on-site to submit a joint recommendation. If Lergen viewed it like all the other papers received by the Achievement Assessment Department, it was truly just another formal document. If anything, it seemed a bit unusual for them to assign an alias.

Naturally, as a member of Personnel, he had a duty to maintain fairness and objectivity. It wasn't as though he didn't appreciate the valuable acts of self-sacrifice Lieutenant Degurechaff took in combat up north. She had completely dedicated herself to a delaying action and tied down an enemy unit. While she ultimately wasn't able to detain them until reinforcements arrived, she defeated one and possibly two others in a bold move that stopped the enemy assault. Though she ended up literally covered with wounds, she fulfilled her duty and diligently supported her allies the whole time. As large as the Imperial Army was, it was rare to find such commendable acts of self-sacrifice.

Chapter **I**

Normally, Lergen would have no cause for hesitation; on the contrary, he would have drawn up the documents to expedite the process for her to receive distinctions. But unfortunately, Lergen had known of Second Lieutenant Tanya Degurechaff ever since she was a first-class student at the military academy. She didn't exactly leave a good impression on him.

It happened during one of the many occasions Personnel Division business took him to the academy. That was when he saw it unfold. Small rather than petite, the girl was young enough that it would have been perfectly appropriate for her to still play sweetly with toys. But instead he witnessed the surreal scene of her roaring, brandishing her computation orb and scattering a line of cadets. That was the one and only time that he had ever questioned his eyes.

Normally, a simple mental note stating *She's a gifted mage who skipped ahead* would suffice. In fact, his initial impression was *There really are precocious child prodigies out there.*

In spite of sympathetic voices that had reservations about deploying a child whose age hadn't yet hit double digits to the front lines, the army's empirical evidence strongly suggested that mages matured early to begin with. In times like these, the authorities were perfectly willing to send grade school boys and girls to the front lines as long as they were talented mages and had volunteered. Of course, the applicants accepted into the military academy didn't receive special consideration for their assignments. This prodigy had performed within her abilities while demonstrating her devotion to the Empire. Under normal circumstances, that would have been the extent of it. *Under normal circumstances.* But when he really thought about it, the situation was terrifying.

This child—this young girl—had yet to reach ten years of age. The thought of her flying around the battlefield like a seasoned soldier was inherently chilling. While Lergen didn't mean to speak poorly of the academy, he wanted to ask the girl's instructors whether they had created a killing doll instead of preparing her to become a magic second lieutenant.

For one thing, typical officer cadets exhibited massive inconsistencies between their actions and words. For all their bravado, newly appointed officers were surprisingly useless. It wasn't uncommon that all anyone asked from the overly enthusiastic cadets was to not hold back the veteran officers. But Second Lieutenant Degurechaff was a textbook example of "a woman of her word." Since her days at the academy, she had shown glimpses of surprisingly realistic values.

According to the instructors Lergen pumped for information, after learning of the policy for first-class students to instruct second-class students, she proclaimed that she would weed out the incompetent fools. The enthusiasm wasn't uncommon for first-class students, and so the instructors initially laughed it off as healthy enthusiasm; however, Degurechaff stayed true to her word, to such extremes that it made the blood rush from the instructors' faces.

While out on a field training exercise, a second-class student started a minor quarrel and foolishly contradicted First-Class Mentor Tanya Degurechaff's orders, moronically underestimating her young age and outward appearance. Lergen witnessed the moment she attempted to carry out her duty as his commanding officer and literally moved to execute him on the spot for insubordination, as dictated by military law. That incident marked the moment Lergen felt that out of all the countless Imperial Army magic officers, Tanya Degurechaff was a dangerous one worth remembering.

Of course, the insubordinate cadet should have been severely punished. Regulations and training formed the very heart of the Empire. If no one heeded them, the foundations of the army would crumble. When an issue concerned fundamental doctrine, standard officer attitude was actually for instructors to take a firm stance.

In fact, an officer's pistol historically served as a tool for punishing desertion or insubordination. There was no need to argue that maintaining discipline among one's subordinates was one of the major duties assigned to an officer.

But even so. Degurechaff took it too far when she screamed, "If you're too dim-witted to remember orders, how about I split open your skull and pound them in for you?!" and drew a magic blade on the insubordinate cadet she had pinned down. Lergen was certain he had seen the blade coming down the moment the instructors rushed over and pulled her off. If they hadn't stopped her, she definitely would have killed the man.

Perhaps Degurechaff made an outstanding officer on the front, but she was definitely not of sound mind.

In terms of her humanity, she had a loose screw. Perhaps that was an ideal trait for soldiers off fighting wars on the battlefield. In reality, few possessed personalities innately suited for combat. Hence, the Imperial Army, along with the armies of other nations, trained people as soldiers through regulations and drills before finally recognizing them as trained combatants.

In that regard, Degurechaff was blessed with great talent. It was annoyingly obvious to him, precisely because Lergen worked in Personnel. She embodied the ideal officer from the army's perspective, from the way she calmly used a nearly self-destructive maneuver to the way she loyally carried out her duties. Of course, she was clearly hazardous in some ways.

In particular, she greatly strayed from the army's desire for unit cohesion. Degurechaff's way of thinking was dangerous enough that it wasn't possible to trust her to act on her own discretion, so Lergen was forced to consider her a potential threat. She was truly war hungry.

"…This is no joke."

Realizing that he would be in the minority as far as his views were concerned, Lergen was nonetheless driven to have the proposed decoration reconsidered.

The girl had held the line until reinforcements arrived, ultimately fighting so hard that she was hanging on by a thread when infantry searching the area found her. Such a feat was definitely worthy of praise, but considering her disposition, he was convinced that was the natural outcome. As for the way she fought, it was hardly surprising that she had followed the textbook to the letter by putting up a noble resistance. She had extensive gunshot wounds all over her arms and legs, and there were signs that she had held her computation orb with her teeth. In short, this indicated that she had made the levelheaded strategic decision to buy time and desperately defended her vitals while resisting enemy forces for as long as possible.

But that was precisely the problem. Having finished reading the documents, Lergen couldn't help but bury his head in his hands. It was true that Degurechaff was horribly dangerous. Yet at the same time, based on the principle of rewarding excellence and punishing inadequacy, he couldn't overlook such an outstanding accomplishment. It would be unacceptable if he did.

It was unclear what the future held, but considering the achievement that earned Degurechaff these recommendations, she would most likely receive the glorious Silver Wings Assault Badge. The Northern Army Group probably regarded this as the greatest deed in the initial phase of the war. During a critical phase in the early battles, a crisis occurred. Enter a mage from the academy, performing exactly the kind of distinguished exploits the military hoped for to boost morale. She'd gotten real results. And the story was absolutely perfect. It was an honor for a mage to be awarded an alias, and so soon in her career. He immediately understood that she'd been given the elegant nickname "White Silver" because everyone was thrilled.

While Degurechaff might not be a hero for boosting morale, Lergen still had to exercise both positive and negative discipline. He took pride in being fair and true to his duty. Yet for the first time, he was torn between his emotions and his obligations as a military bureaucrat.

A child honed into the perfect weapon is terrifying. The only way to use Degurechaff is to turn her on the enemy. I'll build you up as a hero. I'll respect your exploits as much as possible. I'll permit you to act on your own discretion to the best of my ability. I'll support you however I can to make certain you can fight. I'll do all of that. So please, I'm begging you, fight on the front.

Is it right to bestow honor and influence on a soldier I can only possibly hope to control with a prayer?

"…If only this was one rung lower," Lergen grumbled in spite of himself. The Silver Wings Assault Badge provided massive influence and recognition in the army.

This decoration was one of the most valuable distinctions of many the Empire had to offer. Of course, merit awards were also presented out of honor and courtesy for years of continuous service or at certain points in a soldier's career. Still, it was true that the decorations for courage and remarkable devotion to the nation were viewed more highly. (This tendency was attributed to Empire-like fortitude and utilitarianism but could have simply fallen under nationalism.)

Long ago, each individual received a crown of laurels for his or her brave actions. But with the modernization of the army, this was switched to the current decorations. Among these decorations, the assault badges honored soldiers who fought with dauntless courage in field operations. Normally in a large-scale offensive, the unit that served as vanguard would receive the General Assault Badge, while whoever among them who clearly contributed the most would receive the Assault Badge with Oak Leaves.

A soldier holding the Assault Badge with Oak Leaves was viewed as a core member of the unit and trusted unconditionally. But even that honor could not compete with that of the Silver Wings Assault Badge. After all, it was reserved solely for those who were like archangels coming to the rescue of allies in crisis. Even the nomination requirements differed from the normal assault badges.

Nominations for the Silver Wings Assault Badge were not submitted by the candidate's superior officers. Generally, the commanding officer of the rescued unit would nominate the fellow soldier out of overwhelming respect. (Though in most cases, the highest-enlisted officer of the rescued unit would do this.)

But that wasn't even the most unique aspect of the Silver Wings Assault Badge: The majority of its recipients were already deceased. In other words, the bar was set so high that the badge wasn't awarded unless the soldier heroically fought under such perilous conditions.

Could an individual rescue a unit in dire straits? How would one pull that off? Was such a feat possible through normal means? Needless to say, the answer became clear at the sight of the photographs taken in commemoration of the Silver Wings Assault Badge recipients. For the most part, the badges were pinned to the recipient's hat resting atop their rifle. Official regulations said the only decoration that could be presented to the rifle and hat in place of the deceased was the Silver Wings Assault Badge, so it wouldn't be an exaggeration to say these restrictions alone indicated a bitter struggle.

As a result, regardless of a Silver Wings Assault Badge recipient's rank, it was appropriate for officers and soldiers to show them respect. The badge connoted that level of honor.

I'll admit it. Bluntly put, I dread what will happen if we give Degurechaff that kind of clout. She's simply too different. At first, he had suspected she conformed too well to an overzealous recruitment agency's wishes. Wondering if she had been indoctrinated with fanatic patriotic beliefs, he went so far as to have an acquaintance in Intelligence investigate her orphanage. But it came up clean. It was an ordinary orphanage that could be found anywhere, up to typical standards, and the staff were sensible enough. If anything stood out, it was that they provided average nutrition, since donations and the like had created some leeway for the administration.

In other words, the basis for Second Lieutenant Degurechaff's loyalty to the army and will to fight was neither a means to escape starvation nor an inclination toward violence caused by abuse. Out of curiosity, he checked her responses on the question-and-answer section of the military academy entrance exam only to find that she—this monster in little girl's clothing—had said, "This is the only path for me."

Overflowing devotion and loyalty to the nation. Nothing short of a magnificent display of what the military looked for in an ideal soldier. Continuous training and a desire for self-improvement. All those things were worthy of praise. A soldier with any one of those traits would make Lergen perfectly happy as an imperial officer managing human resources.

If an officer has a combination of them, we're delighted. That's precisely what the army wants. But ironically, now having seen those qualities made incarnate, Lergen realized that highest form of the Imperial Army's desires was simply another way to describe a monster. And it filled him with fear.

He didn't know what she was implying with "This is the only path for me." One of the logical theories he had conceived was that perhaps she was trying to sublimate her overflowing lust for murder into something practical. Who could say for certain that she wasn't born hungry for war, and the army was the only path that could sate her appetite?

Who could guarantee that she wasn't a loose cannon who would enjoy the sight of dripping blood and fly off on a journey of carnage? Even if she conducted herself like an ideal soldier in every way, the overall picture suggested she had to be crazy, or at least abnormal.

Naturally, he understood that you couldn't fight a war with tranquil serenity. It wasn't as if he didn't know from experience that only those who snapped or were truly mad could fight without getting nauseous. But what if someone enjoyed it?

He had once heard that as far as a murderer was concerned, both theory and practice were nothing more than a difference in aesthetics. Meaning a serial killer conflated their theories with actual implementation. At the time, he had laughed it off as a rather wild opinion, but he understood all too well now. Sadly, he had come to understand. *At best, Degurechaff is an anomaly, fundamentally different from the rest of us.*

Maybe that's what a hero is—someone divergent from the average person in some way. There's nothing wrong with celebrating a hero, but we will never teach "Follow the hero." We cannot afford to foster that. The military academy is a human resources development organization, not a place for creating lunatics.

>>> **SAME DAY, IMPERIAL ARMY GENERAL STAFF OFFICE, WAR ROOM** <<<

The General Staff came to a formal decision to award a certain mage officer a medal, and not only was this one of the rare occasions where the Silver Wings Assault Badge was presented to someone other than a corpse, but also the judgment was handed down with unprecedented speed. The recipient was even given an alias. But while one area bustled with the award ceremonies that accompany victory, a heated debate was filling the tense air in a corner of the General Staff Office—the General Staff's First Conference (War) Room, where guards refused entry to all unauthorized personnel.

To be exact, two brigadier generals stood in fierce opposition.

"I absolutely oppose! If we make a concentrated commitment like that, we may lose the flexibility to respond swiftly, a risk which greatly outweighs any merits!" A manly soldier in his prime stood and roared in unending protest. His pale blue eyes overflowed with such confidence that he seemed arrogant, but anyone who met his gaze realized it was always fixed on reality. The General Staff regarded Brigadier General von Rudersdorf as an officer whose balance of confidence and ability made him exceptional. Now, this man cast aside his reputation and all but leaned over the desk as he continued howling in protest. "We have more than enough troops on the field already for a running fight! We should maintain tactical flexibility while applying a reasonable amount of pressure. That's all there is to it!"

"Likewise, I must voice my protest as well. We have successfully destroyed the enemy's forces in the field. What more is there to accomplish through war? We have already met our national defense objective." Furthermore, he agreed with the need to maintain tactical flexibility. With his quiet disposition and scholarly outward appearance, Brigadier General von Zettour gave off a sensible impression, characteristic of a man who measured himself as a soldier. He joined the debate, speaking as matter-of-factly as a mathematician reading his finalized results.

"Both of our brigadier generals make valid points… Would you care to comment, General von Ludwig?" Presiding as the chairman, Adjutant General Marchese felt that both brigadier generals presented arguments that sounded too reasonable to simply overlook. Naturally, the adjutant general was experienced enough to ignore opposing views in the debate if he chose to do so.

However, it wasn't as though Marchese didn't have his own cause for concern. Considering the General Staff's stance would have primary influence over the commander in chief's office, it was worth digging deeper. As such, he had prompted a statement from Lieutenant General von Ludwig, chief of the General Staff, who advocated a large-scale offensive. He intended to hear all sides.

"Prudence is all well and good, but we haven't caught a whiff of mobilization from our neighboring nations. If we want to conduct a large-scale offensive without the restraint of the given conditions, isn't this a prime opportunity?"

The chief of the General Staff had risen, a troubled look on his face. He appeared mildly confused that two of the subordinates for whom he had high expectations were rising in revolt against him. Yet he was also angry. As a result, he was trying to figure out how he felt, so what everyone saw was his bizarrely perplexed expression.

"Lieutenant General, sir! At the very least, we should limit the scale of mobilization! A full mobilization would destroy the fundamental premise of Plan 315!" Rudersdorf strongly objected.

His concise criticism stemmed from the Empire's geopolitical situation. The Empire was the only great power surrounded by other world powers, so in terms of national defense, it was in the difficult position of always accounting for the possibility of a multifront war.

Then there was the historical background behind how the Empire built its reputation as a new military power. Compelled by fear and geographic necessity, the Empire had to pursue military superiority to withstand a two-front war.

"I don't mean to simply parrot General von Rudersdorf, but we should not alter our policies for national defense, including Plan 315," added Zettour.

Assuming the Empire was surrounded by potential enemies on all sides, efficiently moving and managing troops along interior lines became its only defense option. The minutely detailed plan called for mass mobilization to neutralize a single potential enemy's field army with forces superior in both number and quality. Thereafter, the military would prepare to take on the other hostile countries. This was defense policy Plan 315. In order to get them through a nigh impossible two-front war, it had been fine-tuned down to specific train schedules—the plan was something of an artistic masterpiece for the Empire. To put it another way, it would take a massive amount of time to build a new plan if they scrapped this one.

"Zettour, we must avoid sending in forces piecemeal. That hardly needs to be said."

"I am fully aware of the foolishness of gradual mobilization, but I find it questionable to claim we need to deploy our entire force now that we have destroyed the enemy's field army."

On the other hand, Ludwig's argument also stood to reason. Given that the Kingdom of Ildoa, the François Republic, and the Russy

Federation showed no real signs of mobilizing troops, the stage was set to completely crush the Entente Alliance. If the Empire was going to strike, it should go all out.

But as for launching an immediate offensive, Zettour's notion that they had achieved sufficient victory contradicted Chief of the General Staff Ludwig's opinion.

"I agree with Brigadier General von Zettour. Victory is within our grasp, so the question we should be asking is how to exploit its fruits! If we needlessly mobilize troops without a clear plan, the tactical objective will be too ambiguous. I fail to see how that will benefit our national defense." Rudersdorf didn't feel they needed to add to their achievements. The question he posed was simply how to best utilize their gains once they had an understanding of the situation. While that wasn't exactly the main point of his proposal, he too was concerned that the army would needlessly compromise their well-established national defense policy without a plan.

"Rudersdorf, as long as the commander in chief doesn't give us directives, the General Staff can only pursue expanding its military gains."

"General, with all due respect, it would be unspeakable to conduct a military operation that lacked a clear tactical objective. I am strongly opposed to a reckless large-scale invasion that could consequently ruin our defense policy," Rudersdorf replied.

Zettour agreed with an outright bitter expression on his face.

"Opportunity waits for no man! We are prepared to settle the territorial dispute over Norden once and for all with this campaign! We can resolve the Empire's geopolitical problem!"

The cheers that slipped out from a portion of the attendees were not wholly unjustified. Zettour had painted a luscious picture of the future by presenting the opportunity to free the Empire from the ever-present problem of being surrounded on all sides by other nations. If they dealt a devastating blow to the neighboring Entente Alliance, they could successfully eliminate one of the potential threats facing the Empire. It was a prime opportunity to resolve a geopolitical problem that had haunted them for ages.

"Objection! We should not go through with this at the cost of our established defense program!" The point Rudersdorf fiercely made struck at the heart of the disagreement. Should they try to secure a safe future at the risk of jeopardizing their current defense program? "The Empire's goal is national security. Seeing as we've established a de facto border with the Treaty of Londinium, the issue might as well not exist."

Zettour went so far as to coolly say that they should forget about the Entente Alliance. In other words, he didn't want to open the can of worms the Treaty of Londinium had shut.

"There's no need to do what the enemy wants! Should we not rather follow our own plan? Would you have us squander all of our preparations?!"

More importantly, as Rudersdorf vehemently appealed to those present in the conference room, this decision would affect the very fundamentals of the Empire's national defense.

Plan 315, which the General Staff had continually altered over the years, was the Empire's only viable defense policy due to the country's geopolitical environment. Surrounded by potential enemies on all sides, the Empire made the desperate decision that no matter which country set off the invasion domino effect, it would resolutely defend its territory through coordinated counterattacks. In truth, it was unable to conceive any other defense plan with a high chance of success.

"Will you pass up the chance to break free of this encirclement, if only partially?"

"If we could weaken the Entente Alliance, we would be able to concentrate more on the east. And to the west, we could mount a somewhat less tense line of defense against Albion, François."

But they continued their arguments one after the other with no end in sight. The debate stemmed from the General Staff's inescapable desire to seize this opportunity; they could finally break free of their stalemated country's defense strategy. *If we act now—if we act right now, for the first time since the founding of the Empire—we could resolve our military problems in one fell swoop.*

"Fortunately, none of the powerhouses show any indications of mobilizing. I believe that if we act now, we can eliminate the root of the Empire's problems."

They had no way of knowing whether or not this decision was for the best—at least not at this point in time.

[chapter]

II

The Elinium Type 95 Computation Orb

The skies above the Kruskos Army Air Corps Testing Lab, southwest of imperial capital Berun, are noisy as always.

Orb and scepter once brought about miracles that were recorded only in lore. Now, thanks to scientific investigation of these myths, it has become possible to replicate those marvels, and thus modern magicology was born. The field discovered a method for changing the world through the use of computation orbs. In a physical world bound by three dimensions, the technology actualizes phenomena by applying the appropriate amount of stimulus to the right location. To give a simple example, you can flick the flint wheel of a lighter with your hand, or you can do it with the power of magic. Once you understand the mechanics, it's possible to reproduce any number of magical wonders. Yes, magic has become a technology.

Naturally, the principles of the fundamental elements, such as mana and interference formulas, are still not very well understood. Magic engineering was pushed to achieve remarkable progress in order to secure military advantages and established as an academic field following a decisive breakthrough in the Empire. By combining mana with an analog arithmetic unit, they created computation orbs. Unlike in the age of legends, it's clear what locations, methods, and degrees of power are required to cast magic.

The quintessence of this technology would probably be its practical application in aviation formulas that allow a mage to levitate without a vehicle. By generating propulsion, it thrusts the operator into the air and keeps them balanced. If they feel like it, mages can mimic witches riding on broomsticks. Rifles with fixed bayonets are more convenient than scepters as focuses for casting. Well, firearms are also good for shooting battle formulas in long-range combat.

In any case, engineers replicated miracles with technology. An extremely wide range of militaristic applications was also recognized. The importance of the orbs had been widely acknowledged for a long time, which is why the technology race between the world powers grew so fierce.

As the pioneer in the field, the Empire naturally participated in that race.

It's a day with clear skies but strong winds. My current altitude is four thousand and climbing. Roughly half of the scheduled tests for the day are done. My situation is more favorable than last time, when I nearly died after my parachute failed to open due to humidity, but I'm not in the mood for this—especially not under such demanding conditions where a slight lapse in concentration could cause the computations to fail and the orb's engine to catch fire.

Fighting to keep my face from twitching, I cautiously maintain a cruising ground speed according to the plan. As long as I keep clearing tests without incident, I have to keep going. And that means ascending.

Yes, I have to continue climbing using the "new model": an absolutely unreliable, horribly flawed prototype orb.

Is this the joy of holding the world in your hands? The access to the world's laws that the orb symbolizes is an elaborate operation that demands finesse. Under orders to oversee that process—using something that has no tolerance requires the utmost care—Tanya is getting her hand ripped to shreds.

If it weren't for advances in medical science, she would be stuck spending her life with only her left arm.

Holding an unreliable orb isn't much different from holding a grenade. The end result is obvious. That's why Second Lieutenant Degurechaff is so loath to be doing this. She heaves an inward sigh as she flies.

"The engine exploded! It's on fire! Abort the test! Abort the test!"

Yet another day of piercing shouts from Control and Tanya's agonizing groans echoing across the sky.

How did I wind up in this mess? It goes back to when I was ordered to the rear after getting injured in the north.

Second Lieutenant Tanya Degurechaff was still recovering at the time, and she considered where she would be reinstated a matter of life and death. She had fought hard, creating something of a war record for herself, and even received a medal... That could be beneficial for my future promotion, but it entailed the delicate problem of potentially trapping Tanya on the front lines.

"I'll review it now."

So when I received an envelope and opened it, the thought running through my mind was *I just hope they don't redeploy me to the front.* But my fears turned out to be unfounded. The envelope contained a document from Personnel with undated orders for domestic service. In other words, the orders weren't official, but they would take effect once dated and signed by a superior officer. This was the so-called informal job offer by army standards.

"Rejoice. It's unofficial notice of your domestic assignment with the combat instructor unit, along with a request that you be lent out to headquarters as technology inspection personnel."

In sum, the proposal wasn't bad. In fact, it was rather ideal: a domestic position that was, for all intents and purposes, rear service. But the instructor unit and tester positions were still associated with a strong career path. She could tell they held her in high regard.

Most importantly, getting assigned to the domestic combat instructor unit had many benefits. As the Imperial Army's most elite group, not only were its members given the best equipment, but it was also a holy land for combat research. The unit was a great place for me to hone her skills—an excellent environment for improving the chances of survival as much as possible. Even if Tanya had to teach, it was a perfect position from which to steal other people's techniques. To top it off, an attachment to the instructor unit would be no stain on her record.

The vague temporary transfer request to serve as technology inspection

personnel for headquarters wasn't so bad, either. Headquarters was practically the epitome of rear services. As long as I was a tech verifier there, I
could hide out in the rear behind the excuse of conducting tests.

If there was anything to nitpick about, it would be that a position in
the Railroad Department or General Staff was even more preferable due
to the low probabilities of accidents in both. But it was such a minor difference, the compromise seemed more than acceptable.

"I intend to respect your wishes as much as possible, but is it safe to
assume there are no objections?"

Perhaps the commander respected Tanya's wishes as a matter of form,
but in reality, the decision had already been made. There was no expectation that she would reject the offer. It would be inexcusable to turn
down the positions after they had been served up on a silver platter. The
only three options were "yes," "oui," or "ja."

"Yes, I have no complaints. I humbly accept my deployment orders."

"Excellent. You will test a new model at Supply and Logistics Headquarters. As a formality, you will transfer there from the instructor
unit," the commander said before scribbling my acceptance onto the
document. He proceeded to sign off on the orders and hand them back;
on paper, my transfer was complete at that point. How efficient. Perhaps
the whole "unofficial notice" was a formality in its own right.

"Nonetheless, I'm sure you must have some things you want to ask.
Permission for questions granted."

I always love a sensible superior. He deserved my admiration.

"I appreciate it. In that case, first I'd like to ask why you went to the
effort of assigning me to the instructor unit."

Normally, wouldn't a position at headquarters be good enough? I
couldn't help but wonder.

Of course, I was more than happy to have a career in the instructor
unit, but I was keen to figure out the politics and circumstances that led
to Personnel giving Tanya not one but two great positions. I didn't want
to accidentally step in a pile of trouble later and take a nasty spill. But
the answer to Tanya's question was quite simple, if exasperating.

"Ace or not, sending a child to the front is bad for optics."

...I knew the brass were a bit slow, but it took them that long to catch on? I'm technically a child. Meaning I should be cared for. Apparently, the bigwigs had finally woken up and smelled common sense.

"So you're telling an ace to go be a decoration in the rear?"

Obviously, showing too much enthusiasm over getting away from the front lines would be bad, but I needed to confirm the situation. If things were going the way I hoped, I would be set with optimum conditions for her survival plan. Wonderful. Truly wunderbar. Right then, I felt as though I could reach an understanding with all the people of the world. I was so thrilled behind Tanya's cool expression that it made me worried that I might get strange ideas.

"What a novel opinion, Lieutenant. It never would have occurred to me."

With those words, Tanya was confident her predictions were on the mark. I didn't know what the higher-ups were after, but at least the superior officer before her hadn't denied her conjecture. That meant she was probably in the clear. The safety of service in the rear was truly wonderful.

"Do excuse me."

"The higher-ups think highly of you. That's why they've made you a position in charge of developing the new model."

Actually, it was within the realm of common consideration from Personnel to assign a capable mage back from the front to instruction or tech development. In that sense, it was a plausible reason for transferring a young soldier from the front. Probably anyone in the army would accept it without issue.

I'd caught a break, but still, what was this about a new model? I doubted they would use Tanya as a guinea pig, but at least it would be reassuring to know what kind of technology she would be inspecting.

"May I inquire about the new model?"

If he said it was confidential, I would simply have to back down. Still, I needed a certain level of preparedness. You take far less damage when you have warning before you get hit, as opposed to a punch out of the blue. In order to personally brace for what was coming, I wanted to know what Tanya was getting into.

Not to mention I was terribly curious.

"Hmm, I was only told it's a prototype computation orb."

"I see. Thank you."

All of those things wound up to be undeniably true. Tanya is in the safety of the rear conducting various tests on a new computation orb. Her commander never told a single lie. But neither did he mention that the orb is as unreliable as an Italian "Red Devil."[9]

And that's why I'm suffering like this now.

At twelve thousand feet in airspace southwest of imperial capital Berun, I've already broken the maximum operating altitude for existing computation orbs. Without an orb specially outfitted for the single-minded pursuit of record altitudes, operating this high up shouldn't be possible. The oxygen concentration is distressing, and if that isn't bad enough, my body temperature is seriously low.

Taking so much time to acclimate at 6,800 has come back to bite me. Humans aren't designed to survive for this long so high up.

"Lieutenant Degurechaff, are you conscious? Lieutenant Degurechaff?"

With a heavy head and a leaden, sluggish body from the low oxygen level, even just responding to Control over the radio seems like a horrible bother. Even dressed for the cold, I can only conduct experiments at this altitude carrying an oxygen tank, an aerial radio, and an emergency parachute.

A single thought fills Tanya's mind: *Whoever thought it's a good idea to send an unprotected human this high should come see what it's like for themselves.*

"More or less, but I won't last long. Frankly, I've concluded that it's impossible to go any higher unprotected."

It's a good 21.6 degrees colder than on the ground. Oxygen concentration is just under 63 percent. Whether or not someone can temporarily withstand this altitude for air combat maneuvering is unclear, but it's a space that's definitely not for humans. The typical computation orb

---

[9] **Italian "Red Devil"**   Another term for OTO Mod. 35 grenades. These Italian grenades, notorious for their rate of misfires and accidental discharges, were feared by friend and foe alike.

has a maximum operating altitude of six thousand feet in the first place. Any higher and it can't produce the propulsion necessary to break free of gravity.

This is why Tanya estimates that mages have roughly the same level of air superiority as an assault helicopter. In fact, the gap in altitude has even convinced the Empire that combat between mages and aircraft is unrealistic. The barrier it presents is that insurmountable.

Of course, if the concern is purely altitude, and I have a special orb designed for reaching record-breaking heights, things might be different; however, what Tanya is currently testing isn't a specialized tool for exceptional climbing ability but a military tool positioned as the "new model," created in the pursuit of versatility.

But even though the new model, Elinium Arms Type 95 computation orb prototype, is intended for the army, it's creating ludicrous propulsion that usually isn't even possible. The actual method it uses to do that is extremely simple and cliché. It follows the usual engine development scheme: If one is too weak, use two. If two won't cut it, use four.

In the end, minus the "tech research" stamp to indicate that it is indeed a prototype, the orb doesn't look all that different from any other. Design-wise, it's still a spherical hunk of machinery the size of a conventional orb, packed with countless gadgets.

But what really matters is on the inside.

"Worst of all, this absolutely guzzles mana. Its magic conversion efficiency sucks."

Instead of gasoline, computation orbs use mana; a piece of gear with four engines would consume four times the usual amount of mana. But expanding a human's mana reserve isn't as easy as installing more fuel tanks, which means the operator will get exhausted much more quickly. Maybe this prototype has revolutionary capabilities according to its specs, but the practicality of an orb that demands the impossible and leaves the mage extraordinarily fatigued is questionable. Not only does it consume four times the mana of a conventional orb, but it's also hounded by the technical problem of synchronizing its four cores.

Since the developers have successfully miniaturized the cores, the orb itself is barely any bigger than its peers. Surprisingly, it maintains the same compact size of regular orbs and can fit in a mage's pocket despite the contents. It's very easy to handle.

I have to respect the technology that allowed the researchers to shrink down the cores to such an astonishing degree, but as the one using the orb, all I can comment on is how unbearable it is. Miniaturizing a delicate device means losing whatever tolerances the original had. If tuning the quad-core synchronized activation isn't bad enough, the shrunken orb cores make for an unreliable system with poor stability.

So while the mana consumption for this new model should be four times the norm in theory, it actually needed considerably more. Including mana leakage, even a conservative estimate puts the expenditure at six times the usual. While the fact that I'm not used to being this high is probably a major factor, the altitude test alone invariably leaves me feeling horrendously drained, as though I've exhausted all my energy in air combat maneuvers. As I rapidly become more fatigued, it's also getting harder and harder to breathe.

But upon receiving Tanya's bone-weary report, the radio spits back an engineer's utterly uncaring voice. "Lieutenant, can't you climb a bit higher? Theoretically, you should be able to get to eighteen thousand."

The curse *damn mad scientist* echoes silently in Tanya's heart as she scowls instinctively at the command plane carrying the evil mastermind on the radio. I can only imagine how refreshing it would be to shoot it down. Tanya heaves a sigh as she fights the truly tempting urge.

The voice belongs to Adelheid von Schugel. He is the chief engineer overseeing the prototype, as well as a bona fide mad scientist. It frustrates me that I have to restrain myself from shooting him down because it would only create more problems and resolve none. All Tanya can do is lament life's absurdity. Getting stuck testing this engineer's invention is a prime example of that.

"Dr. von Schugel, please don't be unreasonable."

For a person to climb any higher, they would need heated, not just insulated, clothing. And based on my experience in actual combat, the orb would be rendered impractical the moment I needed to fly with an oxygen tank strapped to my back. It's obvious that it would only take a single shot to the air supply to give everyone besides Tanya a pretty exciting show.

Let's assume a mage uses a formula to generate air and could withstand this upper realm without heated clothing or an oxygen tank. If that output depends on the computation orb, it would make the already inefficient device burn through mana even faster. The possibility of sustained combat operations is exceedingly doubtful with the anticipated level of magic consumption compared to existing orbs, and due to issues such as low oxygen concentration, there's a high risk of losing consciousness during maneuvers.

Thus, a parachute is critical, and while that's fine for conducting flight trials in our own territory, an immobile, barely conscious mage lugging around a parachute is a sitting duck in combat. Even if the operator did reach the ground, their safety wouldn't be guaranteed. If they landed in enemy territory, they were sure to be taken prisoner.

Not to mention there's no small risk that the parachute would catch fire or fail to open due to humidity. Tanya herself went through hell just to find a trustworthy parachute.

"You should still have enough mana. Likewise, the stress on the computation orb is within permissible levels."

Alas! This engineer—unfortunately the type of eccentric only interested in his inventions—apparently feels that theoretically permissible values are all that matters.

"Doctor, this thing doesn't have enough tolerance! Who knows when this defective junk will burst into flames?!"

For a soldier with experience in life-and-death dogfights, reliability is always more important than theory. At least for Tanya, even just recalling the last test climb disgusted her all over again.

That was truly awful. I lost balance at four thousand feet the moment the cores slightly desynchronized. Supposedly it happened due to a minor disparity in the magic bypass circuits' conduction velocity. The bypass circuits used for research were built with vastly more precision than the existing ones used for combat, and yet they couldn't fix the disparity? When I learned of the apparent cause, I seriously wanted to scream. How unrealistically precise are you trying to make this thing?!

Chapter **II**

Any mana that can't be controlled by the computation orb's inner mechanics will go haywire. As a result, the cores, unable to withstand the overload, blow up in a chain of magic explosions. Luckily, I was able to quickly suppress them with a spare computation orb I brought as backup.

But I was only able to handle the crisis because it had happened at around four thousand feet. Up at twelve thousand, where the ambient temperature is too cold to move around in (the air was thin on top of that), I'm not sure I could hold on to consciousness. In the event that the prototype orb catches on fire at this altitude, if I can't get it under control, I'll end up sharing an intense kiss with the earth.

Even if Tanya doesn't have any attachment to her first kiss as a girl, nobody would want a kiss like that. Isn't it common sense, in a totally normal understanding of the word, to toss something if it can't be controlled? But life isn't that easy for someone with professional obligations.

I'd throw it away in a second if I could, but the prototype computation orb is a mass of secrets. I'd never get away with it. The moment I lost it, a mountain of preemptive measures would be taken to secure secrecy.

And after all, it was the duty of the tester to safely recover the prototype if at all possible—which was why I have to be careful to control it in a way that keeps accidents to a minimum. Using this tolerance-less orb is hard to describe, but if I have to compare it to something, it's like riding a unicycle through a ring of fire across a tightrope while juggling knives.

You'd have to be stupid or suicidal to keep climbing with such an unpredictable prototype. Of course, a combination of the two is also a possibility.

But apparently, my candid opinion as a tester is immensely disagreeable for the chief engineer.

"How dare you call my greatest masterpiece 'defective junk'!"

Naturally, even Tanya could honestly recognize the machine's outstanding specs.

A system with quad-core synchronization was once only theoretical, so the mere fact that the chief engineer realized it, albeit poorly, is a testament to his terribly fine skills. Then he succeeded in shrinking the cores to their current size while retaining the functionality of conventional models. From a purely historical standpoint, that is truly ingenious. I'm willing to hail it as the greatest technological breakthrough since unraveling the link between the orb and scepter.

So I'm begging you, could you please keep the users in mind when you're making these things? As far as I'm concerned, it doesn't matter how high the performance is—people shouldn't be forced to conform to the doctor's invention. It's possible to order someone to adapt to their uniform by altering their physique, but that only works if the size isn't too far off to begin with.

"Look at application, not the specs! You at least need to give redundancy a bit more consideration!"

The general assumption is that military equipment will be used under the intense circumstances of war. The army wants *dienstpferd*, not thoroughbreds.

"Do you realize what you're saying?!! Are you trying to desynchronize the optimized orb?!"

"Dr. von Schugel, please don't yell over the radio."

"Silence! First you must take back that insult!"

The explosive exchange of verbal abuse echoes across the test airspace, albeit via radio. Aaaah, not only is he fanatical about his field, but he also has the mind of a brat. I want to cradle my head in frustration. This guy, of all people, had to be the chief? It makes my head hurt. If I were in charge of personnel affairs, I would have at least ensured a managerial officer capable of controlling that tech freak was appointed chief so he could rein him in.

But in reality, this man is the chief, and I am the lead tester. I have no objections to the Empire's meritocratic evaluation system, but I sincerely wish they could at least take administrative skills into consideration. I just want to scream, *It's high time you figured out the difference between technical and administrative roles!*

"Like I said…"

My dissatisfaction with the Empire's administration rose from my prior experience as an administrator ages ago. At the same time, as long as I'm a soldier forced to abide by given conditions, there's no choice but to quietly endure. But as the price of distracting me, the migraine-inducing argument is cut short.

"The temperature of the engine—the cores—is rapidly increasing!"

Tch! Ahhh, damn it! The way trouble arose from such a brief irregularity makes me want to groan. The orb's cores are on the brink of chaos. When synchronization failed, I lost control of them. Without a moment to waste, I urgently cut off the mana supply and perform an emergency discharge of the energy inside the computation orb. It's possible to execute these measures with a single motion.

Fortunately, safety mechanisms were implemented as a result of the lesson learned last time, and they're more effective than anticipated. During that earlier test, there was an explosion and the engine caught fire, but this time I just barely manage to stabilize the circuits. Still, that doesn't mean the mana inside the computation orb will simply discharge without causing any harm.

The desynchronized orb cores crash mana against one another from all directions, and the circuits blow instantaneously. But what luck! The reinforced casing I repeatedly requested was completed in time for this test, so I narrowly avoid sustaining any real damage.

And so, a look of relief appears on Tanya's beautiful face as she radios back the controller about following procedure to descend, sounding annoyed. "Control, are you aware of the situation? I'm releasing my parachute."

I have plenty of altitude, and this is near the imperial capital, a noncombat zone at the rear. Under such conditions, it's safer to open the parachute than scramble to activate a spare computation orb while falling.

In the capital, I can float leisurely down without worrying about getting shot at. In this case, all I need to do as I come down is hang tight and prepare for landing. But just as my parachute opens, and I begin to slowly glide down...

"Rog— Hey, Doctor, stop it! Get back! Please get—!"

Upon catching the sound of a stupid argument over the radio, Tanya couldn't help but look up at the sky and waste some precious oxygen on a heavy sigh. This is clearly the sound of a struggle for the radio set. Apparently, a certain someone is throwing a fit trying to forcefully snatch it away.

Did Chief Engineer Adelheid von Schugel obtain genius in exchange for good sense? While there are plenty of cases where an individual's character isn't correlated with their capabilities, I never expected to encounter someone this bad.

Either the world hates my guts, or I'm cursed by the devil. Well, given something as unscientific as magic exists, I'm going with the devil—Being X.

"Lieutenant Degurechaff! It happened again?!"

Apparently, the signaler's noble battle ended fruitlessly, and the evil scientist has swiped the radio set. Even so, I have to appreciate that he fought bravely to defend it from the doctor. But since that battle was unsuccessful, I have no choice but to exercise my right to self-defense against the mad genius. I never dreamed my world would become a place where I needed to save myself.

If I have to put it into words, *Where is, repeat, where is law and order? The world wonders.*

At this moment, I feel the utmost respect and admiration for jurists. I genuinely wish someone, even a formalist, would restore legal order.

"If I may speak freely, that's exactly what I'd like to say!"

After all, the bizarrely intricate system prevents even simple explosion-type magic formulas from properly activating. Actually, the number of times the malfunctioning system exploded on the ground outnumbers the times I've managed to create an explosion with a formula.

When they told me that I would be conducting test flights, I never thought I would end up once again recognizing the greatness and struggle of flying. I'm not one of the Wright brothers, but this has made me realize anew how the pursuit of flight technology is intimately tied to the risk of a fatal crash. At least those pioneers flew personally, shouldering the danger upon themselves.

Chief Engineer Adelheid von Schugel makes others do it for him. And to top it off, he's so self-indulgent—I couldn't believe my ears when he claimed that safety features lacked functional elegance.

The moment I was finally able to manage proper evaluations, albeit barely, he added strange test items and tasks. That was when I impulsively submitted a transfer request. Unfortunately, it was denied. Why? As immensely unfair as it was, apparently I was the only one who had even managed to get any testing done. In fact, my contact at Personnel Affairs actually told me to forge ahead atop the corpses of my fallen predecessors when he admonished me.

I assume he meant it figuratively, but apparently he meant exactly what he said. The front lines seem more promising in terms of survival. Just the other day, I heard that I now qualify for the Wounded Cross Badge.

"It's your lack of concentration that causes these problems! And you call yourself a soldier?"

I've endured Schugel's insults and fought the inner desire to launch into a screaming fit of curses. I certainly didn't join the army because I wanted to, and it isn't a fun profession, but I did indeed join.

"I assure you, I'm an imperial soldier! However, a soldier's duty is to wield weapons. By no means does that include coaxing some defective junk to work!"

I had originally perceived the job of an imperial soldier as waging war with a computation orb in hand and a rifle over the shoulder. By no means did I ever think it entailed carrying faulty machinery and blowing up without warning. Even soldiers have the right to complain if they're issued a broken rifle or a computation orb gone haywire. At least, that's certainly the case in the Imperial Army.

Not to mention reliability and durability are imperative for a mage's equipment in the harsh environment of modern warfare. That's common sense, even among new officers. And it extends beyond mages—sturdiness and dependability are supposed to be top priority for all military equipment. Bluntly put, a bizarrely elaborate, one-of-a-kind item isn't suitable for combat.

It's the same as how a race car designed in the singular pursuit of bleeding edge performance can't withstand the grind of general everyday use. A delicate, intricate weapon that can't tolerate rough handling by soldiers is practically meaningless on the battlefield.

"What was that? Did you call it 'defective' again?!"

Naturally, it isn't as though the army doesn't understand the necessity of technology inspection. And sometimes, to exhibit its technical might for propaganda, the Empire would produce trial equipment that specialized in a single area in order to shatter records. If it's racing to break a world record, that would be one thing, but the prototype orb issued to Tanya is known as the "leading next-generation candidate," making versatility absolutely essential.

Does this mad scientist even take weapons development seriously? Isn't this more like a hobby for him? As Tanya questions the chief engineer's common sense, she can't help but wonder how Supply and Logistics Headquarters could go along with this.

The world truly is a mysterious place.

"What part of a computation orb that randomly breaks—at this altitude—could be considered a legitimate weapon?!"

If an aircraft's engines suddenly stopped, everyone would call it a "killing machine."

If the defects were particularly awful, it would even acquire renown as a "widow maker." But this computation orb has even bigger problems than that. After all, it's nigh miraculous to get the thing to run at all.

Not only is it prone to malfunction and breakage, but also its output is unstable, and overall, it's completely unreliable. I can't help but feel that this thing shouldn't even be called a weapon.

"Only because you oafs smash them left and right! How do you break my precision instruments so fast?!"

"Because you build them so fragile. Do you know what 'military usage' means?"

This mad scientist definitely does *not* understand the term. Admittedly, though, he has managed to fulfill all the specs that the army requested.

Although it only holds true on paper—and only to a certain degree, at that—the prototype has a functional altitude that makes it possible to intercept bombers. This capability would once again dramatically increase the strategic value of mages. Immediate applicable firepower would be quadrupled, theoretically. The attack potential of mages would skyrocket.

But that's all assuming the damned thing works properly. It should be a given, but frankly, an orb that's a work of art or requires lab maintenance is useless. It's tempting to ask if all the chief engineer wants to make is a thoroughbred that only needs to deliver top performance for a brief moment during a race.

Normally, computation orbs are precision instruments that work fine if they receive basic maintenance once a month. Mobilizing the entire technical staff to work on an orb after every use is absolutely outrageous—by which I mean the full technical staff of the research institution equipped with the most substantial rear support facilities. Namely, the Supply and Logistics Headquarters. The doctor must have forgotten the meaning of *maintenance*.

Not only did he miss the desired maintenance standards for the front, he wasn't even in the ballpark. The fact that this is an advanced prototype must imply that Tanya is expected to perform a certain degree of certification. But I'm endlessly amazed by just how many of its application problems can be resolved.

"Why don't you understand how revolutionary the technology behind synchronizing four engines is?"

"I'm perfectly willing to admit it's revolutionary. That's why I keep telling you to make me one that actually works."

"Theoretically, it does work! Why can't *you* use it right?" He's more like an academic scholar than one of the top engineers working in the field. He spouts exasperating nonsense with a straight face.

Based on Tanya's personal views and her albeit somewhat biased theory on human resource management, in the event there is a scientist at her workplace in the future, there's only one thing she needs to watch out for—simply put, whether the person is nuts or not. Before even worrying about administrative abilities, first things first: Can they manage the basic communication needed to work in a team? Just that one point.

Incidentally, people say there is a fine line between the brilliant and the insane, but I feel like it's actually fairly easy to tell them apart. If by the end of a conversation you're filled with the urge to empty an entire magazine into someone, they're nuts. If you can hold another amicable conversation with them, they're brilliant.

"Dr. von Schugel! I want it to reach a level fit for practical use."

"That's precisely why we're conducting these experiments! Haven't you ever heard of the PDCA Cycle?"

...It would feel so wonderful to knock him out of the sky with my backup orb. Anyone who provokes this sort of thought is a mad scientist. If the voice of reason wasn't holding me back, I definitely would have dirtied my hands.

Needless to say, I know all about the PDCA Cycle. Design a plan (plan), try it out (do), evaluate the results (check), and implement improvements where needed (act)—a commonly known process. It isn't as if I have objections to using this completely ordinary method.

In fact, I'm all for following even stricter procedures. I desperately want to tell him to at the very least give his creations a proper once-over.

As the one using the orb, I can say the defects aren't the kind that can be fixed with minor improvements. The orb has too many serious glitches, problems, and flaws. The thing is such a mess that despite my obligation to secrecy, I seriously would hurl the damn thing away if it weren't for the safety mechanisms built into it.

To top it all off, the safety mechanisms in question aren't necessarily up to standards. It had gone off without a hitch, and Tanya had avoided the worst outcome. But this thing couldn't completely contain the mana. If the circuits do blow, the orb will be rendered useless, so I always have to keep the worst-case scenario in mind.

The absolute worst would be if an explosion ignites my oxygen tank; that would not be fun. Based on past progress, I've also been issued improved parachutes made from fireproof, tear-resistant fabric. But even these don't guarantee safety 100 percent of the time.

If Tanya falls unconscious, there's always the concern that the parachute might not open automatically. Or depending on the scale of the explosion, there's the risk of getting caught in the ropes and asphyxiating before ever hitting the ground.

Humans have learned through experience that, as indicated by Murphy's Law,[10] anything that can go wrong will. If an office employee has the ability to cause trouble, trouble there shall be. For example, it's common knowledge in personnel management not to keep a bankrupt employee in a department dealing with finances. In the same vein, flying with an orb that can explode at any time is like sitting around waiting for the blast to happen.

Upon landing, I decide to submit a transfer request in earnest this time. An emphatic nod reveals the depth of Tanya's determination. Even if the worst should come to pass and I fall out of favor with my superiors for a time, I swear that I'll negotiate with Personnel.

As things stand, a hundred lives won't be enough for her. The assignment to the instructor unit is Tanya's only hope. I used my affiliation with them as a shield and begged to assume my duties there, but begging didn't cut it. There's a very real possibility I'll become a human sacrifice to one of the mad scientist's experiments unless I give up on unofficial overtures and submit an official transfer request.

I gotta send that transfer request—and as fast as possible.

And so, immediately after I land and fulfill my obligations, I pick up my pen.

⟫⟫⟫ **IMPERIAL ARMY SUPPLY AND LOGISTICS HEADQUARTERS, TECHNOLOGY DIVISION** ⟪⟪⟪

The transfer request adhered to the official format. Magic Second Lieutenant Tanya Degurechaff's application conveyed a dire sense of urgency. As a sophisticated bureaucracy, the Technology Division within Supply and Logistics Headquarters had to accept and process any officially submitted transfer requests.

---

[10] **Murphy's Law** According to popular belief, the rule of thumb "If anything can go wrong, it will" was first phrased as "If there's any way they can do it wrong, they will," by Captain Edward Aloysius Murphy of the United States Air Force while conducting research.

General consensus was that she was very serious about wanting to transfer. This was not surprising, seeing as this was—imagine—her fourth request if they included unofficial overtures.

Her previous unofficial attempts were wishes unaccompanied by documentation, so the staff had gotten away with calming her down, but with each attempt, she grew more earnest and imploring. This request was bound to come eventually—it had only been a matter of time. Nevertheless, upon reading Second Lieutenant Tanya Degurechaff's transfer application and petition, all the managerial staff at the Supply and Logistics Headquarters's Technology Division were left holding their heads in frustration.

"So what should we do? These are all official forms, you know. Should we give it to her?"

The soldier had commendably allowed herself to be soothed each time in the past, but submitting this request showed that she had reached the limits of her patience. As far as Personnel was concerned, there was leeway in the Northern theater, so they were in the middle of assigning young soldiers random posts in the rear out of consideration for political and international standing.

As such, it would hardly be any trouble at all for Supply and Logistics Headquarters to reassign Degurechaff to a random posting. But while it wouldn't be hard to find her a new post, she was too valuable in her current position to let her go.

"Out of the question. She's the only one even marginally capable of meeting Schugel's standards."

Chief Engineer von Schugel was outstandingly proficient despite having only his talent, or rather, nothing besides his talent, to call upon. Development of the next-generation orb combined basic-level data collection with the objectives of creating and certifying advanced technologies. He had managed to meet the standards indicated by the Technology Division, at least in the planning documents, despite how ambitious (to put it mildly) they were.

"Good point. Shouldn't we also take into account the fact that his research might finally come to fruition?"

His brilliance was prominent even in the Empire, which had pioneered in magic technology research through scientific observation. Even as magic engineering gained recognition as an independent field of science, there was still room for error, and many elements remained vague. Schugel had made great contributions by pushing the field down a focused if rocky path and then improving on it.

If, as an extension of his methods, they considered purely the research aspect, it was clear beyond a doubt that the data and theoretical values Type 95 achieved had borne fruit in the form of great progress. That appraisal, however, only held true in terms of research. Groundbreaking advancements might have sufficed for a research institution, but Supply and Logistics Headquarters wanted a product that could withstand military operations, so they required more comprehensive judgment.

"Conversely, even if she can manage to operate the Type 95 prototype orb, it would be a shame to run someone with that kind of talent into the ground."

"We should look at the long run. Such excellent testing personnel are irreplaceable."

The voices drifting from the department heads expressed concern for crushing an invaluable mage of such talent. In actuality, competition between nations was driving rapid advances in military technology development and innovation, so while it was rare to sacrifice valuable lives in the name of scientific progress, it did happen.

Weapons development was put on tight schedules due to national defense concerns, which resulted in the occasional accident in an overworked section. The list of people who died while on duty was by no means short.

"Agreed. If we look at the long run, the acquisition, cultivation, and retention of capable mages is also a subject of concern for the Empire."

"And if I might add…I realize her age shouldn't be taken into account, but no matter how talented she might be, she's still a little girl. It pains my heart to make her Dr. von Schugel's toy."

Another major factor for the Empire was that in the navy and mage forces, both of which were under pressure to expand, individual polish could only be achieved with long-term training. They could

Chapter **II**

mass-produce computation orbs or warships, but it wasn't so easy to cultivate a competent, highly experienced core team.

On this point, not only did Degurechaff fall into the youngest age group in the army, but she was also an academy graduate with actual combat experience. All of this made her truly valuable. It would be a waste to ruin her. Additionally, Elinium Arms wasn't the only factory striving to be chosen to manufacture the next-generation imperial standard-issue computation orb, and that created a problematic political situation. Everyone present had to hope they could prevent the media storm that would arise if they allowed the promising recipient of the Silver Wings Assault Badge to die on duty.

Above all else, Degurechaff was simply too young in the eyes of anyone sensible. Even if they didn't make it a matter of conscience, there was the possibility her talents would dramatically improve with time. The skills she had already demonstrated made it clear that she had a promising career in the military. If they asked themselves whether they should throw her to the dogs, the answer was no.

The higher-ups might have permitted her temporary transfer, but they made their message loud and clear by appointing her to a position in the instructor unit: *You're free to monkey around with her all you want, but send her back alive.*

"But the whole reason we're stuck agonizing over what to do is that the Type 95 orb is too promising to lose!" The words slipped from the mouth of one participant with his head buried in his hands, summarizing the group's predicament.

"In reality, it has also been a fruitful endeavor. The technological achievements are by no means insignificant."

The anticipated returns from the research were gigantic enough that the Empire was willing to tolerate a certain level of risk. That was precisely why they poured money into the Type 95 budget like water. And after investing a massive amount of capital, they were finally beginning to see a glimmer of potential.

When it came to military technology, the Empire dominated. One of the central pillars of its technological supremacy was its revolutionary advances in magic technology. That potential had implications. The returns would be massive, so wasn't developing the project worth the cost? They already had proof of concept for the synchronized orb core technology. With that alone, it would be possible to dramatically boost mage capabilities.

"I will acknowledge the significance of quad-core synchronization, but we hardly have any idea if it will ever be practical!"

Naturally, even the opposing faction was willing to acknowledge the project's technological significance. It wasn't as if they didn't appreciate its revolutionary nature. Nor did they deny that the Empire profited greatly from devoting itself to backing the scientific analysis and cultivation of magic. But in their opinion, certain aspects regarding the development of Type 95 made it too expensive.

After all, regardless of its theoretical values, user feedback indicated that it was too problematic for practical use. And besides that, the thing was packed with so many cutting-edge, revolutionary mechanisms that it was liable to surpass not only the "next generation" but possibly even the "next-next generation." When the idea of it being practically implemented at this point came up, it seemed like an unlikely story. That was precisely what had them going around in these endless circles.

What eventually brought that debate to a halt was the consideration of a single report.

"Have you read the technical report? Lieutenant Degurechaff's analysis is rather insightful. No matter how much mana you had, it wouldn't sustain the orb."

The test report submitted for Type 95 displayed keen analytical skills and even a hint of profoundness that seemed to be backed by experience. The office was shocked to think a ten-year-old could have written it. Some even questioned whether she had done it herself.

That said, the actual content of the report was fitting and immensely perceptive. And as far as they could find, she had written it herself. At the tender age of ten, Degurechaff was too young to attend military prep school, but she was a mage with average mana capacity. Based on her talent and the amount of mana she possessed, she was practically guaranteed a promising future. But even this precocious, capable magic officer was crying that she couldn't make it work reliably.

"Its range, increased power, and ability to activate multiple formulas are all excellent improvements, but it's worthless if those things detract from its usability in prolonged combat to a critical degree."

The goal may have been technology inspection, but a magic consumption rate that rendered combat maneuvers unsustainable meant the quad-core engine design was simply flawed. Perhaps it had enhanced instantaneous firepower, but that was unacceptable if it came at the price of drastically reducing the amount of time combat could be maintained continuously.

In a sense, it could be said that a healthy evaluation mechanism was at work here. Part of what made technology inspections important was catching flaws in advanced equipment such as this. That said, if the issue was excessive mana consumption due to a structural problem with pouring mana into multiple orb cores, there was nothing to be done for it.

"From the very beginning, our objective has been to verify and test advanced technology. It's still within acceptable parameters."

The pro-development faction, on the other hand, was willing to admit that the project was lacking when it came to combat sustainability. However, that was of no particular concern, at least at the inspection level, if they specified that the objective was proof of concept. The engineers in the faction felt that the restraints on usage weren't terribly important.

The technological race with the surrounding great powers was so heated that in everyone's heart of hearts, they had a great desire for Type 95 to ensure technical superiority for the fatherland. If trailing behind in innovation presented a grave threat and gaining the advantage ensured overwhelming returns, they would want to keep pushing forward. If they evaluated the project based on potential, they could have approved all the costs related to Type 95.

"Its technological significance aside, the army can't afford to fiddle around."

The thing is, only the engineers engaging in development and the researchers supporting them felt that way. The troops, who used a variety of different weapons and weren't terribly gentle with them, had their own theory. As it was, normal computation orbs already cost as much as their most powerful weapons. This one-off special-order prototype frequently broke down and had blown through its initial development budget a long time ago.

It had already consumed unbelievable sums of money, and they were increasingly hesitant to invest more. If they shifted the budget elsewhere right away, wouldn't it still prove more cost-effective? Such assertions made perfect sense. The Empire was powerful, and while its military budget was by no means meager, it was finite. Since funds were limited, efficiency was required.

"What about the potential to convert mana to a fixed state? Isn't that more than enough reason to continue development?"

"Do you intend to send him off in pursuit of alchemy? We can't afford to waste our limited budget and manpower on this forever."

They were never able to see eye to eye about whether it was possible to sustain mana and store it. In theory, it made perfect sense. Even Schugel acknowledged that the orb's voracious consumption of magical power would impede continuous combat.

As a countermeasure, he figured if he could store mana the way chemical energy was stored in batteries, that would solve all his problems. People were constantly trying to make a breakthrough in the transformation of mana to a fixed state in reality only to give up on the impossible task.

By optimizing mana through a computation orb, a mage could superpose interference effects upon reality with their will. That interference creates a concrete phenomenon. This was principle behind the formulas mages used.

Naturally, the magic mages cast is temporary. Say someone wished for an explosion, and that creates one. Not only is it a temporary phenomenon, but also the mana that caused the explosion disperses, making it impossible to hold on to the mana. If it were possible, the mage would have only needed to will the phenomenon to remain in the world to fix it in place.

Concepts along those lines had been entertained shortly after the practical usage of computation orbs became viable. But each time the idea of using mana to fix mana in the world was attempted, the failures only multiplied.

Though researchers were often optimistic, there were mountains of papers describing failed implementations. All the great powers that had put serious effort into the idea thus far had already abandoned it.

By interfering with the world with one's will, an object could be created. It sounded easy enough, but telling a mage to actually do it was akin to telling them to defy the laws of nature and perpetually bend the laws of physics. At that point, it was venturing into the realm of alchemy from the stories of yore.

In other words, that was how far-fetched it sounded, at least to the row of realist soldiers. In their eyes, the overly hyped new technology was plain suspicious. The theory itself was also quite old.

In a sense, the theory stemmed from a technological dream that should have been left to future generations, much like alchemy, but it had become so notorious that not only soldiers involved in weapons development had heard of it but also anyone working in magic.

Bending the laws of nature and maintaining that state required a massive amount of mana. In order to raise the amount of mana that could be poured in at once, phenomena had to be cast with at least two cores. Likewise, fixing phenomena required another two cores. As a result, fixation required perfect control of at least four synchronized cores that were also performing their own tasks in parallel. Up until now, all of that had been merely theoretical.

"He's already realized quad-core synchronization. You can't deny the possibility."

"As it stands, we can't count on it reaching perfect synchronization. Lieutenant Degurechaff is the only one to have had any luck with it, and even the mission capable rate she's achieved is unsatisfactory."

This was precisely why the pro-development faction and the group that suggested pulling the plug reached completely different conclusions despite observing the same results. The former saw a glimmer of hope, while the latter dismissed it as futile, and both conclusions were logical to a degree. Realistically speaking, an orb that had trouble with each and every test was unreliable. Of course, there was no such thing as a perfect first prototype, so a certain number of problems were expected.

But such a frequent occurrence of major accidents was unprecedented. Based on what they discerned from the reports, it seemed like Degurechaff was hanging on by the skin of her teeth. And despite risking life and limb on these experiments, she had only just barely managed to operate the orb.

This alone was proclaimed a remarkable improvement on existing progress, which made it clear how "well" it was actually going. As such, when a number of soldiers were about to protest that it was a massive waste of money, a certain mid-level officer from Personnel who happened to be at the meeting posed a question from a slightly different perspective.

"I can't help but wonder—why her?"

Superficially, this was an innocent question. On the other hand, it certainly brought up an intriguing point. Magic Second Lieutenant Tanya Degurechaff's career wasn't bad, but there were plenty of soldiers with superior credentials. Perhaps if they compared her to the previous testing personnel to see why she was the only one to succeed, they would get their answer. Once this occurred to them, they saw the value of delving into this modest question.

"No, you have it backward. We should focus on why she succeeded."

At this point in the conversation, the director of Supply and Logistics Headquarters, who was leading the meeting, brought up one of the most obvious questions of all. "Why did she get selected? Who chose her?"

Without a doubt, the Personnel Division at Supply and Logistics Headquarters approved the assignment, so someone must have dropped off the paperwork. And that paperwork should have included the reason behind her selection.

At their superior's question, younger administrators flipped through documents and found the personnel assignment form. It had gone overlooked thus far, but it contained all the answers.

"Chief Engineer von Schugel chose her personally. Apparently, he claimed she had the highest chance of successfully operating the orb."

"How would he know that?"

Given all the previous testers' failures, there had to be something convincing him that Second Lieutenant Degurechaff could do the job. Why did he specifically want someone like her from the front lines? Was it something unique to her? Was it her skills? Something else entirely? It was a truly intriguing question.

But the answer Chief Engineer von Schugel wrote on the form was exceedingly simple. "...It says that since she is not set in her ways with the conventional orb, he figures she wouldn't treat the prototype the way other soldiers treat their orbs."

Well, the orb *was* brand-new. His logic was perfectly rational. The quad-core synchronization system was a whole other animal, so trying to conduct mana the same way as before would prove difficult.

It took a child's malleability to understand that even if conducting the mana felt awkward, they shouldn't fight it. Someone as precocious as Degurechaff had a good sense for conduction and comprehended the logic behind it, and not only that, she could pull it off. The logic was nice and sound.

Assuming they understood everything up to this point, that was precisely why the whole row of participants let out the same groan. It was the groan emitted in the face of an unpleasant truth.

"...Hey, there aren't all that many skilled mages out there who are unaccustomed to conventional computation orbs."

That went without saying. Even if they turned human resources upside down searching for such opportune mages, there would be painfully few who met those conditions. Naturally, the minimum requirement for the orb to be issued as the next-generation standard was for the majority of existing mages to be able to use it. If it couldn't reach full operational capability, there was no point.

The implications were that using Type 95 was a hurdle too high. Until the training system could be overhauled and all the active-service mages retrained, the next-generation model would be useless. It was also more difficult to use than the existing computation orb, so the drills used for the new recruits also would need to be reevaluated.

Even assuming they could accomplish all that, the orb's mission capable rate, reliability, and cost were enough to give them second thoughts about mass distribution. Considering the level of craftsmanship the devices demanded to function, they would be accidents waiting to happen.

"We don't have an infinite budget. Are we placing too much emphasis on versatility?"

"We've already achieved innovations in orb safety mechanisms and other areas. Don't you think it's about time we called it quits?"

In conclusion, perhaps it would be wise to call off development or, at the very least, scale it down. It was hardly surprising when that opinion began to dominate the conference room.

No matter how alluring the technology, the army had no choice but to abandon the project if it couldn't be implemented in the near future. The Imperial Army didn't have the budget, manpower, or resources to play around.

"The promise of amplifying firepower is just too enticing. Couldn't we just do dual core instead of quad core?" Naturally, those who would regret halting development still couldn't shake their lingering attachment.

"That's a good point. If there were only two cores, wouldn't it make synchronization that much easier?"

"Relatively, yes." Compared to quad-core synchronization, coupling only two cores together would of course be easier. Ironically, the solution came from a member of the technology department who was part of the pro-development faction. "But even then, we believe lackluster mission capable rates would be unavoidable due to its complex structure."

The mechanics for synchronization itself had been innovative and complex from the get-go. They couldn't really hope for an improved availability rate.

"In that case, it'd be quicker to just have mages carry two computation orbs."

"They're useless if their operation is spotty on the front. From the looks of it, we're not ready for synchronization technology yet."

They stopped further development. At that point, it was the natural decision.

》》》 BEYOND THE REALM OF PERCEPTION **《《《**

"Gentlemen, I fear the situation is grave."

This was the godly realm. And in one corner of this realm, the gods were genuinely distraught. Their distress was sincere, even benevolent.

"As you already know, the number of pious humans is decreasing rapidly."

"It is immensely difficult to balance religion with the advance of civilization."

Some guided man to higher planes of existence. Others intervened as little as possible. Regardless of which method they subscribed to, a growing number of limitations threatened the continuance of the life-and-death cycle system.

In particular, the more advances people made, the happier they were and the more their faith crumbled. For the system, there could be no worse nightmare.

"How did the test fare?"

"Not good. They may have perceived it as a supernatural phenomenon, but beyond that…"

A radical archangel and some others had advocated for generating supernatural phenomena to restore faith to the hearts of the people. Believing they should follow the example set with Moses, they had been experimenting, but their results were far from successful. Science would probably be able to explain things someday.

The phenomena exceeded the people's comprehension *at that point in time*. It was simply unexplained and, as such, nothing more than a subject for investigation and research.

"I had a feeling it wouldn't go well."

"I wonder what the issue is. In the past, all we had to do was talk to them and they would understand that we were gods."

"Sometimes they would even call on us."

Yes. They should have spoken to the people when they were deeply religious. Then they would have been able to communicate their divine will. Not only that, some people would have called out to the gods of their own accord. Now there were none. There were hardly any voices truly seeking salvation.

How had it come to this? When an answer proved evasive even upon extended consideration, it was important to go back and reexamine your successes. That statement was in and of itself extremely logical. As such, their noble ideals and sense of duty led them to take action, and they investigated everything from the age of myth to modern times. To them, the age of myth was just another memory of the past. Naturally, they could recall each case one by one to examine if they so desired.

"...Isn't divine grace what made it work?"

The conclusion was very pragmatic, in a way.

"What do you mean?"

"In the past, back when human civilization was terribly undeveloped, we intervened to protect them from catastrophes that would have been impossible for them to avert on their own."

In the contemporary world, storms no longer posed a significant threat to developed countries. Not even a hurricane could crack their foundations, let alone destroy them. Frankly, for the majority of nations, high winds and heavy rain would only manage to paralyze the cities.

It was a completely different environment from the age when a single storm could devastate farms, wash people away, and leave entire families destitute. Hence, the gods took care not to intervene more than the humans wanted, and because of that, they were being forgotten.

It was essential to encourage mankind's self-reliance so they could develop higher-order cognition. Yet for the longest time, no one foresaw this would lead to a lack of faith.

In ancient times, the people would praise progress as divine favor. The Roman Empire existed right alongside the gods. After the fall of Rome, the Church ruled the Middle Ages in the name of God; however, advocates for the divine right of kings argued that sovereignty was bequeathed by God. This caused the Church to gradually change its doctrine. Then, out of religious faith, scientists began to seek the truth of the world created by God. Before anyone knew it, mankind had completely lost their belief, although that was no one's intention.

"Yeah, lately the civilizations in the mortal realm have been progressing nicely, so we decided intervention could stunt their development and left them to their independence."

"Isn't that precisely what makes it hard for them to recognize our existence?"

They didn't particularly mean to hinder mankind's development. Really, looking at their original plan, they wanted them to progress.

Chapter **II**

We must seek the order created by God. The natural sciences stemmed from that objective, so the gods had actually been all for them. Mankind would evolve from mindless worship to reverent devotion with greater understanding. That logic would allow them to reach higher-order intellection. The gods even considered it a first step worthy of commemoration.

However, if it was having the opposite effect, that could cause extremely serious problems—they were inevitable. Too many worlds had cultivated only the natural sciences.

"Hrm, that would make things difficult."

The whole group grew pensive. If they couldn't resolve the issue with fairly minor corrections, they feared it would be excessively laborious. This was a tight spot. And they foresaw it getting worse the longer they neglected it.

"Does anyone care to propose a way out?"

The cherubim never failed to disappoint, and one of them explained the plan he had racked his brain to devise. He asserted that for the most part their basic policy was fine. In essence, if they had a system that could compensate for lost religious faith, they would have no problem.

"As such, we really should refine one point and revive their faith."

The proposal was accepted almost unanimously. However, considering their previous policies, it felt like they had run out of specific ideas.

"This plan makes a lot of sense, but what precisely should we do?"

"I'm not sure, but perhaps we should give the world a new holy relic?"[11]

"Hmm? What do you mean?"

They had already deposited as many in the mortal realm as there were stars in the sky. The numbers may have differed slightly between a nation or region, but they had already invested more than enough in the things. In terms of promoting faith, it wasn't a very successful method. At best, the relics were prized as historical curiosities.

"The current relics are treasured, kept under lock and key. They're

---

[11] **holy relic**   Bones, objects that created miracles, and whatnot. This is a touchy topic, so I'll keep the jokes to myself.

unable to adequately fulfill their role in making divine grace known to the masses."

The gods didn't know that. After all, they had long lives. They still remembered giving the holy relics to people, but it wasn't as if they constantly kept tabs on the artifacts thereafter. Upon looking into the current state of affairs, they had finally discovered that the items had been relegated to decorative purposes.

"I see. No wonder they've forgotten religion and prayer. In a way, it's rather ironic..."

The gods were becoming dispensable. That's all there was to it, yet they couldn't help but feel a flood of mixed emotions. They had no intention of unilaterally forcing religion on people. But if they didn't boost faith, the system was in for rough times. So to help people come to understand on their own that faith was necessary, shouldn't they periodically deposit divine relics where they were needed?

The gods thought this was worth a try.

"In that case, let us bestow the holy relic they need upon the world and teach them how to pray."

"Great idea. Let's do it right away."

"I have just the thing."

The decision was made very quickly. Though the gods were patient and laid-back by nature, they were taking this situation seriously. Because of that, they carried the whole process out wholeheartedly, neither cutting any corners nor getting bored halfway through in the way gods sometimes did.

"Oh?"

"There is a human in the mortal realm researching an item that is just a step from the godly realm. Given another one thousand years, it could be successful."

"Ah, a singularity. Were you able to contact this human?"

It was extremely rare, but in the past, too, on all the worlds, humans had appeared who neared the godly realm in pursuit of natural sciences. The unusual phenomenon was remarkable these days, but not without precedent. And this human seemed to be the most appropriate specimen for this test.

"He must have realized he has a long way to go. When I reached out to explain the works of God, he was exceedingly impressed."

"So are you suggesting we send down a holy relic there?"

"No, it should be a miracle."

"A miracle?"

Apparently, there exists such a thing as news that is both good and bad. This is Magic Second Lieutenant Tanya Degurechaff's unfeigned sentiment upon receiving the notice.

While only an unofficial notification, the higher-ups are indicating that they aren't going to provide additional funding. The implicit suggestion is probably that they intend to ax development of Type 95. At the same time, the Personnel Division is sharing their intentions by telling me to focus on my upcoming duties with the instructor unit. This is exactly what I want.

I should be thrilled by the termination of this flawed orb's development and my return to the instructor unit. The only problem is that this is only an unofficial notification, not an official decision. But it's probably already decided. Since I won't have to risk my life anymore, the news couldn't be better.

The bad news is that since the research can't continue no matter what happens after this point anyway, the mad scientist has become defiant and decided his department should conduct experiments that were previously suspended as too dangerous. If only he would get depressed or discouraged so he could become more docile! But such hopes have proved meaningless, and this mad scientist even seems to be equipped with the ability to tune in to radio waves from somewhere.

Out of the blue, he starts shouting that he's received divine inspiration from the heavens and begins yelling, "Now we can do it!" In his usual frame of mind, however, even the mad scientist deemed this experiment too risky. If in his agitated state he insists on going through with it, this can't possibly go well.

It doesn't help that the other engineers have been shaken by the impending end of development. What engineer isn't eager to see the fruits of their project? Full of those sentiments, they make only half-hearted protests. It's all too easy for the mad scientist to get his way.

I've managed to survive up until now, but I'm unable to stop them from forcing me to conduct an experiment that any sane scientist would certainly frown upon as suicidal. We'll be testing the fixation of materialized mana phenomenon to spatial coordinates via overlapping compound interference. "Mana fixation" for short. It's the product of one soul's crazy imagination.

Apparently, the ultimate goal in developing Type 95 was originally to conduct this experiment successfully, but it was considered so unlikely to succeed that nobody took it seriously. It's hard to imagine this ending in anything but failure. The theory itself is well-known for being plausible. It isn't as if Tanya had never heard of it before.

Type 95's delicate internal structure means it will inherently be frail and suffer from a poor mission capable rate and ease of maintenance. In order to overcome those shortcomings, I would need to use mana to recognize a phenomenon in this world, then secure and maintain power via fixation.

Theoretically, Type 95's quad-core synchronized system means that the technological groundwork to make such a thing possible has already been laid down. Tanya's doomed attempt to reach Type 95's ultimate technological goal will still hold great significance in terms of exposing its flaws.

When the engineers told me that, I thought it sounded similar to a bureaucratic explanation of budgetary provisions. They usually sound quite clever. But now I have no doubt they were only doing this experiment because the mad scientist is curious. Even if I form an argument to point out the obvious obstacles involved, it would be futile; surely the loon has no intention of calling off the test. He's desperate for it to go well, and he has to be pushing ahead based on unhinged judgment that relies entirely on luck.

"Lieutenant, you're ready, right?"

Of course, he has to understand what level of danger is involved. So how in the world can he crack such a gleeful smile? I suddenly question

Schugel's sanity. An urge comes over me to tell him to take a good look around.

We're in one corner of a vast live-fire exercise range with absolutely nothing man-made nearby as far as the eye can see. If I go out of my way to look for evidence of human activity, all that catches my eye is the recording apparatus and the doctor. The rest of the team appear to have accurately assessed the danger—they're currently at an observation station considerably removed from the test site, monitoring the situation only through the on-site viewing device. No one's willing to run through the standard signaling checks. In other words, all the personnel have taken shelter on the assumption that Type 95 will explode.

Hence Tanya's apparent misery as she continues to suggest canceling the experiment. "Doctor, can we please just not do this? According to calculations, the worst-case scenario has the entire exercise range blowing sky-high."

Schugel is the only one with unwavering faith that Tanya will pull off the nigh impossible task of attaining absolutely perfect control. The thoughtful development team is kind enough to have a fully equipped medical team on standby. Their elaborate preparations include a highly experienced critical care team and a full-scale field hospital.

"Scientific progress always has its sacrifices. Naturally, it won't just be you—I'm here as well. So what's the problem?" While everyone else feels apprehensive about the experiment, this one man, Chief Engineer Adelheid von Schugel, retains his cheerful smile as he makes that statement with confidence. How glorious it would feel to smash my fist into that cheerfully smiling face of his.

Maybe you want to get blown to smithereens by your own invention. Talk about getting what you deserve. What I want to know is why I'm stuck killing myself with this mad scientist. Isn't a compulsory double suicide a bit too much? But Tanya manages to express those feelings in a genuine but socially appropriate, roundabout way.

"Honestly, I wish you would employ that grace for something else."

"…? A scientist must stay loyal to their pursuit. Now stop complaining and start the test."

But evidently, the moral madman is too much for Tanya. If that's how you're going to be, then go ahead and die if you'd like. Just do your best not to inconvenience those around you. If that's too much to ask, at least don't bother me.

"I'm a soldier, not a scientist."

Tanya is only working as a soldier. Under no circumstances does the job description include committing suicide with a scientist.

And in a sense, the scientist has the perfect response to her protest.

"Then consider it an order. Now, get going." If Tanya is a soldier, she should obey the orders according to chain of command. He's completely tied her hands with that, but he's absolutely right.

"...Supplying mana to Type 95 now."

Having resisted in every way possible, Tanya laments her misfortune as she begins slowly, carefully pouring energy into Type 95.

"Observation team, roger. Our prayers are with you."

It's common courtesy to say that, but now the words have taken on an ominous tone. The fear that Type 95 will explode at any moment is plain in my expression. Frankly, I feel like my life is in greater peril here than back on the battlefield.

Both a mage's tough defensive shell and the protective film for deflecting direct hits are cast using magic orbs. The thought that I'll have no protection when the orb explodes is worrying me to no end.

But upon seeing the indescribable emotion contorting Tanya's face in response to the anxiety for this absurd situation, Schugel dares to smile. Tanya feels as though it's virtually the first time she has seen the doctor smile reassuringly out of consideration for her. His expression almost seems to be telling her to relax.

"What? No need to worry. This is practically guaranteed to work."

When Tanya sees how he has the pure, innocent, dangerous gaze of a cultist, skepticism transforms into blaring alarm bells in her head. I should steer clear of that crowd...

"...Doctor, what makes you so confident?"

If he's simply a psycho, it would come as no surprise. The problem is that his insanity threatens to involve Tanya in an immense, inexcusable crisis.

"What? It's quite simple."

The doctor flamboyantly opens his arms, acting as if he's about to start expounding upon a simple truth. That alone is enough to send chills down Tanya's spine. Confidently preaching the truths of the world with innocent eyes? That is something fanatics do. The type that's immersed in some dangerous religion.

"...And what might that be?"

The most dangerous move to make when dealing with a blind believer in something is expressing agreement or denial. I was taught back in my human resources days that if I ever needed to peacefully force resignation from an employee under the influence of a cult, it was necessary to avoid affirming or denying their beliefs. The idea is to remain distant and leave no room for misunderstanding.

Thus, all Tanya can do in this situation is try to prolong the conversation using the gentlest voice she can muster.

"I am the chief engineer. Lieutenant, you are the lead tester. That is to say, if we work together instead of standing at odds, we can do anything."

All cult members are just like this. They only say reasonable things in an even tone with an innocent expression at the very beginning of an encounter.

"The other day I received a divine revelation."

"...A divine revelation?"

Yeah, figures. I was afraid of this. Hmm. It's probably just a figure of speech. But this ominous premonition—the voice of reason—won't stop screaming. I've got a bad feeling, like super-dreadnought-class bad.

"That's right. If we say a prayer to God for success, those who believe in him shall be saved."

".........Ugh."

I groan in spite of myself, although I braced for this. Before realizing it, I also heave a massive sigh.

He just said to ask God for success? A scientist just told me to pray? Thinking that far, it quickly occurs to Tanya how unlikely this scenario is. Did the chief engineer lose his mind over the project getting terminated? That's entirely possible.

Realizing as much, I judge that regardless of orders, it's too dangerous to go through with the experiment. In a split-second decision, I curb the flow of mana and initiate safety mechanism activation to prevent the orb cores from going haywire.

"I am told it's important to be humble, free of arrogance."

But the safety mechanisms won't activate. Feigning calm externally, Tanya can't hold back her shock as she looks again at the orb in her hand. It's the same all-too-familiar prototype orb she conducted countless tests on. Multiple safety features could clearly be seen…and aren't activating? In which case, they've been disabled…? He just had to mess with it, didn't he?

The only one who could have done it is the peacefully smiling chief standing before me. He's serious about this. He's so crazy to begin with that it takes me a moment to fully realize.

"Isn't this a wonderful opportunity? Let us join in prayer for success."

"Doctor, aren't you an atheist?"

"The god of invention came down to me. Now I'm a devout believer."

Crap. Things really do look hopeless.

The Type 95 starts acting wacky, much like its creator. I've been controlling its coating with mana but can't any longer. Something about the circuits doesn't feel right, either. At this rate, the mana will hurtle straight down the path to chaos. And the safety features I normally rely on aren't functioning.

"……………"

If I try to extract the mana manually, it'll throw the whole system off-balance, resulting in certain collapse. So despite realizing how dangerous it is, I have no choice but to keep feeding the engine energy. But at this rate, I'll eventually lose control. I'm caught by this dilemma, but it seems as good as settled that the orb will go berserk in the near future.

…At this point, I can't stop myself from imagining my unpleasant fate in vivid detail.

"We're sure to succeed if we become believers of invention and pray."

"…By the way, what would happen if I don't pray?"

"Well, I suppose we would both become martyrs," the lunatic replies simply. The dangerous smile on his face indicates he would undoubtedly embrace martyrdom with pride. It could be described as the ecstatic smile of a suicide bomber.

Chapter II

"We should call for a medic right away. Or would you rather I simply put you out of your misery?" From Tanya's point of view, if she's doomed to die anyway, at least she could kill this lunatic with her own two hands. If she takes him out as she's being killed by his defective orb, at least she won't be the only one suffering a loss. An enticing prospect. Granted, it isn't much of a fair deal, but market principles assure me it's better than winding up completely in the red.

"Calm yourself, Lieutenant. Have you not met God yourself? If we both trust in God, we'll be saved."

He says this at the very moment I'm winding up to make my hidden desire to kill him a reality. Tanya stops short. Whoa, wait a minute.

"The energy coefficient is rapidly destabilizing! The mana is out of control!"

"This is insane! The cores are about to melt! All personnel evacuate!"

The observation team is shrieking. Tanya can't hear the screams as anything other than noise, but a second before she falls unconscious, she definitely feels it—

I swear I can feel that damn devil—Being X—grinning at me. Oh yeah. It's a supernatural being who plays with the laws of nature. It's the vile devil, who toys with human lives.

"You set me up?! Damn you, Devil!!!"

"After much deliberation, the Lord has approved of causing a miracle during the—what is it you're developing again? Elinium Type 95?—that thing's activation experiment."

When I come to, I'm in a familiar space, and at some point, an entity slightly more intellectual than Being X approaches me. The reason for my visit this time is directly connected to the mad scientist demanding to conduct such a reckless experiment.

But he's only a mad scientist, not a religious fanatic. Based on how he was acting just before the accident, he's a victim, too. It's probably Being X and his sect pulling the strings. They must have been manipulating him, at least as far as this experiment is concerned. Not that I feel a particle of sympathy for him, let alone a full ounce.

"Ahh, I see."

The entity before me only seems decent compared to the one that came before it. In other words, this one is more like a fanatic capable of holding down a conversation. I can't let my guard down. I'm basically dealing with someone steeped in a religion of one kind or another. At the moment, I don't care if he's a god or devil.

What I need to watch out for is the very likely possibility he'll try to push his values on me rather than discuss things rationally. His values are completely insane. He might seem intelligent, but the core of his nature is no different from an incompetent worker's.

I should eliminate him immediately. If he's at least an incompetent bum, I can put up with him. Still, competence notwithstanding, all religious fanatics are diligent workers. It would be a truly praiseworthy virtue if not for the insanity.

"Allow me to congratulate you. The Lord has determined that you have led a sinful life out of ignorance. He has decided to guide you down the righteous path."

"I'll pass on that."

…Wow. A fastball? I figured he was up to something, but pitching an incredible fastball down the middle? Messing with people's lives is quite honestly a lot of fun, but it's completely unacceptable for me to be on the receiving end like this. Why can't I decide how to live my own life? Isn't my existence as an individual the least I should be able to control?

"Oh, set your mind at ease. Doesn't your distress stem from the fear that you'll be forced to act against your will?"

Well, it's hard to say. I'm not sure how to describe this sense of trepidation. It's true that I resisted the idea of being forced to follow a path determined by somebody else.

It would also be immensely humiliating for these beings to control my mind or lead me to think a certain way. Mass hallucinations should only be shared among the people who want to get intoxicated by a particular story. If there's profit to be had in illusions, we'll invest in them; if there isn't, they aren't even worth taking an interest in. And if any crazy people become a threat, I can always kick them awake and make them guzzle down the sludge of reality.

As an individual, I have to firmly resist this attack on free will that compels participation in mass hallucinations. Freedom. I'm free. I don't want anyone to violate my freedom.

I would hate to act against my own principle and violate the freedom of others, but honestly, I can deal with that. The thought of someone else violating *my* personal freedom, however, is absolutely intolerable. I was once equipped with the resources and connections to protect that freedom. Now I possess certain powers to defend it, coupled with an appreciation for the significance of its value.

"As such, worry not. We shall bless your computation orb so that it may bring forth miracles. You shall use it and feel the grace of God. Surely that will enable you to offer him words of prayer."

"'Words of prayer'?"

"That's right. The words for praising the Lord were forgotten by your ancestors. It is through no fault of your own that they were not passed on to you."

"Well, that's obvious. Although I think there's more to it than that."

Where the heck does that reasoning come from? Someone give me a proper explanation. And right now, if possible. You can even interpret or run it through a translation machine. Since it's a rush job, I'll pay extra, and I'll even throw in a tip, so someone please make it clear what this guy is saying.

"As I said, the Lord has made it so words of prayer shall flow from your lips, his voice shall be heard by your heart, and you shall believe in miracles."

"...That sounds like a really nasty form of brainwashing."

Let's try to sort this out. These evil guys threw me into this world. They may as well have abducted me. And since I haven't caved, they've come up with a new scheme. They're going to make me use a cursed computation orb. And the more I use it, the more it'll consume my soul? Oh, screw that.

As if that isn't bad enough, they have me in a nasty predicament. They had me in checkmate the moment I realized accepting their offer might be my only way to survive the war despite the price I have to pay.

These beings are like glory seekers, stirring trouble just to dash in and save the day. Insider trading doesn't hold a candle to this unscrupulous foul play. For them to get away with this absurdity would be no different than wiping law and justice off the face of the earth. Perhaps I should try to be the representative for the mortal realm's core values.

"We won't actually force you to do anything. You will simply be able to offer prayer in earnest upon experiencing God's miracles. Such is the blessing the computation orb in your possession has received."

It must take a lot of nerve to say that. You hurled me into an environment where I could die at any time in some war and then tell me you aren't forcing me? That's like telling someone in a desert not to drink water. You might as well tell me to die. In other words, threatening me much?

"I see. By the way, what happened to my real body?"

"You people are being protected by divine grace. Go now, you'd best set forth. Spread the name of the Lord."

And on that creepy note, my consciousness is pulled back to the mortal realm. In a most unfortunate turn of events as I snap back to reality, I'm greeted by the face and voice of the last person on the planet I want to see. If I were an imperial judicial clerk, I'd immediately create a law that states mad scientists are to be executed by firing squad. It would be my duty to pass such a law for the sake of the Empire; I have no doubt of that.

"We were in the presence of the Lord! It's a miracle! Blessed are those who believe!!"

The dangerous gleam in the mad scientist's eyes makes me worry he might burst out shouting, "I am the new prophet!" No, he might actually believe he is a prophet now.

"Calm down, Chief."

I'm begging you, please shut up. There's no need to emphatically boast that you've scientifically proven a mad scientist can change jobs to "religious fanatic." Please, get out of my sight.

"Oh, Lieutenant Degurechaff. The experiment is a success!! Let us exalt God's name together!!!!!"

Alas, he may have become a religious fanatic, but he's also still a mad scientist. He's batty for his beliefs.

"Come on, come on. Show me the miraculous gift of God!"

"Degurechaff to Control. Is Type 95's control formula functioning normally?"

I'm hoping they could call this all off due to technical difficulties. But a curse has been placed on this device by more or less supernatural beings. How easily they could trample my hopes and wishes. Alas, how powerless humans are...

"It is, as far as I can tell, but that could be due to issues with the observation apparatus."

"Maybe. I guess we don't have much choice. We should probably seal up Type 95 and examine it back in the lab."

Excellent. Caution is an indispensable quality in engineers. While it's hard to forgive the way they all abandoned me and ran for the hills, I can come to terms with that now. If their survival leads to the end of this experiment, then I'll allow it.

"Bite your tongue! Activate it right this instant, Lieutenant!!"

Thus begins the struggle. Seriously, can't this damn mad scientist catch a friendly bullet or have an unfortunate accident one of these days? Actually, I'm sure he's gotten mixed up in more than a couple situations like that, so why is he still alive? I sincerely doubt this is true, but could he be a pawn for Being X and his clique? I know he's my enemy, but is he my mortal enemy?

"...I'm activating it. Theoretically, it will either work or the whole lab will blow up with us."

"I'm afraid that joke wasn't funny, Lieutenant."

It wasn't the least bit funny. Mostly because I was dead serious. But seeing as this thing is cursed, I don't understand how this could end well.

I run mana through the computation orb's circuits and begin synchronizing the four cores. The energy flows absolutely smoothly, no difficulties whatsoever. As for the core synchronization, it's so effortless I do it without thinking. The mana loss is undoubtedly on par with the theoretically projected value.

Now I get it. Just going by its specs, I have to admit this truly is amazing. Definitely worthy of praise. But, although it's truly regrettable, this thing is cursed.

"Oh, great are the wonders of the Lord. Praise the Lord and the glorious name of God," I shout, the emotional words pouring from my mouth. Every cell in my body suddenly yearns to praise the Lord.

"It worked? …It actually, really worked?!"

When the observation team plunges into a whirl of astonishment, their shouts of wonder finally bring me back to myself.

"…What did I just do?"

What was I just thinking? What did I say? Did I offer praise? To that thing?!

"Oh, Lieutenant. We share this faith, don't we? It's a miracle! A miracle!"

"A miracle?"

"Give glory to the Lord and bear witness to his miracles."

Everything that transpires is like a living nightmare. Ultimately, I'm cursed, I have a horrible time, and in the end I finally—finally—get released after we finish collecting a certain amount of data. I don't care where I go as long as it isn't there. I just want to get away.

As if to grant my wish, the Republic to the west goes out of its way to declare war. Just the notice I've been waiting for. It arrives right as I'm about to despair for the world. My mind is saved.

But I guess the easy life is hard to come by.

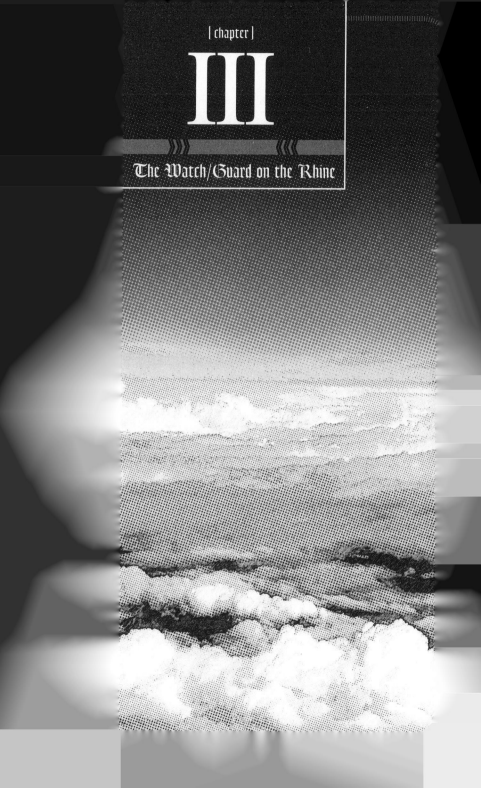

The sky over the Rhine Front... Among the mages soaring through it is Magic Second Lieutenant Tanya Degurechaff. If anything separates her from the others, it's that she's been ordered to fly solo.

Why was I given such orders?

Because the higher-ups are idiots.

And so I'm flying around the front lines alone.

The whole sad story of how I was sent here can be told in three sentences. Perhaps this is unexpected for the Empire. But as someone hastily selected for deployment due to the higher-ups' lack of foresight, I can't really let it go as simply "an unanticipated turn of events."

I've learned from my experience against the Entente Alliance on the northern front that there's no cover in the sky. Clouds are about the closest thing you can get. And as for defense, mages are lucky they're tough.

But just because I'm resilient doesn't mean I'm immortal. If someone asks me to stand in front of a high-penetration sniper rifle or a machine gun with a caliber that breaks the scale, my answer will be a flat no. Solo assignments are worse for mages than any other branch of the military. Nevertheless, the brass ordered Tanya to fly alone in hopes of drawing out a strategic delay.

How can a lowly second lieutenant possibly dodge the order? All I can do is adhere to my employer's regulations like a salaryman. I want to weep for the lack of such a noble concept—a soldier's right to refuse. As for my aerial combat maneuvers, my diligent training in the academy earned me the ACM Skill Badge. Whining that I can't fly isn't a valid tactic at this point.

And so, no matter how loath she was to go, Tanya nevertheless scrambled to fly ahead of the land forces. She would serve as airborne early warning and a scout for the forward warning line. Western Army Group's Control Center gave her the call sign "Hawkeye." It was certainly preferable to "Fairy."

"Hawkeye 03 to Command Post. Please respond."

Hawkeye 03 is my temporary call sign as a member of the early warning team. With eyes like a hawk, my job is to fly ahead to search for enemies and notify the advancing troops if I find any. Other than that, I'm supposed to maintain a fixed distance from the approaching enemy and continue gathering intelligence. Depending on the situation, my duties might eventually include taking on the role of forward air controller to guide direct support groups.

Unfortunately, though, I have to admit this job is tougher than I thought it would be. I didn't realize I'd have to work so hard just to contact the controller of the area I've been assigned to.

"…Hawkeye 03 to Command Post. Please respond."

Ever since the surprise attack, radio communications have been growing more and more chaotic. With that in mind, perhaps I'm lucky that ground control eventually connects to one of Tanya's repeated—and exasperated—calls.

"This is Seventh Provisional Field Command. Call sign Lizard 08. Reception is poor but not a problem. Hawkeye 03, send your traffic."

Basically every single type of unit targeting land forces wants to take out the enemy's eyes in the sky—aerial mages—first thing. The situation is essentially the same as the one I experienced on my mission in Norden. If an army fails to secure air and magic supremacy, it's akin to losing their ability to see. Lone magic officers are preyed upon more than any other unit of the military.

In a military operation, the first course of action is generally to eliminate interference, not that you can afford to neglect anything.

"Roger, Lizard 08. I can hear you on my end as well. Commencing support mission now."

"Thanks, Hawkeye 03. Glad to have you! We've been needing another pair of eyes."

And that makes what's coming next even worse. Now I have to kill the excitement of troops who are sincerely thrilled to finally get decent support.

"Hawkeye 03 to Lizard 08. Sorry to say this so soon, but don't expect much help from me after all. I've picked up a large group approaching fast from up ahead."

As a solo mage under enemy assault, it's out of my hands. If I get attacked the moment I arrive, then I have to defend myself before I can provide intelligence support.

Personally speaking, Tanya feels no desire to take pointless risks out of some desire to sacrifice herself for the greater good. She focuses as much as she possibly can on ensuring her safety. Anyway, if it's necessary to fly solo, then the moment enemy detection is confirmed, fleeing becomes the name of the game.

So although I hate to draw attention, I gain altitude using the power of the Type 95 computation orb, which has been issued to me for field tests. As always, I take advantage of my acceleration abilities and ascend to a certain point, where I can quickly dart up and out of range of any hostile enemy aircraft sent after me. At the same time, in anticipation of anti-air fire from the ground, I form the best protective film I can beneath me; a single hit would probably be all I can take.

The altitude I choose for my survival is eight thousand feet. That's the upper limit for combat operations, which were made possible by the protection of the Lord and Type 95. According to the mad scientist, this is the fruit of a miraculous collaboration between the hands of God and man, but the details of how this technological innovation was accomplished are immensely unpleasant for a certain free-spirited individual. Not only is this device cursed, but the most vexing part of all is that Tanya has no hope of escaping the duty of being its dedicated tester, since she's the only one who can operate it.

Well, there are other ways to look at the situation; someone might describe it as being "in the care of providence" or "blessed," but Tanya adamantly refuses to think of it in that light. There are reasons for that I don't even want to talk about.

In a manga I read a long time ago, a member of a crime syndicate whispered that secrets make a woman beautiful, but that's an unmitigated lie. The more Tanya uses this orb, the deeper it engraves this "faith" or whatever in her mind. With no choice but to praise the Lord, I'm dying for my inner self to be free again.

Well, before I start to think about this stuff too much, I should at least do the job before me. It's time to get down to business. This is what it means to be hounded by reality until you lose your inner freedom.

"An approximately company-sized group of mages is rapidly approaching from three o'clock."

Tanya conveys what she can observe of the enemy to ground control as she gains altitude, all the while grinding her teeth and vehemently cursing the ineptitude of the higher-ups in her head.

Tanya was out here with a target on her back due to their failure to notice the François Republic's attack coming from the west. Their gravest error was committing forces to trample the Entente Alliance in earnest. They had faithfully followed the theories of force concentration, pursuing battle in their desire for ever greater military achievement. Some even had delusions of annexation, it seemed.

Thanks to that, they left their own country unguarded, stupidly inviting an invasion from the west. I can't help but laugh.

Normally, according to the Empire's defense plan, it's fine for the north to just focus on delaying operations. The Northern Army Group is responsible for the northeastern front; lately, there's been an argument that they should support the Eastern Army Group against the Empire's primary potential enemy, the Federation. If each individual army group was prioritizing defense, reinforcements would be only sporadically available, and they would have no hope of achieving total victory.

As such, the General Staff had apparently schemed to take advantage of the unanticipated large-scale invasion and cut down the Entente Alliance with a single stroke by mobilizing reserves on a grand scale.

Mobilizing so many troops, however, rapidly altered the situation. "The art of war is of vital importance to the state," but the Empire's foolhardy mobilization showed poor judgment at a time when established national strategy called for caution; whether it liked it or not, its actions had provoked the surrounding countries.

In the same way the Empire hoped to proactively take out the Entente Alliance to gain future national defense advantages, the François Republic decided to take advantage of the opening and launch a preemptive strike of its own. Only an idiot could say they didn't see it coming.

To the Empire, the mobilization was surely meant to address the problems between it and the Entente Alliance. The neighboring nations are nervous about the Empire's ever-present interest in increasing its military might, however, and consider the prospect of a break in the encirclement terrifying. Not to mention that François Republic, to the west, is unable to overlook the Empire's overall goal. The long-smoldering border disputes and territorial issues between the two have erupted into localized wars on multiple occasions in the past.

The chains binding the cornered Empire are beginning to loosen, and what if the master isn't home because he's out trying to pry them off? Fully aware of the gap between its own military strength and that of its potential enemy, the François Republic believed that it could not miss this opportunity.

Ironically, it did the exact opposite of the Empire, with its huge debate about whether or not to break from the existing military strategy. In the François Republic, they had no choice but to go on the offensive to ensure the effectiveness of their own strategy.

"I've also got a battalion-sized ground unit at one o'clock. Also, multiple unidentified aircraft are approaching fast."

That's how Tanya has ended up flying, forced to use this new orb she doesn't even want, while facing swarms of incoming hostile mages.

"Lizard 08, roger. Take immediate evasive action."

The relationship between the Empire and the François Republic is such that they both have a fairly good idea of the cards in each other's hand. Naturally, the François Republic can predict that the Empire will confront the encirclement via interior lines. As a result, its defense strategy focuses tightly on how to defeat the interior lines strategy of its potential enemy.

The solution is quite simple. Before the Empire completes its large-scale mobilization, the Republic's core standing army would storm and subdue the Empire's western region, the source of a great deal of its industry and military power. That would drastically cut down the Empire's war potential. The Republic's strategy also includes taking action if the Empire invades a third nation.

Strictly speaking, the Republic's position gives it no choice but to frame all its actions as responses to the Empire. If the leaders let the situation be, they would eventually have to contend with an Empire free of northeastern pressure. As such, they have to act now, while they can still gain the upper hand.

Oh, I get it. From a purely historical perspective, it's possible to say the northern front will be decided in one blow. It would really only take a second. Anyone with common sense, even an amateur, could clearly see that the war is going to end soon.

The Entente Alliance's resistance wouldn't amount to anything, and it would be forced to surrender to the Empire. That snapshot of the future is too realistic for the analysis to be flawed, but a specialist would have told you it wasn't quite right. A few months *is* a bit fast for a country to fall into ruin, but strategically, it's also far too long to have your main forces tied up.

In a few weeks, mobilization would be complete, and the troops would be able to march in great numbers. Under those circumstances, an offensive would become a seductive option for the François Republic. It's akin to the Empire's conviction that it could use the Northern theater to break the fetters that had kept it bound to their defensive policy for years. The François Republic is equally confident that, with this one move, it can eliminate a significant threat that has been plaguing its fatherland's national defense for so long.

The Empire is prioritizing victory in the Northern theater. In other words, the higher-ups are insisting this is a strategic decision... Really, they either foolishly failed to foresee this scenario, or it did occur to them and they underestimated the probability.

The war has been recklessly directed in the first place. The stupid radio stations and newspapers were celebrating the sweeping victory on the Northern theater with dreck like, "This is the Empire's secret plan to avoid a multifront war, and the roar of artillery heralds the birth of a new order," and now, thanks to the sudden attack, they're slinging daily propaganda about the diabolical François Republic. But the people on the front lines don't care about propaganda; that's only good for making jokes about the brass to kill time in the trenches. They want to yell, *If you can afford to broadcast propaganda all the way to the front, get more men and supplies over here.* They're the ones in trouble if the higher-ups keep arguing about causes and ideals instead of facing reality.

"It looks like the vanguard mages have spotted me. They're still coming up fast."

Reality is cruel but also simple. The forces in the Western theater are basically a punching bag until the main forces return. The Empire has reached the limit of its resources. The proof is the special deployment of the instructor squad from the forces at home and the evaluation unit that assesses the practicality of preproduction models.

Really, the instruction and research-oriented units are meant to improve the overall quality of the army from the rear, not to fight on the front. Sending them in is usually a taboo that only a nation nearing its end would violate. Of course, these units are universally skilled, which makes them great problem solvers. And that's why, with the nation in a panic over the unexpected development, Tanya got thrown from a homefront research lab to the front lines.

"Lizard 08 to Hawkeye 03. We'll send reinforcements immediately."

"Hawkeye 03 to Lizard 08. I'd appreciate it, but I won't hold my breath," Tanya acknowledges as she promptly begins to withdraw. She's allowed to run this time. No need to tough it out.

"Leaving this airspace."

"Hawkeye 03, good luck!"

Out on the battlefield, incoming reinforcements might seem like a ray of hope, but I know all too well from both personal experience and history that more often than not, they don't make it in time. It's the epitome of stupidity to count on unreliable backup and risk one's life with wishful thinking, so I give my undivided attention to retreating.

Chapter **III**

"Hawkeye 03, roger."

The hand I've been dealt is discouraging, but I know I need to confront reality, even if it makes me reluctant enough to pull a face. The impatience and conflict in Tanya's blue eyes resemble that of a philosopher yearning to explore the wisdom of mankind; the groan that slips from her adorable mouth in that immature voice, her indignation at the unfairness of the situation, embodies the innocence of a child.

"...Ugh..."

Tanya Degurechaff's worries are quite simple. She's angry that the duties dumped on her exceed her pay grade, and she's distressed by her evil workplace that fails to comply with safety regulations. She would accept the existence of unions, and she wishes with all her heart for the creation of labor laws.

Part of the issue is my personal conflict with the army's goal-oriented rationale. Armies generally supply aviation personnel with high-calorie diets as a means to relieve fatigue and maintain the concentration necessary for withstanding consecutive days of intense combat, and that's great. In the Empire, too, mages and pilots have to be provided high-calorie diets.

But I'm not so sure I want them to make me take Pervitin. And "hesitant" doesn't even begin to describe how I feel about my orb as a trump card. The fruit of the collaboration between Being X and the mad scientist could poison my sharp mind in a manner far more insidious than any drug. Really, I should have gotten rid of it.

That's how desperately I don't want to use Type 95. I really hate the idea of relying on that damned computation orb steeped in the grace of God. But what if I need it to survive? Truly the ultimate choice.

This was supposed to be a day like any other for the 228th Reconnaissance Mage Company commanded by First Lieutenant Michel Hosman. The François Republic Army had successfully conducted a surprise attack, and this company was its forward-most advance guard. Even if the "surprise" was beginning to wear off in places and the mission was transitioning to assault, the spearhead's duties didn't change.

Crush the Imperial Army's eyes as it attempts to recover from the chaos, and cut off their communications while you're at it. Their duty was to isolate the enemy and prevent the formation of an organized line of resistance, which would help later troops widen the breach. It was the same assignment these veterans and First Lieutenant Hosman had received the previous day. Yet on a real battlefield, unlike in war films or novels, there was no foreshadowing what would come next.

"Golf 01 to CP. I've encountered an enemy sentinel."

"CP, roger. We think it's local direct support. Upon elimination, continue searching for the enemy's main forces."

Luck isn't on this guy's side. That was First Lieutenant Hosman's impression. After all, this sentinel was up against a whole company of mages, and it was Hosman's company, the vanguard for an entire army. It was obviously not a fair fight. That was why the enemy mage had been focused on running ever since detecting the company's approach.

Seeing that response, Hosman immediately recognized that their opponent was extremely accomplished and excelled at quick decision making; the lone mage had already climbed to the impractical altitude of eight thousand feet. And that was why Hosman couldn't help but consider the enemy unlucky: Soldiers never lived long without luck, no matter how skilled they were.

"Golf 01, roger. But that mage sure was bold, climbing up to eight thousand…"

Nobody could last long up there, but it was their only avenue of escape in the face of a whole company. Hosman was also perfectly aware of that fact. To shake off pursuit in a confrontation like this, their opponent's only options were to flee where hunters would be hesitant to follow or to fly erratically low to the ground and trust everything to fate.

Units advancing over long distances were usually loath to expend the energy necessary to climb that high, so the sentinel had assumed they would avoid that option. *Not bad.*

"Only little kids can get away with crying, 'It's too high! I can't reach!' Let's get to work, men!"

They couldn't very well let an enemy mage escape to fight another day. Considering their mission, there was no way they were backing down.

"Everybody got that? Okay, Platoon Mike will eliminate the sentinel.

Chapter **III**

Everyone else is conducting recon-in-force with me. We're gonna bust right through."

With the Empire's warning line spread so thin, the Republic had a good chance of victory. That was the guiding light for everyone participating in the operation, regardless of rank. They couldn't waste time on a provisional defensive line when the main enemy forces could return.

That was why the reconnaissance mage units were crucial to disrupt the enemy lines. They would start with the usual recon-in-force, which entailed initiating contact with the enemy to gather intelligence, but they were then expected to also create openings to break through. Knowing that Republic victory rested on their shoulders, they were determined not to get routed.

"Wilco, we'll catch up with him right quick."

After the platoon leader's acknowledgment, Platoon Mike climbed rapidly. Naturally, operating at eight thousand feet would be exhausting even for the Republic's elites. Standard combat altitude was four thousand, though if they really pushed it, they could tolerate six thousand.

In this sense, their enemy was doubly clever for choosing eight thousand. First, the chase would exhaust Platoon Mike, reducing the overall strength of the recon-in-force mission to two platoons. Also, the sentinel was making significant contributions to the wider battle by distracting the enemy and dragging things out. *We're taking on a respectable opponent.*

"Engage. Fox 01, Fox 01!"

The silence of First Lieutenant Hosman's thoughts was suddenly shattered by radio contact from one of his men. As company commander, he followed the calls for long-range magic formula fire. At the same time, the enemy soldier in front of them performed a new maneuver after realizing that escape was improbable. The bandit abruptly circled around to rush Platoon Mike as if descending upon some prey. Apparently the lone mage was taking the offensive.

"Fox 02, Fox 02! I can't believe it! He dodged that?!"

The confused voice of his subordinate on the radio contained both surprise at the enemy strike, as well as the shock of his shot missing. As

Hosman speculated about their enemy's intentions, the distance between Platoon Mike and the mage shrank considerably.

Hosman was in a somewhat-removed position, but when he confirmed the platoon had cautiously begun combat maneuvers, he was certain they were on top of it. Was the enemy trying to squeeze more time out of them by engaging at close quarters? As a tactic that could be employed immediately, it wasn't a bad choice. But unit Mike was a platoon, not a company. The coordination of a platoon was too tight to easily disrupt, and the difference in their combat potential made it hopeless for one mage to take them on alone. Hosman respected the courage and resolve, but it was a reckless maneuver.

"Enemy incoming! Disperse! Disperse!"

That very moment, Platoon Mike spread out to shift to a formation more suitable to close combat. Their objective was eliminating the opposition's eye in the sky to support follow-up Republican attacks. Their plucky opponent couldn't have known it, but the reconnaissance mage company's mission had been all but accomplished the moment they made visual contact. *Take out the eyes.* If they could do that, even if they were held up for a bit, they would be fine.

"Three rounds of interlocking fire! Get your formulas ready! Nail 'em! Fox 03! Fox 03!"

The coordination and skill of Hosman's subordinates were textbook ideal as they deliberately kept some distance in order to intercept the charge and maintain cross fire. The enemy mage had entered the line of formula bullet fire. Even if he had superior speed, Hosman's men were ready and waiting. It wouldn't be hard to nail him.

But what happened next was something no one could have predicted. It was definitely a direct hit. Regulated fire of military-grade explosive formulas, which could easily strip off a mage's protective film and even chip their solid defensive shell, had hit the target dead-on.

"Fox 03! Fox 03! Shit! The bastard's so tough!"

The moment the formulas in the multiple bullets activated, the flames should have swallowed up the enemy mage for sure. But even so...

That *thing* continued its advance without missing a beat, casually closing the distance as if it were flying through an empty sky. By intuition, not logic, they sensed something bad was happening. However, as civilization had advanced, humans as a species were no longer in touch with their animal instincts.

"Mike 3! Check six! Check six! Ahh, damn it!"

In a blink of an eye, the bandit had rushed Hosman's subordinate. Absurdly but undeniably, a magic blade sprouted from the man's chest. Then, in a single, unenthusiastic motion, as civil as someone cutting up their dinner, the blade sliced clean through him.

"Pan-pan, pan-pan, pan-pan!"

"What is that thing?! What?! It's—! Agh, Fox 04!"

A tangle of radio calls. *What was that? What the hell was that?* Hosman watched the unfolding scene through his binoculars. He couldn't believe his eyes. In terms of air combat maneuvers (ACM), Platoon Mike was the best in his company. They were being given the runaround? "It can't be...," he muttered in spite of himself. *Can a mage really move...that fast?*

"Mike 1? Mike 1?"

By the time Hosman realized, Platoon Mike was half-paralyzed. One and three were down, and the engine of four's computation orb seemed done for. He had stalled and was falling. Two was barely hanging in there covering for four and wouldn't last long, either.

"Shit, Bravo, Golf, turn back! Turn back! We have to cover Mike!"

There was no way First Lieutenant Hosman could stand idly by while his men were in trouble. He abruptly ordered the platoons in his command to race back at full combat speed to support Platoon Mike.

But inside, he wondered, *How?* No matter how much individual abilities differed between mages, could there ever be a fight this lopsided? He had heard that some imperial mages were armed with specially tuned computation orbs and had naturally high mana output.

But even then, the most they could take was a two-man team. Supposedly even those Named monsters mostly specialized in hit-and-run tactics. For someone to face a platoon head-on—and capably—instead of picking off the mages one by one was inconceivable.

"Enemy in range!"

As the company commander, though, Hosman didn't have time to lose himself in those thoughts. The enemy was already within shooting distance. The question on his mind had nothing to do with the fight, so he pushed it aside and called out sharpshooting formulas at long range in flight formations. It was a little far, but with a hail of bullets from two platoons, they couldn't miss.

Their opponent must have understood that as well and began taking textbook evasive action, which was perfectly fine. There was only one problem. Just how was that mage flitting around as if gravity didn't exist?

"Fox 01! Fox 01!"

But the most unbelievable thing—no, the utter nightmare—was how resistant the enemy's protective film was. Although the recon company had prioritized accuracy due to the long-distance nature of their shots, they had combined, albeit imperfectly, explosion formulas with the guidance formulas. Even if their target dodged all the shells, there was no one who could completely avoid the fireball blotting out the sky.

But the enemy didn't seem to be in any pain and returned fire unfazed. Hosman had to wonder if it was a joke.

"I'm going in! Cover me!"

Golf 02 probably felt like they weren't getting anywhere, so he charged with magic sword in hand. Certainly no matter how tough someone was, they'd have to take some damage from a close-quarters slash with a magic sword. If the platoons couldn't finish the enemy off at range, con-centrating their fire was also a reasonable strategy.

"We got 'em! Fox 02, Fox 02!"

They agreed and advanced, ready for a midrange brawl where it would be difficult to take evasive action. At the same time, they executed the Named Killer, an internationally famous tradition of the Republic's and the epitome of fire discipline. The support fire was six sharpshooting formulas with an explosion formula as a smoke screen, and they all made a direct hit—or rather, it should have.

"He's still fine?! Of all the ridiculous—!"

"Golf 02! Break! Break!"

The enemy mage was still up and running even after the combination of restraining and enveloping midrange fire. *Those sharpshooting formulas can pierce subpar defensive shells easily. How can anyone still fly after that?* Though he could hardly take it all in at once, he didn't have time to ponder the question.

As for Golf 02, who had tried to charge in close, he just barely managed to escape the tiger's jaws thanks to Mike 02's cover fire. Then the enemy mage shot through two protective films like they were nothing and took the men out of the fight.

"It's a trap! You piece of shit!"

Hosman had been had. He didn't like it, but he knew it was the truth. *Evading by climbing to eight thousand feet was a trick to divide our forces. Common sense says combat maneuvers are impossible at eight thousand... but that's been proven false. We walked right into this. My men are being taken out one after the other, and it's all my fault.* Chewing his lower lip, he was having trouble swallowing his fury at the deaths of his subordinates, but he understood the situation they were in. They had encountered a monster—an unknown Named.

"Mayday! Mayday! Mayday! We've encountered a new type of enemy!"

"Shit! And they said this would be easy! Golf 01 to CP, this is an emergency! Tally one unknown Named! Requesting reinforcements and permission to RTB!"

》》》   IMPERIAL ARMY TECHNOLOGY RESEARCH LAB BOARD OF REVIEW   《《《

When building a new weapon, it wasn't enough to simply implement the latest technology. Production cost, maintainability, and mission capable rate were all matters of life and death. Even so, many elements were difficult to evaluate without using the weapon in actual combat.

To the General Staff, the fighting with the François Republic that had broken out in the west was a horrible disaster, but to the Type 95 development team, it meant a highly anticipated chance to try the orb out in the field. The engineers awaited the results en masse, and the Type 95 proved itself—it blew past their expectations.

"How did the battle go?"

"Very well. Six downed, three defeated, three missing. According to the observer squad, it's incredibly doubtful that the three who went missing will make it back to their base."

They had assumed it would be impossible. After all, the experiment had only succeeded thanks to a miracle. But the test run had yielded surprising results. Type 95's achievements were worthy of all the praise the elated technology personnel were heaping on it. They could hardly stop grinning.

Of course, the skill of the user made a big difference. Second Lieutenant Degurechaff certainly had the skills of a Silver Wings Assault Badge recipient, but that alone shouldn't have been enough to overcome such a disadvantage and get such impressive results.

"She basically took out an entire company by herself."

She didn't defeat all the mages, but she had still repulsed the whole unit. She was overwhelmingly superior in a fundamental sense, nothing more. The theoretical values had indicated possibilities, but she had made them real.

"Yes, to think it's come so far…"

From a commonsense perspective, the results could only be described as incredible. The orb was nothing short of revolutionary. This technological innovation opened the door to a whole new universe of combat.

"Right. Judging from its record at Elinium Arms, I was expecting it to have major issues."

The officers who had questioned continuing development were now commenting in wonder, almost self-deprecating. They had been so worried about this thing, but when they saw what it was really like, the results were so good that all previous failures could be forgiven. If it could perform this well, everything was fine. They could even lower the cost via mass production.

"Oh, it has issues all right."

The tech department grandly threw a bucket of cold water on them and their admiration. They understood Operations's feelings all too well. They were excited by the revolutionary technology, so they were hoping for a revolutionary improvement in quality. But unfortunately, it was all a fantasy.

They had to wake everyone up from the dream.

"What do you mean? It achieved far more than we'd expect from a solo flier."

"Right. This thing could change mage combat as we know it."

Certainly, Type 95 had achieved stellar results. That was a fact. In terms of performance, it was in such a league of its own that you could call it a next-*next* generation orb. That was made possible by quad-core synchronization. The quad-core engine's demonstration of mana fixation in actual combat and the possibilities inherent in that were enough to make Operations drool.

After all, the technology to stabilize mana and store it like bullets was of immense tactical value. The ability to freely use stored mana effectively removed the barrier of mana capacity.

"My understanding is that all the worries and criticism raised in the past have been proven false in combat," a General Staff officer muttered.

Really, the achievements spoke for themselves. Quad-core synchronization made quadruple output a reality, increasing combat potential to a whole new level. After seeing the technology was usable, Operations had to have it.

"We only have one successful case. The project has been a huge failure, unless we say the goal was simply to verify the technology."

But engineers didn't deploy Type 95 in order to convince the army to adopt it. They just wanted to see what kinds of issues would come up in actual field use, so when war broke out in the west, they sent it to the front. They had focused on the tech and never even considered mass-producing it.

"What happened in the other cases?"

The most successful case was also the *only* successful case. If anyone asked about the prospect of mass production, they would have to raise doubts as to whether they could reproduce their success. Users of mage technology were already a chosen few, but even then, an orb with only one successful operator couldn't have much chance for mass production as a weapon.

"In one of the worst tests, there was an explosion in the lab, and we lost a whole platoon."

The things were constantly blowing up—one defective circuit would cause them to self-destruct. If someone could manage to coat the orb with mana, it could take a beating, according to the actual combat trials. However, the success rate of that critical step was hopelessly low.

The worst accident had occurred during a synchronization failure; four times the usual mana had detonated and blown away the platoon doing the testing—a group of elites including instructors from Central and members of the Advanced Technology Inspection Corps.

"...But it can shoot bursts of mana, right? That's too appealing to give up on."

"The only one who can use it is Lieutenant Degurechaff. The best anyone else has managed is not getting blown up."

As developers and engineers, they were ethically bound to push back. Even the engineers who had requested to continue research had only cared about the technological revolution. After their impulsively inquisitive minds had been inspired, Chief Engineer von Schugel and his team had spent their days focused only on testing the limits of what was possible. But when they took a moment to think calmly, they were the ones who best understood the orb's dangers and difficulties.

Of course they understood—they built the thing.

"But you have one successful case, right? Can't you just replicate it?"

"...I told you we almost lost Elinium Arms! Even the successful case of Lieutenant Degurechaff was a total fluke—though I shouldn't be saying that as an engineer. We still don't even really know what happened."

Analysis of observed values made it clear that mana fixation via quad-core synchronization was more dangerous than anyone had imagined. The experiment was a miraculous success, but they had measured enough mana to know that if the test had failed, the entire Elinium Arms Factory would have been blown to bits. It was obvious to anyone with a modicum sense that they couldn't afford to repeatedly fail an experiment that would cause destruction on that scale.

"A fluke?"

"Just when a runaway mana reaction was about to melt the cores, the interference waves harmonized, and moments away from liquefaction, the cores synchronized."

For the engineers, it was a frustrating result. They didn't know how, but they had managed to succeed. By some fantastic stroke of luck, the uncontrollable mana had just happened to straighten itself out; that was as far as they could grasp. Even if they wanted to verify the results further, all they could tell was that it was a coincidence.

You could propose that it might be possible to duplicate the results if they lost control of the mana and then adjusted accordingly...but that was a conclusion. It was impossible to make conclusions about these results. They simply couldn't be duplicated. This was like seeing a lightning strike that just happened to carve a splendid sculpture and then trying to re-create it with human hands.

"So the rampaging mana stabilized itself. Basically, it was a miraculous coincidence."

The fact that Chief Engineer Schugel noted in the experiment report "We owe our success to the power of God" showed the extent of that miracle. Something that was by all rights impossible had occurred, and it just happened to do so beyond the reach of human understanding.

Even Chief Engineer Schugel, who created Type 95, had given up on continuing development, saying, "Going any further would be blasphemy, an insolent act in defiance of God." Even the hard-core techies concluded that you probably had to be chosen by God or something to use that computation orb, which goes to show how hard it had to be.

"So what does that mean?"

"We're currently using something we don't understand without understanding it, and it hasn't been easy."

In other words, that was about all they knew. Whether unraveling the principle behind the orb or reproducing it, a vast amount of time and effort would be required, and on top of that, their probability of success wasn't worth betting on no matter how they calculated it.

"It might be better to just glorify Lieutenant Degurechaff as a hero."

"...I agree. That could help us out in a bigger way."

Fortunately, Second Lieutenant Degurechaff had earned her Silver

Wings Assault Badge at quite a young—frankly, tender—age. Praising her abilities for publicity would be much easier than trying to show off the flawed orb.

I, Viktoriya Ivanovna Serebryakov, am an early riser.

"Visha! Get up, Visha!"

"Urgh, morning, Elya."

Technically, that's because my gorgeous friend always wakes me up. The ever-kind Elya is taller than me, *and* she has curves in all the right places even though she's so thin. Not only that, but she also doesn't get low blood pressure in the morning—she's always full of pep.

I'm only a centimeter shorter than her and just as slim! God is just so unfair. Elya and I have the same lifestyle, so I really don't get why certain parts of her body are so much more developed than mine.

Anyone fresh out of the Cadet Corps wants to stay sound asleep in their warm beds as long as they can. That's because one of the only fun things about cadet school is staying up all night chatting with your dorm buddies. Elya is one of the girls who really loves it. I go to bed before her pretty often.

But then she always gets up earlier. How does that make sense? I guess it's just one of those differences between people. I can't do anything about it no matter how hard I try.

I probably sound like I hate my good-natured friend, but really, I don't.

In general, joining the Cadet Corps is voluntary, but anyone eligible to become a mage is basically forced to enlist and thrown into the fray. So this unlucky cadet was bound by the strictest rules and continually chewed out by demon drill sergeants. Of course I blamed God at the time, but I couldn't stay mad when I'd met such a great friend.

Sadly, my time with my good buddy is scheduled to end today. It hasn't sunk in yet, but today, we'll be assigned to our respective combat units. I hope we end up together, but that's probably too much to hope for.

It's less like we're wearing our uniforms and more like our uniforms are wearing us, but we're still real soldiers. For whatever reason, fate gave us magical potential.

And so, we've become Imperial Army mages, pride of the Reich. Well, technically, we're newbies. Before I knew it, I was tossed into the dormitory of the Western Army Group as a reinforcement for the Rhine Front.

My duty as a soldier is to serve indefatigably in the west as a shield for the beloved fatherland at this critical juncture...or something. I'm an imperial subject, too, I guess, so I do think maybe I should fight for my great country, but it doesn't feel quite right. Maybe that's only natural since I was born in lovely snow-white Moskva. Well, the hazy remnants of my memory are just a torrent of red, which isn't very fun. My parents turned to relatives for help, we thankfully managed to escape the country, and that's my story. I was too young to really remember much, but I might be lacking qualifications compared to imperial soldiers actually born here.

That said, I'm so grateful to my aunt and uncle for taking me in. I'm second grateful to God for giving me my daily bread.

"Let's eat!"

Our diet here is different from the rear, but I already got used to the less-than-fresh veggies and the canned goods you tend to find at the NCO mess halls near the front. On the first day, I cried because the food tasted about as awful as combat rations, but lately I've been enjoying it just fine.

"Visha, did you hear that the platoon you're assigned to is getting a new leader?"

Mealtime is fun since we get to chat. Given the circumstances, it's no wonder we're interested in discussing our assignments.

"Really? Isn't this kind of a weird time to add a new platoon leader?"

"It's definitely true!"

"Elya, calm down."

Of course, so much of the chatter is gossip. I heard that once you get to be a vet, you can catch wind of your own assignment and your buddies', and I bet it's true. But as you might imagine, mages fresh out of the Cadet Corps, mere NCOs, can't tell right from left in the army.

Still, I'm interested in my assignment, and my friend has an uncanny ability to overhear things.

"But seriously? We're supposed to be reinforcements. Would they really make a whole new platoon on the front lines?"

"Logically, no, but this has to be true, Visha. I heard personnel officers talking about it!"

I do wonder where Elya just happened to hear all this news. It isn't like they're elementary school teachers chatting about their classes; would officers from Personnel really discuss assignments in front of other people? ...*I shouldn't overthink it.*

"Elya...sometimes I wonder if you're a ninja from the Far East."

"Ha-ha-ha-ha-ha. A woman has her secrets, Miss Serebryakov."

"Well, whatever. So do you know where this new platoon will be deployed?"

"Oh, so...it's not a new platoon but a replacement for one that got wiped out. You'll be okay, though. Supposedly the leader is a veteran with Silver Wings."

For a second, I don't understand what she said. I'm normally easygoing, but when I come to my senses, I'm so shocked that I can't help a knee-jerk reaction.

"Silver Wings...? You mean the Silver Wings Assault Badge?!"

"Wow, your eyes are like saucers."

"What?!"

"Visha, your faces are always so funny."

I'll have to thank her later for keeping her burst of laughter quiet so we don't draw attention from the other diners. But wow, someone who is still *alive* got the Silver Wings Assault Badge... An awesome imperial soldier? More like an awesome human being.

"You must know about your own assignment, too, right?"

"Yup. I'll be supporting the artillery as part of an observation squad. Of course, I'll be making tea in the back!"

"Hey...you never know what'll happen if you're not careful."

That said, the news that my friend will be somewhere safe makes me envious, but I'm still relieved.

"Uh-oh, if we keep lollygagging like this, our time'll be up. Chow down, Visha!"

"Yeah, you're right... Hey, where'd my caramel go?"

"Oh, you hadn't eaten it yet, so I helped you."

Yes, this maddening mischief maker is my precious friend.

>>>   (A FEW DAYS EARLIER) IMPERIAL CAPITAL   <<<

"Reassignment?"

I'm being transferred away from the technology research department and from being treated like a guinea pig as the dedicated tester of the Type 95 computation orb. Magic Second Lieutenant Tanya Degurechaff has longed for this notice—waiting out days that felt like years—and is pleased as punch to accept. Her application must have finally, *finally* been approved. My mind will be freed. I'll leave this place and head to the new posting immediately.

"Yes, a reassignment. Guess the brass isn't about to let an ace just hang around. You're going to be leader of Third Platoon in the 205th Assault Mage Company."

Considering resources are so low that even the instructor unit has to join the battle, there's nothing I can do about ending up on the front lines. Actually, as someone fresh out of the academy, leading a platoon, even in the thick of battle, is much better than getting abused as a guinea pig.

Finally, I'll apparently have subordinates. Now I can delegate tasks I would have had to handle alone in the past. And in the worst-case scenario, although I'd lose favor with the higher-ups, using them as human shields is a possibility. I mostly hope they aren't incompetent, but either way, this is cause for celebration.

"And congratulations, Lieutenant. It's not much compared to the Silver Wings, but in recognition of your recent achievements, we have decided to award you the Aerial Assault Badge."

"Thank you, sir." Tanya gives a cheerful salute and a smile that makes her look like the little girl she is.

In high spirits, I return to the dormitory and set about packing luggage. Of course, soldiers don't have many personal belongings to begin with. Even though she's biologically female, Tanya feels that clean and neat is good enough for clothes. In fact, her uniforms are the only clothing she has. Since none of the existing sizes fit, she just has to apply for a clothing allowance and get them made to order.

It takes less than an hour to pack my officer travel bag. I briskly tell the manager of the dormitory, where I was staying during my temporary assignment, about the transfer; show him my orders; and thank him for taking care of me while I lived there. With that, my moving preparations are complete.

Then I head straight for my designated unit. These are frontline orders. They require me to forgo annoying social obligations like farewell parties and take up my position as quickly as possible. Hence, after receiving permission to fly from the Air Defense Identification Zone, I immediately take my bag and race across the sky toward the assigned rendezvous point.

Fortunately, though the army is facing a crisis, this is still only moving between bases in the rear. The short flight ends without incident, and less than two hours after my departure, I arrive and present myself to my new company commander.

"Magic Second Lieutenant Tanya Degurechaff, leader of Third Platoon of the 205th Assault Mage Company, reporting for duty."

"Thanks for coming, Lieutenant. First, allow me to welcome you. I am company commander, First Lieutenant Ihlen Schwarkopf." He confirms that I've arrived as ordered and completes assignment procedures as he welcomes me. While keeping things businesslike in adherence to military regulations, we casually appraise each other. We're both soldiers, and soldiers don't get to choose their allies. Thus, it's logical to assume that they won't last long on the battlefield if they don't at least get to know each other.

"Commander Schwarkopf, sir, pleased to be serving under you."

"Great. Let's get to it, Lieutenant Degurechaff. Do you have any experience leading a platoon?"

One thing that makes Tanya happy at a glance is that her commanding officer appears to be an extremely orthodox mage. He is a first lieutenant. Judging from his age, he has probably served a decent amount of time. And from the medals he's wearing, it's easy to gather that he has a wealth of combat experience. The decorations commending his participation in several minor conflicts, especially, provide a certain level of assurance. So my first impression is that he isn't an inept superior, which would be scarier than the enemy. Since I can't choose my commanding officer, if he ends up being like the legendary soldier who ruined the Burma-Imphal front, I may decide to take action and mourn the ensuing "unfortunate accident."

"This will be my first time, sir."

Schwarkopf is also observing Degurechaff. He can't deny being a bit puzzled to see a little girl appear before his desk in the company command office. All he has heard from above is that they would send him a mage from an instructor unit at Central who has combat experience on the northern front.

Schwarkopf figured they would give him a seasoned veteran. It's safe to assume that a second lieutenant from an instructor unit would have worked up from noncommissioned officer status, and a veteran should be reliable in any situation. Plus, as a recipient of the Silver Wings Assault Badge, whoever the brass sent would have to be a capable soldier with a wealth of combat experience. That's why when Schwarkopf laid eyes on this kid younger than his daughter announcing her arrival with a perfect salute, he wonders what he'll do with the difficult platoon. His original intent to give her the command had relied on his expectation that she would be a veteran...

"...Lieutenant, I'll be frank."

If the records don't lie and there isn't any mistake, the second lieutenant waiting at attention for him to speak is a significant asset who has splendidly distinguished herself in battle, and she had been dispatched to deal with the worsening situation on the western front. But being a great athlete is different from being a great coach, and Schwarkopf fears this situation is similar.

"The 205th Assault Mage Company is meant to have three platoons, but during the early days of the war, our numbers dropped to less than two, and we've been operating undermanned ever since."

To replace the lost men, a new platoon leader and fresh members have been assigned to the company. Schwarkopf knows he can't complain, even if every member of the platoon is a raw recruit, but that's precisely why he hoped the leader would be an experienced veteran.

"...Can you command a platoon of recruits straight out of the Cadet Corps?"

To cast the situation as it currently stands in a pessimistic light, the platoon will consist of a child leading greenhorns. It would be not only ineffective but also deadweight—worse than deadweight. Needless to say, if the Empire's forces could simultaneously babysit and wage war, they wouldn't be having such a hard time.

He asks the question partially out of doubt; whether an immediate change in personnel is necessary or not will depend on her answer.

Degurechaff's response is simple. "Please give me the order." She keeps her reply short and speaks in an even, matter-of-fact tone. Yet her eyes shine back at Schwarkopf with nearly arrogant pride, rejecting his misgivings about her ability. "I will give you results."

Her reply also shows her unfaltering self-confidence. It surpasses his expectations. The first step toward trust is believing that if this combat veteran says, "Give me the order," the order will be carried out.

"Well, you've got the Silver Wings Assault Badge. I'm expecting a lot out of you!"

"Yes, sir!"

A living recipient of the Silver Wings Assault Badge from the instructor unit is worthy of that much trust.

Tanya, for her part, surmises that Schwarkopf only accepted her response because of the decoration she's wearing. In other words, the entire worth of Second Lieutenant Tanya Degurechaff can be summed up by the badge.

In that sense, she's truly grateful to have received the Silver Wings. Apart from the "White Silver" moniker that comes with it (which I never wanted in the first place and am more than eager to get rid of), and

Chapter **III**

the sanity checks it forces onto me, nothing about my current situation is harmful, and I have a good reputation.

Well, I should probably welcome this. Beneath the face of a soldier, Tanya is calculating. Goodwill and praise are better than hostility and insult, at least.

"All right. I'll go ahead and explain the situation."

"Yes, sir."

Having gotten more or less good impressions, they decide for the present to trust each other enough that they can focus on their respective jobs. Next, it's time for work.

"As you know, the Great Army's main forces are urgently being reorganized and assembled."

The Empire has fallen into disorder in the immediate aftermath of the François Republic's surprise attack, but overall, it mostly held its own in the early battles. That doesn't change the fact that the troops are under pressure, but the national defense policy calls for interior lines strategy. In that sense, though it's true the Western Army Group has received reinforcements from remaining units at Central, they have completely fulfilled their duty of delaying the enemy.

"While that is the case…it will take some time to reach the western front."

There's only one problem: The reserves and standing troops, who are supposed to be the counterblow, have all been invested in the north. The top General Staff members wanted to resolve the Norden issue with one push, but the original national defense plan is falling apart.

"All the Western Army Group can do is hope they arrive soon, but we have to assume it will take a while."

Originally, the plan called for Central to send three divisions within twenty-four hours of mobilization orders, including one Imperial Guard division as vanguard, and within seventy-two hours, seven more divisions to follow. Within a week or so, the Great Army itself would invest an overwhelming force—twenty divisions of their dignified regular troops and enough reserves for sixty divisions.

That's why the Western Army Group never imagined a need to slow down the enemy on their own for a month. And of course, since they don't have the reinforcements from the plan, even if they only fight to delay, they'll have to do it in a way that minimizes their casualties.

The only plan the Western Army Group has prepared is a defensive battle limited to large-scale resistance.

The General Staff forgot that while investing the Great Army in Norden, and the price has been higher than anyone imagined.

The fact that the higher-ups have mobilized the instructor unit in an attempt to establish western defenses shows how panicked they are. They even sent out Type 95, a military secret that wasn't supposed to leave the lab, under the pretext of continued evaluation with Tanya; really, they just wanted the muscle.

Perhaps the rapidly changing war situation gave them no choice, but if they're in so much turmoil they can't prioritize confidentiality, there's no way they can carry out the defense plan as it was envisioned.

The Great Army, the main imperial attacking force, was deployed to the north in its entirety due to an error in strategic judgment. Even if it only took a short time to reorganize and redeploy the troops, that was far too long from a military perspective.

"How is assembling the Great Army going?"

It's obvious that their difficulties stem from the lack of a plan for this unforeseen need to deploy troops. Even a minutely calculated operation is difficult to execute without hitches, so handling this situation off the cuff seems nigh impossible.

Inevitably, the current pace of assembly is not ideal. In this situation, the delay of reinforcements and ensuing impact on the front are matters of life and death for the Western Army Group, as well as critical concerns for the imperial soldiers who have to suffer the brunt of the attack before the Great Army arrives.

"Not good. They're short on vehicles in the north, so they need about two weeks to redeploy the units to the west."

Schwarkopf seems to doubt they'll really be only two weeks late. Experience has taught him that HQ always gives optimistic estimates when it comes to the number of reinforcements and their arrival time.

Redeployment sounds simple enough, but it involves more than just reorganizing the units and setting up a new chain of command; the units need to be replenished and resupplied before they can go anywhere. It's no easy feat. Just transporting an army consumes resources—not only fuel and supplies but also intangibles such as soldiers' energy.

That's why Tanya isn't surprised when her superior matter-of-factly explains, "We've given up on delaying along the western line. We're switching to mobile defense."

Once you determine that buying time won't cut it, adopting a mobile defense strategy is a natural step. Normally, you would base the troops in rear locations that are reinforced against long-distance enemy artillery and use the distance you withdrew during the delaying battle for defense in depth.

"Lieutenant, I doubt I need to say this to you...but this is a classic example of something easier said than done."

"Yes, sir, understood."

The original interior lines strategy calls for the defensive line to obstruct the enemy's advance and for the Great Army reinforcements to surround and annihilate the forces that have penetrated too deeply into imperial territory. But that line has already collapsed, and they're now fighting a defensive battle on thin ice, which is not much fun at all. Probably the only enjoyable defensive battle would have been the one fought behind the famous Maginot Line,[12] perfect for shut-ins. You could have just holed up in there and wait for the war to end.

To Tanya, this is a problem that goes deeper than a strategic level failure. If you're planning on fighting using attritional containment tactics, then it should probably have dawned on you to tighten up your border with forts instead of going for a strategy that will fail before the fighting even starts. If command actually assumed that the François Republic would be content to overlook the threat of their exterior lines strategy collapsing upon the defeat of the Entente Alliance, that naivety would leave Tanya dumbstruck. Lower-ranking soldiers like Tanya and

---

[12] **Maginot Line** France put a significant amount of money into its defense budget (3.3 billion francs in the year 1930) to construct this defensive line. The sad thing was that Germany went around it, so the units holding it were unable to participate in the war in a meaningful way. Though they did a bang-up job securing the Maginot Line, the enemy chose to go through the Ardennes and Low Countries to wallop them—what a pitiful fort. It's a classic example of how even a great idea needs great execution to be any good.

Schwarkopf are stuck paying the price of that miscalculation in blood, which is something they can't tolerate.

"We are soldiers. If the brass tells us to do something, we do it."

A patriot might argue that the nation's leading strategists work against the country by dint of their incompetence. Tanya doesn't house even the slightest intention of dying for the Empire. I always have to make exemplary remarks that go against what I truly feel, acting out the expected role to help myself succeed. To that end, I would even give a Tsugene-esque[13] speech, though I despise his incompetence. If it came down to it, I would even shout, "Patriotism is not a crime!"

I can blather about those things as naturally as breathing, and that plus Tanya's doll-like appearance is enough to suggest my patriotism to anyone listening.

Most importantly, the majority of soldiers detest the idealists throwing around words like *patriotism* and *brave loyalty* in the rear, but to them the sentiment of loving one's country is sacred. Combat veterans who earned their praise in the field swear to defend their country. In extreme conditions, they treat that vow as a declaration of faith.

"…Quite right, Lieutenant Degurechaff." Thus, the model imperial soldier is one who indifferently completes their missions in adherence to mission-oriented war doctrine, and those qualities are praised. "Good. Back to the topic at hand, then."

"Yes, sir!"

He must at least be able to tell that I'm not inept. With a deep sense of satisfaction, Schwarkopf is able to relax a bit. The situation is unpleasant to be sure, but here's a good asset.

He has to take units that were mobilized at the last minute with no clear strategic direction and fight a defensive battle. He's lost a great number of his already harried troops, the replacements are deadweight

---

[13] **Tsugene-esque** In Japanese, *Tsujiinkyū*. A joke about the awful tactical planner Masanobu Tsuji. It's used for people who are only halfway competent. Due to his ability to take action and his—for better or worse—inflated pride, in a nutshell, he was toxic. His collection of arbitrary actions teaches us how important discipline is in military units. Even so, he was never punished and actually rose in rank; the world is full of injustice.

recruits, and their leader is a little girl? For just a moment, he feels like looking to the heavens in despair, but for Schwarkopf, the mere fact that Degurechaff is an officer who can get things done makes her one of his few valuable resources.

"The 205th Assault Mage Company has been selected as a mobile strike force in the mobile defense battle."

Schwarkopf and his company's skilled fighting and finesse during the initial battles have landed them on the mobile strike duty; their job is to rush around putting out fires, and it will require playing more roles than ordinary units do.

"We are the linchpin of the counterattack. That's a big responsibility for us to share. I look forward to seeing what you're made of out there."

"Thank you, Lieutenant. I'll do my best to protect the fatherland."

Tanya looks at Schwarkopf with her innocent blue eyes and speaks of noble ideals and contributing to the nation with her childlike lips.

Of course, Tanya's words don't have an iota of sincerity; I just know it's a line someone in her position should say.

Tanya knows how awful the trenches are—even if my sources are war films and books from another universe—so she's happy to be a counterattack reserve instead of stuck in one of them.

Certainly, holing up in some fieldworks fortified with reinforced concrete seems like the safer option at a glance. I can understand why amateurs would think that. The invention of the machine gun gave defense the advantage, and to anyone who knows that, the defensive position is unquestionably strong. No one ordered by General Nogi to capture Port Arthur with swords would hesitate to make an "accident" happen. Humans are much frailer than concrete and iron.

At the same time, it's important to remember that the base at Port Arthur was destroyed by heavy naval artillery. Fortifications on a battlefield have the fatal structural flaw of being immobile. History teaches us that that no matter how sturdy the fortress, before siege artillery it's nothing but another target. Given the previous point, Tanya knows that being part of a mobile unit out in the field where they can run anywhere they need to in a pinch is safer.

Even a mage can't attack a well-defended stronghold at close range and get off easily, but I also know that stronghold will get pummeled by artillery. And I'm also aware that attacking the enemy vanguard is safer, if only in comparison, since they'll be exhausted from breaking through the defensive line.

Thus, Tanya makes false declarations of loyalty, while the only thing she truly welcomes with joy is her assignment. Raising her chances of survival even just a little is undoubtedly a happy occurrence.

"Great. Any questions?"

"Yes, sir. Will we be sortieing from the defensive line or the rear?"

There's one point worth bearing in mind. Mobile strike forces come in two types. One is positioned in the rear and responds quickly to seal enemy breaches. The other sets off from a forward position to catch the enemy around their backside. The difference between the two is whether you can kick back and relax as counterattacking personnel in the rear or have to dig trenches and build fortifications while under the constant threat of enemy attack. They are two completely different environments.

Of course, the unit that has to seal the breaches will take some damage since they do have to charge up to the front lines, but generally, the act of launching a counteroffensive in the first place usually means they get to enjoy numerical superiority. In other words, I won't need to worry about being sent on counterattacks if the situation is overwhelmingly bad.

"Rejoice, Lieutenant. We'll be on the forward-most line."

"What an honor."

This is the worst.

Mobile strike personnel on the front? Meaning they would have to defend the line and double as distraction during the counterattack? No number of lives could be enough. If she were defending from a trench, she could use the nearest people as shields, but she can't do that if she leaves the line to be a decoy. Pincering the enemy with the guys from the rear might sound great, but we would only be glorified targets.

"I never doubted that would make you happy. We may also need to help defend the strongpoints, depending on what the situation calls for."

As expected. Should I be happy? I'm not thrilled that my ominous hunch was right on the money. As a way to hone my crisis management skills, this assignment won't be bad, but I would rather never need to use them.

"So we'll prioritize mobile strike operations but also support the defensive line?"

"That is correct."

Am I supposed to just accept my fate? Let myself be exploited as part of the mobile strike force after being stuck on the line? There should be a limit to how much you can overwork someone. I'd like to demand better working conditions or at the very least an increase in base pay.

Of course, I don't have any problem with performing duties covered by my contract, but this is a bit much. I'd like to be adequately compensated.

"However, our mission isn't to eliminate the enemy, just repulse them. We don't need to bend over backward to surround and annihilate them."

"This is the worst. Assembling the Great Army must be going rough."

"Oh, you can tell?"

"If we make our only objective to delay enemy forces and don't adopt a mobile defense aiming to exhaust them, we won't last long enough. Even the stupidest freshly minted officer could see that."

They couldn't possibly conduct a successful delaying defense along the whole huge front. Without using a mobile defense strategy to exhaust the enemy forces, it would be impossible to suppress the enemy; things are so dire that the Empire would have to risk allowing raiders to get through at one location and attack them there. At least they would be organized, so it probably wouldn't be as much of a disaster as the latter days on the eastern front in World War I, but I still have to brace myself.

"…That's one way to put it. Well, there's no cheerful way to fight a war, anyway. Here's who is in your platoon."

"Thank you, sir." Tanya takes a mental deep breath and looks over the list of her first subordinates ever, but it's so ridiculous, it makes her brain freeze up. It dawns on her that she's reeling. The only reason she doesn't instinctively hurl the document away is due to excessive shock, rather than a triumph of reason. In words, her thoughts would be, *This is too much!*

"My understanding was that there was a general lack of key personnel in the Western Army Group and that because of this, the only replacements we could get for the third platoon were rookies with zero experience, but I have to correct myself… Perhaps we should call them untrained recruits?"

"I see no problem with that. This means your platoon will be extremely rough around the edges. I want you to make defending the position your main duty."

These mages have only completed Cadet Corps basic training, and we're rushing them into a combat unit? Anyone with half a notion of how mage battles work would laugh it off as an April Fools' joke. With four to a platoon and twelve in a company, mage teams prioritize skills over numbers more than anyone else. Even someone with innate mage potential would only be in the way as a newbie with nothing more than basic training. This is like taking a guy with only the most basic army rules and regulations beaten into him, putting him in a plane, and telling him to fly. It'll be worse than a turkey shoot.

I see. By having us on defense, he's telling me that he doesn't consider them fit for combat. It'd be irrational to expect anything out of this unit, so it's a valid conclusion.

"Commander, a humble suggestion, as platoon leader, if I may..."

"Lieutenant Degurechaff, I realize fighting a war while babysitting is a lot to ask, although it's weird to say that to you..."

"I have to say that, frankly, I would be more useful fighting solo than in that platoon."

I get that the platoon lacks training, but you're telling me to make it a stationary force? They can't handle mobile battles, so you're telling me to defend the base while reeducating and training them? Isn't that the same as ordering me to let the incompetent hold me back?! Tanya vehemently protests this crisis with indescribable rage. Unless the regulations that she learned at the academy have been revised, childcare is definitely not in a soldier's job description.

It would be safer to hurl these novices into no-man's-land and free myself of the burden. Maybe I should do that if I get the chance. No, I can't judge them without even meeting them...

"As an officer, I have no plans to abandon my command duties, but I hope you will consider the way to use our forces most effectively."

"These guys are backup. If the situation calls for it and the timing works out, we'll send you on guerrilla missions."

Even though he wants her to whip the platoon into shape, he's implying from the start that he will send Tanya on her own if necessary.

"Understood. Are we permitted to abandon our position if need be?"

"Regrettably, we can't pull the lines back any farther."

"So we have to hold it?"

"Command says we can choose victory or Valhalla."[14]

Victory or Valhalla? Is that even a choice? It's just a roundabout way of ordering us to die on the line. No, it's not even roundabout—it's just narcissistic bullshit.

Why should I die for other people? If someone wants to die for me, that's their prerogative, but forcing me to die completely violates my free will.

Freedom reigns supreme. We can be democratic, nationalist, or even imperialist, so long as I'm free. So please, stop issuing war bonds. Financing the war by printing bonds under the assumption the Empire will win just guarantees hyperinflation no matter how the war ends.

Win or lose, I can only imagine the future will be a barrel of fun. How utterly unpleasant.

"Splendid. Both options sound great."

"Fantastic. Then I'll introduce you to your platoon."

Okay, time to greet my allies in this miserable war. If they happen to be in the right place at the right time, I might even use them as human shields, so I have to expect a lot out of them.

And so, though neither of them wanted to, the young lady and the little girl would slurp the same sludge and nibble biscuits so hard they had to chip them apart with bayonets before they could eat them, fighting side by side on the western front under a shower of shells.

My first impression of my direct superior, Imperial Army officer Second Lieutenant Degurechaff of the western front mobile strike army, Seventh Assault Group, 205th Assault Mage Company, was "vampire."

---

[14] **Valhalla** The place where the souls of those who fell in battle join the souls of past heroes. In other words, having to choose between victory or Valhalla means choosing to win or die. Most will end up in Valhalla anyway.

Her skin was so white she looked sick, and her sharp eyes seemed to loathe the sun. It was quite a shock.

The first time I saw her, First Lieutenant Schwarkopf had ordered us to assemble, and as we were standing by, a little kid who looked bizarrely comfortable in her uniform showed up. She couldn't have been a student from the Cadet Corps—she wasn't even old enough to enroll. The cap sitting atop her messily tied hair was too big for her. Any normal soldier who saw her wearing the rank of second lieutenant would have done a double take.

When the company commander introduced her to us, though, I didn't feel like anything was off about Lieutenant Degurechaff. I couldn't quite explain it, but it was like she fit right in.

Still, the moment she turned her icy cold eyes on us like we were objects to be appraised, I shrank from her in spite of myself. People might laugh at me for being afraid of such a little kid, but those eyes reminded me of the way a cat looks when it's playing with a mouse, which creeped me out.

Just like Elya said, Lieutenant Degurechaff was a veteran ace who had earned numerous decorations for her distinguished service, not the least of which was the Silver Wings Assault Badge. She had a thick aura of battle around her, and her face was almost doll-like, it was so pleasant to look at. Vacant blue eyes, blond hair tinged dark gray.

Maybe it was partly because we didn't get much sun on the Rhine front, but I noted in my head that she looked just like a vampire.

She urged us, in a calm, businesslike tone that left no room for mis-understanding, to state our rank, name, and where we last served, and I felt—just a little bit—like I wanted to get out of there. The Cadet Corps had a simple method of categorizing cadets. The army knew very well that volunteers and conscripts wouldn't be on the same wavelength, even if they trained together, so they divided the mages into two classes from the start. Battalion C was expected to eventually train as officers at the academy, and Battalion D would just complete their compulsory service.

My two platoon mates were elites from Battalion C.

"Corporal Kurst von Walhorf from Idal-Stein Battalion C, First Company!"

"Corporal Harald von Vist, also from Idal-Stein Battalion C, First Company!"

I gave my rank and name after the two Cadet Corps volunteers. I didn't wish I had volunteered, exactly, but it was sort of a bummer to say I was drafted right after people who announced they had offered their services to their country. I couldn't just not care like Elya; I wasn't thick-skinned enough to just laugh it off. Oh, God, why must you torment me?

"Corporal Viktoriya Ivanovna Serebryakov from Idal-Stein Battalion D, Third Company."

You could say I felt a bit out of place as the only conscript. I mean, Corporals Kurst and Harald were volunteers from the same company. If we did things the usual way, that meant the two guys with experience working together would be buddies, and I'd get paired with the platoon leader.

That was why I was thinking, as I reported, that it would be great if I didn't get chewed out for being a slow, lazy draftee. So I was momentarily stunned by what the second lieutenant said next.

"You have my respect for fulfilling your obligations, Corporal Viktoriya Ivanovna Serebryakov. It'll be tough, but do your best to survive."

Unexpected words of encouragement—and from an officer I was convinced was so cold, with those eyes more warlike than any I'd ever seen. For a second, I couldn't understand what had happened and froze.

Meanwhile...

"Then, to the fellows who enlisted of your own free will: Since you volunteered, you better not die after Corporal Serebryakov and me." Her calm tone hadn't changed. She didn't raise her voice. But the words she spoke with that emotionless expression were incredibly heavy. "First, I'll make one thing clear. The Empire doesn't have the time or resources to support inept officer candidates. In fact, doing so would be counterproductive."

She was different from all the drill sergeants. The way she talked, it was almost like she was a different species of imperial soldier. Her values ran counter to the ones that had been pounded into me since I had joined the army.

"It'd be a different story if you were forced to serve against your will because the nation needed you, but you're the ones who got in line to don the uniform of the fatherland, so contribute accordingly. If you're too inept to do that, then die."

She must have said all she wanted to say to us speechless, frozen recruits. After telling the company commander that was all, she immediately kicked us outside because we were still just standing there. Before we knew it, though we'd only just arrived, we'd been hurled into the trenches and were getting showered with periodic "deliveries" from the Republican Army.

What awaited us there was a reevaluation of our basic skills as mages. We learned that not only were we not earning our salaries, we were worse than garbage.

Having been thus "straightened out," Corporals Kurst and Harald became rebellious, but they weren't disciplined outright—key word *outright*. After the company commander and the second lieutenant mentioned that they simply couldn't take care of them on the front lines, the pair was assigned to the rear.

After that introduction and a bit of action, I became Lieutenant Degurechaff's buddy as the sole member of her platoon, and we flew together.

Meanwhile, the two other cadets were transferred to a better position. They were double promoted and assigned to defend the company's base in the rear. They could stay safe inside a pillbox as reserves and prepare for the counteroffensive. One thing I learned while flying, though, was that…for artillery, an immobile pillbox is nothing but a sturdy target.

It was when we received orders to flank the Republican unit trying to breach the line while we were under suppressive fire by their supporting heavy artillery. Half in tears, thinking I would never make it out of there alive, I followed the senior members of the company, who were grinning as they charged. I saw a base get blown to smithereens while we got off without so much as a scratch.

Weirdly, not only did barely any shells come our way, but also we didn't suffer any real losses at all before we made contact. After experiencing this over and over, I realized that artillery needs to be used systematically.

It made sense when I thought about it. Machine guns had a better chance of hitting aircraft than artillery. As long as you didn't stumble upon an anti–air cannon position, the only things shooting aircraft were machine guns. Although mages were slower than planes, we were still too fast for the artillery to take their time aiming.

It would probably be a different story if we assaulted a firing position or a pillbox and took heavy zoned fire. But we were taught that when fighting on our own territory, speed is everything. I was lucky enough to learn from Lieutenants Degurechaff and Schwarkopf that the more experienced you get as a mage, the more suspicious you get about defending a fixed position.

In short, artillery is the god we should trust on the battlefield; it's also the god we should never anger. You can't survive unless you make this god your ally and learn how to avoid its iron hammer.

Maybe that was why… My leader is a dyed-in-the-wool believer in firepower, the perfect embodiment of nonnegotiable mobile warfare, and then a mage. The only faith she has rests with artillery.

Could soldiers, by nature a group of realists, believe in God? Her answer to the question was pretty interesting. When I wrote to Elya about it, she wrote back, "Then I am the war goddess in charge of divine will." That answer was so like her, it made me smile. She had a way with words.

We had eyes and ears, so the devout believers crouching on the front line, in the trenches, and in gun nests were promised the divine revelations of the artillery.

With the contribution of the observers, we could call for fire to break up an enemy charge or a bombardment, depending on the crisis. It reminded me of Elya, smiling about her easy job where she could hang out and drink tea. But she was always the nurturing, helpful type, so I was sure her sense of responsibility kicked in and she was hard at work.

Right before we went on an airborne assault, what the company wished for most of all was supporting fire from the artillery. Whenever we received orders to counterattack the Republican Army breaking through our defensive line, we attacked its flank in sync with the artillery's fire to break up the offensive.

I was used to battle now. My only job as a newbie was to follow Lieutenant Degurechaff as she raced ahead. Ideally, we were supposed to be partners, but our commander laughed and said I still needed more training.

"Ohhhh, praise be to God. His name is Artillery! That's about right. Isn't it a wonderful sound?"

First Lieutenant Schwarkopf beamed, praising the artillery as their shells rained down with perfect timing. *Our taste in music seems a tad different—I'm only just able to get through these intense bombardments without the sound freaking me out.*

"Yes, it is God of the Battlefield! God has answered our radio requests!"

"Artillery, Artillery! Thou art our friend! Thou art our savior!"

The ones carrying on, relaxing their scary frowns, were the intense but dependable old hands from First Platoon. Although their opinion that artillery was our savior was a little dramatic, I was learning that it wasn't entirely wrong. We may have been a counterattacking unit, but half of our job was to contain the enemy so the artillery could finish them off.

If we just surrounded them—the rabble, an advancing unit, a defensive unit, or even enemy artillery—the artillery would naturally destroy everything. Witnessing it just once was enough to make you want to pray. *Dear God, please grant me artillery support.*

The artillery prep prior to an assault was always reassuring for inconsolably fearful hearts. One time our support ran late, so our battalion-sized unit, containing various different mage companies, had to go at it with an enemy echelon[15]...and a bunch of things I don't really want to remember happened.

On that note, when there was enough support and enough space between the front and the rear, the weight of combat would grow lighter. Yes, looks like I'll survive again.

---

[15] **echelon** A special term used in the military. During an assault, the foremost party was the first echelon, the one behind them was the second echelon. The term was often used when arranging various military units.

*   *   *

As Tanya gazes at the enemy unit through her binoculars, shells plow the earth right where they were meant to, turning people into fertilizer. In other words, this is the correct way of waging war—taking organic life and rendering it past tense through the use of ammunitions.

"The concentrated fire of a 120 mm really is a spectacular sight, sir. Amen."

"Truly, Lieutenant. Must be the teamwork between a talented observer and the artillery. They wasted no time before firing for effect."

People in any situation find it easier to remain calm as long as things go smoothly, and apparently those on the battlefield are no exception. The edifying teachings of the Chicago school say that all things can be measured using economics, but it's tricky to measure and quantify the effects on health when things go according to plan. When everything is on track, with redundancy limited and no additional costs incurred, it's just wonderful.

The situation unfolding before the 205th Assault Mage Company is a perfect example. Just as First Lieutenant Schwarkopf had said, the artillery is performing admirably. They must be coordinating quite closely—the way they transition from establishing a calibrating shot to firing for effect in only a few shells shows magnificent skill.

Thanks to that, by the time the company arrives at their attack position, the enemy army is collapsing under the artillery's thorough barrage. Normally there would be a chance of retaliatory fire and an artillery duel, but it seems the enemy guns are busy with the suppressive fire from our forward position.

"Lucky us. Our corps level artillery blew up the enemy troops with 120 mm shells, and we just have to mop up the surviving remnants."

"Yes, indeed."

It was just as Schwarkopf said—the company is in luck. For Second Lieutenant Tanya Degurechaff, it's a great day for a war. All we need to do is take out the decimated enemy infantry on a battlefield they already have the advantage on—a simple, convenient mission.

"It's almost time. Company, prepare to attack. We're gonna hunt down the ones the artillery missed."

And so, following her commander's orders, Tanya shoulders her rifle loaded with formula-imbued bullets, grabs her computation orb, and prepares for the assault.

The company is on standby and aware they'll be charging, but right before they leave, even experienced veterans can't help but get anxious. The nervous swallows are a familiar sound in the trenches, distinctly audible over even the shells exploding nearby.

"Let's go to work. If only every time could be this much fun!"

For Tanya, being able to fight against the dregs of infantry ravaged by artillery fire under the lead of a competent officer like Schwarkopf is great—well, relatively. People don't fight wars because they want to.

Ask if she considers herself happy, and you'd learn everything you needed from the string of expletives directed at Being X for hurling such a young, innocent child onto this random battlefield. Still, she has to be objective, so it isn't a mistake to welcome a less awful situation.

"Lieutenant, don't be a picky eater, or you'll never grow any taller."

"Commander Schwarkopf, I rather like having a smaller surface area, since it makes me less likely to get shot."

"…You win, Lieutenant. That's the best excuse for being a picky eater I've ever heard."

For Schwarkopf, who is waiting for the right moment to launch the strike, the banter with Degurechaff is opportune. You don't have to look back at history to know that commanders at all levels consider managing pre-assault stress part of making the job go smoothly.

Schwarkopf's 205th Assault Mage Company may have been veterans of the Rhine Front, but even they still tense up the moment before an attack. So when the light joke relaxes everyone to some extent, the lieutenant chooses that moment to move them out. He alerts the artillery units that they're launching the assault.

Once he gets the go-ahead from Control, the operation is go.

"Okay, everyone. Don't let picky Lieutenant Degurechaff hog all the good stuff!"

Thanking God that the company is able to remain calm and chuckle in the face of the enemy, First Lieutenant Schwarkopf roars with his well-trained voice, "Charge! On me!"

Everyone soars from their assault positions and rushes the enemy troops at a reckless speed.

To unprotected infantry, rapidly approaching mages are a threat just as serious as artillery. Mages have protective films and defensive shells, so a few shots aren't enough to take them down. On top of that, they have no trouble unleashing firepower more intense than heavy weaponry. They are truly tough opponents.

There are a limited number of ways to effectively counter those dreadful mages. One is grenades. If you're lucky, a mage will come into range—and that's it. The best way is to intercept them with a concentrated barrage of fire. Apart from that, infantry units don't have many options.

So from the perspective of the enemy army, whose command structure is already in disarray due to the shelling, even an undermanned company of only about ten mages is a terrifying threat. They probably already have direct support mages to fight fire with fire, but even mages have a hard time on the receiving end of artillery shells.

Lucky for the imperial company, unlucky for the Republican Army, the Empire's 120 mm guns connected with the flying Republican mages, turning them into mincemeat and littering the ground.

"Make sure to target enemy commanders and communications first!"

Isn't that obvious? Tanya thinks to herself, targeting a group of soldiers who seem to be carrying the distinctive backpack-style radios. Like the other company members, she uses an explosion formula to greet their uninvited Republican guests with the warm, welcoming embrace of fire and steel.

Judging from the sporadic return fire, resistance is weak. At most, there's only a handful of isolated soldiers shooting at random. The majority have already given up and turned tail, so all we have to do is sweep through.

Normally, potential enemy reinforcements would be a concern, but this time a mixed group containing another artillery unit and mobile strike team have already taken care of them; the current mission is just mopping up the remaining infantry.

That gives Tanya enough leeway to keep a close eye on Corporal

Serebryakov's combat performance, whereas before she was only able to make sure her subordinate was still behind her. Even under rifle fire, she never drops her defensive shell. Her maneuvers are still textbook, but compared to a month ago, she moves like a totally different mage. That amount of progress isn't half-bad.

I can't help but recall Lieutenant Schwarkopf's comment that this is a combat exercise, using the beat-up dregs of their collapsing enemy as targets. Actual combat really is the best training.

"And just think, not so long ago they were turning green and puking everywhere. It's amazing what you can do with a bit of training."

Never underestimate human potential. Remembering that lesson once again, Tanya can't help but ponder the sacredness of human dignity and free will.

For that reason, she pities the Republican soldiers. What an outdated mess their HQ must be to have ordered them to charge into so much iron. It was demonstrated to the whole world ten years ago during a conflict in the Far East between the Federation and the Dominion that iron dominates flesh.

This is the horrifying thing about people who lack initiative. No initiative basically necessitates lost potential, so it's a sad irony that they took human resources that probably did have initiative—an abundance of human capital—and exported them to the Empire as mincemeat.

It was to the point where I wanted to ask if they maybe shouldn't rethink a bit and recognize the value of human capital according to the market principle.

Unfortunately, everyone in the world is bound by contracts. As an imperial soldier, the relationship between Tanya and the Republican invaders is kill or be killed. It's fine and good for every country's propaganda to praise the noble act of dying for one's fatherland, but I really wish people would understand the utterly obvious flip side—that they have to kill their fatherland's enemies, too.

In terms of precious human resources wasted, there's no greater crime than war, laments Second Lieutenant Tanya Degurechaff, having just robbed several young people of their futures with a magic formula.

Things just never turn out how you'd like, she thinks to herself as her formulas mercilessly turn the fleeing Republican Army soldiers into organic debris. The only word for it is *wasteful*. Even though it isn't her own country, Tanya can't escape the feeling that something is wrong with squandering so many trained youths. Aha, I see why "extravagance is the enemy." Of course one of the ironies of history, in a sense, is that a certain country adopted that slogan and then wasted their human resources. Perhaps there will always be inept leaders frittering away the lives of their most promising patriots.

"Geez, maybe I should focus a little more on the battlefield."

"Artillery plows, mages descend, and the infantry advances." I remembered learning that on a nice afternoon, when I would rather have been sunbathing than struggling to stay awake in a lecture on the history of warfare. But when exactly that was, I didn't know…

Back in the Cadet Corps, the lessons seemed so ordinary as I sleepily listened, but once they became real life, it was horrible. Lieutenant Degurechaff had this disheartened look on her face, but she still unleashed a swift, merciless storm of destruction. I was half-impressed at her superhuman abilities and half simply stunned; it was all I could do just to fly after her, but she managed to handle even the enemies coming after me without taking a single hit.

I knew it was pointless to think about these things at times like this, but this kind of stuff forced me to realize that if the two of us weren't basically in different universes, she would never have earned the Silver Wings Assault Badge.

"Company commander to all hands. In three hundred seconds the bombardment will continue. Fall back."

And then at some point while I was spacing out, the scattered vestiges of the enemy forces had begun to retreat. The battle always ended while I was just flying for dear life. Naturally, then, I had braced myself for the usual orders to pursue, so it was a bit of a relief to answer, "Roger."

Yes, relief. Relief that I wouldn't have to guiltily chase down the enemy. I was different from Lieutenant Degurechaff, who could calmly nail fleeing soldiers in the back with optical sniping or explosion formulas. I was relieved because I wouldn't have to shoot.

When I was doing everything I can just to fly after her, I practically went into a trance, scattering formulas at random with no time to think. But I still hesitated when I had to aim at a fleeing soldier and cast. I mean…I would wonder if killing them was the right thing to do.

Of course, as Corporal Viktoriya Ivanovna Serebryakov, I should shoot, but as Visha, I have no motive.

"We're all here. No casualties. No losses besides gear."

When we landed at the rendezvous point, the sudden release from tension left me dazed. The sole thought occupying my mind was a desire to sleep like a log.

I did wonder if that was all right, as a young lady of a delicate age, but on the front, where there was barely any water, you couldn't hope for something as convenient as a girls' shower room. Lieutenant Degurechaff brusquely muttered, "Sleeping now. Night," and went to bed, so I followed her example and decided to just be thankful I *had* a bed; I was so ready to rest.

But it turned out God wasn't so kind. We were suddenly called to assemble. Before I knew it, we had all gathered.

"Good. Okay, company, I have some bad news."

Uh-oh. I couldn't help but grow tense as Lieutenant Schwarkopf matter-of-factly—unsympathetically so—continued talking. Even with my limited military experience, I had learned that there was no worse sign than a commanding officer going on matter-of-factly.

"We've received an urgent message. The 403rd Assault Mage Company has suddenly entered an encounter battle with two penetrating enemy mage companies."

That meant the company that was tasked with handling the next enemy wave had been attacked. A new enemy had bothered the guys who were supposed to be attacking the reinforcements. My brain was tired, but the sense of crisis got it moving, and soon I was up to speed. There were our troops, the next wave of enemy forces, and the new enemy.

"…And the reinforcements?"

"The artillery is pounding away at them, but the observer is being chased by enemy direct support mages and can't properly assess the impacts."

The conversation between superior officers made me predict a horribly bad future. *Ah, I have to fight again,* I sighed as I comprehended the situation.

"So we have to rendezvous with the 403rd. We're moving out immediately."

It was just one thing after another. And plus, it's not so easy to rebuild the will to fight once you've relaxed. The company commander continued, heedless of me and my scattered thoughts.

"At the same time, we have to rescue that observer who's under attack. He's requested backup. That reminds me, you experienced something like this up north, didn't you, Lieutenant Degurechaff?"

"Yes, sir, and I'm not looking to repeat it."

Observing for the artillery was almost like painting a target on your back for enemy mages. Any veteran would repeatedly tell you how critical it was to take out the artillery's eyes, because then the guns were nothing to be afraid of. If you were the eyes for the ruler of the battlefield, your fate was being the first to get shot at.

...Elya, you liar. You're not safe in the rear having tea!

Observers got targeted to a shocking degree. What terrified me more than anything was that even Lieutenant Degurechaff, who could calmly weave through a hail of bullets, had been seriously injured when she was an observer. That was how intensely the enemies came after them.

Another way to think of it was that this observer, in the same position as Elya, was in serious trouble. It wasn't at all logical, but a voice was telling me I had to save him. I didn't really understand the feeling, either.

So I had to do my best in this rescue operation. Newly determined, I stretched and took a deep breath to wake up. But I only *felt* different. On the outside, I still looked like a dead-tired kid.

"I see. Well then...Lieutenant Degurechaff, as a Silver Wings recipient, is the rescue possible?"

"Not even counting any potential delays, it would be difficult."

"Even if you used Type 95?"

"...I'm fine, but Corporal Serebryakov looks to be at her limits," Lieutenant Degurechaff responded, a bit resigned sounding, after glancing at me as I stood there dazed and motionless. "I don't want to be an inept officer who takes her subordinate out on a rescue mission only to lose her in addition to the one we're supposed to be rescuing."

"Then break up the pair. No, never mind."

The emotions contained in her words were hard to pin down. Maybe disappointment, maybe concern, but in the end, what she'd simply stated was that it was impossible. And the way Lieutenant Schwarkopf changed his mind mid-response said it all. A pair was the basic unit.

If Lieutenant Degurechaff flew the rescue mission solo, I would be faced with an aerial battle with at least two mage companies. Assuming that units over the border would have backup was elementary. Without my buddy's help, my chances of survival as a squirt with no support were slim.

Even if I wanted to go on the mission, I was standing there in front of them all, tired and absentminded after the last attack. That was why they rejected the idea. That was where their hesitation came from.

When I realized that, I shouted. I didn't understand the urge very well myself. "Commander, if I may!"

"Corporal Serebryakov?"

"I'd like to volunteer! I volunteer for the rescue mission!"

Lieutenant Schwarkopf sounded suspicious. Well, I had interrupted my superior officers, which could get me punished. I never would have dreamed I'd do something so impulsive, that I had that kind of guts.

"Corporal!"

"I'm an imperial soldier, too! While it's presumptuous of me to say so, I believe I can handle this mission!"

Lieutenant Degurechaff's short reprimands would usually make me go limp, but even her harsh tone couldn't stop me this time.

"Commander, please let me go!"

"That's what she says, Lieutenant."

"Lieutenant Schwarkopf?!"

Her shocked yelp and her eyes, usually half-closed in disinterest, now popped as wide open as they could go—the way she objected to this unbelievable response made her look somehow closer to the ten-year-old girl she was.

Apparently even someone who seemed so cold on the surface had been worrying about her subordinates.

"I'll have Schones's squad escort you. Move out."

"But…Lieutenant."

"She's made up her mind. I understand your concern, Lieutenant, but any more just makes you overprotective."

Lieutenant Degurechaff looked astonished. *Maybe she's more emotional than she lets on.* The thought was impertinent, but her expressions were so funny that I couldn't help it. Though it wasn't what I should have been focusing on at the moment, I felt I sort of understood my friend who teased me for my funny faces.

Lieutenant Degurechaff's vampire-like coldness had faded, and a little bit of distress took its place.

It was weird to realize just then how unexpectedly important I was to her. And it was a bit late in the game, but it also struck me what a young girl it was taking care of me.

"Understood. I'll do my best."

"To save the day in a crisis is the dream of every mage. Good luck."

"And to you, Commander."

With that, the main body of the company left. Lieutenant Degurechaff saw them off and then turned to me with an admiring smile.

"Well then, Corporal. Are you ready?"

It was a good smile. For some reason, seeing that expression, I couldn't help but think that she really did have pointy teeth like a vampire's. But I still smiled back, proud and confident. That's right, I made up my mind. I won't abandon anyone.

"Yes, Lieutenant."

"Good. Then it's time to go to work. Sergeant Schones, I'll be making good use of your team as well."

"Sure thing. We've got more experience on the Rhine Front than anyone."

"Damn Intelligence to hell! How could they tell us this area is under-defended?!"

The combatants were nimble. Graceful from a distance. But in reality, the imperial mages were desperately taking evasive actions as the observer cast his optical formula with a shower of mana glow. This was

finally shot number four. They had been picking off enemy observers for a while now, but it hadn't affected the artillery's accuracy one bit. From the sound, they were probably firing 120 mms. Worst-case scenario, maybe some 180 mm or 240 mm as well.

The ground forces trying to leave the fighting area were in disarray, and the enemy was having a field day. Their breaching formation may have been ideal for speed, but it made them vulnerable to fire.

Their only advantage was direct mage support that let them focus on breaking the line. Unfortunately, Control couldn't get around to assisting them, so they were intercepting about as well as if they were shooting at random with their eyes closed.

Though they had taken out the solo enemy observers, a warning must have gone out. There were limits to how well jamming could be maintained. Enough time had elapsed that they had to assume that a decent intercepting force or quick reaction force was on its way. In the worst case, their own retreat would be cut off in addition to the ground troops'. That was how much time had gone by.

"If you got time to flap your lips, cast some formulas! You bastards!"

To support their infantry's retreat, they had to neutralize the enemy artillery somehow. And that was the problem: How? The simplest way would be to attack them, but from the scale of the bombardment, it seemed like corps level artillery.

If it were artillery attached to a division or a battalion, charging in prepared to die would give them a chance, but corps level artillery would anticipate anti-mage combat. That's why their only option is to hunt down the weak points, the observers. But not only did that take a lot of time and effort, the effects weren't immediately obvious.

"Aye, sir. Agh, there's only so much we can do with opticals. Give us authorization for explosion formulas."

If they blew up the whole area with explosion formulas, that would catch any observers hiding on the ground, too. They didn't have time to scan the surface for each optical cast. Not only did they have to drop their altitude to a certain extent, but also they had to do multiple flyovers to ensure they didn't miss anything. At first they caught them off guard, but their enemies weren't stupid. The ones who expect their opponents to be fools are the real idiots.

News of their attack must have spread quickly, so the other observers had probably gone into hiding. Finding them would take a terrific amount of effort.

"At this rate, we won't even be able to get half of them."

Hence the idea of blowing the entire suspicious zone away. That was one valid method. Actually, in the preliminary stages of artillery battles, both sides would send out scouting parties to search for the enemy position and lay down high-explosive anti-personnel suppressive fire. If they were lucky, they might take out the observer squad. But this method presupposed a certain amount of firepower.

Basically, they would need at least an entire mage company sustaining maximum available firepower. That would certainly give them a boost, but it would be too heavy a burden for the current forward direct support unit. And if they suppressed them with a formula big enough to burn up the whole area, it would seriously hamper them in sustaining combat later.

"Out of the question. In the long term, it will just make finding them harder."

But in the long term, it was really not their day.

"Detecting high mana! Suspected reinforcements—mages—coming up fast!"

"Ah, damn it! Forget hunting observers! Get ready to intercept!"

They were scattered and exhausted. Military doctrine would emphatically recommend avoiding combat in such a state, but logic was first and foremost idealistic. Things wouldn't be so tough if it were actually possible to follow doctrine in combat. Since the leading army had yet to finish extricating itself, if the backup were to retreat, literally everyone would get killed.

Of course, the ground units had been retreating since the moment they failed to break through, and an overhead view of the battleground showed the entire army was pulling out, but mages could move far faster than troops on the surface.

They could just see the observers returning to direct the batteries and take out their ground army while they were fighting off the reinforcement mages.

That was why they had to secure this airspace. There were some battles you couldn't run away from.

"All units, our observer is down. I say again, our observer is down."

Hearing that, Second Lieutenant Tanya Degurechaff makes an irritated face and mutters, "Just great."

If only we had sortied slightly earlier or even a bit later is the lament that crosses my mind.

All I can do is curse the terrible timing. They didn't make it in time to help their ally but have come too close to the enemy to turn back now. This will be all pain and no gain.

"...As you all just heard, unfortunately we didn't make it in time, but that just means our job is a bit different."

"Lieutenant Degurechaff, isn't this too much for one platoon?"

Sergeant Schones, on loan to Tanya from the company commander, gives a warning. According to the latest from the Combat Direction Center, they've lost contact with a mage; they're sure he was shot down. Before his signal went dead, he reported a group of enemy mages that looked like at least two companies. In a sense, retreating is the correct answer despite the danger of being pursued. They were dispatched to perform a rescue. If the object of the mission has been taken out, there's no need for them to stick around.

"Sergeant Schones, your opinion is correct in most cases, but not in our current situation."

Common sense would never have them undertaking this fight as a solo platoon. Even Tanya would turn on her heel and return to base if there was enough distance between them. But rather than risk pursuit and be constantly watching their backs, it's better to take the initiative and strike.

"I can't deny that we're outnumbered...but we don't need to wait around for the enemy to regroup and assemble."

Taking out enemies one by one is an elementary war strategy.

"From the way they're moving, the penetrators are probably two companies equipped for long-range movement."

They're probably elite forces, but they've come a long way on high alert. Surely they're more than a little tired. They had to break through the Empire's defensive line and save energy for the equally long trek back to base; that greatly limits the amount of energy they can expend in the fight. Meanwhile, the imperial mages can put up a fierce defense and then just wait for friendly forces to pick them up afterward. If the artillery makes it to their position in time, a cleanup bombardment could be arranged.

Of course, even if the enemy is exhausted, I can't count on them to be careless. Still, the body often betrays the will. My platoon's chances of victory are not slim. More than anything, the enemy is scattered due to the sweeping operation. Their units are too spread out and can only coordinate in groups up to platoon size.

Although this battle is following directly on the previous one, the mages from the Imperial Army can go full throttle since they're on defense. Meanwhile, the Republican side has to operate on enemy territory with limited support and supplies. Assuming even numbers, the scale will still tip heavily toward the Empire.

"In other words, this is a simple task of taking out one exhausted platoon six times."

Maybe it's a slapdash strategy, but they have the supplies. They even have support, though not much.

One-on-six sounds hopeless, but one-on-one gives them a chance. If they do some damage despite their numerical inferiority, the army can't ask for anything more.

"Okay, guys. I'll take three platoons. The rest are yours. This shouldn't be too hard."

I can't expect to wipe them out completely, but it's a perfect opportunity to rack up points by taking out one at a time. It's a good chance to put my capabilities on display.

The rescue was a failure, but thankfully, we've got the artillery battery behind us—a little energy to spare. I heard they even saved some shrapnel shells for us. How perfect! I had been upset that I didn't get away with using my exhausted partner to refuse the mission, but I guess you never know when you'll get lucky in life.

Still, Tanya thinks, with a glance at the face of the subordinate behind her. Corporal Serebryakov may be nervous, but she's flying steady. She's skilled, yet she was drafted. She didn't join up because she wanted to; she's a young girl who was pressed into service. I would never have dreamed a corporal with such a background would volunteer for combat. Was it out of a sense of duty? Patriotism? Love for her buddy? Someone willing to do jobs above their pay grade is a promising human resource.

"Are you trying to monopolize the title of ace, Lieutenant?"

"Good question, Sergeant. Nah, just if I take out ten more, I'll get a bonus and time off. I'm about ready for a vacation."

If my score breaks fifty, I'll earn a special break—specifically, two weeks off, plus a bonus and a raise on top of that. I would be given flextime and authorization for limited discretionary action. Five downed makes an ace; fifty downed makes an Ace of Aces.

Unfortunately, testing Type 95 muddied my memory, and I'm also sniping from artillery bombardment range. That meant that inevitably many of my scores have been unconfirmed. Still, at least some had been acknowledged, so I'm currently at forty.

The best thing is that with these clean results, I won't be put on trial for war crimes. Even after the war, it won't be a problem—how about that! In other words, killing one person is a crime, but killing a pile of them gets you a medal. Most people would find that inconsistent, but economic theory makes it acceptable.

"Once I get it, I'm going to take it easy and splurge on gourmet food. Sorry, guys. I want to go have a leisurely beer hall lunch."

"I can't even tell you how jealous I am," Sergeant Schones jokes with a nod. Corporal Serebryakov and the other team member smile, somewhat at a loss.

That's how it's meant to be, though. After working to accomplish something, she should be allowed to enjoy the fruits of her labor. Winners on vacation even get to eat tasty food in the rear. There are opportunities to dine with corporate managers. In short, she would be in the best environment to build social capital. Just wonderful.

"I feel bad since you're accompanying us as a favor, Sergeant Schones, but...well...first come, first served."

Schwarkopf, concerned for their lack of manpower, dug into his hurting personnel pocket and lent them this squad. Maybe it's only two people, but in mages, that's more than a little muscle. It also means that the Empire still has the resources to make a considerate gesture.

In other words, I still have time to fall back to the rear. If I don't take my chance to go back now and get stuck here till I'm worn down, all that would be left of me is happy times in a psychiatric ward. I definitely don't want that, so I have to make winning the war my objective and be ready for anything.

...Can we win?

True, the Empire is a war machine of unparalleled precision. Just like the Germany I knew, if they fight against a single country they'll surely win. Fighting on two fronts is not impossible. But though those facts speak to their military strength, they don't guarantee victory.

After all, this is one nation against the world. It's less like a world war than me versus the rest of the world. Can such a war be won? Honestly, it'll be difficult.

"War is only fun when you're winning," Tanya says.

"Oh? And here I thought you would enjoy the despair of the defensive line."

...I could consider it if it would advance my career.

But frankly speaking, I can't rapid-fire miracles. Type 95 is the crystallization of a curse. Even if I use this thing—and I don't want to—it doesn't mean I'll win for sure.

"I'm a soldier. I go where I'm ordered." Company staff fulfills directives. Similarly, if military officers don't swear loyalty to their country, at least as a formality, they're in violation of their contract. Tanya was forced to fight this war. Who would take such a gamble with their own free will? Her answer is short and to the point—

"Sorry to butt in, Lieutenant, but you don't like the war, either?"

—but perhaps unexpected, because Corporal Serebryakov takes the rare step of joining their conversation, looking puzzled.

"Of course, Corporal. Even I prefer a quiet life. What about you, Sergeant Schones?"

"I'm with you, Lieutenant!"

Maybe it's part of his plan, but Schones jokingly gives a smart-looking salute. Mainly he does it to ease the other pair's bizarrely tense mood. Nicely accomplished. No wonder they say an outstanding NCO is invaluable.

"Well, that goes without saying. All right, time to plan the welcome party."

After wrapping up their conversation, Tanya rapidly ascends to combat altitude. Her wish for tranquility and her hatred for the ones who disrupted it are making a storm in her heart. Who actually *wants* to carry a rifle and fight? Her fury is intense.

Let this cursed world go to ruin. Well, let everything except me go to ruin. If that's not possible, may I at least avoid ruin, she mutters in her head as she races across the sky.

"What's your plan, Lieutenant?"

"Let's give them a grand reception. We'll treat them to lead and mana glow."

Lead is a government expense, and wasting the budget will lower her evaluation, but investing resources via sales effort is part of business. The costs of entertaining clients can be expensed because they are a necessity. So if something is a necessity, they can use as much as they want as long as they get results. If mages can mass-produce enemy corpses, no one would complain about how many bullets they use.

I do worry about the stomachs of the finance officers. I feel genuinely bad when thinking of their stress. I really do, so I hope the people in charge of mental health will help them out.

My job is to spend money to defeat the enemy; the finance officer's job is to come up with the money. And our mental care is the task of professional support personnel. In an ideal world, everyone contributes in their own way. We should praise order and applaud economics for foreseeing this evolution of the division of labor.

"Should we check if they have passports and visas?"

"Yes, let's."

That's right, the law of war shouldn't invalidate border control laws. If someone crosses the line the Empire has determined to be its border, it goes without saying that the newcomer will have to go through immigration. How careless of me, needing a reminder from my subordinate.

"Okay, that's our signal to begin. How about we make it a contest?"

"Hmm, then let's say whoever downs the most enemies wins. If you can beat me, I'll steal the commander's secret wine stash."

I remember when I peeked into his tent one time, I saw wine so fine it looked totally out of place. He must have won it in a card game, but it shouldn't be too hard to convince him to give it to someone for a job well done. If he refuses, I'll just abandon civil tactics. Sure, I may not be old enough to drink, but I still know a good bottle when I see one.

"Well then... All right, if Lieutenant Degurechaff snags the win on her own, we'll all give you our allowances for today."

"Hmm, not bad. Not bad at all. You're on!"

>>> **THE RHINE FRONT** <<<

My head felt heavy, and my consciousness was hazy. My unit? My subordinates? I no longer had the wherewithal to worry about them.

It was all I could do to stay conscious through to the next second. Though I'd quickly deployed a refracting optical decoy, I was still performing more evasive maneuvers than was deemed safe.

Though I just barely managed to maintain control, the company, proud to be one of the Republic's finest, was at the mercy of a single enemy. Everything had happened so fast.

"Mayday! Mayday! Mayday!"

First was the distress call notifying us of enemy contact. I'd never heard the forward controller scream like that.

"Break! Break!"

The commander instructed us to scatter. Nothing would be stupider than all getting shot at once from a distance. Even though we obeyed immediately and had trained to pull it off, it wasn't enough. I'd cocked my head, unable to spot the enemy, and my buddy got his upper body blown off.

"Sean?!"

"Bandit! Angel 12!"

"Angel 12?!"

I scanned the sky for the source of the attack, and when I found the bastard, I was speechless. Twelve thousand feet, an altitude that made the practical limit of six thousand for mages look like nothing.

Not only was it a harsh environment where oxygen concentration was roughly 60 percent of ground level, but the bigger problem was that you would run out of mana. The aerial mage limit for practical maneuvering was six thousand for good reason.

"Impossible! It's not a fighter plane?!"

"Fucking hell, it's definitely a mage."

We wondered if it was maybe a plane, but no, there was no doubt about it. We detected mana particles and glow. It was definitely an aerial mage.

The air up there was thin. The temperature was low. Running out of mana was fatal. Acclimating to the altitude was also a hurdle. While it was hard to believe, the enemy mage had overcome all those things and was managing to fight a war. I couldn't stop thinking that the leisurely soaring figure was an incarnation of imperial military might.

"Climb! We're climbing! We'll engage at eight thousand feet!"

My unit was completely exhausted. Eliminating an enemy observer squad had worn down their concentration, and they were also worn down from being in the air so long. If two forces of equal numbers and strength fight, the odds are in favor of the side that is better rested—that's simple logic.

The Empire's aerial mages were known for being elite, whereas our side had a tendency to make up for inferior quality with quantity. And this enemy was something else. Even if we were to attack at peak performance, we'd probably still be in for a tough fight. For starters, approaching an enemy at twelve thousand feet was impossible.

"Captain, that's—!"

"There's no other way!"

In theory, aerial mages had a slight edge over aircraft.

But that was at altitudes below six thousand feet. Aerial mages were able to use magic, but they were still just flesh-and-blood humans. In combat at high altitudes, they were nothing but targets.

"...No wonder the AWACS is going crazy."

"Right. That guy's...insane."

I see. The enemy mage is far from normal. I could understand why the airborne early warning and control system (AWACS) was going nuts. I mean, according to the standard aerial mage rules of engagement, it wasn't possible to ascend beyond 6,800 feet. No, *it actually is impossible.* Six thousand feet was the limit for a proper fight to the death with computation orbs and rifles. I'd heard that in the rare cases of aerial mages from highland regiments, fighting above seven thousand was possible, but this was on another level.

This was twelve thousand. At that altitude, even fighter pilots would need oxygen or they'd black out. The air was simply too thin. The only reason you would ever climb that high was an extreme emergency evasive action.

Even if we managed to shoot down the enemy mage, getting back would be hopeless. But this time, we had to go.

"If we can't suppress that imperial, our ground forces won't be able to get home."

"You're right... We have to do this."

It was true for more than just aerial mage battles: Letting the enemy get you from above was fatal.

So all we could do was climb. If we couldn't at least get him in range, we would be stuck as prey. Whether we would eventually run or fight, we first had to climb. But running wasn't an option. We had to buy enough time for the ground troops to retreat, otherwise it was possible we would all be wiped out. We were left with no choice from the start.

"This is all-out war. Don't even worry about getting home."

I would fight until my mana was depleted. Most importantly, I had to avenge Sean. I couldn't let this enemy get home alive.

"Crush that mage! Don't stop until that bastard crushes you!"

Was it an order or a scream? Either way, our commander was determined.

We would either take out the enemy or be taken out. Those were the only two choices.

"Bravo, engage!"

The Bravo team joined the fight. We would probably all be destroyed, and I wanted to curse God in spite of myself. I felt like a real sorry wretch thinking this pain in the ass could have backup.

"...Oh my God!"

But my long-distance observation formula showed me something even worse. I searched for our target's mana signature in the library. The hit I got was far more horrible than reinforcements.

Registered Mages, also known as Named... The aerial mage world was small. A company was only twelve members. Even a battalion was only thirty-six.

That was the kind of world it was. If you shot down five enemy mages, you were called an ace, and when your score hit fifty, you'd be recognized as an Ace of Aces. Units with six or more aces and individuals with over thirty kills crossed a threshold. Crossing that threshold meant being registered by foreign armies and perceived as a formidable adversary.

Named dominated the battlefield. The only viable ways to counter one were to employ overwhelming resources or an equally strong or stronger Named. To the men on the battlefield, nothing was more reassuring than having friendly Named mages in the sky. For those reasons, enemy Named were given individual names and caution was urged.

To the Republic, "Registered Mage: Name—'Devil of the Rhine'" meant sheer calamity. A registered enemy aerial mage had been recognized as a strategic threat. Among them, the Devil of the Rhine was the one everyone was most eager to avoid. It had been a mere two months since he had been spotted on the front, yet he had already accumulated over sixty points.

Especially horrifying were his skills with heavy mana spatial detonation and precision optical sniping formulas. Units would lose half of their soldiers just from falling for the "fish bait" strategy snipers commonly use. The nastiest thing was that many of the mages had suffered wounds that nearly kept them from returning to base at all.

We didn't want to lose such precious resources, so aerial mages received intensive care, but almost all of them died. Not only did that consume vast amounts of medicine, but also it tied up the medics, which led to a shortage of care for ground force soldiers.

On top of that, losing so many mages was becoming an issue from a tactical point of view. A single actor was taking on an entire military and their strategy. What could you call him besides a devil? He had to be taken out by any means necessary.

Naturally, it would be reckless to engage at twelve thousand feet, but at eight thousand, we had a shot. We may not have been at 100 percent, but we did have the numerical advantage. Plus, the guy was flying at twelve thousand feet—no matter how extraordinary you were, that was impossible to do without pushing yourself too hard.

Degurechaff definitely didn't expect the enemy unit to come charging at her.

They had looked so exhausted and scattered. She couldn't imagine them having any energy left, so she thought she would pop them one by one from a distance, but apparently she counted her chickens before they hatched. Charging under these circumstances was utterly reckless, but it was also terribly effective.

"Devil of the Rhine! Today, today we take you down!"

"...I don't believe we've met."

Tanya is bewildered, but for some reason, the enemy's will to fight is centering on her.

Genuinely puzzled, I proceed with my tactical considerations. My opponents' maneuvers are nimble and unpredictable. Precision sniping will no longer work.

It would be best to switch to either explosion types capable of targeting an entire area or spatially targeted guided formulas. *Target locked. Adjusted for relative velocity.* She unconsciously chooses the optimal attack using the Elinium Type 95. *Rebuild neural linkage network, ion concentrations normal, meta-motor cortex parameters updated. All systems green.*

"*Nicht!*"

Multiple faint early targeting mana signals detected. Formula types include invisible guided shots and spatially casting blasts. The enemy is close enough to engage, but I was distracted by pointless chatter and didn't realize!

Signal alarms scream in my head. I immediately start up casting processes in parallel using the Elinium Type 95 cores. Even though I know it will cause a system imbalance, I pour energy in as fast as I can. Meanwhile, she begins erratic evasive maneuvers automatically. Just as she gets out of the way, her previous position erupts with mana glow.

Some of the formulas seem to have been explosion type, and the shock waves create wild turbulence.

"Mmkay. What's all this now?"

I think maybe it's a highland unit, but can they climb straight to eight thousand feet without acclimating? Despite the vertical distance between them, they have me in range. Worse, I'm outnumbered. If they're going to charge, then it seems the enemy is tougher than I thought. Convinced of my opponents' skills to some extent, I immediately create an optical decoy.

While casting that, I initiate evasive maneuvers in order to prevent them from predicting my flight path. But even after a number of illusions, a magic shot comes flying at my actual body. How is their disciplined fire so accurate so fast?!

"That shot missed? What a monster!"

These guys are obnoxious, shouting like that on the open channel. Wait, they must be doing it on purpose. They're capitalizing on their numerical advantage. They want to distract me with radio chatter, but I won't fall for that again.

Shooting magic in volleys is a combat style that imperial mages avoid, since they rely more on individual skill.

The Empire boasts superior quality, but the Republic has always made the most of their numerical superiority—for example, the perfectly ordered formation before her eyes. These have to be some of the Named we're always warned about.

I check the mana signatures against the library. My irritating guess was right on the mark. These guys are such a pain that the combat instructors warned everyone about their fire discipline. I am clearly going above and beyond my pay grade.

"CP, this is urgent. The enemy company is Named. I say again, the enemy company is Named."

"CP, roger. I've got reinforcements heading your way. Don't work too hard."

Well, that's good news.

I should probably be happy they didn't tell me to go die. In military creature society, courage and a loud voice are the things that get you praised. When you're in an insane group that respects the foolhardy over the cautious, it's rough to be the sane one. But this is all for my advancement. I have no choice.

"Reinforcements acknowledged, but this is my battlefield."

I don't want to, but I have to at least rush them. Otherwise, it could adversely affect the evaluation of my achievements in this battle. Now that I recall, I wonder how the Kwantung Army was able to puff up their self-image so much. That said, I can definitely get ahead if I act like them. Nobody who calls themselves a patriot is worth a damn.

True patriots demonstrate their love for their country through actions, but the fakes express it in words. To get ahead, you have to do both. Patriotism is a really handy tool, and tools are meant to be used.

"Our mission is to eliminate the rabble violating the Empire's borders regardless of whether they're from the Entente Alliance or the Republic—we don't discriminate."

Elinium Type 95 comes with a curse that corrodes my mind the more I use it. In exchange for performance, I have to exalt the self-proclaimed god, Being X, with all my might. The only silver lining is that since I'm employing the Kwantung Army promotion doctrine, I can at least make it sound like patriotism.

But there's really something wrong with the army if the more you copy those big-talking Tsugene guys, the more you advance. That's gotta be why there are soldiers who actually want to take part in something as stupid as war.

Really, no one should long for peace and an idle life more than soldiers.

"Spatial coordinates acquired, potential evasion paths calculated, expansion chamber magic filling normally."

They want to leverage their numerical superiority and hunt me down. I doubt taking out one at a time will work against Republican mages. If I try, they'll probably gang up on me. They take pride in their perfect coordination, after all.

I was unbelievably lucky to have the chance to pick them off and thin the herd at first. I can't expect an opportunity like that again, so I need to switch up my tactics. In short, I just need to treat this clump of guys as a single target instead. Time for some giant killing.

I don't need to fiddle around with my aim. I can just target the whole area.

"CP, requesting theater warning for spatial detonation."

"CP, roger. Will issue a spatial detonation warning."

Elinium Type 95 is capable of storing mana via its system of four synchronized cores. With an explosion formula cast at full throttle operation with that stock of magic, it's possible to superpose interference across the entire war zone. Of course, that means full throttle operation of a flawed orb—something stupid is bound to happen.

"Sergeant Schones! Prepare for impact!"

In addition to blowing up friend and foe indiscriminately, it would litter the area with mana noise and reduce visibility with smoke, isolating soldiers. It would throw organized combat into chaos, making all coordination impossible, so I can't just go using it willy-nilly when fighting on a team.

The tactic is so disruptive, in fact, that the instructor unit was kind enough to comment that apart from self-destruction, there was no use for it. If, however, the fight is one versus a group, it can blow away the group's organization and turn the fight into one versus multiple individuals. Thus, the verdict is that the formula causes nothing but problems in team battles but it's not bad to have on hand when low on manpower.

"Be gone, impertinent foes. This is our Empire, our sky, our home."

I should be able to get positive evaluations for proclaiming my nationalism to the entire area.

Coincidentally, the military also generally approves of religious faith, so I might as well make use of Being X's curse to get ahead. I'll just have to accept it this time, even if I scream in agony as my freedom and dignity are trampled.

"If ye come to disrespect the fatherland, we shall pray unto God."

The enemy mages begin spreading out. They create a zone of interlocking fire from either side; rather than concentrate their shots on Tanya, they plan to torture her to death in midair. On top of that, as a precaution against ordinary explosion formulas, the spread is wider than usual.

"O Lord, save the fatherland. O Lord, grant me the strength to defeat my nation's enemies."

They can pin me down even after all those intense maneuvers up this high? These guys are war crazy. Geez, if you like it so much, you should just split into two sides and kill each other.

Why do they have to get other people involved? Did no one teach them not to be a bother? There had to have been some major flaws in their education. Education decides a child's future; they need to take it seriously.

Or maybe they're rational, economical people like me, using war to advance their careers and aiming to survive. Wait a minute. If that's the case, shouldn't I do my best to negotiate for a profitable outcome…? How could a logical, economically minded person like me nearly forget the pursuit of profit? Is war so harsh that people lose all reason?

Profit is everything; that's self-evident. In short, negotiation is key. If you blow up the other party before you start the dialogue, there won't be any of that.

By the time this dawns on Tanya, she's overwhelmed by how easily her reasoning had been impaired by war and how far she'd gone down the path to losing her humanity. Unless your hobby is fighting to the death, killing someone without getting anything out of it is pointless. Right, this isn't a zero-sum game, so building cooperative relationships should be theoretically possible.

Then instead of earnestly slaughtering one another, it would be more logical to rig the game. We'll move from a savage world of killing and being killed into a world of reason. Surely the fabled "win-win" solution is possible.

We can't go overboard. Just as economists were able to determine through statistics that Japan's national sport was riddled with fixed matches, our deception will one day be exposed, but by the time a third party sees through our plot, the fighting will be long over. Economists have plenty of other things to be working on during a war, and most of the time those things are extremely important.

"Save us from the heathen invasion. O God, grant me the strength to slay our enemies."

I have to just keep singing meaningless praise to make it look like I'm using a formula. That way I can conceal my intentions from CP for a while. If this goes well, all I have to do is settle the negotiations while they can't tell what I'm doing due to the mana noise.

Things are coming together. Noting that, Tanya thinks for a moment and then decides that the proper time for her message might be at hand.

Perhaps they will open the door to negotiation, and things will go well for both sides. No one can call themselves an adult if they are bound by preconceptions. Maybe she's only been looking at Republican soldiers as stereotypes.

People are more than appearances. Surely we need to gain a thorough understanding of people's true inner selves to interact with them properly. All individual personalities are one of a kind and thus deserving of respect.

Even in the middle of a war, if it might be possible to negotiate with someone, you should be sincere with them. Of course, negotiating with the enemy will naturally get you court-martialed. Forsaking combat is treated the same as fleeing before the enemy; you have no way to talk yourself out of the death by firing squad that awaits.

However, if I can avoid needless combat as an upright individual, I'll accept the personal risk. If I can make myself understood, I'm willing to forgo opportunities for promotion and time off. I'll earn them by defending myself from war-crazed maniacs.

Most importantly, the amount of risk and labor involved here is clearly unfair, given my salary. I have no obligation to do work above my pay grade.

In the unfortunate event that I can't make myself understood, I'll have to take them down and have a nice vacation eating tasty food in the rear. It's a crying shame I can't drink wine, but the region back there is famous for the way it prepares sautéed fish. I'm sure it'll be exquisite.

"Attention! You are trespassing on the Empire's territory." For now, let's start with a couple benign remarks. "We will do our utmost to defend our fatherland, because behind us are people we must protect."

Apparently a soldier's duty is to protect their country's people. Though some armies are violence machines and some belong to emperors, soldiers really are usually protectors of their nation. Well, there are also cases like Prussia, where the army possesses the state instead of the state possessing the army, so it's not a hard rule. But the generalization sure sounds good.

"Answer me this. Why do you wish to invade the Empire, our homeland?"

She says it like a reprimand, but she actually wants an answer. I'll get the negotiation ball rolling. I may be talking to the enemy, but this is still innocuous enough that I can explain it away.

I wonder what their response will be, but all I get is a barrage of curses and a hail of bullets. Are these guys really just a bunch of dumb, war-crazy animals? I can't help but doubt their sanity.

So these people aren't modern entrepreneurs I can calmly pursue a rational outcome with? Or perhaps they, too, have lost their humanity in the war? If that's the case, how sad. That means I have to play along with these war-loving fools—the worst possible scenario.

She wants to request overtime pay, along with extra compensation for being placed in this hazardous working environment, but she doesn't know who to invoice... I realize it's immature to throw a fit, but I want to cry.

"This is CP with a warning for the theater. Watch out for mana noise."

CP is kind enough to issue the warning Tanya requested. And she has accumulated enough mana. All right, if these guys are logical, economically minded fellows, they're sure to value one over zero.

Who knows? Maybe they're the prudent types who won't take a risk while the radio signal is good. Even if they get bombed first, rational fellows like that will undoubtedly choose a reasonable solution if they survive. At least, *I* would choose a reasonable solution. Maybe I should get this over with. Knock it off with the hesitation and delays and get things moving. Focus on controlling all the mana I saved up and accept the noise in my thoughts.

"O saints, believe in the blessings of our Lord. Let us be fearless."

Tanya feels drained at the sudden release of loaded mana. She wants to scream as all the energy is sucked out of every one of her cells, but Elinium Type 95's curse prevents it. Still, she can't get over how weird it is for pain to be forcefully converted into religious ecstasy.

The sensation of joy and agony blending to rattle your mind is a horror beyond description.

"Lament not your fate. Oh, the Lord has not forsaken us!"

The full-body pleasure and the uncomfortable deprivation of my freedom finally reaches an intolerable level. If she could, she would curse him, but her mouth is probably only capable of praise. It annoys me, but the one thing the commies got right was to call religion a drug.

The Chicago school of economics says drugs should be regulated by the economy.

That said, my problem isn't that I want to stop but can't, it's that if I stop, I'm likely to die. It's the biggest pain in the ass. The Chicago school doesn't consider the case of a drug where if you quit you instantly die.

"At the distant end of our journey, let us reach the promised land."

A process similar to a thermobaric explosion starts up instantaneously. The mana has reached its pressurization limit and gushes out at an immeasurable rate. As the boiling magic explodes into freedom, the scattering mana makes contact with the open air and triggers an unconfined magic explosion. The abrupt changes in atmospheric pressure could collapse lungs and cause pulmonary congestion, and the combustion drops the already low oxygen concentration to fatal levels.

Oxygen deprivation and carbon monoxide poisoning at eight thousand feet would cause even the hardiest aerial mages to black out and fall. Anyone who manages to maintain consciousness would experience agonizing pain. Collapsed lungs, carbon monoxide poisoning, and the complications from the steep drop in oxygen hurt like hell.

"Ngh...gaghk...gagh..."

Even Degurechaff, who was out of range, has trouble breathing as the oxygen concentration falls. If the mages in range are still able to fly, that won't last long. The free-range magic explosion creates mana noise over a wide area.

Not only does it cut off communications, but also it makes sustaining flight formulas difficult, so continuing the battle is impossible. Although smoke limits her visibility, it's easy to imagine the state of her opponents who have received a direct hit.

"Attention, fighters of the Republican Army: This battle is over."

So Tanya attempts to suggest they surrender. She has to wonder if after all that there are any survivors, but it doesn't cost her anything to try.

Well, if there are no survivors, I can take my accomplishment of annihilating an entire company and enjoy a tea break in the rear.

"If you surrender, we'll guarantee your rights as prisoners according to the Worms Convention."

The Republican Army, which had a strong tendency to rely on numerical superiority, had extraordinary faith in their Named. They could put up a fight against the imperial elites, after all. Due to their rarity and strategic value, they were deployed in the most critical battles, and their bravery was known far and wide.

The 106th and 107th Reconnaissance Mage Companies of the Forty-Second Magic Brigade belonging to the Fourth Aerial Mage Division were also famous for their skills. Until recently, at least.

"The tactical council regarding the recent annihilation of the 106th and 107th Reconnaissance Mage Companies is now in session."

Initially, the Republic had assumed that the Imperial Army's powerful magic units, including the Named, were deployed on the front lines against the Entente Alliance, so it should have been impossible for its Named and equally elite troops to be wiped out.

Chapter **III**

And yet, that was what happened. It happened despite their over-whelming numerical advantage—and at the hands of a single mage. When the news came in, no one could believe their ears. They thought it had to be some kind of mistake.

"While the 106th and 107th Companies were engaged suppressing enemy observers, an enemy mage unit came to intercept them."

They had sent Named units out of necessity due to the long-range nature of the invasion. The mission was too difficult and strenuous to give to anyone else. As hard to believe as the news was, if a numerically inferior unit had inflicted massive damage on them, it was possible it would have repercussions for the entire war.

It was no wonder the ranking members of the General Staff, who understood that fact, looked so grim.

"What I'm handing out now is a report combining the logs from recovered computation orbs and survivor accounts."

The expressions of the magic officers who had done the analysis were even darker. To prepare the data, they had had to review the computation orb logs and recorders.

The debriefing of the survivors was limited since some of them were severely injured, but what they had heard was shocking.

If the information hadn't come straight from half-dead survivors, it would have been hard to believe. No, they wouldn't have *wanted* to believe it.

"...Anyhow, first please take a look at this recording of the battle."

"Mayday! Mayday! Mayday!"

That was the emergency distress signal used when encountering an unexpected enemy. The frontline combat controller, whose job was to remain calm and clearheaded at all times, was shrieking. It might have been funny if it had been a newbie, but he was a veteran. He had been the first to report 106th's defeat and the one to request assistance for retreat. Thanks to him, the survivors of the 106th and 107th companies could be recovered.

"Break! Break!"

The screen, though awash in static, showed the unit promptly following their commander's order. The aerial mage officers who had done the analysis still found it difficult to accept the reality of what followed.

At that moment, according to the log, the user was sniped from a distance far greater than was thought possible. It was hard to believe.

The 106th was performing erratic evasive maneuvers.

"Sean?!"

The screen kept jerking around due to sharp changes in flight path. During that short time, several soldiers were shot out of the sky.

"Bandit! Angels 12!"

"Angels 12?!"

And then, incredibly, an attack from twelve thousand feet. They had already received this information as an emergency report. The issue was that an imperial mage had climbed to double the current standard. If it was true, all of their aerial mages would be rendered virtually powerless.

"Of all the... It can't be."

No one was sure who had spoken, but the sentiment was universal. The number twelve thousand momentarily paralyzed their brains. It was too extraordinary.

In fact, the unit had wondered if their opponent was a fighter plane, but it was undoubtedly a mage.

After performing a series of optical-processing techniques on the video, they had managed to make out the standard-issue Imperial Army rifle and signs of an unknown computation orb.

The distance kept them from getting a clear view of the enemy soldier's features, but they could make out an incredibly small silhouette. Still, the way that mage cruised so calmly, like the ruler of the sky, told them no one could interfere.

Then it was confirmed that the 106th's opponent was a Registered Mage. Even worse, this was a new Named who had recently appeared in the theater and rapidly racked up achievements. All details were unknown. They didn't even know what sorts of tactics this unfathomable threat would use, much less how to counter them.

They had kicked Intelligence's butt to get a reinvestigation under way, and so far they had found several unconfirmed reports that had been previously dismissed as frontline rumors—things like a lone enemy soldier taking down an entire company, a mage flying at an impossible altitude, and so on.

It was a war zone, after all. They understood some of the intelligence coming in was confused, but it was too bad the unusual nature of their opponent was delaying their identification attempts.

"Damned Devil of the Rhine!"

"Cut it out. Captain Cagire, who is the Devil of the Rhine?"

"An unknown enemy Named. We can currently identify them only by their magic signature."

The intelligence officer had paled at the sudden question. If they were only able to identify this enemy by magic signature alone, that meant they knew nothing. This was as good as admitting to the other high-ranking officers present that everyone in Intelligence was incompetent.

They could get the gist of what had happened by analyzing the logs of the computation orbs used in battle. In other words, either the intelligence officers had neglected their duties or nothing had been recorded.

"Did you analyze the logs?" The chief of staff, who was running the meeting, asked the obvious question. Essentially, *Are you bastards so inept that you couldn't even do that much?!*

"We've inspected seventeen, mainly from recovered orbs of mages who were shot down, and the survivors have all been debriefed." The response from Intelligence, however, made it clear that they had done a proper job. They were the ones who sent the notice that an unconfirmed mage had inflicted heavy damage.

They formed a special task force and even launched an operation to retrieve the bodies of fallen mages who hadn't been recovered. As a result of that effort, they were able to recover a number of computation orbs and investigate the wreckage to see if there was any salvageable data.

…But they didn't find anything useful.

They had a mountain of evidence indicating the mystery mage's existence, but they had no idea what he was like.

"…So only a magic signature? What does that mean?"

"Almost no one survived an encounter close enough to see him. The

majority of people who lived were shot down while they were still outside of firing range."

Every mage that approached the Devil was hit with enough force
to leave them with full-body burns. When the computation orbs were
retrieved afterward, the tough outer shells had melted, and their cores
were damaged. To inflict that level of damage with conventional
weapons, you'd have to pull out either the big guns or a metric ton of
explosives.

There was a mage out there who could both eliminate opponents at
close quarters with overwhelming firepower and snipe precisely at great
distances. This Named had been classified as a strategic-level threat, and
although they didn't know the mage's identity, they had registered the
Devil of the Rhine in their library by magic signature alone.

The "Devil" alias was given out of the hatred and fear of an opponent
they couldn't see. And it had only been two months since the first sighting in this theater. Yes, if the records were correct, the Devil had been
deployed just as the Republican Army had attacked, and had already
scored more than sixty.

Troops on the front line had even sent an earnest request for a Named
extermination squad composed of their own elites.

"Moving on, this is footage recorded by a computation orb moments
before it failed. Miraculously, the member of the 106th it belongs to
survived."

The video showed an enemy figure casually evading the volley fire of
an entire company. The shots seemed so unlikely to connect that everyone wondered what the soldiers were aiming at. Incredibly, despite the
cross fire, the enemy was flying so calmly it looked almost graceful.

"...Is that...dancing?" The movements were so mesmerizing that
someone murmured unknowingly.

A spectacular amount of magic glow filled the air, but the enemy
dodged its many sources with elegant ease. Irritatingly, not a single shot
seemed to hit.

They didn't know who had come up with the alias, but Devil of the
Rhine was very fitting. No ordinary person could weave through a setup
like that and fight back without seeming to be in any danger.

"Is that mage too quick for our disciplined fire to land any shots?"

"Could their mobility really be that much better than ours?"

The Republican Army had developed their fire discipline in response to the known superiority of imperial mages. Working as a team, its troops could shoot down the overconfident enemy mages who tended to stick out.

Although it was a doctrine premised on numerical superiority, the Republican Army considered it a solution. It figured there wasn't a mage in the world who could stay in the air once the barrage began.

"The Devil evaded spatial detonations, too. Most likely after detecting the attack during early targeting and getting out of there with no time to spare."

"You mean the enemy performed evasive maneuvers in a few seconds or less? Wouldn't that mean this mage could dodge all guided magic attacks?"

The basic concept in disciplined fire was to use a large volley of guided missiles to severely limit the enemy's ability to evade and try to get a direct hit. At the same time, the unit would estimate the velocity of their opponent and use exploding formulas along a wide area in their flight path to catch them.

If they couldn't lock on to or measure their opponent, however, it would be almost impossible to shoot effectively. They fought like a team—organized and continually coordinated. In other words, against an opponent on whom those tactics didn't work, there were far fewer benefits to fighting in groups, though not zero.

The officers in the meeting gasped as their chests tightened. Not only had the observed mana value of the enemy computation orb gone way past the limit, but the mana was reducing—concentrating—and amplifying. Collisions of mana triggered by overlapping compound interference were creating...multiple glows?!

A single imperial mage had called on enough mana for several casters.

"The observation apparatus also returned a value that was off the scale."

"Absurd! If that's the case—"

His comment cut off abruptly. They were all witnessing data that indicated a mana fixation reaction was occurring. The immeasurable profusion of mana denoted a phenomenon that mages and nations had attempted to achieve but finally given up on.

In theory, it was impossible for a cast mana phenomenon to access spatial coordinates. Attempting fixation was madness. Nobody thought it could be done.

"...It can't be! Impossible!"

The technology officer, who understood the significance better than anyone else, began denying reality, as if he had come unhinged. This was no longer mage technology but something from the realm of myths.

"If ye come to disrespect the fatherland, we shall pray unto God."

The zoomed-in figure shocked them all. The picture may have been blurry and full of static, but what it showed was unmistakable.

"...It's a child!"

The mage could still be described as quite young, yet she proclaimed annihilation and doom. Together with the mana reading, her cry was an omen of destruction.

Supposing this god you pray to exists—is it the devil or the god of destruction? Everyone cradled their heads, inspired to cling to the Lord.

"O Lord, save the fatherland. O Lord, grant me the strength to defeat my nation's enemies."

However, the sentiments were pure. Her gaze was utterly innocent. Could she really be an enemy mage? She was only looking to God for help.

"Save us from the heathen invasion. O God, grant me the strength to slay our enemies."

Should we really not be allowed to exist? they wanted to ask. Her gaze was that pious and judging.

"Attention! You are trespassing on the Empire's territory."

She spoke with the solemnity of a shrine maiden delivering a divine message.

"We will do our utmost to defend our fatherland, because behind us are people we must protect."

What she said was backed by a sense of responsibility. It was as if defense was her only duty. And they could feel her fervid desire to protect the ones behind her.

It was to fulfill that duty that she had stood before them.

"Answer me this. Why do you wish to invade the Empire, our homeland?"

Perhaps the 106th had sensed disaster; they concentrated their firepower to stop her with all their might. They tried to prevent her from casting even a little longer.

"O saints, believe in the blessings of our Lord. Let us be fearless."

But reality was cruel. Fate was not on their side. Assuming God existed, he was smiling on her.

"Lament not your fate. Oh, the Lord has not forsaken us!"

The converging mana suddenly began to flood the observation apparatus with noise. That meant there was enough mana accumulated to agitate space.

"At the distant end of our journey, let us reach the promised land."

It was as if her words were both the key and Pandora's open box. The officers watching stopped thinking entirely as the monitor emitted a dreadful flash. Eventually, the computation orb was damaged, and the video cut off.

"…Dear God, have mercy on our souls."

O God, is this…what you wanted?

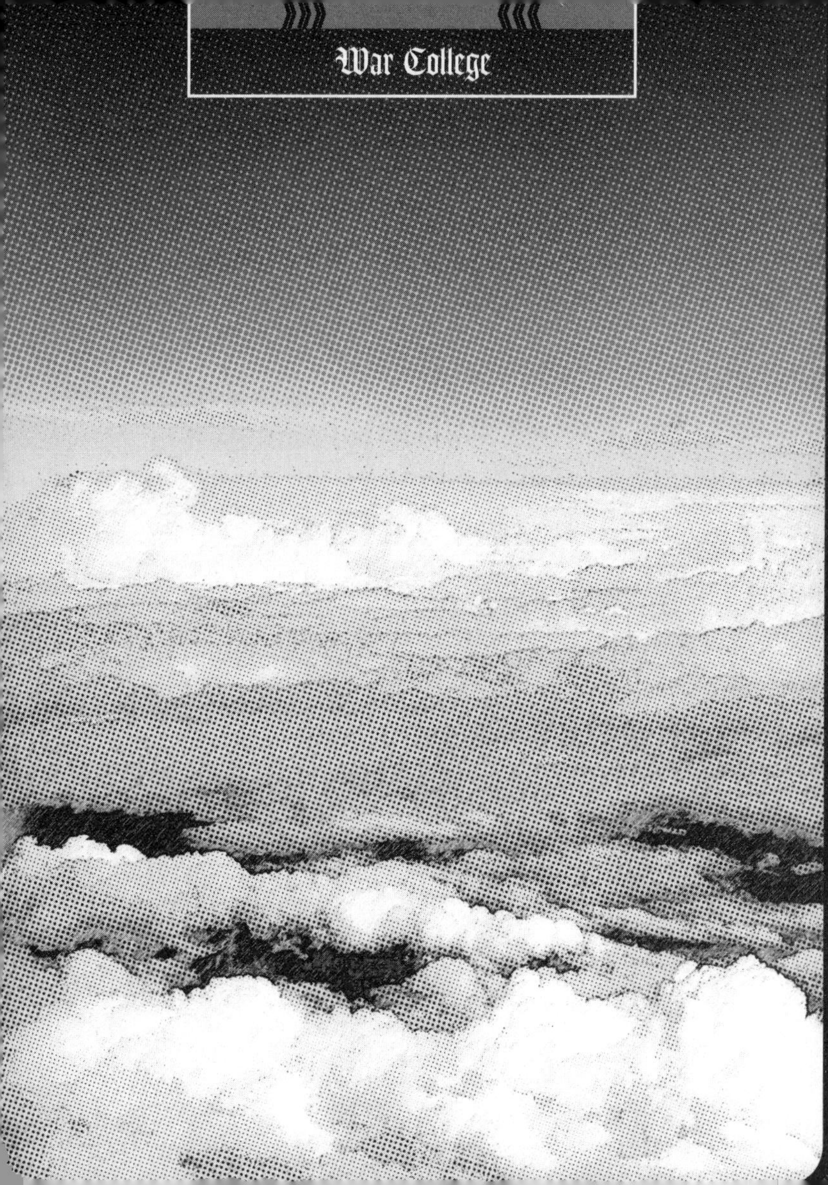
War College

"It's the appointed time, so I'd like to begin the Imperial War College Admission Committee's third round of reviews." An instructor from the war college is leading the meeting, and the row of committee members are all talented key figures in the army. The Empire has a long tradition of investing people and time in the selection of next-generation leaders.

The result is outstanding commanders at every level trained to a high standard of excellence.

"Today we'll be reviewing candidates up for reexamination."

For that reason, war college admissions are discussed as a matter linked directly to national strategy and defense. Naturally, they spare no effort to discover the ideal candidates, considering multiple future placement options during the process.

The army values diversity, so the committee holds second and third rounds of review with different members for candidates who don't pass. It would be a horrible loss for the Empire if an exceptional candidate were dismissed as unfit.

And history has proven that this process is the correct one.

Many people, including distinguished officers of both the army and navy, have become central figures in the armed forces thanks to the multiple stages of assessment. General Möltke the Great is such a fine commander that the reviewer who selected him said the greatest accomplishment of his military life was "discovering the magnificent Möltke the Great," but he still received severe criticism to the tune of "I can't imagine this candidate becoming a soldier" and only barely managed to squeak by in the third round.

Chapter **IV**

"As usual, I hope we can make this a lively debate and hear from the perspectives of the front lines, the General Staff, and the war college."

And the Imperial War College traditionally chooses to downplay the question of how many rounds it takes someone to pass.

Two recent examples are Zettour and Rudersdorf, both selected in the second round. There were apprehensions that the former was "too scholarly and thus not suited to becoming a general," while the latter, despite being acknowledged as "sharp and dynamic," was criticized for his "tendency to daydream." Both of them were accepted *after* those remarks were made.

Nevertheless, the two of them are now treated as geniuses and entrusted with the future of the army, so much so that they are on the admissions committee. Due to cases like these, it is even said that candidates who pass in the first screening, with its very general standards, won't amount to very much.

The army is thorough, as evidenced by the way they weed out mere dogmatists and allow people who are dropped in the first round to be accepted in the second or third rounds.

"We'll start with the request submitted by Major von Lergen from Personnel to reassess a candidate who passed in the first round."

The Empire is so thorough that a candidate accepted in the first round would normally never be deemed unfit.

That's why everyone is so confused.

For a moment, no one can help but look at the presiding war college instructor with bafflement. The request is to reassess a candidate who already passed the first round and doesn't even require a second. What exactly is Major von Lergen trying to say? The war college instructor has to continue the meeting, but he probably doesn't know himself.

"During the first screening, which is done anonymously to ensure impartiality, the candidate up for review was given a 'superior' rating."

The first screening consists of multiple reviewers examining documents from which all personal information about the candidates has been omitted. The reviewers are given only a list of the candidates' achievements and evaluations from their academic advisors and Intelligence. That eliminates any bias, which makes it possible to examine the candidates more or less accurately.

Eventually the personal information would be released, and the committee would make the final decision on which officers would advance along the army's elite track. The screenings have to be strict and fair. Naturally, receiving the best evaluation possible means the candidate lacks nothing, according to the army.

"But the major has objections and has requested a reassessment. We're holding this review in response to that request."

The comment indirectly implies that he finds it hard to understand why the reassessment is happening. In all reality, if the request hadn't come from a section chief in Personnel who was able to investigate candidates in more detail, it would most likely never have gone through.

Previous disputes regarding the suitability of first-round admissions took issue with how ordinary the candidates were. That's why it's no surprise the instructor sounds skeptical. Very few officers received "excellent" scores in their anonymous evaluations, much less "superior"—Major von Lergen is raising doubts about the top nominee.

If the candidate were the child of an influential officer or someone with noble connections, it might make more sense to worry about bias. Cases of suspected favoritism are rare, but they are not unheard of.

The candidate in question, however, is the orphan of a soldier. It goes without saying, then, that there are no influential relatives. The ones who made the recommendations had no prior relationship with the candidate; neither were there any ties to factions or nobility. Not only that, all the recommending officers were straitlaced veterans who had achieved much in the field and never caused any problems.

Closing the door on a self-made officer with such outstanding records is not in keeping with the tradition of the military. Everyone turns to Major von Lergen for explanation.

"Major von Lergen, I'm curious to know what criteria informed your decision. Looking at the records, I can only conclude he's a fantastic candidate." He sounds somewhat amused, but Brigadier General von Rudersdorf is voicing the question on everyone's minds: *Why?* "Given the recommendation from his unit, his standing at the academy, the background check from Intelligence, the military police investigation report, and his achievements, this officer is exceptional. I wonder what the problem is."

Recommendations for achievement exist to select distinguished officers. Young—fledgling, really—officers are chosen in the hopes that making the best use of the army's talent will result in many future benefits.

The candidate's unit recommendation consisted of unreserved praise. Academic records revealed a slight lack of practical training compared to some candidates, but superior combat experience made up for that. In terms of simply fitting the requirements, this officer was worthy of being considered a top candidate. And in fact, the review score was nearly perfect.

Even Intelligence and the military police, who were usually so particular, both came back with the highest praise. How many times had that ever happened?

"Hmm, how to say...? I believe, and I think many of you agree, that he's one of the most promising candidates we've had in recent years—uncommonly good." In other words, even Brigadier General von Rudersdorf, who prides himself being contrary, has a hard time understanding why such a great candidate would be doubted. If the reassessment request hadn't come from one of the top elites in Personnel, who was known for his intolerance of flaws, everyone would have shouted him down.

"True, the candidate has performed at the highest level in every area, but nevertheless, I find this a difficult one to admit." Major von Lergen, however, declares that he asked for the reassessment despite acknowledging all the candidate's strengths.

"He came in second in his class, hasn't made any trouble for the military police, and according to Intelligence, he's a patriot. And they guarantee he can uphold confidentiality. He even got a recommendation from his combat unit!"

Naturally, to the committee, Lergen's objection can only be a joke. To preserve candidate anonymity, decorations and what years they attended the academy were redacted, but this one's records are such that they practically guarantee an award of Aerial Field Service Badge or better.

After all, a recommendation from a combat unit requires excellence of both character and skills.

"If we drop this candidate, we won't be able to admit any new students this year." The solemn comment accurately represents nearly the entire committee's thoughts. *Brilliant* is the only word to describe a candidate with such ability, achievements, and evaluations. If they were to throw out this one, they would have to disqualify everyone else as well.

"I've decided to make an exception and reveal the identity of the candidate this time. Take a look at this." Unable to let things go on like this, the chief of general affairs in Personnel hands out the document in question. As a rule, candidates remain anonymous for reviews, but he has the authority to reveal their identities if circumstances warrant it.

He doesn't know Lergen well, but he wants to at least give him a hand, even if he's basically doing it in good faith to safeguard the major's career.

The candidate is a rare (and that's an understatement) Silver Wings Assault Badge recipient and was also nominated for an Aerial Field Service Badge for frontline accomplishments. Such an officer would normally be wholeheartedly welcomed as a future leader.

The problem is that the one who achieved all these things is a child of eleven. Any sensible officer would hesitate to send a little kid into battle. The general affairs director figures Lergen is opposing her advancement due to her age. That is about as much as he understands of the situation, but he agrees to declassify the information.

"...You mean a kid did all these things?" Her age is enough to stun even Rudersdorf. By that point, it seems that everyone understands how abnormal this is. The room abruptly quiets down in confusion and astonishment.

She became a magic first lieutenant at age eleven. Graduated from the academy second in her class. Received the Silver Wings Assault Badge and was recommended for the Aerial Field Service Badge. Was recognized as an Ace of Aces with sixty-two downed (plus thirty-two assists) and nicknamed "White Silver." And she's working in the instructor unit?

They wonder if they should laugh. A résumé like that makes her a prodigy.

"Cultivating magic officers is a pressing matter, but her age gives you pause, correct?"

More than a few of the committee members feel she is too young. They aren't sure they can entrust her with command of a whole battalion. More importantly, even though there has long been demand for more magic officer training, some people criticize magic officers as shortsighted.

"Yes. She may be a competent magic officer, but whether we can use her as a commander is a different question."

Excelling in a highly specialized field is hard enough. Plenty of aerial mages boast outstanding individual capacities, but surprisingly few of them make decent commanders.

No, a magic officer's high competency doesn't necessarily make them a great superior. Not all famous athletes become great coaches. The qualities required for commanders are different from the ones it takes to be an individual ace.

Thus, some of the officers interpret Lergen's doubt as a response to the girl's age and ability level. From those angles, there is indeed room for debate.

But her reviewers dismiss those concerns. "She's plenty talented. And her achievements, unit recommendations, and so on fit the requirements perfectly. She has nothing to find fault with." Her records include her experience leading a platoon with no mistakes. Well, if she couldn't even lead a platoon, there wouldn't be any point in officer training; more people than you might expect get tripped up there.

That said, at this point, considering her unit recommendation, it wouldn't be right to express doubts as far as her command ability was concerned.

"She's an officer from the accelerated training program. Her tactical knowledge might be too specialized. Maybe it would be better for her to do advanced officer schooling first."

Some of the generals still raise doubts. She took an accelerated course, after all. Even if she can put what she knows to use in actual combat, she could have holes in her knowledge. Regardless of whether she can give simple instructions at the tactical level, does she have the appropriate skills to give commands that take complex situations into consideration? It's only common sense to wonder.

But the reviewers who rated her so highly during the anonymous screening stand their ground. "Her graduation thesis was 'The Logistics of Swift Deployment.' The Railroad Department thought very highly of it."

As of her graduation, there is already proof that she is capable of debating strategic issues—the thesis in question.

For a cadet to write on such a subdued topic was rare; usually they preferred something more rousing. Considering the results she had attained on the battlefield, it was even stranger. During the anonymous review, everyone figured the candidate had to be someone with extensive field operation experience if they could write logistical analysis like that. Anyone who read it would assume it was written by an expert and think no more of it.

And when people who knew logistics read it, they were impressed by the superior writing and viewpoint, even if they didn't want to admit it. The outline was simple and clear. She emphasized gathering resources and said that supply lines should be secured through depot organization and a standardized distribution process. She argued that efficiency should be a top priority with the goal of eliminating all long-term storage, except for emergency supplies.

After her criticism of hoarding resources in the rear, she proposed a way of managing essential matériel that would support continuous combat on the front lines. Apparently, it was common knowledge in logistics that the Railroad Department had read it, loved it, and practically begged for her to be assigned to the team.

In fact, a number of skilled field officers reviewed the paper and gave it high praise. They said that anyone who had ever launched an offensive from the front line and run out of supplies had a keen understanding of where it was coming from.

Rudersdorf, always worrying about operation logistics himself, was no exception. No one assessing the anonymous candidate would have ever imagined that she was only eleven.

"Sorry, one thing. I hadn't given much thought to who wrote it, since information about the author was classified...but it wasn't a research report from the war college?"

"No, she wrote it in the academy."

"Excuse me, but do you really think any further deliberation is required? I can't see the need for it myself."

If she can debate on topics in logistics, it's hard to call her shortsighted. Rudersdorf cocks his head. The longer the discussion goes on, the better the candidate looks, and the fewer reasons to doubt her remain.

Then, and perhaps it's to be expected, Brigadier General von Zettour breaks his silence, looking as if he can no longer stand by. He doesn't particularly raise his voice, but his tone is dissatisfied, to be sure. "Here's a question. It appears that the candidate previously received a recommendation to advance to war college from Brigadier General von Valkov during her field training as a cadet, but Personnel rejected it. Can someone explain what happened?"

As far as Zettour can see, aside from her age, First Lieutenant Degurechaff is an excellent candidate and fits the bill with no problem. She even received high evaluations from some officers while she was still a cadet.

Valkov admired her performance in the conflict zone so much that he recommended her for war college admission. Though Zettour had only met him in person a handful of times, he sensed the man's intelligence during those conversations, and it was hard for him to imagine that Valkov would make a deeply erroneous recommendation.

And furthermore, as far as he can tell, she was regarded highly throughout her entire career, and her abilities have never been doubted before.

"Why wasn't she reviewed at that point? Who rejected her?"

"...I rejected her for her age and lack of achievements."

Zettour nods as if he expects Lergen's answer and turns a stern eye on him. "Major von Lergen."

"Yes, what can I do for you, sir?"

"I don't want to go on a tangent questioning your impartiality, so setting aside the initial rejection, why did you request this reassessment?"

Lergen's objection is so problematic his fairness is being called into question. Zettour doesn't outright say it, but everyone is wondering the same thing. She has so much talent, so many achievements. She is an outstanding officer. How could he doubt her?

"Because I have serious qualms about Lieutenant Degurechaff's character."

Lergen can't shake a bad feeling he has about her. His experience assessing numerous officers tells him something is off.

And that uneasiness has solidified into a deep distrust. He is determined not to let this abnormal girl be appointed to the heart of the Imperial Army.

"Are you saying that despite knowing she scored extremely high on both her psychiatric evaluation and Intelligence's test of her ability to maintain confidentiality?"

"Yes."

Of course. She would *pass both the psychiatric evaluation and Intelligence's assessment. Not only that, she might even be religious enough to get complimented on her piousness by a priest—most soldiers wouldn't ask God for forgiveness in the middle of a fight.* Still, that only means no one has been able to detect her abnormalities.

"Are you questioning the results of the tests?"

"That's right, but I don't doubt the tests themselves. I concede that the results are adequate."

I'm sure the tests all came up with the right numbers—that's not what's abnormal about her. Well, I understand the issue anyhow. That psychiatric evaluation is meant to test adult military professionals, not weirdos like her. So I'm sure those numbers are the result of a fair and carefully conducted test.

And that's precisely what's abnormal.

"Major von Lergen, I'd like to take the opportunity to remind you that everything you say will go on record, and then ask you to confirm something."

"Yes, sir."

For Lergen, both going on record and doing major damage to his career are frightening prospects. Really, as one of the best of the best racing down the elite track, he would rather avoid these sorts of arguments.

But he has to say something—the urge has taken hold of him. His entire body, his soul, warns him of something like a natural enemy to him as a human being—something alien, an abnormality that can't be allowed to exist.

"Why do you doubt Lieutenant Degurechaff's character?"

"I've seen her three times."

The first time, he thought she was an outstanding officer candidate. The second time, he thought she was a terrifying officer candidate. The third time, he was sure she was an insane officer candidate.

"In an official capacity or privately?"

"All three times came about due to my military duties. I saw her three times during inspections of the military academy."

There is probably no cadet who has made a deeper impression on me, and there probably never will be. She's at least abnormal enough that I can say that. Coolheaded and logical, patriotic and egalitarian, devoutly religious yet a liberal. Though all of those are praiseworthy qualities for a person to have, she's warped. Something about her is strange and twisted.

"Are you claiming that she's done something wrong? Or did she say something?"

"Please look at the remarks from her instructors. The word 'abnormal' is scribbled at the top."

Her academic advisor, who had interacted with her the most, had left an interesting memo. Though he gave her excellent scores in every area, he'd scribbled the word *abnormal* as a personal note. Was it her character that had made him uneasy? Instructors often point out students' deficiencies, but writing *abnormal* seems unthinkable.

"…Hmm, so there is a reason? Please explain." Even Zettour relaxes his accusatory stance and shows he is willing to listen—although it is only because he feels it necessary to confirm the facts from an impartial point of view.

"She's abnormal. I've never seen an officer candidate with a fully formed personality and perspective who regards people as objects."

She's just like a perfected machine. She takes orders and carries them out to the letter—an ideal officer. Despite that, she understands reality—I've never heard her spout any pointless theories. I just can't believe she's normal.

And that's why she was capable of what I witnessed when I saw her the third time.

"Did you ever think it might be some quirk of a genius's mind?"

"She definitely comes off as a genius in combat. In fact, General von Valkov and Intelligence jointly recommended her for the Iron Cross Second Class."

More than anything, something about that kid as a newly commissioned officer seemed wrong. Lergen exercised his full authority to investigate and found indications that she had participated in actual combat even before she was commissioned as a second lieutenant.

There were very few clues, but when he put them together, his suspicion of her involvement in an intelligence operation deepened. The recommendation may have been dismissed during the application-processing stage, but they wouldn't have nominated her for an Iron Cross Second Class for no reason.

"...You mean during her field training?!"

This surprises everyone, and a stir goes through the room. It is difficult to believe no matter what, but the rapid growth of her career over such a short time lends it credence.

During her field training—in other words, when she was nine—this child saw action and came out of it with a nomination for an award? If they heard it anywhere else, they would write it off as a bad joke. The abnormality here is this nonsense coming up during a review of candidates who may hold the future of the army on their shoulders.

"When I grilled Intelligence, they hinted that they might have involved her in some kind of top secret operation."

A border conflict zone... It is a rather dangerous place for an officer candidate to do field training, but...well, still probably fine. But the long-range penetration training makes even the hardiest soldiers scream—and doing it in actual enemy territory?

A march in full combat gear in the middle of the night to an isolated friendly base across land crawling with barbarians—you'd never expect a cadet to lead that sort of operation. Lergen wrung the information out from an acquaintance from Intelligence, and even he had assumed it was run by a battle-tested warrant officer.

Well, it made sense. It was only natural that Intelligence would look to such a capable leader for help. They probably never dreamed she was a cadet doing field training. Now Lergen has a hunch that the medal application was withdrawn after they belatedly realized that Tanya was only an officer candidate.

"...You mean to say that a cadet was involved in a field operation that led Intelligence to apply for her decoration?"

By now, no one can ignore how anomalous she is. The intelligence officers fend off glares by shaking their heads as if they know nothing about it. But it's common knowledge that Intelligence's right hand doesn't know what its left hand is doing. They have to know that they'd come up with something if they investigated—their faces became awfully pale a few moments ago.

"If possible, I'd like to get that information declassified."

"I'll check on it. And? If that's it, I'm pretty sure she's just an outstanding officer." *We'll ascertain the truth of this matter.* That's what the chairman means, but he is already convinced. That is why none of this makes sense to him.

Why is Lergen so skeptical about an officer with whom, aside from her age, they have no issues—not with achievements, performance, or anything else?

"While attending the academy, she pulled a magic blade on someone for insubordination."

"…Isn't it the senior cadets' responsibility to smack the rebels into shape?"

To come out and say it, although military law prohibits taking punishment into one's own hands, there are unwritten rules. For example, injuries incurred during training are "accidents," and they happen quite commonly in sparring matches against upper classmates.

It's not a nice way to say it, but if the committee is going to punish her for that, almost half of the army deserves some kind of similar criticism.

"She really meant to pry his head open. If the instructor hadn't stopped her, she would have turned an able soldier into a disabled person." Lergen suppresses the urge to shout, *No, this is different!* and explains. He knows no one could possibly understand unless they were there.

"Major, if we believed everything the trainers said, the army would be full of corpses by now."

Trainers hurling excessively harsh words at new recruits was business as usual for the army. Of the verbal abuse marines and aerial magic officers hurled at recruits during drills, *I'm gonna kill you!* was still on the cuddly side. In the army, it wasn't rare to see instruction that completely rejected a student's worth as a human being.

Nobody bats an eye when threats like, *I'm gonna crack your head open!* and *I'm gonna blast your empty head off!* echo out over the training grounds. And corporal punishment isn't just endorsed.

"Even if she tended to go to extremes, that's a bit of a mean evaluation."

"Considering her age, you could say she has great self-control."

If it were only words and some threats. Frankly, if that were all, most of them would go by what they know and think it was cute. But they hadn't see her with their own eyes.

Actually, they probably even think they are being considerate by not court-martialing people for every failure to obey.

After all, disobeying a superior officer can, at worst, result in capital punishment by firing squad. To put it a different way, they believe it's kinder to the new recruits, who might not have great judgment, to punch them out rather than execute them.

"Hmm, well, if your worries are her age and capacity for self-control, then I suppose I understand."

They aren't going to change their minds at this point. Everyone can agree there is an issue with her age. Coming down hard on a new recruit as the major commented may have been overkill, but it was still within bounds of the permissible. And it isn't as if they don't understand his concerns about her unusual ability.

But actually, by putting her through war college, they can offer her education in areas she lacks and grow her into a remarkable, competent officer. That much is certain, they think.

"Major von Lergen, your views are too subjective. Yes, I must say you're lacking in objectivity."

Despite all the debate and reservations, she will still be admitted.

"I recognize that you were trying to be fair. I'm surprised that someone like you would get so caught up in superficial impressions."

"Well, nice investigating. We'll have to grill Intelligence."

No one understands that he brought her up as a problem in earnest. Most of the committee thinks he took this tack as an indirect way to criticize Intelligence; with the way army politics works, a personnel section chief can't very well censure them openly.

Everyone is sure, though they don't state it outright, that he requested this reassessment in order to bring up this murky business he discovered while conducting his review of the candidate. The evaluation from Intelligence reflected some sort of secret operation in the past. Certainly in that case, it would partially have been an oversight of his part, but discovering it would work to his credit. And instead of going after him, Intelligence would end up having to issue an apology.

In other words, the main thing that would register for people was that the personnel section chief did his homework. Basically, he had managed to remain impartial while questioning Intelligence's secrecy.

"Nice work, Major von Lergen. We're not going to reassess her, but we will talk to Intelligence again."

"...Thank you."

And so, contrary to Lergen's intentions, no one tries to stop the candidate's admission.

Tanya's days continue on the forward-most line of the Rhine Front in the west—being woken up at any time and thrown into interception missions. As she gets splattered with mud and blood, the smell of gun smoke clinging to not just her hair but her entire body, she is promoted to first lieutenant. The raise in base pay, though small, is a good thing.

But the part that makes her ecstatic is the accompanying notice that she has been admitted to war college. Luckily, perhaps it should be said. First Lieutenant Schwarkopf assures her that considering Corporal Serebryakov's proven combat ability, he will recommend her for the officer track so that Tanya can go to war college with no worries. She is glad she can get away without acting like she cares about her subordinate.

As for the notice itself, getting recommended for admission to the war college is an honor, so that's a dream come true. To be eligible, you have to be at least a first lieutenant, so she doesn't even qualify at the moment; apparently, some commendable personage nominated her when recommending her for achievement. Mentally giving thanks to Personnel for their mysterious workings, she naturally accepts the enrollment, which means a transfer to safety in the rear.

And so...

First Lieutenant Tanya Degurechaff, eleven years old on paper, has a second opportunity, at least in her subjective memory, to enjoy the life of a college student. To the world, she must look like she's skipped a few grades, but in reality, it's my second round of college. From my perspective, it won't be very hard to fit in.

Strictly speaking, of course, a war college is quite different from a typical university in terms of both educational mission and curriculum. But in Tanya's view, it means getting to study in the rear, blessed with three hot meals a day and a hot bath to soak in. What a comfortable life compared to the front lines.

And to Tanya, a war college and a university are essentially the same thing. As long as I can use signaling theory to market her value as human capital, there is no difference between the two. Not only that, my theory is that war college is even better than a normal university in some ways.

Certainly in terms of Tanya's professional future, it's a sweet deal to not only not pay tuition but also get paid by the state to go *and* have a career track all laid out for her at the end. So war college freshman First Lieutenant Tanya Degurechaff merrily devotes herself to her studies. Though an elementary school backpack would be more appropriate to someone of her stature, she seems strangely comfortable in her military uniform carrying her officer's bag.

Ever since her experiences in the war zones, she can't go anywhere without her standard-issue rifle and computation orb, so after finishing a few routine tasks, she grabs those as well and heads off for another day at school. Of course, she knows she's supposed to bring writing utensils to campus, not her rifle…

Still, at some point, she's started to feel incomplete without her gear within reach. She never knows when there will be a chance to shoot the mad scientist, a rabid believer, or Being X dead. Therefore, she feels it's both imperative to consider everywhere a battlefield and be ready to seize any opportunity, and impossible not to.

Yes, her battlefield is everywhere. That's precisely why the war college accepted even a little skip grader kid like her so naturally. Even if it isn't her intention to look tough, it's difficult to make light of an officer back from the field wearing the Silver Wings Assault Badge and constantly exuding that battlefield tension.

On top of that, she uses her free time to disassemble her rifle and give it a good cleaning, unconsciously gritting her teeth, dreaming of the moment she will kill Being X. And her response when another officer notices her and asks why she always has her rifle is definitive.

Looking up with a perplexed expression that makes her seem her age, she says, "I may have to stake my life on this equipment at any moment, so I can't relax unless I have it with me. I.e., because I'm a coward."

"…You mean you don't feel safe unless it's within reach?"

"Yes, sir, something like that. Please consider it the childish habit of a baby who won't let go of her favorite blanket, and laugh."

Yes, that's probably enough to leave a solid impression. Thus, it doesn't take long for everyone to perceive First Lieutenant Tanya Degurechaff as less a child than a soldier back from the front lines—that is, they treat their classmate as a frightening but reliable fighter who smiles as she discusses national defense, arguing about the best ways to eliminate enemy troops.

"Morning, Mr. Laeken."

I only realize she's approaching when I hear her voice. I really can't even sense her. I do have a little combat experience, but I guess I've gotten pretty soft compared to the officers just back from the front. Or is she simply that great of a soldier?

"Good morning, Lieutenant Degurechaff. Beg your pardon, but do I see you have your rifle again today?"

In my time as a warrant officer, I've seen a lot of commissioned officers, but probably none of them have as bright a future as she does. She's barely over ten and enrolled in the war college, which they say is unheard of. Well, it's incredible that a kid that young would even have enough career experience to be a first lieutenant in the first place.

But I guess the world's a big place.

I was just as good as everyone else on the battlefield, but here's an officer who can get around my back. Lieutenant Degurechaff is clearly not the type of officer you can judge by looks. I hear she brings her rifle and computation orb to school every day and leaves them with the on-duty commander of the guard.

The reason she can't be without her weapons must be related to her combat experience. There are some guys who come back and have psychological issues that don't let them leave their weapons, but her case seems different. She doesn't seem like she would be particularly nervous without them.

Basically, she's making a habit of carrying her weapons. That means she must be ready to do battle at any time, but—and I'm repeating myself a bit—she did receive the Aerial Field Service Badge very young. She's well trained and addresses noncoms properly.

Next time I'm on the battlefield, I won't separate enemy soldiers out by age—if I don't shoot, I might die. I'll count that as one lesson learned.

"Yeah, it's embarrassing, but apparently habits are hard to break."

I know the feeling. Until I finally got used to sleeping in the moonlight, I was always unconsciously looking for cover. I knew I was safe, but the habits you create while you're fighting for your life don't fade so easily.

"Not at all. I think it's wonderful."

Actually, it means she has a good grasp of the important things on the battlefield. Understanding those while keeping a grip on your sanity is a test for green second lieutenants. On the battlefield, harsh reality crushes the rules they believe in.

Bravery, glory, honor—all those ideals get covered in mud as they fight to the death, and a handful of exceptions make a name for themselves. The secret that those few know is that it's not so hard. All they have to do is listen to what the noncoms have to say and offer opinions that will garner them respect and admiration. But there are really almost no officers who can do that.

"Thanks. For someone working their way up, nothing makes me happier than some reassurance."

That's why I have to look past this little girl's exterior, honor who she is, and assist her with sincerity.

If an officer can appreciate the effort it takes to climb the ranks, they grow. Understanding that fact, I faithfully fulfill my duties as commander of the guard and pay respect to the small yet illustrious first lieutenant.

"But with all due respect, Lieutenant, may I ask what brings you here? As you know, today is an off day. There aren't any classes."

It's what is generally known as the Sabbath—in other words, Sunday. Most pious believers go to church, and some go to confession. I hear this first lieutenant is often praying in earnest at church in the morning. Actually, I've seen her staring raptly at an icon more than once.

"Yeah, it's something straightforward. I want to use the library; the reference room at the dorm isn't enough."

Although it's an incredibly simple observation, Lieutenant Degurechaff is really, truly hardworking. Even the grumpy head librarian commends her knowledge, curiosity, and desire to learn, so I guess this girl is the epitome of what a soldier should be. I even heard from my former superior that the General Staff's strategy section was blown away by her analysis of the lessons of war and reexamination of basic tenets.

I wonder what she's got crammed in that little head of hers. She really impresses me.

"I beg your pardon. Then as usual, please leave your weapons here before making your way in."

Normally it's too much fuss to look after officers' personal effects; keeping an eye on them takes effort, so I don't usually want to do it, but this first lieutenant is different. A soldier has no greater friend on the battlefield than their rifle. And for a mage, their computation orb is just as invaluable. Watching over these is an honor, so I don't even notice the workload.

"Thanks. Then if you'll excuse me..."

After quickly filling in the application and accepting the proof of storage receipt with a practiced hand, Lieutenant Degurechaff proceeds onto campus. I glance after her, and even from behind, I can see that although her stride is small, she steps with confidence. Her narrow shoulders seem incredibly broad. The thought that such an officer trusts me enough to hand over her brothers-in-arms with no hesitation makes me happy in spite of myself.

"She's an awfully cheeky little bed wetter."

But an idiot shows up to rain on my parade. He doesn't understand how lucky I feel. It's amazing that she's a commissioned officer so young, and this bozo doesn't possess anything to commend him on besides his age.

"Are you stupid? She may look young, but it's not piss she smells like! She's got the scent of combat around her, gun smoke and blood."

215

So even a sergeant with combat experience can be this naive. Achieving that level of perfection as a soldier takes enough skill and love for battle to rival the old-timers. To put it a different way, even if you despise war as a human being, there has to be something about it that you love, or you'll never be able to understand her.

"Sergeant, is that all you think about her?"

"Huh? No, of course I think she'll make a great officer."

Of course she'll make a great officer. If she were my battalion commander I'd gladly follow her. Whether on an assault or breaking up a penetrating enemy force, performing delaying action or even rearguard duty—I'd follow her anywhere. War loves her.

She'll make her mark—her whole unit is sure to get the highest honors. I'm convinced. I know because I've observed so many officers: She's what they call a hero.

"Pay attention, moron. She carries two computation orbs, but she only gave you one!"

But there's no use trying to explain that to a numbskull like this. She turned in her rifle and backup computation orb as a compromise to respect my duties. It's virtually her right to keep the other orb, the one she's used the most.

So, yeah, I don't feel like pointing that out to a guy who doesn't even notice that I tacitly allowed her to take it because I understood.

"Maybe she kept it unconsciously, but boy, she doesn't let her guard down."

"If the Officer of the Week finds out, there'll be trouble."

...*Agh, is that still all you think of her...?*

Tanya's mental state as she walks the increasingly familiar war college campus is a bit complicated, as usual. If a human loses their sense of shame, they become shameless, which is dishonorable to a social creature. In that sense, being ashamed is a phenomenon that's particular to social creatures.

Which is why... Ugh, how embarrassing... Though I'm intent on revenge, I know I can't be proud of carrying my rifle with me everywhere.

So after an instructor indirectly chided me for it, I've taken to leaving my firearm with the commander of the college guards. Tanya compromises by carrying a combat knife specifically made for non-magic battles, so she's never completely unarmed.

Still, it would be a lie if I said the way they look at me when I go to turn in my weapons doesn't bother her. I don't like being exposed to their amused glances, as if I'm some weirdo under observation. But considering they have a point, there is nothing I can do about it.

Maybe it's my imagination, but I can't help but feel the guards are laughing at me—*Here's that dork again, bringing her rifle to school.* But Tanya can grasp why they might stare at a fully outfitted mage wandering around the rear. I can't get upset if it's something I would do myself.

Still, I have a reason for always being prepared that I can't tell anyone else.

It's a simple issue of dignity. If my rational mind gets buried in faith, my sense of self will fade; I can just see myself becoming Being X's toy if I don't keep my raison d'être[16] clear.

This guy calling himself God has a lot of time on his hands if he's playing with dolls, but the one being played with isn't going to stand for it.

So to clarify and renew her knowledge of her enemy, Tanya has been going to the nearest church on Sundays for a while now and cultivating her hatred before a false idol of Being X. Inside her, a chorus of curses joins her unbounded loathing—a healthy state of mind. That is the individual Tanya Degurechaff's response to the manipulator of humans, Being X. She takes her rifle with her so that if a chance materializes, she can shoot him, but unfortunately she never runs into him there.

Of course, I know that's an unproductive way for Tanya to spend her time. Even so, if I neglect the practice, it's possible Elinium Type 95's curse will turn Tanya into a pious believer. She needs to take care of her mental hygiene; it's an unavoidable necessity to ensure her mind abhors the mere image of Being X.

Slacking off on that would be the same as slacking off on breathing or abandoning thought.

---

[16] **raison d'être**   A reason to exist. The firm line demarcating you as you.

"…Hmph. So we don't want to be dolls?"

Tanya has an unwavering belief that human dignity lies in thinking. The human race, evolved from monkeys, feels that thought is what sets them apart from other species and makes them human.

That's why she can't understand why believers assume they are blessed and abandon rationality.

The moment a person loses the capacity to think, to question, Tanya considers them no longer human but a machine. And that is why the individual Tanya Degurechaff reveres thought, loves debate, and sneers at dogmatism from the bottom of her heart.

So of course she laughs at the fanatics, the blind believers. She can't stand that those dumbasses are just like the blind followers of Communism and other dogmas (essentially another type of religion) who built mountains of corpses through social experimentation—the feeling stems from her views on humanity. Thinking is sacred because trial and error is inherent to existence. When unthinking people force their dogmatism on others, she wonders how stupid the world could be.

Being X, who is trying to make her the vanguard of that sort of dogmatism, is nothing but her sworn enemy; she can't allow him to remain in this world.

That said, she is still rational enough to realize that spending all her time building up her hatred is unproductive, so for the time being she'll set that aside and push ahead with her studies.

Tanya is ambitious, in the sense that she's doing what she can do now with her eyes on her future. Hence the frequent library visits. She walks down the already familiar halls, exchanges salutes with the staff she knows, and heads straight for the library.

"First Lieutenant Degurechaff, coming in."

She puts her hand to the library door after giving the usual notice of her arrival. Since a rank of at least first lieutenant is required for admission into the war college, she's simply the lowest of the low. Although it is Sunday, it wouldn't be strange for some others to have arrived ahead of her. There could be superior ranking officers inside, so she always has to conduct herself smartly.

"Hmm?"

Chapter **IV**

Tanya's daily efforts to extend the proper courtesies are rewarded. A soldier with a scholarly air and nearing old age looks up from a mountain of resources as she walks in.

The insignia on his shoulder indicates he is a brigadier general and, judging from his clothing, probably an important one. The fact that one of his rank would be there digging through maps and records—well, it's unsurprising considering the quality of the materials at the war college. Research for military strategy always ends up dependent on the war college library. When one of the higher-ups needs some data, they often visit. There are mountains of records and papers that aren't allowed to leave the premises. If they want to browse those materials, they have to come in person.

"Ngh— Please excuse the interruption, General."

Tanya chuckles to herself in her head at this one-in-a-million chance meeting. No matter the era, it never hurts to have friends in high places. And if you are trying to meet people, it's essential to go out and increase your chances.

That said, it's a terrible shame that my external age is so young. It makes me hesitant to go anywhere alcohol could be employed. Obviously if such a little girl were present, anyone would have a hard time enjoying their drinks—it would defeat the point.

On the other hand, she's able to make a good impression by having her act so put together at such a young age. It is difficult for me to capitalize on her appearance because I have to consciously behave like a child, though.

Children are already another universe I don't understand, so little girls might as well be alien life-forms. She can smile in a pinch, but that is about it.

Now that she's blessed with an opportunity, she will not hesitate to take full advantage.

"Oh, you can just treat me like an older alum for the moment."

The man who returns her salute sounds less like a soldier and more like a philosopher who would be more at home doing research. He is probably straitlaced in some sense, but as far as she can tell he seems friendlier than bad-tempered.

"Thank you, sir. My name is Tanya Degurechaff. I'm a student here, and I was granted the rank magic first lieutenant by the Empire."

"I'm Brigadier General von Zettour, deputy director of the Service Corps in the General Staff Office."

The Service Corps in the General Staff Office! He's one of the top dogs in the rear! I'm so lucky.

"It's an honor to meet you, General."

She's pretty sure she can say that and mean it. After all, they have about as much clout as the guys who run General Staff Personnel. In a corporation, they'd be the ones running administrative strategy.

The only word for this chance to meet an off-duty officer from there is *lucky*.

"Hmm, Lieutenant, are you in a hurry right now?"

"Not in particular, sir. I'm here for the purpose of self-study to acquire knowledge."

She manages to control herself and obediently states her purpose instead of jumping up and down. Luckily, between her need to satisfy her intellectual curiosity and errands to research laws and ordinances, she is here quite frequently, so it isn't out of the ordinary.

"Great. If you'll give me a moment of your time, I'd like to get a younger person's opinion on something. How about it?"

"Gladly, sir, if I'm not interrupting."

"No, it's fine. Relax."

"Yes, sir."

Perfect, he's interested in me, too. It's so much easier to talk to someone when they're interested. This will be infinitely better than giving a presentation on personnel cutbacks to a bunch of execs who oppose the idea because they don't understand the necessity.

"I've heard a bit about you. It seems you've been quite busy."

"My reputation is undeserved, sir."

That agonizingly annoying nickname "White Silver" has convinced me the army needs to reconsider its taste in names, but apparently it does attract attention.

It seems like getting some name recognition will be good for my career

as a young elite, although the nail that sticks out gets hammered down. I need to keep an eye out for ways to keep my fame under control.

"Hmm? I think everyone intends it as a fitting appraisal... Oh, but let me ask you this."

And apparently even false reputations can contribute to a good first impression. Even if it is just a casual whim of this brigadier general who has taken a slight interest in Tanya, he is going to ask her perspective.

"Lieutenant, you can give me your subjective opinion. How is this war going to turn out? What's your view?"

Two soldiers having a conversation about the state of the war. Well, that's a kind of military small talk. Sticking to safer topics isn't a bad idea, according to common thinking.

But he's taken an interest in me. If I can give him an honest opinion, he'll see me as motivated. Of course, the barrier to entry is having something smart to say.

"That's a very broad question, sir."

So showing that I'm both assertive and deliberate by confirming the aim of his question is critical. In the military, everyone will like you if you consult with your superior officers often and report everything. If you don't know something, admit it and ask. That kind of attitude seems particularly useful in the army. These imperial soldier creatures have a tendency to be bizarrely obsessed with accuracy.

Since that's how it is, instead of trying to gain points, I'll put effort into not losing them. You can't get promoted just by speaking up. You need to pay attention to the minute details *and* make your voice heard.

"Hmm, you're right. Let me rephrase it. What shape do you think this war will take?"

"My apologies, sir, but I don't believe I'm in a position to comment."

And you should always stop yourself from commenting on things outside your duties. For example, human resources shouldn't butt into sales's business, just as sales shouldn't butt into human resources's. It's important to know your place.

"It's all right. This isn't an official consultation. Just tell me what you think."

"Then with your permission, sir..."

I really don't want to say anything, but refusing any further would be rude. It would be worse than anything to come off as someone too inept to have anything to say. Remaining silent and expecting him to understand would be naive—a super-dreadnought-class fantasy.

Human beings have two ears but only one mouth. In other words, when dealing with someone who is willing to listen, one mouth is plenty. Unless you open it, your ideas have no chance of getting across.

"I'm sure it will turn into a world war."

Rule number one of making a presentation: Declare estimates with confidence. And while it's important to be creative, make sure your forecast is reliable. A presentation is meaningless if your points don't reach your audience.

"World war?"

"I believe most of the major powers will become involved, so the fighting will take place on a global scale."

Will this be this world's first world war? Well, there's no mistaking that the major powers are going to have a serious fight. It's definitely going to be big.

In that case, perceiving it as a "world war" is only common sense. World powers will clash with world powers, seeking hegemony. Each side will fight like they mean it, for sure. So showing I'm not taking things lightly, that I'm facing reality, is more likely to work in my favor.

"…What makes you say that?"

"Though the Empire is an emerging state, compared to the existing powers, we boast quite an advantage."

It's also important to avoid convoluted explanations. The only way to prevent pointless meetings is to thoroughly establish common understanding.

In that sense, this brigadier general seems very smart—so much so that it's surprisingly open-minded of him to have a conversation this serious with a first lieutenant. But then, that's precisely why he's worth talking to.

"If we were to fight each nation one-on-one, we would surely come out victorious."

"Right. Against the Republic, we could win."

He said the hard part for me. "Against the Republic" can mean that it might not hold true in other cases. Since the superior officer hinted at their other potential enemies, it's easier to continue the conversation.

Genuinely impressed by that nuance, Tanya realizes she is perhaps talking a bit much. She even senses that in the army, where you don't really get to choose your subordinates, they invest in their juniors more than in the corporate world.

This perspective was impossible for me to have had when I was doing layoffs in human resources, so I should take this lesson to heart. In the army, unlike in a company, you don't get to choose your subordinates—all you can do is educate them.

"But actually, it's difficult to imagine the Commonwealth and the Russy Federation simply standing by. I'm not sure about the Kingdom of Ildoa."

"...They shouldn't have any direct interests in the current war."

And with that Tanya reconfirms what is already obvious. Yes, this is good. This is fantastic. This is what you call an intelligent conversation. It's the type that doesn't occur unless the person you're talking to is interested in finding out how smart you are. This is delightful. It's what being an adult member of society is all about.

"Not direct interests, no. But they will be forced to confront the question of whether they will allow the birth of a dominant state or put a stop to it."

"A dominant state?"

"Yes. If the Reich, situated in the center of the continent, eliminates the Republic, we will have not a relative advantage but absolute superiority."

I can consider this to be similar to how it was possible for imperial Germany to defeat France and the Russian Empire. Was the British Empire stupid enough to let that happen? If it had been, that island nation would be treated like a backwater about now.

Instead, they participated in the war because they understood the severity of the situation. Won't the great powers of this world join the battle as their national interest dictates?

"So if we can't get rid of the Republic quickly, in a way that doesn't give other nations enough time to interfere, the fighting will trigger a domino effect of other countries getting involved."

"I see. You may be right, but isn't the alternative that the Republic ends up the dominant state? They shouldn't want that, either."

Ngh. Agh, I didn't say enough, so he filled in for me. If I assume he's taking my youthful appearance into consideration, I've been pitied. I can't make any more mistakes.

Hang in there. Look him straight in the eye and answer clearly.

"I agree. That's why I think they'll try to make it so both the Empire and the Republic fall."

"You mean other countries will intervene?"

"Yes. I imagine it will start with financial assistance to the Republic. Other conceivable methods include providing them with weapons and dispatching volunteer troops."

Think of the famous lend-lease[17] policy and how wars are financed. English and France won, but they were still in a precarious position by the end. Considering that, the Empire and the Republic would have their fun little war, and the natural result would be for everyone else to intervene right when the pair had exhausted each other. If they wanted to, they could even pretend to be good Samaritans about it.

"...Aha. I'm beginning to see what you mean."

"Yes, I would think the general plan of the other powers would be to lend large amounts of money to the Republic and then intervene to take down both of us in the end."

States are honestly so evil. They take good people and turn them into members of an evil cult. We need to consider their potential for grossly warping people's true natures.

For example, the hateful Soviet and East German secret police caused massive harm to human nature. Behold society's fear under the eye of the Stasi! Freedom. Give them mental freedom! It's high time the human race realizes that individualism is the only path that will save the world.

---

[17] **lend-lease**   A wartime service that allows mainly allied countries to rent everything from weapons and supplies to bases and land. They key word is *rent*, so they would only be borrowing. But to the opposing side, it doesn't matter if these are rentals or not—if the enemy's war potential increases, that's a problem. Everything is supposed to be returned, but as you can see from the example of the Soviet Union sometimes failing to pay back the United States, things basically have to be offered with the assumption of taking a loss.

"And if the Empire overwhelms the Republic?"

"It's very likely that its national security policies would say to team up with other powers and intervene directly. Even if they can't do that, they may not hesitate to intervene on their own."

The noble proposition of freedom of thought may be important, but I can't take this intellectual conversation lightly. I have to keep up the appearance of stating well-thought-out views.

"I see. That's a fascinating conjecture. How do you think we should handle things?"

"Well, I haven't come up with a plan..."

Actually, when I have ideas, I submit them. If I could give him one now, it could be a seed for my advancement, but unfortunately I lack the military expertise. Well, perhaps military creativity should be left to Napoleon[18] and Hannibal. As a good, peace-loving individual, there is nothing wrong with that.

"So I would learn from history and try to make peace, and if that was impossible, I would make limiting attrition a top priority."

"...You mean you wouldn't try to win? People will question your will to fight."

Yeah, he's right. That was an awfully careless thing to say. In the manner of a university professor, I spoke a bit too passionately. I can't believe I would say something that brings my will to fight into question in front of the director of the Service Corps in the General Staff, of all people. Was it really my mouth that said it? That was such a huge mistake, I want to shoot it off.

This could hurt my career. No, I once heard that cowards get overworked on the front lines. This is very bad. Truly bad. Somehow, without letting any distress show on my face, I need to indirectly state in an utterly calm tone that that is not my intention. At the same time, I'll probably still be at risk unless I say something kind of brave to show off my fighting spirit.

"In a literal sense, yes, General. But I don't mean that we shouldn't

---

[18] **Napoleon**   France's great revolutionary soldier and politician. Just like Germany's fellow with the toothbrush mustache, he's an example of how an outsider manipulated the powers that be. This one lost, but he is well regarded, so you won't get thrown in jail for talking about him in France.

aim for victory. It's a problem of definitions; we must deconstruct our assumptions."

"And? Go on."

"Yes, sir. I believe that if we aren't defeated, we should define that as an Empire victory, since our national defense plan would have worked."

"So in your opinion, how do we achieve victory?"

"We carry out a thorough bloodletting and crush the enemy's ability to continue fighting." Tanya seemed to specifically choose words soldiers liked to hear—*carry out, thorough, crush*—groping for a way to speak realistically while projecting that she was full of fighting spirit.

"You mean annihilating the enemy field army?"

Annihilating their field army? Well that would be ideal, but it's not an easy task. In other words, this question is a trap. In order to show him I'm not just taking a hard line because I think that's what he wants to hear, I have to dare to disagree here.

"That would be ideal, but quite difficult, I imagine. Perhaps we should make attrition of enemy human resources our goal and devote ourselves to positional warfare defense?"

"Can we win that way?"

"I don't know. But we wouldn't lose. And saving up enough extra energy to deliver a decisive blow at that point would increase our strategic flexibility."

I can't declare we can win. But this is the best thing I can say so he doesn't interpret my answer as saying we'll lose. I put the words *decisive blow* in there as insurance. I need to keep making comments that show my motivation to sock it to the other guys.

"Hmm, how intriguing. But what would you do if the enemy arrives at the same strategy?"

Now. Now's the time to be assertive. Once someone shows an interest in you, the final impression they take should be the strongest. If that's the case, I need to make my aggression clear and gloss over the extremely inconvenient truth that I am lacking in the will to fight department.

"Yes. Having considered that possibility, I propose switching our main strategy on the battlefield to infantry defense and mage offense."

"Mages may have destructive power and impact, but I don't think they're suitable for capturing positions."

"I agree; however, the objective isn't to occupy but to eliminate enemy soldiers."

To put it another way, the combat maneuvers would be carried out not to extend our sovereignty over enemy land but to exhaust and eliminate enemy countrymen. We need to acknowledge the reality that in all-out war, cutting off the root of the enemy's ability to continue fighting is the only path to victory, and we should develop measures to achieve that.

In World War I, Germany slaughtered Russia and hit France and England hard—they were overwhelming the other countries on the tactical level. The biggest reason it eventually lost was that it ran out of strength. When in addition to France and England, they had to fight the United States, it was precisely because they knew they couldn't win that the German General Staff gave up.

They realized that even if their lines hadn't broken, they could no longer continue fighting and had no choice but to accept their defeat. So they lost. There's an important lesson to be learned from this memory. That is, how defeat looks in total war. No matter how well you compete on the lines, if your country runs out of power, you can't continue the war. It's not a question of mentality but the limits set by the laws of physics.

"As such, I'm convinced our main purpose should be to exhaust enemy soldiers with tactical disruption and penetrating raids from aerial mages."

Honestly, I think penetrating raids are crazy talk, but as long as there's a slim possibility that mages could succeed with them, they're worth proposing. Besides, I won't be the one doing them; if it's just unreasonable blather, I can keep it up all day.

Take a look at Tsugene! Didn't that idiot get promoted at home for doing whatever he wanted in Manchuria and Mongolia? Or the general who forced the Battle of Imphal! They called him the best spy for the Allies, full-of-shit-guchi, brute-guchi. Or wait, was he the "I'm dying" scammer general?

Didn't he say he was dying and then get money in an out-of-court settlement? Mm, maybe not—I can't remember... Well, whatever. If I can be that irresponsible, life'll be a cakewalk.

But unfortunately, I'm a good person. Since I haven't abandoned that much of my humanity, I'll draw the line at this plan, which should be doable based on my experiences so far.

Ahh, I'm such a sensible person. I'm just a bundle of good intentions. Yeah, I am undoubtedly justice incarnate. I'm a long-suffering martyr boasting an utterly wholesome character, who seeks goodness and peace.

"Hmm? The mage mission wouldn't be support?"

"In positional warfare, mages have firepower on par with artillery and agility that outstrips infantry. They're the ideal branch for hunting enemy soldiers."

To be honest, mobile defense was tough. I learned very well what a pain it was to combat war junkies, for instance, when I had to fight those Named. If there is a god, he should erase that whole bunch before declaring himself. Any species that enjoys killing its own members is insane.

In other words, there's the end of my explanation of why Being X isn't God. Ahh, what can I do to escape the devil? If the devil roams a godless world, we're basically in Armageddon, right?

"If you want to win while minimizing your own losses, then perhaps the Attritional Containment Doctrine? Mages are best for that."

"I see. You sure know how to sell it."

"My humble thanks, sir."

Now I should probably back off a bit. But his reaction's not bad. He's hunching slightly to write something on one of his documents, so it doesn't look like he's going to press me further. This is great.

If I can talk my way out of things, perhaps I should consider a career as a negotiator. But my area of expertise is human resources. Going for depth gets you a better salary than breadth, but hmm.

Maybe I should start planning my life after the war; maybe I should learn a trade. Now that I think of it, I'll definitely have to earn some qualifications. How can I change jobs when my résumé is, "Mage with a wealth of combat experience. Can handle a fight to the death any time, any place"? Like, what kind of gang are you trying to join?

Every era has the same issue with finding occupations for ex-soldiers. If Tanya doesn't invest in herself now, she'll have trouble later. It's precisely for that reason that she's going to the library, to learn about laws so she can earn a legal professional qualification or something similar that will keep her fed in the future.

"So hypothetically, if you were to use mages as the linchpin of this Attritional Containment Doctrine, how many would you want?"

...Maybe I shouldn't be planning my life in one corner of my brain. I answer the question without really considering its aim. "I'm sure a battalion is the right size. It wouldn't be a huge logistical burden, and it has the minimum force necessary."

"Interesting. Well, I'll think about it. Young people's opinions are always interesting."

"Thank you, sir."

Not realizing what just happened is a basic error. Normally, Tanya would definitely feel something was off and try to somehow avoid the incoming trouble. But this time she's careless. Yes, even though carelessness causes all the most horrible errors in life.

>>>> THE IMPERIAL CAPITAL, AT THE DESK OF THE DEPUTY DIRECTOR OF <<<<
THE SERVICE CORPS IN THE GENERAL STAFF

When in doubt, learn from the lessons of the past.

The military man Zettour has learned so much from history that he's criticized for being too much like a scholar, but he does it because the strategic principles of the past contain pieces that can still be applied.

And because Brigadier General von Zettour is so familiar with history, he has a nose for recognizing indescribable yet fundamental change. He has learned from history to sense a shift in the tides. You could call it a feeling that the existing paradigm wouldn't quite work for dealing with the national defense strategy issues the Empire is currently facing.

He believed the teachings of history should be used as a guiding light, and they told him change could be coming.

The difficult-to-grasp question of what will change is a distraction for most imperial soldiers. Given that most of them are expected to deal with the circumstances right in front of them, that's no surprise. Considering the traditional way of thinking in the Imperial Army, which only cares about how well each individual carries out their missions, Zettour is certainly heretical.

But regardless of his academic leanings, he has proven himself with outstanding achievements. The Imperial Army is open to welcoming all kinds of people as long as they can demonstrate skill as officers.

And that's why Zettour is respected even within the General Staff.

The sight of him lost in thought at his desk has become a type of featured attraction at the General Staff Office, and no one thinks to interfere. The staffers who work under him are used to seeing him open up a philosophical text and sink deep into thought once his work is done.

Ever since the war started, they have all been busy with urgent tasks, but now that both the northern and western fronts have stabilized, the lull creates some spare time, so they can finally breathe.

None of the officers have rested since the war began, so the General Staff officers are finally given a short break as well. The younger staffers dash off in high spirits for the beer hall, where they make liberal use of their salaries because how else will they spend them? The older staffers take off as well, finally getting to spend some relaxing time with their families.

What both groups have in common is that they take their first vacation in a while and enjoy it to the full.

But the day they return, they find their superior officer, who clearly hasn't slept a wink, immobile and staring feverishly at his hastily scribbled notes. The officer who remained on duty tells the puzzled staff that about half a day ago the brigadier general returned from the war college and has been scowling at his notes ever since, as if he has forgotten everything else in the world. Puzzling, indeed.

"General von Zettour?"

The field officers can't bear to see him like this, but even when they try to talk to him, his bloodshot eyes only wander over the notes spread out on his desk. There isn't any other way for him to process the shock he has received.

At first, he thought she was just an officer with an interesting, novel idea, and that her proposal, which he had written down, was just another way of looking at things.

As he thought more about it on his way back to the General Staff Office, he was impressed by her view that the conflict between exterior and interior lines might reach a head.

But as he continued to ponder these ideas, he understood that his thoughts were beginning to grasp something. Then he realized—that even if he didn't want to, he had to admit that the notes strewn across his desk contained an inconvenient truth.

He's shocked that she can speak so lucidly on the direction the war will take, when even the General Staff is unsure. Where did such an accurate understanding come from? As far as Zettour knew, Brigadier General von Rudersdorf was the one most sharply hinting that the tides of war would change, but even Rudersdorf didn't seem able to see things as clearly as First Lieutenant Degurechaff had proclaimed them.

She said that this was a world war, and that total war would be inevitable. Anyone else hearing that would say she was deluded. But he has the feeling she just put into words the changes that the Federation and the Dominion were hinting at. She fully understands the "something" that both Zettour and Rudersdorf were feeling, though they were unable to explain it.

It's a borderline delusional plan but strangely persuasive.

She said it as if she'd already seen it happen. And Zettour has to agree with the analysis and understanding of the situation that provided the foundation for her conviction.

Suddenly, he realizes that a number of staffers are eyeing him with concern. *I can't make a scene in front of my men*, his usual officer values clamor, but he has received such an intellectual shock that he is still reeling from the aftereffects.

Not in the mood to shrug it off as nothing, he lets his actual feelings slip. "It's world war, men. Do you really think we'll go to war against the entire world?"

"Huh?" The lower-ranking officer's expression says, *What's gotten into him?*

As awkward looks appear on everyone's faces, Zettour wants to tell them he can't believe it either, but that would be more awkward. Besides, his experience and knowledge judge that young brain's horrific picture of the future to be a valid prediction.

Yes. Zettour knows the words of this child—who would look more natural cheerfully laughing—can't be laughed off.

He heard of that officer, that…little girl, during the war college admissions process. He felt lucky to have run into her on campus, but when he tried to test her in conversation, the result was Pandora's box.

"Sorry. I can't reveal the source, but I want you to consider this possibility."

"…It's an awfully extreme prediction. Radical even…"

Though he is giving orders, he understands his subordinates' perplexity far more than he would like. Even he hadn't considered the possibility of the entire world and the Reich plunging into war, and why should he have?

How extreme could you get within the bounds of reason? And "radical" was exactly right. But the more he thinks about it, the more horrible the possibilities that flicker across his mind.

Something like that could never happen. I'll find a hole in it somewhere, he thinks.

But, hypothetically—only hypothetically—what if…what if she were right? In that case, the Empire would have to go to war against the world, literally.

If that happens, it wouldn't be a bad idea to give her a battalion. If we can't win unless we go insane, then we'll just have to do that.

"…The one thing I didn't want to be when I grew up was a horrible person." Suddenly aware of his own thoughts, Zettour is shocked. Send a child to war? That would be the worst sort of shame for a soldier. Yet he was assuming it as a given.

Ahh…I regret being so incompetent.

The position of a high-ranking General Staff member in the military is a specialist position. But you can't only be a specialist. What the Imperial Army's General Staff seeks are military specialists who are simultaneously generalists with insight into a broad range of related fields.

Of course, at the very least, you have to understand the combat situations as well as the rear. For that reason, officers on the elite track frequently encounter transfer milestones.

Major von Lergen, stationed in the hub of this activity—Personnel at the General Staff Office—is used to transfers. After all, from the perspective of his career, as important the role of a section chief in Personnel is, it's only a milestone on the way to his next position.

In the Imperial War College Admissions Committee meeting, he showed himself to be keeping an eye on multiple departments, and that was assessed favorably in the General Staff Office—although it was a valuation of his familiarity with other departments as a generalist, not his skepticism of the candidate, which was what he was hoping they would consider.

In any case, you can never have too many skilled generalists in a war.

Before long, he's promoted to lieutenant colonel. And to Lieutenant Colonel von Lergen, who has risen at a quicker pace than usual, they offer a position as a high-ranking staff officer in the Operations Division of the General Staff.

Although his role isn't specified, a position under a high-ranking officer where he would get to be involved in the drafting of various overarching plans is proof of the army's high opinion of him. And right upon reporting for duty, the lieutenant colonel would get a taste of the traditional slave driving.

The Operations Division is a body at the center of the army within the General Staff. The General Staff building stands in a quiet, prime location in the imperial capital. Its exterior tranquility, appropriate to its accumulated history, belies its awfully hectic interior.

"Congratulations on your promotion, Colonel von Lergen. We're glad to have you."

"Thank you, General von Rudersdorf."

"Well, we're going to work you like a horse, you know. No matter how many people we get, it's never enough. Take a seat."

Felicitations upon his arrival and promotion. He has taken his orders; gathered up his things; and with his bag in hand, entered Operations, where he is met by the deputy director of the division, General von Rudersdorf, himself. Despite the long strings of hardworking days familiar to every General Staff officer, the general grins energetically and urges him to take a seat so they won't waste time.

The moment Lergen sits down, Rudersdorf launches into the topic at hand, as if they really have not a moment to lose.

"Okay, Colonel. This is sudden, but I'd like you to go straight to the northern front. Here are your orders."

Though he knows of the general's reputation for quick decisions, even Lergen doesn't expect to be dispatched immediately upon reporting for duty.

"As you know, the strategic confusion has had serious repercussions on the way things are going up there."

But Lergen wears the staff braid, too. It isn't just a decoration. He instantly adapts his mind-set to the situation and refocuses. In almost no time, he's listening closely to his superior, leaving no word unnoted.

"Well, it's no wonder given we're suddenly performing a large-scale mobilization for an offensive on a front where we weren't planning on attacking."

Imperial Army is paying a steep price for misjudging the situation. On top of tensions in the west, the massive unexpected deployments of the Great Army are having dire consequences.

It's easy to imagine the difficulties the armies in all theaters are facing as a result.

The strength of interior lines strategy is movement across domestic territory, but it can't be pulled off without extensive preparation. If conditions deteriorate, they can't avoid chaos.

"There's nothing so atrocious and wasteful for a nation than people who aren't fulfilling their duties getting paid in positions they aren't suited for. Naturally, we've reshuffled."

As a result, most of the General Staff members who advocated for one big push have been dismissed or demoted. Of course, the ones who did their duty without any gross errors didn't get it quite so bad, but the current mood is definitely favorable for promoting promising talents.

It can be said that Lergen himself, considering his rapid advancement and important post in the General Staff, is one of those who is benefiting from the situation.

"It's ironic that we're shorthanded, but it does mean we can give a promising officer like you somewhere to flex your muscles. That's why we're having you go up north."

"So my orders are to gain an understanding of the situation?"

All things considered, the reason a General Staff member from Operations would be sent to the north would be inspection. Even a new staffer can understand that orders like this under these circumstances mean the higher-ups want data for long-term planning.

And it's all according to the basic strategy the Empire traditionally keeps in mind—of breaking through two fronts to the best of their ability. That is, one of the fronts will surely need to be prioritized, and the higher-ups probably want information to decide which one.

"Exactly. The western front has stabilized, but we still don't want to be fighting on two fronts for too long."

"So we need to decide which one to settle?"

"Exactly. After you see what's happening up north, go make observations in the west." The general nods as if to say, *Very well.*

As far as Lergen can tell, his response was satisfactory. "Yes, sir. I'll go immediately to the north."

High-ranking staffers keep a bag packed with a change of clothes next to their desk so they can be ready to follow orders at any time.

Lergen learned from senior officers, so when he takes his orders, he grabs the bag he faithfully packed according to tradition and walks out the Operations Division door. Of course, he never imagined that his preparations would come in handy so soon.

"Good. Oh, and, Colonel. Take a look at this on your way up."

"What is it?"

"A paper Zettour passed along. It's worth a read."

"Understood. Then if you'll excuse me, sir, I'll be going."

Lieutenant Colonel von Lergen leaves straight from there, taking a military vehicle to the station. He boards a train bound for the north, which departs not too much later. He sits in the first-class compartment reserved for high-ranking soldiers, takes out the paper, and reads the title: "Predictions on the Shape and Direction of the Current War."

For a moment, he remembers the Deputy Director of the Service Corps Brigadier General von Zettour's scholarly face, and the title brings back fond memories of the texts accompanying lectures on the history of war. Zettour's habit of deep thought is famous enough that Lergen has heard of it.

So perhaps it makes an intriguing point, and that's why General von Rudersdorf read it and recommended it to me. That is Lergen's interpretation, but as he reads, his eyes glaze over.

Not only that. As he reads further, his expression grows confused. It's the emotional disturbance of fear and astonishment. He can't help his shock, as if he has just been whacked in the head.

"What...is this?"

Is this...? "The Current War"? Wait, is this kind of war even possible? his mind murmurs, profoundly doubtful.

...It is. The answer comes from his professional consciousness.

As far as Lergen knows, Zettour isn't the type of officer to go around shouting wild nonsense. On the contrary, he is rather restrained. It's the General Staff's common view that reality should be analyzed and understood. That scholarly yet realistic officer is warning them of a world that is, simply put, one of global war. *Outrageous.* How happy he would be if he could just laugh it off.

But Lergen, head in his hands, moaning in spite of himself, is forced to confront reality. These kinds of strategy papers always entail furious debate; as a member of the General Staff, he's aware what a dilemma exterior lines versus interior lines is.

Naturally, he understands how world war is possible if the parties faced with the Empire's interior lines strategy were to discuss how to beat it.

"In that case...this is saying that the current war will inevitably develop into a global conflict?"

The Empire would be under siege. The problem of its fragile national defense environment, stemming from political factors, gives those in charge of it a never-ending headache. It's why they are still concerned about national defense despite having a military superior to those of nearby powers.

But the countries encircling the Empire also have the security issue of having such a powerful neighbor.

Naturally, the Empire anticipated them to construct a united front, employing an exterior lines siege strategy with the aim of dividing the Empire's forces and tipping the power balance.

Those loose chains are the thing threatening the Empire. In order to crush the siege slowly strangling them, it has turned to interior lines strategy.

It also cut off its diplomacy efforts—agreements such as its alliance with the Kingdom of Ildoa and its nonaggression pact with the Russy Federation—long ago. Normally in a situation like this, most countries should have been hesitant to negotiate, fearing a local flare-up.

But is that really the case? If the Entente Alliance were to drop out, François, with an active conflict zone, would be forced to resist the Empire's pressure on its own.

The question of whether the cunning Commonwealth would obediently ally with François is another that can't be answered easily. To maintain the balance of power, it would probably join in support, but it is entirely possible they might aim to take both the François Republic and the Empire down at the last moment.

Once that was pointed out for him, he can't deny the possibility that all the other sparks blazed up in a chain reaction.

Russy and François are allies, historically, but a rift has grown between them over communism. The Empire seized that opening to make their nonaggression pact with the Russy Federation. From the François point of view, that pact means it has to count on the Entente Alliance to restrain the Empire with a second front.

And that's why the Empire is stuck fighting both the Entente Alliance and the Republic. And if, fatally, the fall of both the Republic and the Empire is the only outcome of this war the other powers will accept...? It's possible that the one thing they won't allow is a hegemonic state overwhelming all the others.

With his knowledge and experience, Lergen can hear the gates of world war opening. *It's possible.*

And then, when we wage war against the world... The concept of "total war" comes naturally to mind, along with something else—something unfathomable but snickering like a witch.

Chapter IV

Total war: when a country finds it necessary to mobilize all of its power to accomplish their goals in battle.

The desire to refute the paper suddenly wells up inside him, but the inference it makes is based on the truth.

The nature of war will fundamentally change; ammunition and fuel consumption will drastically increase. The things he saw and heard at the General Staff Office backed all of that up. It's undoubtedly the truth—especially considering the Western Army Group has already gone over the projected weapons and ammunition usage in a head-on clash against another power.

A striking amount of combat casualties? Yeah, that's also right. I heard our recruiting speed is already hitting a wall. We're losing so many more men than expected that the peacetime recruitment plan is already failing.

We would have to fight under the assumption that we will expend large numbers of weapons and soldiers. There would be vast consumption of personnel and waste of matériel on a scale that could destroy the national economy. Yes, consumption *of human lives. Not even "sacrifice" but simple, numerical "consumption." Will this insane struggle go on until one side or the other collapses under the burden?*

He's suggesting a type of war in which people and things are consumed until you go completely bankrupt, plus the idea that this would be taking place on a global scale? Normally, such a prediction would be considered delusional.

If I agree with this, what awaits us is a horrifying world where people will be numbers—disposable products. But this argument has a lot of parts that seem plausible. Still, when I think about what it would mean to accept it...

No. Of course, it's possible to criticize both the total war and world war theories. But for some reason this still feels realistic. I want to deny it, but there is something in here that is undeniable.

But why? Why can't I deny it? I have this bizarre sensation sticking in my throat.

"...What is this weird feeling?"

I should be somehow familiar with both total war and world war. Er, there's no way I could be familiar with awful things like that, but I definitely have some memory of them. It's like I have a memory in some other sense...

"Somewhere, I—no, I'm…forgetting something? No, something is bothering me."

Did I see it in some other paper? No, that's not it. I just now heard the words total war *and* world war *for the first time. I just learned them.*

Then are there some similar concepts? I don't remember anything like that. The closest thing was…yes, something I read in an SF novel. So is it derived from some experience I've had? I barely have any frontline experience, though…

I was in the field up until I reached first lieutenant, and after I was stationed in the Commonwealth as a military attaché, I've been serving in the rear. Did I hear something in the Commonwealth? I wrote a mountain of reports while I was there. I remember them all very well, but I don't recall any concepts like those… Am I overthinking this? I'm sure I've seen some part of this before, though…

Even in the middle of a war—no, precisely because it is wartime, capable staff are a must-have. That's why money is being poured like water into staffer education. As one of the students benefiting from that funding, First Lieutenant Tanya Degurechaff is on the traditional staff trip as part of her military education.

Mainen is a well-known hot springs getaway. Though its bathing district has made it famous as a health resort since ancient times, it's located right next to a harsh mountain region that always has a coat of snow. On one of the nearest mountains overlooking the peaceful town, Tanya is among the war college students getting put through the mill.

She is the only female and the only child who made it through the admissions process. Honestly, she doesn't sense as much subjectively, but as a biological fact, it can't be denied. But in the far-from-gender-free world of "ladies first," Tanya with her outwardly girlish appearance is, albeit only relatively, blessed compared to the other students.

A simple example is when they spent the night in a village on their hike. The men not only slept in a pile, but they were forced to dig trenches to do it in. Fearing the army's reputation, the superior officer allowed only Tanya to borrow a bed. She was also allowed to use the local army facilities.

Chapter **IV**

Basically, apart from the mage branch, the army is a man's world. Actually, even most of the mages are men. Of course, there are rules and regulations about the treatment of women officers. And naturally, the dense army regulations you would expect from the Empire include provisions on how women soldiers are expected to behave.

That said, most of the few women soldiers who existed before mages were from the imperial family. Drafted under that assumption, the regulations envision an imperial princess and her attendants rendering only nominal service, so they feel outrageously out of date. As you might imagine, the rules for mages on the front lines, where the members of the imperial family would never be sent, have been overhauled in recent years to make them more practical in combat situations. The regulations for treatment of women officers in the rear, however, still read much like an old-fashioned guide to manners, since most of the women in those positions were nobles or imperials.

And since so few female officers continue on to the war college to begin with, no one has bothered to update the war college rulebook—the regulations drawn up for imperial family women remain wholly intact. Even if they're so outdated you want to ask how many decades or even centuries ago they were written, any rule in the Empire that hasn't been amended or abolished is enforceable. Maybe it could be counted as an adverse effect of bureaucracy, but the law in the Empire is to follow the rules that exist, even if they privilege certain people. For that reason, they've practically rolled out a red carpet for Tanya on this trip.

The purpose of the trip is simple: endurance training under extreme conditions that dull the ability to think. Tanya knows that most of the operations that staffers running on fumes come up with are Tsugene-esque nuclear land mines. So it makes no sense to the instructors to treat First Lieutenant Degurechaff like a woman when she's strong enough and has such a wealth of combat experience. And there are no stipulations in the now classical regulations concerning women war college students about how to treat magic officers. In other words, they can't ignore "Women officers should be provided with appropriate accommodations," but if there's no rule stating, "Women mage officers should not be made to carry heavy loads," they can weigh her down just as much as the others.

For that reason, since mages can use support formulas, she was ordered to attend in full gear with a dummy heavy machine gun. Essentially, go climb a mountain in your normal full gear plus a nearly fifty-kilogram machine gun, to boot. If Tanya suppresses the urge to cry child abuse, there's no legal issue with it.

Of course, there's no hiking trail—they're in the region where the alpine troops train. You can only conclude that the one who designed this system was a sadist. Even the lightly equipped alpine infantry is groaning about this uphill trek, but the students are being made to do it in full gear.

But teleologically, it isn't a mistake.

Still, wouldn't it be better to not completely exhaust the staff? she can't help but think.

"Viktor, say an enemy built a defensive firing position on that hill. You're ordered to make a swift advance on them with a battalion."

But the education is thorough. The tired officers are mercilessly quizzed about hypothetical combat orders.

"Propose a strategy."

A firing position on that hill? If it was up there, we wouldn't be able to break through or go around, would we? We'd either have to make a dejected retreat or use the heavy artillery to pummel them from a distance. Or maybe have mages charge in.

"It would be difficult to break through. In order to move swiftly forward, I propose going around."

But apparently the impossibility of a breakthrough is as far as First Lieutenant Viktor's weary brain can get. He will employ the textbook detour strategy. Well, it's true that from the looks of it we would never succeed…

That said, I can't imagine going around working any better. There's not very much cover, and the enemy is on higher ground. Before you could "move swiftly forward," you'd be shot like sitting ducks.

"Then try it, if you can."

"Huh?"

"If you think you can get around them in this steep terrain, I'd like to see you try it, dipshit! I'm telling you to look at the topography!"

Naturally, the instructor's angry shout sounds tough, but Tanya doesn't have time to savor the sweetness of another's mistake.

"Degurechaff, what would you do?"

Damn it! You owe me, Lieutenant Viktor! If you had just answered properly, no one would have gotten yelled at. She wants to glare at him, but as long as he's at a loss, the heat's on him. Even if Viktor is useless, he's a good lightning rod. I should use him like that, not tear him down. Right now I need to prioritize getting through this situation.

"Do we happen to have heavy artillery support, sir?"

It's important to get a basic handle on things. I can't imagine an infantry battalion would be bringing infantry guns into this mountainous region, but if the division has its own artillery, we could expect support. Or the corps artillery would be fine, but knowing whether we have support or not is crucial...although I'm sure he wants us to think about what we would do if we didn't have any.

Still, if I don't show that I'm trying to confirm what cards are in my hand, he'll yell at me, "Why didn't you consider heavy artillery support?!" for sure. I get it, but it's stupid.

"We'll say you don't!"

"My first idea is to make a large retreat and then maneuver around along a different ridgeline."

Then the best thing to do is avoid unnecessary casualties. Luckily, depending on the ridgeline, it won't even take any longer than any other tactic. More importantly, there's no need to launch a reckless attack. Ordering a charge against a position with a good field of fire is not only reckless but cruel.

Can guys like that get jobs in the General Staff? All I can say is I hope not. In any case, the only way to beat firepower with flesh is by having more soldiers than bullets...

"And if you don't have that kind of time?"

"...My second idea is to employ skirmish tactics with mages and infantry. The mages can take out the emplacement and the infantry can back them up."

Aerial mages could definitely capture the position. We'd have been ready to take casualties, but it would be much better than trying to break through with infantry alone. I mean, I'm an aerial mage. If you're asking me what I would do if I were in command, then it's not unreasonable for me to have mages with my infantry battalion.

Well, maybe my answer was a little sneaky, but...

"That's fine. Now how would you capture the position if you only had infantry?"

"Huh? 'Capture' it with only infantry, sir?"

...Did he trap me? Before Tanya knows it, he's ordering her to win with nothing but infantry.

"Yes. I'll give you a minute. If you don't want to sleep outside tonight, better answer quick."

Now he's just talking nonsense. If it were possible to capture positions with infantry, we wouldn't be spending all this time worrying about positional warfare. You're seriously telling me to take the hill under these conditions?

With no engineers? No mages? Are you just telling me to do this Three Human Bullets–style? I don't even have to think about it.

"Sir, I think capturing it would be impossible."

For a second, all of her classmates' expressions change. Most of them were mulling over the problem, and the word *impossible* is a shock. After all, that word could put the instructor in a bad mood. It's a comment that could lower Tanya's academic standing.

I've got a bad feeling. Why couldn't he have picked on Captain Uger or one of those guys? I want to put my head in my hands and moan about my bad luck, but I can't because my hands are full of heavy machine gun.

"What? What do you mean?"

Like a certain Empire of the Sun, our army has a reputation for bayonet charges, and if the opponent's interdiction fire is weak, maybe something could be accomplished with them. But rushing a Republican Army defensive position with bayonets would just be kicking a hornet's nest. A night assault is conceivable, but a mission on battalion scale in the dark mountains could end with us all getting killed. If we think that far and still can't calculate a decent chance of success, the answer is that it's impossible.

"What is a staff member? Going back to basics and considering my duties and obligations, I believe capturing the hill is impossible."

She makes sure she has some remarks ready to shift responsibility. People learn from mistakes. She isn't about to repeat her error of talking too much to the brigadier general in the reading room. She will make impossibility a factor of her duty, not her lack of fighting spirit.

"A staff member's duty is to pursue the best possible plan."

In other words, according to the General Staff, capturing that emplacement is impossible. It can't be done. That's what I'm saying, anyhow. Of course, a staff member has to come up with operations that will win. But there are any number of obligations that can be used as excuses.

"But piling up casualties in vain would be the most abhorrent thing I could do."

If he shouts at me that we prioritize victory over soldiers' lives, I won't know what to say, but at least I've done everything I can to avoid looking like I have no fighting spirit. In the academy, we were told over and over—and, for some reason, over again—to love our troops.

Weirdly, now that I think of it, I feel like they emphasized this the most when talking to me. It would be a shame if it was because they thought I didn't understand that we have to educate our subordinates since we can't choose them.

Anyhow, I have my excuse. My cause is just enough. I can stand tall this time and say what I think.

"In light of that, I would say that in this case, attacking the hill should be avoided."

The instructor turns a glare on her, trying to figure out how serious she is. I have zero intention of screwing around. Any businessman can stare back with that look in his eyes. The only other thing you need is the nerve to not back down under the intense gazes of soldiers and the like.

In other words, being used to it is half of the battle. The other half is having a heart that believes in inner freedom.

"All right. I'll make a note of it. Okay, we march!"

Ack, so he's going to make a note of it after all? I guess soldiers don't like the way businessmen think. Ahh, what should I do?

I want to believe I faked him out okay, but I have the feeling getting noted isn't a good thing...

The Primeval Battalion

"We've finally curbed the deterioration of the situation on the western front."

Brigadier General von Zettour, who was in charge of the Service Corps, was in conference room 1 of the General Staff Office relaying a report that gave everyone the first cause for relief in a very long time. The dire situation in the Western theater had marginally improved.

"We do, however, remain somewhat cornered overall."

A map on the wall of the conference room showed that the western army was still stubbornly holding out. Their failure to make the first move had allowed the François Republic to push back their lines, but at least the advance toward the Rhine industrial region had been stopped. Of course, the fighting strength of forces on the front lines was nearing the limit; the dogged resistance had left nearly every unit with casualties. They were on the cusp of resorting to prematurely scraping together new units and rushing them from the capital in piecemeal deployments.

Slowly but surely, pressure was increasing along the whole line. Even some of the rear positions were within range of strikes by enemy mages.

"The assembly and redeployment of the main forces of the Great Army is complete."

The Western Army Group had held out even longer than the national defense plan, Plan 315, imagined they could, and they'd succeeded in buying a decisive amount of time. It was just enough for the Empire to deploy the Great Army, its primary fighting force. The reorganization of the lines was proceeding apace.

This entailed, of course, a large-scale redeployment from the north to the west, but the railroads were an even bigger bottleneck on mobility than they had feared. As a result, everything was behind schedule. That said, with the defensive wall of the Great Army, there was still time to reorganize.

"...Although we've only just managed to make it in time."

But the faces of the General Staff did not look happy or relieved. They and Zettour were all aware of the problem facing them: the difficulty of responding quickly in the time they had. Time, time, time. It was one of the great, ever-present challenges in waging a war.

Yes, the Great Army had been redeployed in time, but the General Staff recognized that the situation had gotten down to the wire. Though they had counted on moving their forces efficiently via interior lines, it was proving harder than anticipated. That meant they couldn't hope for the strategic flexibility they had expected to have before the war began.

The standing forces from Central were meant to compensate as relief forces, but the western front had shown that deploying such a small force would be like tossing a thimbleful of water at a raging fire. Even if they could respond quickly, numbers were a huge problem.

"The Service Corps has to recommend that we focus on developing a unit capable of rapid response."

"Operations concurs that we need a mobile force that can be used at will and that has a measure of firepower."

Essentially, they had to make the Great Army easy to move. That was the military's unanimous opinion. They wanted to adjust the rail schedules to enable the smooth transport of troops on a vast scale. After all, the Empire's strategy, focusing all their strength on one front to achieve victory there, would succeed or fail based on speed.

But there was also a pronounced desire for a better quick reaction force, a reserve unit that could move quickly to address any situation, as Brigadier General von Zettour had calmly suggested and Brigadier General von Rudersdorf had seconded. It was critical to have a unit that could help fight fires when large-scale deployments would be unable to address a problem in time.

"In addition, the Service Corps suggests we look into a national defense strategy predicated on the assumption of fighting a two-front war."

Zettour's sudden additional suggestion was a reevaluation of where troops were most needed. That is, the risk that one front would fall apart while the other was achieving victory had become too great in recent years. There were many in the Service Corps, Zettour chief among them, who harbored doubts about the interior lines strategy, believing there were limits to how long they could pretend it was working.

Wasn't it time to change the military's doctrines and prepare for a two-front war? They felt it was no longer feasible to have regional commands mainly focused on defense and use the venerable Great Army for offensive maneuvers.

"I don't have any objection to research as such, but…practically speaking, we must absolutely avoid the opening of a second front."

But the ironclad rule against dividing one's forces had been constant in every era. Bring all your power to bear on one enemy, and once you've dealt with them, turn to the next foe. The General Staff saw this as the golden rule of their interior lines strategy.

Above all, Rudersdorf and Operations had a hard time denying the effectiveness of overwhelming the enemy with an all-out frontal attack by concentrating their forces.

"Operations agrees with building a shelter against every storm, but we need to prioritize finding a way to avoid a two-front war."

"It'll be difficult, considering the Empire's geopolitical situation, General von Rudersdorf."

"I can't deny that. But what you're proposing, in the worst-case scenario, would leave all our lines undermanned."

Gain partial superiority and employ the regional armies to buy time until overall victory can be achieved. It was a strategy born of the Empire's history as a polity surrounded on all sides, as well as simple geopolitical necessity. If the nation was powerful enough to put up fierce fights on two separate fronts, this wouldn't have been a problem to begin with.

"And what if things don't go so well? We have no choice but to shore up the regional armies until we can improve the functionality of our interior network."

Although the regional forces were decently sized, the Republican Army had nonetheless brought the ones in the west to the brink of destruction. The fact also loomed large that if the Great Army hadn't arrived in time, the critical western industrial area would have fallen. The interior lines strategy hinged on the premise that one front could hold the line.

Hence, Zettour and the Service Corps' claim was not necessarily mistaken that their most pressing task was to strengthen their defense.

"At present, a large-scale restructuring of military districts would be difficult. Does anyone have any other ideas?"

Reorganizing military districts was a massive undertaking even in peacetime. Trying to reorganize commands while actively fighting a war was next to impossible. It was like trying to switch all the forwards and fullbacks around in the middle of a soccer game. The best you could hope for would be chaos.

"In that case, I'd like to propose the creation of a quick reaction force. We need a unit with improved ability to theater-hop, one we can deploy when needed, where needed."

The idea of a quick reaction force was one some had been advocating for some time. There had always been those who wanted a unit on the scale of an army that could move fairly rapidly to wherever the fighting was. The Service Corps had been pulling for it recently, in particular, rallying around their deputy director, Zettour.

"That's something Operations can agree to. Depending on the scale, that is."

Operations, which had to deal with the practical employment of troops, was able to see eye to eye with the Service Corps, recognizing the need to improve their ability to react quickly. Up until now, the Great Army was intended to fill that role, but it had grown too large. Without the heroic fighting of the western army, the western industrial area would have been captured, and the Empire would be drafting provisions for peace talks.

"On that point, the Service Corps suggests beefing up the reserves by strengthening Central troops. The prompt resistance from the Western and Central Army Groups was truly superb."

That was why Zettour was making his recommendations now. They had always avoided the step of creating a standing reserve that they could deploy in an emergency to the west on the grounds that it would leave soldiers idling, but with necessity closing in, no one could argue.

"We would also have to consider the eastern and southern regional armies when conducting the reorganization."

"Absolutely. It's not right for only the troops in the west to get all the medals."

"It's skewing the war college's admissions recommendations by achievement, and they're getting more of the assignments to Central. I'm sure it irks the regional armies."

As with any organization, there would be a great many things for the Imperial Army to consider if it was going to do any restructuring. It was true that the Western Army Group had been getting an overwhelming number of decorations and bonuses because of their stalwart fighting. Budget limitations meant there were only so many awards to go around, and the other regional commands were getting the short end of the stick. It had already begun to warp the officer corps. Some officers were being surpassed by not only their own former classmates but also those who had started after them. Thanks to the flood of recommendations to the war college, the Eastern Army Group had grudgingly given up some of their slots to the west.

"I wouldn't underestimate the effect this is having."

"Indeed. Discontent is especially rife among the Eastern Army Group. They're bearing the brunt of it."

As Personnel pointed out, this was not an ideal situation from a human resources perspective. Soldiers were being left behind while the Western and Northern Army Groups amassed achievements. Those who had once been treated so well for their crucial defense of the eastern border suddenly found themselves paid less, their ranks lowered. It was only natural for them to feel upset. Brilliant deeds in battle were all well and good, but the fear of being surpassed by juniors and peers was a significant worry, though it lurked below the surface.

"The Eastern Army Group have had nothing to do with either the Entente Alliance or the Republic. They *are* holding down the eastern border, but people look down on them as freeloaders."

"Lack of combat experience is another problem. We need some kind of balance."

The soldiers' feelings were an issue, but the real problem was the imbalance in combat experience. It wouldn't do to fight the entire war with troops from the Western Army Group. They had to assume the troops in the east would engage at some point. It would be a waste to have them watch from the sidelines until a battle began in their region.

Yet transferring large numbers of veterans from the west to train the men in the east was equally out of the question.

"In other words, you want to create a unit with some degree of flexibility, drawing mainly from the Eastern Army Group?"

In that case, the most realistic proposal would be to take a unit from the Eastern Army Group to form the quick reaction force. What Rudersdorf of Operations wanted to confirm with Personnel was whether they felt forces from the east should be used to form this new unit.

It wouldn't be real war experience, but it would be more beneficial than leaving them totally bereft of any sense of meaning to their fight. On top of lessening the burden on the Western Army Group, it was also liable to reduce the amount of squabbling over the budget.

"So we'd like to attempt this on the scale of a division. Consider it an experiment in strategic mobility."

Even so, the suggestion would not go without debate. Zettour's group was very interested in this experiment in rapid deployment, but matériel was limited. If people agreed to the idea but not to the scale, consensus would be hard to come by. They proposed experimenting on the division level in conjunction with the Railroad Department, but that was too much to ask during a war. It had revitalized interest in a quick reaction force, but the opposition was entrenched.

"I'm against it. We only have two reserve divisions in the east."

In the eyes of Operations, the idea of pulling troops was out of the question given the limited number of reserves.

"That's too big a scale. Our defense in the east would be stretched too thin."

They took a lesson from the previous failure: During the reorganization of the Great Army, defenses in the west had become fragile. The whole reason the Western Army Group was in such a tough battle was that the assumptions of the national defense strategy had failed to prove accurate. Thus, although the Eastern Army Group was far from the main conflict, it would be dangerous to take too many troops away.

After all, aside from stationary personnel, the Eastern Army Group had only a single army as a strategic reserve. It was only natural that there would be objections when they were already at the minimum possible number of reserve forces and the proposal was to take even more away.

"What if we were to draw from both the eastern and southern armies?"

"Maybe after the situation in the north is resolved."

They would gain some leeway after the Entente Alliance troops in the north had been mopped up. But as a practical issue, although the main Great Army force had crushed the main enemy force, it would take time to truly overwhelm them. To take units from the east and south at this point would be like putting the cart before the horse. It was completely unacceptable to create a rescue squad at the expense of weakening their national borders.

"Then let's just try one part of it. How about putting a battalion of mages under a Readiness Command at Central?"

He appeared to be proposing a compromise, but in fact this was what the Service Corps had wanted all along. The idea of a quick reaction mage battalion had already been suggested by a group helmed by Zettour.

"Your pet project? Very well, I agree."

A battalion-sized experiment didn't leave much for Operations to object to. Their division was primarily concerned with tactics on the corps level; they could compensate for losing mages if it was just a battalion.

And actually, they would even welcome having a battalion of mages they could flexibly deploy anywhere on the front lines.

"You want to pull an entire battalion's worth of mages?"

"The eastern army should have the forces available. Anyway, a battalion of mages would be easier to transport by air. They'd be very easy to deploy."

Some were leery of drawing down the fighting power of the Eastern Army Group, but others pointed out how mobile they would be. A battalion of mages was thirty-six people. It would be easier to transport than a company of infantry.

Even if a unit of thirty-six people needed forty-five days of regulation supplies, the logistical impact would be relatively low. If need be, the unit would even be able to move from the west to the east within a day.

"Very well, then. We authorize the experimental creation of a mage battalion—under the direct command of the General Staff Office."

It was never an idea that would invite much objection.

"We'll pass on the idea of a Readiness Command for now, but let's see how the unit performs."

The Readiness Command he had tried to squeak through had been too much to ask, but they had been permitted their experiment. The creation of a quick reaction mage battalion would almost certainly lead to the creation of a Readiness Command in the future.

"All right, gentlemen, let's proceed to the next order of business."

It looked like he would be able to keep his promise. Zettour surreptitiously sighed in relief. Then he switched gears and focused on the next issue.

》》》   JUNE 23, UNIFIED YEAR 1967, LONDINIUM, _WTN_ PRESSROOM   《《《

The world war has many mysteries.

Materials from the Empire, in particular, are full of questions, owing largely to the chaos of the final days of the conflict. Both sides are believed to have committed wrong, but everything is hidden behind a thick veil of secrecy to this day. I was part of the war, too, as an embedded reporter with _World Today News_. Like so many of my generation who were connected in some way with the great war, I want to know the truth.

It isn't about assigning blame. I just want to know what really happened. I teamed up with some like-minded friends, and together we decided to seek the truth. We pitched the _WTN_ editorial staff on the idea of a documentary.

I have to confess, even I didn't know where to start. Luckily, though, I was able to gain the support of my friends and sympathetic superiors.

Still, the question of how to begin remained. What was the truth of the war? Some argued that it might be different for each person, which left us directionless. Several documents were declassified, but rather than clarifying the big picture, they only raised even more questions.

Initially, we focused on materials from the Commonwealth, which was relatively quick to declassify things. To start with, we tried researching the Dakar Incident from the latter half of the war. It was an action in the south considered by many to be a diversionary tactic.

Famously, all seven of the ships in Commonwealth Navy's Second Squadron, including *Hood*, its flagship, were sunk. How was that squadron sent to the bottom so suddenly? It had to be related to the reason the documents were classified.

We hypothesized that false intelligence led the Empire to concentrate their intercepting forces at Dakar. In other words, the Commonwealth sacrificed Second Squadron to take the focus off a planned ambush of the Empire, who was expected to win the war. Perhaps that explains why the materials were classified.

We theorized that some kind of plot was at work on the battlefield. I had heard rumors of dirty dealings during my time as a correspondent, enough to make me suspect that the documents would back up our idea. We rushed to read the declassified information, but our expectations were betrayed.

"The worst day in the history of the Commonwealth Navy was caused by xxxxxxxxxxx."

Only that single sentence was declassified, and everyone who had anything to do with the army had clammed up and was refusing to comment.

Serendipitously, it was around that time that an acquaintance of mine, a military historian, said something very interesting. He hinted that if I analyzed the battlefield rumors very carefully, I would find the truth.

For example, the eleven-character code xxxxxxxxxxx could be found all over. He speculates that it was the code name of some high-ranking officer or spy. We dubbed it the Eleventh Goddess, after the figure on the tarot card, and began our investigation.

The results were startling. The Eleventh Goddess appeared in nearly all of the Empire's major battles. The earliest instance we could find was from two years before the war. One country's intelligence agency reported her in the area of a border dispute. That led us to hypothesize that it might have referred to an intelligence agent of some sort.

But we noticed something odd. Some of those who had been on the front lines had a strange reaction to the name we picked. They claimed it was the worst joke they'd ever heard.

Perhaps there was more than one meaning behind eleven x's, and they were all getting jumbled together? We took a tip from statistics and tried using context and location clues to deduce the most logical "xxxxxxxxxxx."

xxxxxxxxxx came up most frequently in the Rhine Air Battle (sometimes considered the war's deciding battle). It was feared as the most intense combat zone—"30 percent sky and 70 percent blood"—where mages patrolled the airspace.

As luck would have it, my colleague Craig and I had been dispatched there by *WTN*, so we witnessed the scene. It had many names: "Rhine where the devils live," "the graveyard of the Named," "the battlefield where even silver rusts." They all sound absurdly exaggerated and unrealistic during peacetime, but they're true. I can say from personal experience that there was an honest to God devil on that battlefield.

For example, say I meet a friendly mage in a bar and we get along famously. Just six hours later, he's been turned into few scraps of meat and I'm attending his funeral. This wasn't uncommon. It happened to me three times.

An aerial mage officer I'd grown close to once said, "Humans cease to be human over there"—just before he was killed in battle. I can still remember it so vividly. That battlefield was a collection of every sort of human madness.

The various reports about the battles on the Rhine Front remained behind a heavy veil of *classified*s. That must have been related to the rumors about what happened in that abnormal, blood-soaked world.

In any event, the Eleventh Goddess was a supreme presence in the Rhine Air Battle. We became fixated on her. Despite knowing it is hopeless, we interviewed a number of people who were with the Imperial Army at the time, and as expected, all our investigation revealed was that the wall of *need to know* was far thicker than we imagined. One former member of the General Staff gave us a single word.

He said he wanted us to make it public when we could no longer communicate with him. I wanted to ask what he meant, but when I tried contacting him about it, I never heard back. Let the record state that I haven't been able to reach him to this day.

Out of respect for the promise I made, I'm writing here the word that he told me on the condition of anonymity.

V600.

We're going to get to the bottom of this mystery. We want to know what happened during that mad time.

(Text by: Andrew, *WTN* special correspondent)

>>>   KLÜGEL STRASSE, THIRD DISTRICT, ZOLKA CAFÉ   <<<

Really, time spent on education at the war college is a luxury. For that reason, many subjects get covered only in a cursory way during a war, but by the same token, the curriculum becomes more practical. Some people even feel that's an improvement. A track that normally takes two years to complete has been shaved down to less than one, but it's more intense. As someone currently enrolled myself, I also find it an improvement.

I would like to think my talents are in no way inferior to those of my classmates, but sitting side by side with so many future heroes makes me realize what a vast place the world is. Still, I feel lucky.

My parents didn't force me to be a soldier, but when I graduated from the military academy, they were as proud as if they'd done it themselves. I count meeting my wife, who I'm hardly worthy of, as my greatest happiness.

My daughter, who was just born the other day, is utterly precious.

Perhaps it was being a new father that made me to want to ask about something I'd never paid much attention to before.

I was in a quiet café near Saint Gregorius Church. Just as I was told, a little girl has casually dropped her rifle and computation orb on the table

Chapter V

and is ordering lunch. A member of the military police I know clued me in that she eats here every Sunday.

His theory was that it was because there were no other cafés that happened to be next to churches you could enter with a weapon.

"Captain Uger, what a surprise to see you here."

Suddenly, I find that First Lieutenant Degurechaff has followed the waiter's gaze to me. She greets me with a perfect salute. I return it and approach her seat, ordering something or other from the waiter and pressing a tip into his hand to buy us a little time alone. This won't be an easy conversation to have with so many people around.

"Oh, er, I just heard you always eat here. Do you have a moment?"

"Certainly. Please join me."

As she offers a chair, I notice how well she wears her uniform, not even a hint of affectation. Frankly, it suits her so well that if I saw her in civilian clothes, I wouldn't recognize her. It makes more sense to call her a first lieutenant than an eleven-year-old.

She doesn't appear to have any personal belongings that weren't given to her by the government. Perhaps we can include the newspaper spread across the table and the *Londinium Times* and *WTN* special issue filled with notes. Ah, yes. The war college did encourage us to learn the languages of surrounding countries. The *Londinium Times* and the *WTN* magazine from neutral zones are among the best materials that are easy to obtain. But maybe it's a stretch to call them personal belongings.

"Do you come here often, Captain?"

She stops writing in the newspaper and looks at me. Though I doubt she intended it, a shiver runs down my spine. This small girl is one of the most distinguished of the Imperial Army's mages, an Ace of Aces. Yet as a father with a daughter, there is something I have to know.

"Miss Degurechaff, pardon a rude question, but why did you enlist?"

"Huh?"

I mulled over what to ask her but decided there was no point in dressing it up. That blunt question was the result, but now it sounds too simplistic, and she doesn't understand what I was trying to ask.

Never in a million years did I think I would ever see Lieutenant Degurechaff look perplexed. She's said to wear an iron mask, but apparently she does have expressions. Not many of them, perhaps, but although it's disrespectful to say so, I am relieved to find something human about her. "Er, please don't think of it as a question from a captain. Just a curious fellow student." I don't want her to say what she thinks a superior officer wants to hear. I'm interested in how she truly feels. "With your talent, you must have any number of options. Why the military?"

If she were nothing more than a talented mage, her choices would have been more limited. The army is hungry for capable mages and snaps up anyone with aptitude without much concern for age, so it wouldn't have been terribly surprising if she had been conscripted despite her youth. If that were all, she would have been used as just another weapon.

Still, there should have been time before they pulled her in. It's worth noting that she got into the war college on merit alone. At a mere eleven years of age, she became a member of the honorable Twelve Knights of the war college, albeit the lowest-ranked one. If she had only magic affinity, she would have only been a weapon, but with her talent, she could have been a researcher or an engineer—anything at all. The Imperial University allows early entrance, and not only do they comp tuition for exceptional students, they even give stipends. Every path should have been open to her.

"...My father was in the military."

"Was? So he's... I'm sorry."

The word *was* sticks out to me, and I quickly realize the implication. It's a common story. Death is never far from members of the Imperial Army. Anyone can die at any time.

And each dead soldier has a household, the family they leave behind.

"Please don't let it trouble you. I'm hardly unique these days."

Lieutenant Degurechaff smiles, showing no sign of distress, as if to say she has already adjusted, but I can't help thinking that having to understand so much at that age is tragic. Did she join the army for revenge?

"There was no other way for an orphan like me. We have little choice in the world."

But her answer is one I never even imagined.

"But you made it into the military academy. Surely that means you could have chosen a normal high school."

She has overcome so many hurdles, and at her age. I know some who would have been thrilled to support a wunderkind like her. Why did she say she had no choice?

"Captain, if you'll forgive my saying so, I think your family must have been quite well-off."

"Not really. Happy, yes, but ordinary."

My father was a mid-level bureaucrat, and my mother from an average household. We had no ties to any higher status. My grandfather on my father's side was in the navy, so they were happy when I expressed interest in the armed services, but that was about it.

What Lieutenant Degurechaff says next shocks me beyond words.

"Ahh, I really envy you. An orphan simply has no options. All I could do was scrape by day to day."

In her mind, she seems to be going back to the times she went hungry. Though she doesn't say anything, her whole body exudes an aura that tells how terrible her circumstances were. The atmosphere becomes heavy, and before I know it, my back has hit the back of my chair. I realize I'm being overwhelmed—by an eleven-year-old girl.

"But if your father was in the military...surely, there must be a pension."

"Captain, I'm a bastard child who can't even remember her mother's face. If it weren't for the orphanage, I would be dead in the streets right now."

One of the church orphanages. That explains a lot. Though she had a rough start, she was saved by the church. Is that why she's so passionate about attending? Perhaps that's why she prays so fervently.

But even if that is true...

"But—you know. How do I put this? You're still a child. You should quit the military."

Even if there is no way she can leave in the middle of a war, she shouldn't abandon other potential future paths. These creatures called soldiers are fundamentally idlers by necessity. And yet when the time comes, they have to be prepared to die.

For a child to choose such a vocation is a tragedy.

"...Captain Uger, do you doubt my ability?" she asks me with a pale face, telling me I've gone too far. I made the mistake, if unintentionally, of showing a soldier what amounts to pity. She may be young, but she has her pride and honor.

"Absolutely not! I just can't help feeling it's wrong that a child like you should go to war."

It sounds like I'm trying to defend myself, but I mean it. Her eyes challenge me, but she is still a child, a little girl who should be protected. Who would want to send their daughter off to war?

Just the thought of sending my newborn child to the battlefield nearly drives me mad. Surely Lieutenant Degurechaff's father, who risked his life for the Empire, wouldn't want this, either. As a father myself, I just know.

"It's my duty. So long as I'm a soldier, I can't avoid it."

Her response is calm, an unfaltering declaration. She seems to embody what it means to be a soldier. This is no mere facade; it's as if, with no other way to go, she has built her self-awareness around being a member of the military.

Where is her true self?

"Do you really mean that?"

That is how I end up asking such a meaningless question. But she looks at me, and her gaze is so serious that I know she didn't miss my intention. She could never have said what she did as a joke or a lie.

What's more, she has plenty of combat experience. Her statement wasn't the empty rhetoric of someone who has never seen battle. It was an unshakable conviction coated in lead and gunsmoke.

"Captain, is something wrong?"

She must have suspected something from my worries. She probes, careful to remain polite. I find it almost unbearable.

"My wife had a baby. I hear it's a girl."

"That's wonderful news."

She offers her congratulations, but out of politeness; she even seems somewhat sad. She speaks dispassionately, less out of love for a child and more because congratulations is what an auspicious event demands. It's as if that world has nothing to do with her.

"When I look at you, I can't help but wonder if my daughter will go to war."

She has already opened up quite a bit. I even think she has shared her genuine feelings. But to my disappointment, I'm still running up against an impassable barrier of contradiction and uneasiness. "There's something wrong with a society that sends cute little kids to battle, don't you think?" I hardly know what I'm trying to say. I'm just giving voice to the emotions welling up inside me.

I can see that she's examining me. Honestly, I didn't expect to lose myself to such an extent. But once the words are out, there's no taking them back. After she observes me at length, Lieutenant Degurechaff replies deliberately, like a shrine maiden delivering a divine message.

"Captain, you're a sensible man. I suggest you resign."

It is as if our positions have been reversed.

"I never know what you're going to say next. How can you tell me to leave when it's vitally important for us to put an end to this war so it doesn't continue on into the next generation?"

"You're a man of sound judgment who knows the realities of the battlefield. Your resignation could in fact be an asset."

Think about it, she seems to say, clenching her little fist on the table to emphasize her point. *You should leave.*

"I'm a soldier, too. I don't know how to be anything else."

"No, Captain. You have a rational mind. Let me give you some advice as a fellow student: At least get to the rear before the real insanity breaks loose."

"They would never allow it."

This is war. The easy days of doing work behind a desk are over. And how can I shamefully withdraw on my own, leaving my friends, classmates, and brothers-in-arms? We vowed to fight together. I could never abandon them.

"Captain, living is a battle in itself. You can fight to keep your daughter out of the fray."

"...I'll think about it."

I have no counterargument. I oppose the idea, but I have no further way to express that. This eleven-year-old child has completely dumbfounded me. There are no words.

"There isn't much time. You should decide soon."

"You sound like a member of the General Staff."

"It's the only education I've had."

I must not have been thinking straight. Telling a fellow student at the war college that they sound like a General Staff officer is meaningless. That's precisely the type of role we're being groomed for.

If anything, what I said is a compliment—I have used that sentence in the most incorrect way possible. It makes me realize how profoundly shaken I am.

"...I see. You're right, of course."

You're right. That's all I can muster. I'm taken aback at how lost for words I am.

"Oh, our food is here. Let's eat together."

"...Yes, let's."

When I meet Captain Uger at lunch, he seems agitated by the birth of his daughter. Well, I certainly agree with the notion that becoming a parent leads to major psychological changes.

In any case, now Captain Uger will be dropping out of the promotion track at the war college. Whichever fascist advocated making your case when your opponent was emotionally vulnerable was a devilish genius. Captain Uger had enough tact not to protest the hit his reputation took when he requested a rear-line posting. With him out of the way, I can just barely make it into the top twelve of the college's hundred students. Thanks to that I'll be able to add *von*[19] to my name, even if for only a generation, and become a member of the General Staff.

I'll be able to take advantage of my experience at the war college to get a career. There will be trouble later if I rise too high, but if my rank is too low, I won't be able to act freely. In that sense, getting "superior" ratings and earning the honorable appellation of Knight of the War College seems about right. It's just a question of studying and getting along with instructors.

---

[19] **von**　Added to names of nobles. In modern times, new members of the aristocracy (semi-nobles) add *von* before their surnames in a usage akin to the English *sir* or the French *de*.

Chapter **V**

Considering my fighting spirit has come into question, my current status seems appropriate. I'll have to be a little more assertive. Luck won't always be on my side, so I need to be careful.

At least today I caught a break. I have Captain Uger wrapped around my little finger. And I've been invited to dinner at the General Staff Office tonight, so I'm sure something is up. The food in their cafeteria isn't quite as good as the navy's, but I've heard it's all right. I'll be looking forward to it.

〉〉〉　　　　GENERAL STAFF OFFICE, DINING ROOM 1 (ARMY)　　　　**〈〈〈**

While a couple of classmates from the war college were discussing their careers at a restaurant somewhere in town, a similar conversation was taking place over a meal at the General Staff Office's dining room 1—granted, the latter was constrained by etiquette and tradition.

At one point, the Imperial Army had constructed an extravagant dining room at the General Staff Office. No one much cared for it; soldiers considered it an absolute waste, and officers complained that it was inconvenient. But one word from the navy changed everybody's tune. Someone commented, "The army sure knows how to waste resources—even in their dining halls."

The navy had a laugh, but the army responded by suggesting that there should be less excess in the construction of warships, saying they couldn't understand people who went to war in "floating hotels."

Now the army was so united on the issue that any criticism of the banquet room was practically considered traitorous. Mealtime meetings would be held there just to prove that the army was using the place. Word that the opulent venue would be the site of another lunch meeting reached Lieutenant Colonel von Lergen just as he was setting his briefcase on his desk in Operations, back from his inspection tour of the northern and western fronts. He was accustomed to such conferences—it was the topic of discussion that troubled him.

"I'm against it. I absolutely oppose."

His eyes had nearly popped out of his head when he opened the letter.

He would never accept this. Obsessed to distraction, he had gotten little work done in the morning and hardly touched his food. As the lone voice of opposition among the high-ranking officers at the table, he fought fiercely to defend his position.

"Colonel von Lergen, I very much respect your opinion, but you must be more objective."

Unfortunately, his immediate superior, Brigadier General von Rudersdorf, deputy director of operations in the General Staff, did not support his perspective. After all, this was part of the tactical improvements he had been waiting for. He couldn't be expected to give up so easily. But to Lergen, who had seen the situation on the ground with his own eyes, the proposal was too dangerous.

"Giving her command of the quick response battalion is out of the question. She's the kind who won't stop advancing until everyone is dead. You'd be throwing your mages away!"

First Lieutenant von Degurechaff had been promoted to captain upon graduation from the war college. He had been afraid of this, but there was still time to change things. He had let his guard down, thinking she could still possibly be put in Technology or the instructor unit. He never imagined that the brass would create an experimental battalion under her direct command.

Oh my God! That would be nothing short of a nightmare. She's too dangerous. That paper showcases her true nature.

"Yes, we've heard your objections, but the instructors at the war college say she loves her soldiers."

It was true that some of the teachers at the academy supported Lergen's view. They said she was a bit too fond of combat.

But the instructors at the war college thought differently. They said that even under in the harshest conditions during the staff trip, she looked out for troops and avoided losses. Their conclusion was that she couldn't have done what she did without meaning it. That carried a decisive weight in the General Staff, which was made up of war college grads.

"She has a lust for battle, but she still retains her right mind and avoids any type of loss." In sum, they had judged her character to be superior.

"Don't you think you're overly captive to your prejudices?"

Chapter V

"With all due respect, have you not seen the reports from her days at the academy?"

Unwilling to give in, he had found the most damning documents about her and submitted them for consideration. But Lergen himself was a staffer who had graduated from the war college. He knew without thinking whose judgment would count for more. It was the way of the military to trust those who were closest to you.

"Ultimately, I believe we can say she has matured through education. The war college reported no issues."

If she had been the cause of any trouble at the war college, her evaluations would have been poor. But instead she graduated with honors and was selected as a knight. She was flawless.

"Her behavior isn't the result of education—it's who she really is! We can't possibly entrust a battalion to her!"

He at least had to make his opposition known. He couldn't run away from his duty as a soldier, even if it damaged his career. If she was given a battalion, it was possible that its members would all die by her hands before even encountering the enemy. As a soldier, he couldn't allow it.

"If nothing else, she's too young, and her rank is too low!"

"Lieutenant von Degurechaff's promotion to captain has already been decided. She shouldn't be stuck commanding a company; she's worthy of a battalion."

"The Empire can't afford to let a capable soldier languish. You should know that."

The higher-ups had already made their decision. Once Lergen heard Rudersdorf arguing their point, he knew he was finished. This was to help solve the urgent problem of quick response. The brass was prepared to look the other way if the problems were minor.

"Then she should be returned to the instructor unit or sent to do research. She's a child. Do you not know how innocently cruel children can be?"

He tried taking a different tack. The General Staff traditionally welcomed debate, in the belief that a variety of viewpoints reduced errors.

"Colonel von Lergen, we'll hear you out. But this matter has already been decided."

"It's the General Staff's decision. I believe you know what that means."

Conversely, once the debate was over, no further dissent was tolerated. They encouraged thorough discussion, but once policy was decided, they sought to carry it out with a united front and no hitches. Failure to fall into line meant being expelled from the General Staff.

"...Do excuse me, sir."

So essentially, they've already decided? Lergen's shoulders slumped. There had never been a day that the General Staff aiguillette looked so repugnant to him, but he could control himself. In fact, in principle, it was unthinkable that he would harry Central like this. Still, his sense of unease persisted.

"All right. A new battalion will be formed under Captain von Degure-chaff, as planned."

"Prepare a promotion to major and orders regarding the battalion command to be issued once assembly of the unit is complete."

"That's that. Let's move on to the next subject."

...Will this really be all right?

"Well, seeing is believing."

That's Tanya's honest reaction to the food sitting on the plate the orderly puts in front of her.

She knows it goes by the name *schlachtplatte*. She doesn't dislike the stuff, and it's a braised dish, which is hard to come by on the battlefield. Of course, the heat ruins all the vitamin C, which also tends to be in short supply in the trenches; only in the rear can such an extravagant dish be enjoyed.

This dining room is also used by those returning from the front, and she appreciates the idea of offering menu items you can only get back here. One could argue it was a way of showing that they were getting by with the same amount of resources as were allocated to the front and not just partying.

That much is all well and good.

The problem is the pork, which tastes not so much sour as it does like a block of salt. On top of that, it's undercooked. She can only marvel at how bad it is; if it didn't come with potatoes, she would have simply thrown it in the trash.

To add insult to injury, the bread they served was K-Brot.[20] Apparently, they do it for promotion and popularization purposes, but frankly, the navy's rye bread has better flavor and nutritional value. She would have liked to demand that they just serve the wheat and potatoes separately, like normal.

If she went to the navy cafeteria, she could get better food, she's sure, despite the fact that both places are operating on the same budget.

The reason is simple. The army would never say a word about it, but it's an open secret that because they spent too much money furnishing their dining room, they now have to budget to make up for it. Plus, unlike the navy, the army seems content with subpar food, a situation which does not inspire the creativity of the chefs—not to mention the frequent turnover in cook staff means there's no chance for skill to develop.

Supposedly, they are able to get this K-Brot because it is the cheapest, least popular kind. The food at the army banquet room at the General Staff Office doesn't even measure up to the offerings in the navy's gun rooms, let alone the wardrooms of which it is so proud. She's simply astonished at the army's staunch refusal to accept the navy's point about their budget squandering. Are they trying to beat the Commonwealth in a contest for world's worst food? Even haggis would be better.

No one would ever eat this out of personal preference.

"What do you think, Captain? It's the General Staff Office special."

No, she wouldn't come here out of personal preference, but an invitation from Colonel von Kordel from General Staff Personnel and Brigadier General von Zettour from the Service Corps can't be refused.

"To be frank, sir, I can't help but be impressed—especially the way it reminds me the battlefield is everywhere."

"Ha-ha-ha-ha! A fine answer, don't you think, General von Zettour?"

She has to take care to remain polite in her response to Zettour's

---

[20] **K-Brot**   A new type of bread of which Germany is very proud. Kriegsbrot ("war bread") is one half of the most disgusting field ration, the other half being dried vegetables, aka barbed wire. K-Brot is a healthy bread made by mixing potato flour into wheat flour to increase its volume, but unfortunately it has an acidic taste, among other things. The Empire doesn't want for potatoes, so its armies are amply supplied with K-Brot.

question while revealing her true feelings. She knows soldiers are expected to put up with poor food, but isn't this taking it a little far?

They seem to like her response quite a bit, though. Even Kordel is smiling in amusement. "Perhaps we should call this place the Perpetual Battlefield Café," he muses. "Your attitude is commendable, Captain, but please don't hold back."

"Oh no, I've had my fill. Please don't mind me."

Apparently, they aren't here for the flavor, either.

"Are you sure? You're a growing girl—you need to eat."

"I'm always doing my best to eat, sir, but I have a small stomach."

The comment comes from Zettour, whose position means he can use—and is stuck using—the General Staff Office banquet room. He probably ribs the new General Staff appointees in the same way. Tanya knows that some of the war college instructors like to joke a bit now and then.

But that's only until the meal is finished.

Kordel tells the orderly clearing their dishes to bring coffee and then leave them be for a while; that's when the real talk begins.

"All right, let's get down to business. Oh, and belated congratulations on your promotion, Captain von Degurechaff."

It was Kordel himself who authorized her to be promoted to captain immediately upon graduation from the war college. Now he seems to be making an obvious point of congratulating her.

"Thank you, Colonel."

Tanya was forced to sit in a higher chair because of her stature, but even when she straightens her back, she has to look up to see his face. Still, she expresses her gratitude in a clear voice that is the exact stereotype of what a commissioned officer should sound like.

She knows that in the large organization known as the military, examples are meant to be followed.

And in fact, the colonel from Personnel, whom she has never met before, is giving her a wide, familiar smile. He's only doing it because he's supposed to, but courtesy is never meaningless. At the very least, it's a tool you can use to probe your opponent's vulnerabilities during negotiations.

She speaks grandly, despite the total disinterest she feels. The promotion papers have already been issued.

She knows already, without the colonel's kind congratulations. Just like she knows that the really important matter is the one they are about to discuss.

"Now, we didn't call you here just to say well done on your promotion. There's also the question of your assignment."

Yes. Her path after graduation. The ultimate fate of war college graduates is decided not by the instructor superintendent but by the General Staff—that is, personnel decisions are made by a small, tight clique. Naturally, if you get on their bad side, you can expect to pay for it, but the reverse is also true.

"We'll take your wishes into consideration to the extent possible."

"I appreciate that."

Kordel says they will consider her wishes, but the message is that they will pretend to listen to her. People from Personnel don't usually give completely one-sided orders. Still, no matter how friendly they act, you can't let down your guard. Tanya knows well that these people live in a world of kind artifices. Well, she will just have to respond superficially herself.

"But I'm a soldier. Wherever I am ordered to go, I'll humbly accept."

It's a hollow remark. Saying she will humbly accept any posting is better than rocking the boat. Of course, she also has to take care not to draw the short straw.

"That's good to hear. Here are the papers that have come for you."

The colonel seems satisfied with her response. He carefully pulls out a sheaf of personnel request forms and hands them to her. They are all from frontline units, all desperately in need of both mages and officers, but she does see some units reorganizing in the rear among them. She seems to be very much in demand. Of course, she has no doubt that if she plays her hand wrong, all her choices will vanish, and she'll be sent to the worst possible place.

"Oh, and there's one from the General Staff Office, too."

The final form he holds out to her simply says that General Staff asked for her to be posted there.

"In light of your achievements, Personnel won't force anything on you. Choose whichever you like."

"So I have my pick? It's a tough decision."

Really, it only looks *like I have a choice. The General Staff Office makes the personnel decisions. I guess it was nice of them to let me know how many offers I got.*

She isn't stupid enough not to come when the General Staff calls. There's no way to refuse.

"I can imagine..."

The colonel solemnly urges her to give it plenty of thought. It's all a charade, but he looks every inch an experienced military man offering advice to an eager young person trying to decide the next step in her career. He's a fine actor. Well, she already knew from the moment he started humoring her terrible performance that this was a third-rate script with an obvious outcome.

"...However, there's no such thing as an easy job, in any era."

"Sir."

She remains bolt upright as she replies. He is busy, too. Apparently he doesn't have time to go along with this poorly written drama for too long.

"I don't know what the General Staff Office wants with you. I can only tell you I wish you the best of luck."

"I'm touched, Colonel."

The best of luck. A personal expression. The message contains his own goodwill toward her. Something makes him esteem her highly.

In other words, it's a lie that he doesn't know what they want; she should assume he does. She wants to ask if he has any information, and before she knows it, she finds herself cocking her head like the child she is.

In response, the colonel nods as if he understands, and gets to his feet.

"Very sorry I can't stay for dessert, but I must be on my way."

"Thank you for your time, Colonel von Kordel, I'll see you later."

The colonel hurries out of the banquet as if the discussion is over. Following him with his eyes, Zettour calls over an adjutant he has kept waiting nearby. Taking the stack of papers he is handed, he comes to the most important matter he has called her here to discuss.

"Let's talk about you, Captain. And let's be practical. You're going to be assigned to the General Staff. I won't be your direct superior, but I want you to basically consider yourself to be working for me."

"Yes, sir. Looking forward to it."

It's a calm, matter-of-fact conversation. But even Zettour, who has served for much of his life, would never have dreamed he would see the day when a child of eleven became his subordinate.

Even he had expected her to have a harder time fitting in at the war college. But she had the talent to be chosen as a knight, and given her combat experience, age became less of an issue.

The head of this small captain contains notions that have taught them the foolishness of judging a situation on sight. Normally, that alone would be disturbing. It's so unusual to see such outstanding ability from someone so young.

He doesn't know whether they should praise her original ideas or call her insane.

But can they use her as a commissioned officer? That's the only question in which Zettour and the General Staff are interested. If they can use her, there is nothing further to discuss.

"Very good."

She doesn't even seem hesitant about taking charge of a battalion even though she has never led a company. That suggests that she suspected this appointment was on its way.

He's heard from the war college librarians in the military history archive that she was researching battalion-scale maneuvers. She never would have thought to be so ready if she weren't completely confident. In that sense, Captain von Degurechaff, sitting before him, had become a battalion commander even before the orders came down.

"Captain, the General Staff intends to give you a battalion as soon as possible."

To be perfectly honest, it is understandable if she's eager. A battalion of mages means a certain amount of authority and combat capability that's still small enough to be fairly mobile. Many of the instructors said that she seemed to see herself as most suited for the front lines, and he can see now that they are right. They said that although she valued the lives of her troops, her combat style was bold and aggressive.

So she is both an ambitious field officer and an excellent mage. Surely she's willing to take some troops and do her thing on the forward-most line.

"I'm honored, sir."

But Zettour hopes there will be a larger role to play for the handful of mage officers who graduated from the war college. In a sense, he even sees this as an excellent opportunity.

"Good. However, the battalion you'll be given will be a newly assembled unit of mages."

"Newly assembled, sir?"

"It's just the way the organization works. Get ready—it's not going to be easy."

She will have to organize them, train them, and establish her authority over them. Without the assistance of some older hands, each of those tasks will be difficult. People create organizations, but organizations don't create people.

Thus, those who are capable of organizing things are considered pillars of the Imperial Army. That's why they are making her take on a battalion now that they've succeeded in putting it together.

"That being the case, tomorrow or the next day you'll also receive orders as a formation officer."

They say you should set a thief to catch a thief, and he figures he will take advantage of every system he can. That's understandable—it will take some doing to give a captain who has never led a company a battalion of mages.

The "formation officer" position, for example, is a relic from the Middle Ages, when mercenaries were integrated into the regular army. All you had to do to merit the title was be an officer, no company-commander experience necessary. It's a way of giving someone oversight of several mercenary units. It is also a system left over from three hundred years ago, but since it hasn't been abolished, it's still valid.

As long as it is good on paper, no one will complain. Of course, it's possible that's because no one knows what a formation officer is.

"'Formation officer'? Isn't that a rather antiquated title?"

But Tanya is a sharp one. She recognizes that it's outdated. No doubt she will soon realize that this is a way of using existing systems to cover for what he wants to push through.

I can count on this one. She's so outstanding that if she were a man, I would be happy to marry my granddaughter to her. She is so reliable, in fact, that it's all too easy to lose sight of the fact that the soldier before him is just a little girl.

"It's difficult to give a battalion to a captain. When you succeed in assembling the unit, I'll try to swing a promotion to major for you."

Perhaps he shouldn't really say that. But she will probably work harder if he can convince her that he is on her side. Creating a battalion from scratch is a lot of work. It would be advantageous if she knew she didn't have to be on guard against the Service Corps.

"…So for all intents and purposes, I'm a battalion commander?"

"You just worry about doing the job. I'll handle your assignment and promotion."

Apparently, she hasn't forgotten that she once said she wanted a battalion. She, a first lieutenant, to a brigadier general. There is no question that she is uncommonly determined and confident. And her abilities are the real thing.

She is that rare person who can be both a mage and a commanding officer. He will put her to good use, even if that means enduring the slings and arrows of the other departments.

"May I say something that is liable to provoke antipathy?"

The expression on her face is innocent, but she is being cautious enough to ask. Something liable to provoke antipathy? She's already done that. Though the rumor that she's getting a battalion after appealing directly to the brass hasn't gotten around yet, she sticks out due to her rapid rise through the ranks. But if she is acknowledging the unrest, it means she understands the reality and is asking for help.

"It's a bit late to be worried, isn't it? What is it? Tell me."

"I'll have full authority over the formation of the unit?"

"As I said, we'll do all we can to ensure you get the people and the equipment you want."

The reply to her question is clear. She can do as she likes. If necessary, the Service Corps is prepared to support her. They even got Personnel on board to some extent, as evidenced by Kordel's presence at the meeting. That was the agreement from the start. Measures are in place to accommodate her preferences for personnel and gear as much as possible.

"You can organize the unit however you like. Just keep it under forty-eight members."

He is being considerate; in a sense, it's a way of apologizing for making her build a battalion from the ground up. The sweetest part of the deal is the size of the unit. He has procured the budget for an augmented battalion. He got an exception made, given that this was an experimental unit.

"Forty-eight people? An augmented battalion. Thank you, sir."

"It only makes sense that our quick reaction battalion should be augmented. I was able to wrangle the budget for it on the grounds that it would be a brand-new unit."

All he had to do was whisper, *Can you even use an underfunded quick reaction force?* and Operations agreed to support the project. Although he suspects he also had no small help from Rudersdorf, who respected his aims.

But above all, it was practical considerations that swayed Rudersdorf's decision. A single unit near at hand that can be easily used is far more valuable than multiple forces stationed far away. Anyone would agree.

"The only restriction is that you can't draw people from the Western or Northern Army Groups. That part is nonnegotiable."

The only limiting factor is where the personnel can come from. It won't do to have her plucking elite soldiers off the front lines. That's partly out of consideration for the regional commands and Operations, but it also means that the core members of the new unit will be people without battle experience.

It'll be a good opportunity for the various regional armies to share their experience. All the better if a little goodwill between the armies allows their pipelines to be reorganized. It would benefit the Empire in all sorts of ways.

"We decided to make it a battalion of aerial mages to match your own specialty."

That goes without saying. The orders to create a unit of aerial mages have been practically issued already; it's just a matter of time. Captain von Degurechaff seems to know that as well and says nothing. *Well, dispensing with idle chatter is certainly efficient.*

"Who will I report to?"

She asks exactly what she wants to know. It would be so much easier if I could just say, "Readiness Command," but he can only offer a pained smile.

It certainly is necessary for a commander to think about who they're serving under. Her analytical approach shows how qualified she is. She is asking in earnest, not sarcastically.

"Since yours will be a quick reaction force, you'll be under the direct command of the General Staff. Your formation code will be in the V600s. Any special requests?"

"Not particularly. Please pick whatever is appropriate."

Zero hesitation. Not much interest in codes or ornamentation, then? Although she does seem to understand the necessity of having them, in terms of identifying the unit.

"Then you'll be 601. Basically speaking, you have no superior officer. Be glad. You're reporting directly to General Staff."

"Everything's coming up roses."

"Yes, indeed. Anyone would be jealous."

Being a battalion commander is popularly considered the best job—still able to go into battle as a commander and possessing a great degree of autonomy. Basically, it allows the leader to fight their own war. It's an enjoyable job for those skilled enough to do it.

Reporting directly to the General Staff makes things even better, since much of the annoying bureaucratic tape gets removed.

"How much time do I have to organize the unit?"

"The sooner you can do it, the better, but there's no set deadline."

"I see. Then I'll consider my selections carefully."

As for where they'll be stationed, the north and west don't really have the wherewithal to accommodate them because of their proximity to the main fight, while the south and east tend to be sticky politically. Most likely they'll be fairly removed from those areas, somewhere in between them. Even if his aides would be handling the details instead of him, he can guess that much.

"I imagine you'll be based somewhere in the southeast."

"Understood, sir."

As far as possible from where the fighting is heaviest. In other words, they're giving her a wink that means she has as much time as she needs to train her subordinates. The smirk on Tanya's face reminds Zettour of some unpleasant rumors he's heard about her. Supposedly, her criteria for selecting subordinates are overly strict.

"A word of warning, Captain. You have a reputation for being a bit too choosy with your candidates."

Appearing to lack the strength and talent to cultivate subordinates is a big minus. It's a given in the military that you don't get to choose your colleagues. You simply have to make the best of the situation you are given.

If you can't, then no matter how distinguished you are as an individual, you will fail as an officer and as a soldier. At best, you will be considered a lone wolf and find yourself without a friend to turn to within the organization. The packs will defeat you with their numerical advantage.

"I don't doubt your abilities, but it's not an especially good reputation to have. I suggest you be careful."

"Thank you for your concern."

She has the composure to take criticism in stride. *That's encouraging.* He suspects she already has an idea of who she wants in the unit.

"Well, you earned this through your own efforts. You should be proud."

"Pride goeth before destruction, sir. I try to stay humble."

"Great. I think that attitude will serve you well."

Most importantly, this girl doesn't let promotions and special privileges go to her head. She is relaxed and open; no matter how much favor she receives, she won't lose herself in it but only work that much harder. *She is truly a rare officer. Maybe you could even call her noble.* Nobility has, in truth, always been a way of acting, not just a bloodline. The *von* isn't everything. If the way a person comports themselves is aristocratic, then blood doesn't matter.

"I expect the papers to come through tomorrow. Stay in your quarters tonight."

"You've thought of everything."

I detect a hint of annoyance. Well, it's understandable; her rank seems to change every day.

"Just a gesture of apology on my part. Pay it no mind."

"No, thank you very much."

"I have high hopes for you, Captain. I wish you great success."

She will be granted an experimental unit. It's a serious responsibility, and he really is expecting a great deal of her. Indeed, he hopes his experiment will bear fruit.

V600.

There is no record of that formation code anywhere. With the exception of a classified handful, the materials made public after the war contain every code. Yet there is no V600 series.

The numbering system of the Imperial Army starts with the Central Forces with codes in the V000s. If all the regional armies were added together, that still only accounts for codes up to the V400s. The only exception we could think of might be a unit under Central Technology. But the materials that were made public only go from the V000s to the V500s.

Some experts point out the possibility that V600 was the code given to a special experimental unit in order to maintain an especially high level of secrecy. The fierce technological race that took place during the Great War resulted in a much more advanced world than before the conflict. Winning that race required utmost secrecy. Perhaps they set up a unit outside the normal numbering system so no one would know about it.

That suggestion was worth thinking about. Ender's team got right to work making a list of people who seemed likely to be involved in such a project. At the same time, my own team started working through the documents from the Imperial Army's Technology Division. We hit upon an engineer attached to Central.

We were able to obtain a chance to speak with him in person. His name was Adelheid von Schugel, and he was chief engineer. He headed the project that produced the Elinium Arms Type 97 Assault Computation Orb in the middle of the war, which was hailed as a masterpiece. We heard the devout Mr. Schugel attended mass every Sunday morning without fail. Thanks to the offices of the priest of the church he attends, we were able to get an interview. Luckily, he allowed us to visit, although we would be closely monitored.

Mr. Schugel was a man of intellect, as we heard. "It is my joy to welcome visitors from afar on a day I've prayed to God. It must be what the Lord wishes," he murmured, showing great hospitality to us considering we were intruding on the Sabbath.

Honestly, it caught me off guard. I was expecting an imperial engineer to be more difficult. I confessed my narrow-mindedness in doubting such a gentle person as Mr. Schugel, and asked for his forgiveness.

"You've seen the error of your ways. All things happen according to his will."

He accepted my apology with a smile, and immediately after that we asked him about the V600 unit. But the moment we mentioned it, the military police officer who must have been there to referee the interview prevented Mr. Schugel from answering. There was something there. We were sure of it.

But Mr. Schugel, with a wry smile at the MP, said something completely unexpected.

"The unit code V600 doesn't exist. But go through the records, gentlemen. Journalists need to know their history."

He was smiling wryly when he gave us that baffling reply; we decided V600 must refer not to a unit but something else, and we continued our investigation on that basis. The key was his hint about studying history.

A unit code that didn't seem to exist? No. It really didn't exist. We agonized over it for close to a month before a specialist in military organization put an end to our suffering.

A colleague from the foreign desk introduced us to him, and he recognized our mistake immediately.

"A V number?" he said. "That's a formation code."

In the Imperial Army system, unit formation was handled by the Service Corps, and Operations actually made use of the troops. The important point here is that the people doing the organizing and the people doing the deploying were in different departments. Normally, the latter would simply take over the numbers under which the former had assembled a unit.

For example, say the Service Corps created unit V101 with the intention of replenishing the central forces. Operations would put it to work as the 101st Task Force. But if it wasn't clear where a unit was assigned, they would pick a code that wasn't normally used in order to avoid misunderstandings. So obviously, the formation code V600 could exist even if no unit in the six hundreds did.

That's what confused us. We'd been chasing a six-hundred-unit ghost of our own creation. I hope you'll laugh at us. We thought we had figured out the truth, but look where it got us.

We made an impromptu decision to head for the beer hall to collect information, and I record only that we spent the entire day there. (Sadly, we weren't able to expense the trip.)

Now I understood. The wise Mr. Schugel thought we were onto something. His one mistake was thinking I'd done enough studying to understand his cryptic advice.

But now we were getting somewhere, we were sure. For some reason, we all had terrible headaches, but we started poring over the unit formation paperwork left behind by the Service Corps section of the Imperial Army General Staff Office. And we had no trouble finding what we were looking for.

Among all those neatly organized files, there was only one with the number six hundred, as if it were begging to be found. But it was practically empty. There was just one simple memo:

Attn: Service Corps, Imperial Army General Staff Office
We guide him always, abandon him never, go where there is no path, never yielding, forever on the battlefield. Everything we do, we do for victory. We seek mages for the worst battlefields, the smallest rewards, days

darkened by a forest of swords and hails of bullets, and constant danger with
no guarantee of survival. To those who return go the glory and the honor.
General Staff Office 601st Formation Committee

But what was the unit code that went with formation code 601?
Unfortunately, the file contained only that single piece of paper. The
highly charged prose was unusual, though; normally the Imperial Army
loathed anything that smacked of literary rhetoric.

Anyone who saw it would remember it. Having made up our minds
about that, we began questioning mages who were in the army at the
time. With the very first one we spoke to, we hit the jackpot. But what
he told us was deeply disappointing.

"Oh yeah, that's famous. About the propaganda unit, right? The people who actually applied came back pretty ticked off."

"A propaganda unit?"

"Right. The public relations department wanted a unit that would
'convey the justice and nobility of the Empire' or whatever."

"Hmm, we haven't seen any materials that mention propaganda."

"Well of course you haven't. If people knew they were using a big unit
of aerial mages just for propaganda, there would've been trouble."

"I'm sorry, what are you trying to say?"

"I heard there was a storm of complaints from the Service Corps and
the front lines, and they scrapped the whole thing. It's a pretty well-
known story, as I recall."

Incredulous, we spoke to several other former imperial mages. We half
hoped they'd deny it and half hoped, in resignation, that they'd say, *Oh
yes, I heard about that.*

But—and I don't know whether this is a cruel trick of fate or a happy
accident—the truth turned out to be somewhat different. Several mages
gave us strong alternate accounts.

"Yes, I heard of that. They failed to come to an agreement on the idea
of a Readiness Command, and that was the result."

"Wasn't it a propaganda unit?"

"Nah, that was just a lie. I heard V600 was the code they gave to the
quick reaction force."

"Quick reaction force?"

"Yes, they wanted a unit that could get around faster than the Great Army, but I guess it didn't work out."

That was from a former soldier who served in the central army.

"I think V600 was just a convenient way of referring to the combined Western and Eastern Army Groups."

"Did you hear anything about it being a quick reaction force or propaganda?"

"Those were just bluffs. Happens a lot in wartime, you know."

"So what kind of unit was V600?"

"The short version is that it was a reorganization of the western and eastern armies after they took a beating in the early phases of the war."

"A reorganization?"

"Right. It was easier than dissolving them."

"So what about the other rumors?"

"What I heard was that they were bluffs from Intelligence. To make the enemy worry that they were creating a brand-new elite unit."

This from a former member of the Northern Army Group.

In addition to those things, we heard every kind of speculation, from the utterly plausible to the nearly absurd. We joked with each other that we could compile an encyclopedia of battlefield rumors—but it left us unsure what to do next. The more we investigated, the more new factors bubbled up. I know they say there's no single truth, but this was ridiculous. We were completely lost.

What is correct? I decided to start with that question. We had heard a lot of different things, but something was bothering me. I tried doing a statistical analysis of the accounts we amassed. Sometimes they agreed, and sometimes they contradicted one another. That meant there had to be some seed of truth in the rumors, but they took on a life of their own; now it was possible we might never learn what really happened.

It felt like a microcosm of the war itself. Much has been said about the conflict, and everyone understands that it was an awful tragedy, but the truth of it, what really happened, remains unclear.

V600 and the Eleventh Goddess spurred our confusion.

But could they also have been the very heart of the war?
(Andrew, *WTN* special correspondent)

》》》》 **GENERAL STAFF HEADQUARTERS, FORMATION SECTION** 《《《

An office with a sign that reads "GENERAL STAFF OFFICE, SERVICE CORPS, FORMATION SECTION, 601ST FORMATION COMMITTEE" has been set up in a corner of the General Staff Office to deal with the creation of a new unit. And the office's primary occupant, Captain Tanya von Degurechaff, is confronted with the mysteries of the world, truly at wit's end.

The cause of this is the mountain of application forms that greeted her when she sat down in her made-to-order chair and looked at her desk. The huge volume might make some sense if she were recruiting fresh graduates; the General Staff paid well, so if an open call went out for new alums, even she would have considered applying.

But that isn't what this is. Although she sometimes senses that her feelings don't quite match up with other people's, this came completely out of left field. Figuring there must have been some mistake, she picks up the guidelines that were distributed to all the regional armies and goes over it word by word, but there are no errors anywhere.

We guide him always, abandon him never, go where there is no path, never yielding, forever on the battlefield. Everything we do, we do for victory. We seek mages for the worst battlefields, the smallest rewards, days darkened by a forest of swords and hails of bullets, and constant danger with no guarantee of survival. To those who return go the glory and the honor.

They will be constantly thrown onto the front lines, and the last to fall back in a retreat. It's a declaration of a perpetual battlefield where they will have to force their way into the enemy lines even when it seems impossible, with neither surrender nor retreat as options. And for taking on the toughest battles, she wrote honestly, there would be minimal reward. Surely, she had more than fulfilled her duty of explanation. She even wrote about forests of swords and hails of bullets—the fact that if applicants let down their guard for even one second, they would be dead.

The notice did say that those who survived would be granted medals or whatnot, but that's practically the same as saying they would get nothing at all.

No matter how she looks at it, it's as good as saying, *Please join me on a one-way tour of Hell, thank you very much.* Common sense told her that no one would respond to such a call.

She certainly wouldn't have answered it, and she was sure most soldiers wouldn't, either. That way, she could have stalled for time on the grounds that there weren't enough volunteers. Just a few days earlier, she was marveling that the Service Corps had allowed such an outrageous call for applicants to go out at all.

Mages enjoy top treatment as elites; there was no way they would respond to these ridiculous requirements. It was like sending a want ad to Wall Street that read, "Must work uncompensated overtime; no workers' comp; must be able to work weekends and holidays; low pay; no health insurance. Upon business success, employees are guaranteed a sense of satisfaction and fulfillment. (Chances of success are extremely slim.)" No one would expect any economists or traders to respond to that.

When Tanya sent out the brutal job description, she had counted on killing at least three months gathering volunteers. And yet here she is, confronted with massive piles of papers that tell her there are enthusiastic applicants from every regional army. It hasn't even been a week yet.

"Why did this happen...?" she groans to herself, burying her head in her hands on top of her desk. When she established this office, she requested minimal help from the Service Corps on the naive assumption that the number of volunteers would be small enough that she could handle everything herself—a move she now deeply regrets.

It's disappointing that her plan hasn't worked out, but the bigger problem is the mountain of applications so large that no one could possibly deal with it alone. She fancies herself adept at paperwork, but even she has limits. Unfortunately, it won't be a simple matter to obtain the additional personnel she needs.

In a sense, it's a failure of strategy. Improving the situation with makeshift tricks will not be easy. Part of her wants to know what in the world happened to common sense, but regardless, she has to admit that her assumption was seriously flawed. Yes, Mage Captain Tanya von Degurechaff, formation officer of the General Staff Office's 601st Formation Unit, confronted harsh reality and lost.

To begin with, being entrusted with the General Staff Office's far-reaching plan for the experimental creation of a quick reaction mage battalion was unexpected. For Tanya's part, she had simply hoped to gain some insider knowledge by showing her talent to Brigadier General von Zettour by reporting her reading of the situation. Now she's suddenly found the brass giving her a battalion to do with as she liked.

There were many times she nearly screamed, *I don't understand!* She had murmured the empty words: *As a soldier, nothing could make me happier than to be a part of this,* but deep down, the situation made no sense to her.

The magnitude of what the organization did for her, this powerful backing, is incredible. This situation is like those unbelievable sights that make people doubt their eyes. It's so unsettling, she has the urge to put a rifle to someone's head and pull the trigger just to check if this is reality.

After all, even if her permission to ignore the army's hierarchy to form her unit is only nominal, she has a practically free hand. And the unit she's forming is an augmented battalion. To top it all off, she can set her own deadline.

Tanya is at wit's end, mulling anxiously over all of it, when she catches sight of the phone on her desk and remembers something the busy-ness drove clear out of her head: She has an adjutant. Yes, she's pretty sure she was given an adjutant. Finally recalling that fact, she has an epiphany—*can't I use an adjutant as a secretary?*—and picks up the phone.

"Adjutant, adjutant!"

A week has passed since the little office was established in a corner of the General Staff Office. The moment Tanya remembers her adjutant, she picks up the phone and calls for the officer. Her head is completely occupied with thoughts of how badly she needs more people to help work through the mountain of paperwork. If possible, she wants a dozen of those commissioned military police officers, the nagging ones who never miss a detail.

"You called, Captain?"

Hmm? It's the voice of a young woman, one she remembers.

It makes her pause, but her brain is completely devoted to paperwork. She responds to the voice from the door half-heartedly, without even looking up. But this lady is reporting in for the first time. *I should at least look her in the eye.* When she raises her head and sees a familiar face looking back at her, she realizes her own features are cramping into a startled expression, like a pigeon hit by a peashooter. *It's not part of her usual repertoire.*

"It's been a long time, Captain von Degurechaff. Second Lieutenant Viktoriya Ivanova Serebryakov, reporting for duty."

The woman snapping off a perfect salute in front of her was one of the first subordinates Tanya ever had. As she returns the gesture, Tanya checks the rank insignia on Serebryakov's shoulder and sees she is indeed a second lieutenant. She must have completed the accelerated officer training program and been promoted. After reaching this conclusion, Tanya finally lowers her arm.

"It sure has, Lieutenant Serebryakov. Oh, belated congratulations on your promotion."

"Thank you, Captain."

It's a mild surprise to meet such an unexpected person in such an unexpected place.

"So you're my adjutant?"

"Yes, ma'am."

I see, so the higher-ups are being awfully considerate. Assigning an adjutant of the same gender was already quite thoughtful. She isn't planning on having her handle any personal matters anyhow, but she appreciates the thought that a woman would make things easier on her, even if the gesture is somewhat unnecessary.

In any event, Tanya was merely hoping for a competent adjutant. She's more than happy to have miscalculated. With an adjutant who is not only competent but also warrants a measure of trust, work will go much smoother. She's capable, so luckily I can work her hard.

"Okay, Lieutenant. I'm sorry for the trouble, but I need you to go tell the commander of the guard that I want to borrow a few MPs."

Really, she wants a phone line directly to the military police office, but for some reason phones that can reach outside lines aren't allowed at personal desks in the Army General Staff Office. Maybe it is about maintaining secrecy, but it's tiresome; maybe they just don't want to bother putting in a switchboard.

"Understood, Captain. How many MPs should I ask for?"

"However many are available, but I'd like a dozen if possible."

"Got it. I'll contact them right away."

The interaction went so smoothly that Tanya feels a smile tug at her cheeks. She's annoyed by the amount of work she has to do, but having a useful subordinate will reduce her burden quite a bit. Of course, she can't really say that until they have assembled some manpower. In any case, she has to deal with the fact that there are too many volunteers.

She takes a breath and gives the list a determined second look. Closer inspection reveals that, for some reason, it includes applicants from the western and northern armies, even though she was instructed to choose applicants from forces that are not currently engaged. Given the work involved in sorting through all these applications, it's probably an administrative error. Thinking along those lines, she hits on the idea that the way to fix the problem is to reissue the call for volunteers.

Her plan is to consider all the applications void on bureaucratic grounds, and put out a new notice.

"Right, I'll have to go see the brigadier general right away."

She starts counting her chickens, thinking how just protesting the number of administrative mistakes will buy her plenty of time. But she only gets halfway to her feet before she realizes she is being too hasty.

Wait, wait. You haven't thought this through.

She originally put the call out on the assumption that no one would respond. The urgent demand for combat potential and strict requirements would mean she had to scrutinize those few applications, which was supposed to buy her time. But then a huge number of people applied.

Chapter V

There is a real danger of being accused of taking too much time on the mountain of paperwork if she gets too picky.

So Tanya reconsiders. It would be smarter to form the unit as soon as possible, and then try to drag out their training as long as I can to turn them into a sturdy human shield. For her own safety, the more time she has to prepare the subordinates who will protect her the better. I'll just pretend I didn't see the applications from the west and north. At the end of my "strict screening," I'll decide to let them off this time—lucky them! They were probably forced to volunteer, anyway; they would be just as happy getting passed over and not sent to vicious battlefields where no one in their right mind would want to go. In other words, the best outcome they could hope for was not to be chosen. Overlooking them would surely count as secret good deeds.

I can actually take advantage of the fact that there are so many applicants. She'll put up hurdles to ensure she creates the best possible unit. It'll end up taking a while to form but still retain a high level of quality. If she's lucky, she can waste all sorts of time. At worst, she can expect those who survive the selection process to make reliable shields. This isn't half bad.

Yes. Having come this far, I should focus on damage control. I want to avoid making any stupid Concorde-esque decisions.

Damage control means reducing losses—in other words, not rocking the boat. If she can just do that, there will be no problems. I'll set the standards so high that they'll send even evil deities fleeing.

That's the sort of idea that occurs to someone who's in a bit of a panic.

》》》 **IMPERIAL ARMY GENERAL STAFF AFFILIATED AGENCY, RECEPTION ROOM 7** 《《《

"First Lieutenant Aisha Schulbertz, reporting for duty."

"First Lieutenant Crane Barhalm, reporting for duty."

Two young officers arrived at the capital, summoned from the eastern army. The 601st Formation Committee base had been set up in the suburbs of the city, and they arrived at eleven o'clock sharp, just as instructed. A new elite mage unit was being formed. The applicants had been told to introduce themselves, and the ambitious pair, eager to do their duty, announced their names and ranks with spirit.

"Thank you for coming. I'm Colonel Gregorio von Turner, head of the 601st Formation Committee."

He eyed them over the desk in front of him as if he could see through to their souls, and his battle-hardened aura made the two first lieutenants straighten up unconsciously.

The colonel's gaze froze them in place, but then he nodded as if in acceptance.

"I'm sure you've both been informed of the day's schedule, but there's been a last-minute change of plans."

Even in the academy, changes in schedules and objectives were commonplace.

No doubt they're looking for flexibility. After reaching that conclusion, the two lieutenants focused their full attention on the colonel so as not to miss a word.

"Scrap what you were told about reporting to Training Ground Seven by 1400 today. The two of you should head for the Sixth Aerial Combat Unit's headquarters on the double."

On the double. They figured that was the important part. It had to be a test of how quickly they could respond to urgent orders.

"Furthermore, this goes without saying, but you're both required to maintain confidentiality with regard to the selection process."

A duty of confidentiality, that makes sense, they thought. They began reconsidering how they could travel given they had to maintain secrecy. The city limits were a no-fly zone, but they could probably use regular transportation. Basically, that meant a military vehicle—ideally, one associated with Command or the military police.

"I warn you, if there is any question about your ability to maintain secrecy, you'll find yourselves returned instantly to your original unit with a note on your record."

"Sir!" they both replied.

He had hardly needed to warn them. They quickly withdrew and began conferring with each other.

"The Sixth Aerial Combat Unit's headquarters? Sorry, but do you know where that is?"

"Yeah, no problem. I'm pretty sure they're stationed at the Auksburg air base."

Barhalm had never heard of the unit or its headquarters, but luckily, Schulbertz knew it. Auksburg air base was located on the outskirts of the imperial capital. As she recalled, it was home to a transport unit capable of handling a large-scale mission. No doubt an elite unit would want some connection with the air force. And a base on the outskirts of the city would make the most sense from the perspective of maintaining secrecy.

"So it's on the outskirts, then? How are we going to get out there? I wonder if we can requisition a military vehicle somewhere."

The reasoning was simple to understand, even for a couple of young first lieutenants. But that left them with the challenge of how to obtain a military vehicle. Sadly, they were currently attached to the eastern army. They had absolutely no authority to give orders to other units, leaving them with limited transportation options. And given the confidentiality stipulation, if they showed up at the base in a civilian taxi or the like, they would no doubt be turned away.

"The MP unit attached to General Staff should have vehicles. Maybe they can lend us an extra." Thinking quickly, Schulbertz came up with the idea when she saw an approaching MP salute at them. She trotted over, confirming the officer was with the unit attached to the General Staff. She was sure they would have a vehicle of some kind, and since it would come from the General Staff, there would be no issues with secrecy, either.

"Sergeant, could I trouble you for a vehicle?"

"Of course, Lieutenant. No trouble at all."

The response came just as soon as she asked. Pleased with the efficiency, the pair said their thanks. The MPs saw them off with proper salutes, but the moment the car was out of sight, they all sighed in disappointment.

Their assignment was to see off those who had been tricked and would be flown back to their bases—but there were just so many of them.

"What's this, the fourteenth pair?" he mused. *Man, that's a lot.*

"How many more are there today? I think I heard five."

They had already been asked for a vehicle fourteen times—and that was just that day. Their superiors had ordered them to march around in a visible way. If there were only one or two, they could have chalked it up to bad luck, but with this many, the intentions of the examiner were showing.

"Oh man. I thought at least four pairs would pass."

Could they really not notice they were being tricked and sent back to their units? Those two earnest young officers would undoubtedly be put on a transport departing Auksburg and heading back east.

"Looks like Third Platoon was right."

Third Platoon had bet that no one would pass. First Platoon had bet on four pairs passing. Incidentally, Second Platoon, which had banked on at least half passing, was already out of the running. *Please, somebody pass...*

Thinking of the bottles they stood to lose, the MPs prayed fervently for the applicants' success. They weren't terribly religious, but they felt like leaning on God. No disciple is so pious as a gambler.

>>>> IMPERIAL ARMY GENERAL STAFF AFFILIATED AGENCY, <<<<
RECEPTION ROOM 7, TWO DAYS LATER

"You're saying that V601 was just propaganda all along?!"

A young second lieutenant was shouting in protest, spittle flying at this outrage. His clenched fist looked ready to pound the desk any moment. He had rushed there in hopes of helping the Western Army Group, which were still hard-pressed, only to discover that the eastern army was being given a propaganda assignment?

Everything about his body language made it clear that he thought this was ridiculous.

"Calm down, Lieutenant. Believe me, I wish I could tell you otherwise." The major facing him bowed his head apologetically. Yes, a major was effectively apologizing to a second lieutenant. He was equally concerned about the situation. But even if he couldn't say the words *I'm sorry* to the second lieutenant, he could express it sincerely through his attitude.

"...So you're telling me to just keep my mouth shut and go home?"

"Unfortunately. I'm thrilled at your eagerness. If there's ever an opportunity, I hope you'll volunteer."

The major sounded genuinely sympathetic. Maybe something in his voice reached the young officer, because he relaxed his fist, gave a perfect salute, and bowed upon exiting.

"By your leave, sir."

No sooner had the lieutenant closed the door than the image of the major wavered and then disappeared. At the same time, chairs that had been concealed with optical formulas appeared. The young second lieutenant never had the slightest idea that he was being watched while he was saying his impassioned piece. And that was why the observers were heaving deep, defeated sighs.

"This really makes me want us to work out optical formula countermeasures already," spat a commissioned officer bitterly. He was one of several who had appeared where there was only a wall a moment before. They had been watching the same monotonous third-rate production all day, and they weren't happy about it.

In the test they were observing, morons prattled on without noticing the deception, unfortunately. Their frustration was understandable.

The whole thing hinged on a simple gimmick: the creation of a false 3-D image using optical types. They would project the image of a nonexistent person behind a desk in a corner of the room, then just fix up the rest of the room with camouflage and optical formulas to hide any weirdness. It was merely a matter of finagling the interior design to conceal the strange placement of the desk in the corner.

Once that was done, it looked like the desk was in the center of the room, although it did make the room seem rather small. In the remaining hidden space sat the high-ranking officers, watching everything with obvious displeasure. The second lieutenant had been so sincere, only to have his ambitions betrayed. He had been putting on a one-man show for the distinguished panel of assessors.

Their conclusion was that being a mage didn't guarantee cognitive ability, even on a more fundamental level than common sense. The lieutenant had provided a vivid demonstration of this shortcoming and served as an apt example of the eastern army's lack of battle experience. That would be well and good if the subject of the test were the enemy army, but no general staff would be pleased to see how inept their own forces were.

"Right? Although you can hardly blame them for having tunnel vision."

Captain von Degurechaff shrugged. The members of the eastern army had been openly angered by her annoyed look until just days before, but now their faces were pale.

This was the test to select the members of her elite unit. The fact that almost no one from the east had managed to pass was whipping up a storm of anger.

She said exactly what she thought: "Incompetent, pitiful, lazy, arrogant, unprepared, mentally disabled, inattentive, no powers of observation—the worst kind of freeloader." And her conclusion was "all mages of the Eastern Army Group require reeducation"?

This was no laughing matter, at least not according to the staffers who came in high dudgeon from the eastern army to the General Staff Office. And yet what they found when they arrived was this pitiful spectacle.

"Rather than tell you about it, I think it would be quicker if I showed you," Captain von Degurechaff had said, cordially inviting officers who sympathized with the complainers to be proctors. The test was simple: If the subject could see through the basic optical trick, they passed. If not, they didn't.

The image projected in front of the applicants had no physical form. That could be concealed somewhat by placing it behind a desk, but after watching it all day even the non-mages began to notice something was off. First and foremost, the 3-D image was only pretending to move its mouth when it spoke.

Its synthetic voice, created by Captain von Degurechaff, was spouting fictitious nonsense from the side. If one listened very closely, it was possible to tell that the sound wasn't coming from the front.

Once the trick was revealed, it was irritatingly simple, but almost everyone was taken in by it. The majority of the applicants went to the air force base as they were told and were shipped right back to their units.

By all appearances, the eastern army was not likely to get off without an admonition. In fact, it was quite certain. The ranking officers from the regional field armies who had come to protest ended up bearing the brunt of the General Staff members' critical glares.

"I see now. We came to investigate when you kept failing people, but now we understand."

When Brigadier General von Zettour, deputy director of the Service Corps, turned to the men from the eastern army, his eyes were cold. *What the hell have you been doing over there?* they seemed to demand.

Deception using optical formulas was hardly new. It was even listed in mage textbooks as being especially effective against the Republican Army's disciplined fire. Not only that, but since the Republican Army often used optical formulas on the battlefield, countering them was considered a basic part of every mage's skill set. The fact that the candidates in this test failed to demonstrate even this elementary ability said something about the level of their training.

"Didn't only about half the troops from Central figure it out, even though they've got combat experience?"

"The problem is that almost *none* of the troops from the east could."

As the brass whispered their criticisms, one member of the eastern contingent felt compelled to defend his army and cautiously spoke up.

"If you'll excuse me, might this not be a question of skill rather than experience?"

His indirect question was whether the situation had been brought about by Captain von Degurechaff's extraordinary abilities. At the very least, the eastern army was aware that mages with the Silver Wings Assault Badge were a tiny minority. Hence, it was possible to wonder if the gulf was one of not combat experience but prowess.

"It's a simple illusion created with an optical formula. Such formulas are frequently used as decoys on the battlefield."

But Captain von Degurechaff's matter-of-fact answer said it all. This statement was coming from someone who had survived an entire company's fire discipline using optical deception. It carried an immense weight. And there was no changing the fact that nearly half the troops from Central who had previously seen action on the western front didn't get tricked.

"You just saw them getting manipulated like puppets by something that doesn't exist, a little bent light. Surely you understand why I don't want them in my unit."

"So what are the overall results for the eastern army?"

"Twenty-seven out of twenty-nine pairs were tricked by the illusion and returned to their units."

A nearby assistant read the report dispassionately, and even though they had spent all day watching this comedy of errors, the observers sighed.

Staff from the Service Corps were already fretting about the fact that they might actually need to reeducate the regional armies. Serious doubts had arisen as to whether they could fight a war if the troops were so easily deceived.

"Even with the five pairs out of ten from the central army that passed, that's still only enough for a company."

A mere twelve people passed the initial screening, which was conducted in pairs. Even if she took every one of them, she would only have enough for a company. Just 25 percent of her goal.

"At the moment, I'm hoping for better from the remaining sixty-five pairs in the eastern and southern armies."

Her tone wasn't entirely pessimistic, but her eyes said she didn't expect much.

"Well, this pass ratio won't do."

The verdict negated any optimism. It was as bad for those who heard it as for the one who said it. The commissioned officers from the eastern army slumped in resignation. None of them would have hoped that his unit would be branded inept, but reality was harsh. The mages of the Eastern Army Group could look forward to some cold treatment for the foreseeable future.

"Could you lower your admission standards...?"

"I would have to at least get people who could be useful after retraining. It would take time to assemble."

The openly despairing officers from the Service Corps suggested reevaluating the schedule. More than a few people were glaring at the easterners, silently asking how the hell they had been training. In any event, loosening the standards for admission would inevitably entail more time to set up the unit.

The unit's training period, which was the trickiest part, would have to lengthen dramatically. Calm acceptance of the fact would have been unusual. Bringing veterans together was one thing; training fresh recruits from square one was something else entirely. If the disparity between the members' abilities was too great, it could hinder their operations. Everyone in a unit had to be brought to a uniform level.

In other words, even if they founded the unit on the company Captain von Degurechaff had picked out so far, molding it into a real fighting force would take time.

"How much time, exactly?"

"About a month."

Ironically, it was a word from Captain von Degurechaff that saved the eastern army personnel from their predicament. When she said "a month," all attention suddenly gathered on her, the easterners completely forgotten. Selecting and retraining a unit normally took a terribly long time.

Yet she made this bold claim in front of an assembly of high-ranking officers as if it were no big deal.

She was saying that given a month, she could whip even these useless bumblers into shape.

If any other captain had said such a thing, people would think he was either a liar or an idiot. It took two years to train new recruits. No matter how experienced she was as a mage, it was madness to say this would take only a month.

The words on the tips of everyone's tongues were: *Impossible! It can't be done. Totally unrealistic.*

But the air around Captain von Degurechaff prevented anyone from giving voice to those thoughts. *Just watch me,* she seemed to say. If she hadn't already demonstrated the ability to back it up, the amount of self-confidence she was showing would have been conceited.

Each of the officers there found themselves completely overawed by a girl young enough to be their granddaughter. So powerful and authoritative was her presence that the issue of grilling the Eastern Army Group was temporarily shelved.

"Go right ahead, then. Reeducate them—and be a little rough if you have to."

General von Zettour might have been the only person in the room to have anticipated this scenario. He smirked. *A little rough.* That was his way of saying she could do whatever she wanted as long as no one died.

"Sir."

Captain von Degurechaff was wearing a smile much like that of her superior. It was a savage expression, like that of a vampire with its prey in its grasp—or of a cat playing with a mouse.

"Send today's minutes to the instructor unit as well. I want to have them retrain the southern and eastern armies."

And they were efficient. General von Zettour gave the command almost as an afterthought, but it indicated he had no intention of letting the matter of regional army quality rest. Rather, he intended to thoroughly correct the problem.

"This does not bode well. Going forward, we need to make sure everyone is on the same page with regard to training."

》》》　　　IMPERIAL TERRITORY, ALPEN MOUNTAINS, ZUGSPITZE　**《《《**
　　　　　　　TRAINING GROUNDS

"O Lord, show me the way to guide my sheep."

Eight thousand feet. A height that shatters everything we thought we knew about being aerial mages. The voice that rings out is serious. Anyone who had the slightest thought of resisting has had it trained out of them. Now we are like obedient sheep, driving our half-dead bodies to fly onward. No, we are forced to. I'm partly focused on the tightness in my lungs as I gasp for oxygen, but I still retain just enough concentration to control my orb. This all started—if my fuzzy, rather unreliable sense of time is correct—something like five days ago.

"I'm going to give you all a choice. Either shoot me down, or enjoy your training."

Our bodies exhausted, we were sleeping like the dead. At least we had beds, which was better than my time on the Rhine lines. I thought maybe this was a kinder side of Captain von Degurechaff, but after I let down my guard and went to sleep, I was woken up by a magical assault that blew the entire barracks away. We immediately grabbed our orbs and trowels and put up our defensive shells. When we crawled out of the wreckage, we were met with Captain von Degurechaff's fierce grin. I had gotten used to that smile on the Rhine battle lines, but to encounter it first thing upon waking up was worse for my heart than one of Elya's pranks.

The bayonet of the captain's rifle looked as happy as a vampire on the hunt. It seemed to be waiting impatiently for some mage to carelessly pass out in front of her; despite the darkness of the night, it glimmered in the moonlight. She fully intended to attack when she saw an opening, if the vast amount of magical energy in the computation orb she wore was any indication.

"Have I got your attention? For the next week, all of you will be conducting mobility exercises here on training ground B-113."

Three points were marked on the maps we had been given. According to the outline of the exercise, as soon as it began, we would move as quickly as possible to the first point. The time limit was forty-eight hours.

It didn't matter how we got there—what mattered was that we not fail. Marching was basic; we did plenty of drilling in the Cadet Corps. I could have done without the observer-assisted shelling and magically guided fire bombarding us whenever our mana signals were detected.

It was extremely difficult to march while concealing the signal a mage produced. I was no exception, even though I had gained some experience with it on the Rhine lines. After all, our barracks had been blown to smithereens. Our only remaining possessions were whatever we had on us when we hastily used our defensive formulas. We barely even had any water. And now we had to march without relying on magic? An actual battle would have been easier. It made me want to cry.

But when we somehow made it to the second waypoint, we received orders to begin an optical interception. Word was the artillery had too much free time on their hands, so the training program was being changed.

"Everyone, I'm quite happy to see that not one of you has dropped out." The moment we saw the captain with a rare ear-to-ear smile, we all felt a mysterious chill run down our spines. I knew that smile meant something even worse was coming and cursed God in spite of myself. *No, c'mon!*

Her expression said something like, *You haven't had enough yet? I didn't realize you were such a tough bunch,* or *Seems like I can make this a bit harder.* Curse you, God.

We had no choice but to come to terms with the fact that she would be "kind" enough to step up the training regimen according to our ability.

"You're all so good at this, you've left the artillery with ammunition to spare."

The rest goes without saying. The captain, still grinning, hurled me and all her other subordinates into a pit of despair.

"You wouldn't want them to feel left out, would you? I think you should play with the artillery." She immediately shot an infrared beam using a formula. A training round flew down the line of fire, straight for us—an attack from the artillery against our assembly point.

It was an artillery barrage against a fixed point. An attack so simple it couldn't *not* hit. *You're all so very capable. Even I'm proud of you.* How could she say such things…?

"Really quite splendid. Granted, this is training, but you've still done well evading the artillery's guided fire. As pleased as I am, it won't do for you to go without some anti-artillery training, will it? Training means being ready for anything. So as part of this joint exercise between you and the guns, you're going to defend this foothold as practice. This is a defensive battle. You have fifteen minutes to prepare your position. Oh, don't look so worried. They don't have too many training rounds. I assume they'll run out after firing for about thirty-six hours."

She was as terrifying as she was adorable. Her tone was so sunny, it sounded like she was announcing picnic plans. An instant later, I was rushing to prepare an entrenchment, practically crying. I never dreamed there might be a day a trowel would seem so important to me.

"All right, everyone. If you don't want to die, intercept. Additionally, if you wander off the route, I will personally conduct a magical bombardment against you."

That was when I started to think I really was going to die. Looking back on it now, it shouldn't have surprised me to find that there were reduced-load rounds to "wake us up" mixed in with the training shells. This was Captain von Degurechaff, after all. She was true to her word. *If you don't want to die* was no idle threat.

The artillery opened fire. I thought I was ready, but part of me couldn't help wondering how I'd gotten here.

"O Lord, protect thy servants. Show us thy glory and power."

Except for the captain, who had deployed an almost divinely powerful defensive shell, everyone was tripping over themselves to repel the incoming rounds. Judging by the distance, we had several minutes to intercept them. We had to observe carefully to find the shells on trajectories we could shoot down, and then knock them out of the sky. Easy enough to say, but horribly draining to do.

I think there were seventy-two trainees in total. That was two battalions' worth, but when it came to making observations and setting up a dense shield, we weren't very good at dealing with artillery. And anything we let through would mean immediate, major losses.

The pounding was so relentless it seemed like every battery in the area had been mobilized. If we hadn't realized we needed to pick out the live rounds mixed in with the training ones, we really would all have been killed. The shelling continued intermittently throughout the night, driving us to despair with our exhaustion and limited vision. The worst thing was that even if you did your own job, if your teammate failed to do theirs, you could be blown away along with them. And yet, if you focused only on strengthening your own defenses, someone else could get killed. All we could do was trust our teammates, and those who failed were mercilessly culled. We'd been thrown into an extreme situation that was just like the front lines. In the end, we barely slept at all.

When the thirty-six hours were finally up, the captain pointed to the radio, looking apologetic. "The artillery says they still have more ammo."

The next moment, we heard the familiar sound of something flying through the air toward us. It was very simple: The artillery had begun another salvo. But it came at a moment when we had relaxed slightly. We'd been hanging on by the skin of our teeth, and now we were shaken. My instincts screamed self-preservation, but the price was too high to pay.

We saw once again how happily the captain did what she said she would do. In the end, the barrage didn't last very long, but by that point the number of candidates had dropped to sixty. We set off for the third location on the map. The terms were relatively straightforward: Just go. There were no conditions besides the time limit. In other words, we had as good as no information at all.

"Move carefully."

With only that advice to go on, I imagined the worst. On the lookout because who knew what might happen, we marched on, trembling in fear. Once in a while, an armed bomber company would fly a search overhead, but all we had to do was stay out of sight. For some reason, we spotted military Dobermans roaming around, but we just had to avoid them, too. Of course, everything was avoidable.

Her warning left us paranoid; there had to be something. But as if to mock us, we never encountered any malicious traps. It really was just a march. Of course, the time limit was enough to make us wonder if a bunch of exhausted mages could make it, even at full tilt.

When we reached the third waypoint, utterly spent, Captain von Degurechaff was there waiting for us with a grin on her face. It was time for resistance to interrogation training.

And then, after we had survived interrogation, we were thrown into the Alpen Mountains. It was a nightmare I wish I could forget. I was crying out in a voice no young woman should ever have to make, convinced I was going to die, while the captain marched beside me unfazed. Was she an agent of the devil or of God? It had to be one or the other.

Ahh, I can't believe I have an ally more horrible than the enemy. She's not human. I would bet my life on it. Me and a few others saw it once.

During training, one of our teammates dropped like he was dead. The captain gave him a good kick, and before we knew it, he was back on his feet. I had been staring into the abyss of death myself.

But I saw something else, splat on the ground with a broken leg after an avalanche in the Alpen Mountains at 7,200 feet. I'm sure no one would believe me if I told them, but I saw it.

"You amateur. How does it feel to be a moron who slows down her team because she can't even dodge an avalanche?"

The captain heaped abuse on me. But I know. I saw it: She charged into the avalanche to save me.

Even after my friends told me that she tossed my busted body aside like a used rag, I believe. She is definitely a good commander, even if I'm not sure about her as a human being. Of course, we all laugh and bad-mouth her.

I think we've all gone crazy. Perhaps the captain's madness is contagious. But God gave me a revelation that we would save the Empire. *Be a leader among the apostles who will protect this holy nation.*

What an absolutely insane world. If the captain is an apostle of God, then only the devil can possibly exist. No, we can sense that the mythical gods are beings who have their own circumstances. Doctrine is for the gods. It's not like the gods exist for our sake.

Even so, we don't know everything.

It isn't possible to create elites in just a month. Yeah, all you need is a little common sense to know that.

But I said I would do it in front of a group of high-ranking officers. There's no taking it back.

Under normal circumstances, failure would be a major problem. It would damage my career, maybe even lead to a punitive posting to the front lines. But if I can lead them to the conclusion that the candidates were such low quality that even I couldn't teach them anything, the reverse will be true.

I'm guessing they would want to cover things up, try to pretend none of it ever happened. The Service Corps has authorized me to go to extremes.

If I train them as mercilessly as I can, push them to their absolute limits, they will surely give up.

Then this will end with everyone else getting called gutless quitters. I'll come through unscathed.

Hence, I'll borrow training methods from every special unit known to military history. The American-style stuff includes water acclimation training, but we'll do even harder altitude acclimation training. I'll make them give me all they have.

When that phase is over, next will be the infamous Hell Week. A total of four hours of sleep in four days. It's a cruel method, but when you push people to the breaking point, you find out what they're made of. Mages are capable of compartmentalizing, but there are limits. I'm doing this for a just cause, purging any fools who value themselves over their comrades.

I'm not eager to abuse my subordinates, of course. I'm not so weak-minded as to take pleasure in meaningless violence. Every vicious act will have meaning and a rationale, or I won't commit it.

That's why I welcome dropping out at any time. In fact, I wish they would hurry up and quit! I'm sure they want to escape this pressure, so they should choose to leave! Anyone who makes it through Hell Week goes straight into a week of SERE. It'll be a packed schedule of resistance to interrogation and survival training.

After that they'll have nearly gone insane, so I'm sure they'll give up, but I have a perfect plan for any war-crazy nuts who manage to hang in there.

They'll be dead from Hell Week and SERE, but I'll throw them out on a long-distance, no-magic march through the Alpen Mountains for a week.

Of course, only the absolute minimum sleep and rest will be allowed. I'm basing it on the worst battle conditions on record. How about half water rations? They won't be allowed to carry food, of course. And using their computation orbs will be an instant fail. They'll only be allowed to use a knife—one for every two people.

Perhaps it makes sense if I explain it as a General Staff trip, only harder and more elaborate. Anyone who can't cross the steep Alpen Mountains

in seven days is out. And that's quite a challenge even for someone who is in good health and properly outfitted.

If anyone makes it under these conditions, I must be cursed. But all I have to do is mercilessly fail anyone who makes the slightest error. Then things should turn out more or less the way I want.

And just in case they don't, I've prepared foolproof insurance.

Let me be clear: I don't want to have to resort to this. It's not my intention. There's just no other way that's quite so certain.

So, yes, I overcame my anguish and put this insurance in place.

I've made the new mass-production prototype developed by the mad scientist at Elinium Arms standard-issue equipment. Yes, that walking disaster, Chief Engineer Adelheid von Schugel. It's an early mass-production version of the Elinium Arms Type 97 Assault Computation Orb he's been working on.

I'm confident that we can expect accountability problems from that infuriating man.

Yes, there was a time I thought all that. So why, then? Is life just cursed? Or are the possibilities for humanity just endless? Maybe it's important to have faith.

But please remember, we must completely divest ourselves of wishful thinking. An experiential approach is always instructive.

Please remember. Many of your failures are your own fault. And often, by the time you realize it, it's too late.

Suddenly, I find myself standing on a raised platform. Maybe I'm half-asleep, because just as I'm thinking maybe I should curse my own morning-hating body and its unexpectedly low blood pressure, another irresistible wave of sleepiness assaults Tanya. But then her ears catch snatches of what her mouth is saying.

"As of today, you graduate from being worthless maggots. From this day forward, you are imperial mages. Wherever you go, from now until the moment you bite the dust, you will be bound as fellow soldiers—the members of the army are both your brothers and your brothers-in-arms. Next, you'll be heading to the battlefield. Some of you will never return.

But remember this: Every imperial soldier dies. We exist to die. But the Empire is eternal. That means you, too, are eternal! And so the Empire expects you to put up a never-ending fight."

...*Why do I have to say all this?*

I don't remember saying any of that stuff, but something remains in my memory as if I did. Before and after that is fuzzy. Unfortunately, Tanya has to admit that she has lost parts of her memory, perhaps because she activated the Elinium Type 95 during training. That is exactly why she hates it.

Captain Tanya von Degurechaff, who isn't getting any taller even though she should be growing and has trouble with equipment sizes, can't avoid feeling conscious of her height issue—especially when she is surrounded by battle-hardened women mages (rare as they were) with great bodies.

Good grief. I may be a knowledge worker, but my white-collar job required a certain amount of physical strength. I do pay attention to my diet, knowing that healthy work begins with a wholesome lifestyle, but nothing seems to come of it. Well, not that I would expect to get taller eating K-Brot.

In other words, if as an individual I want to avoid wasting my efforts, I have to grow up. That's what brought me to the military doctor, to find out why I wasn't growing even though I should have been. It's true: Before I knew it, I was even asking the doctor what I should do to get taller.

The military doctor advised me that my growth was stunted because of balance issues between my muscles and training. If I addressed that, got plenty of sleep, and ate well, I would grow, she said. The smile she gave me left me suspicious.

Immediately after, I was seized by an impulse to take my rifle and blow my head off to get rid of those memories.

She was an awfully chubby doctor, for a woman. May disaster befall the General Staff, who choose the worst times to be considerate. Was this woman showing me, *me* of all people, sympathy as a fellow woman? Irritatingly, all of this started when I was accused of resisting the form of oppression known as faith because I was a man. I didn't think it was possible, but was I brainwashed to want to mature as a woman?

No, it's very dangerous to come to conclusions based solely on circumstantial evidence. It's true that I suffered much unpleasantness because of the Elinium Type 95, but I'm pretty sure the thought control is limited to when it's active.

Looking at my records, I can't verify any ongoing manipulation of my thinking. But I do have the sense that something very unpleasant is developing. *Devils! Do you—all of you—mean to trifle with my identity as a freedom-loving individual?*

…The next thing I know, there's a rosary I have no memory of around my neck.

The Holy Mother? Yes, like you see in churches. I understand. I've often seen the sisters handing them out. But I only ever watched.

…Stop fleeing and face reality.

Why do I have this unfamiliar rosary? For that matter, when did I start losing my memory?

This is bad. I really can't trust my memories. For something I got from a church, this thing looks awfully well used. You could say it has a sense of history around it, a presence.

To be blunt, it seems like the sort of thing that—in my world—the church would keep as a holy relic. To the point where I want it as far away from me as soon as possible. If I had my wish, I would donate it somewhere. Anywhere.

…This kind of thing starts to get terribly heavy hanging around your neck.

I know I trained those candidates. It's also true that I intended to pass no one at all on the pretext of a difficult selection process. My memories of that month are clear. But something—something is wrong.

"Maybe my mistake was unconsciously activating it at eight thousand feet."

Yes, my critical error was activating the Elinium Type 95 to go higher. Maybe I should consider the possibility that spiritual corruption can build up. Rather than just manipulating my mouth for a short time, maybe it accumulates in the body like lead does.

"Get tested for spiritual corruption? But on what grounds?"

The military facility that performs our physicals is researching the effects of magic technology on thought. If I can trust them, they announced at a meeting of the Society for RTI Technology that they could tell if someone was having their thoughts influenced. Maybe I should get tested now, while I can still make sane judgments.

But the problem is finding a reason. If I'm seen as a commander with mental problems, it will threaten not only my future career but also my entire life. Women administrators are not uncommon, but in the Empire where gender equality still has a ways to go, their qualifications are always questioned. Any sort of apparent problem would not be good for someone who wants to do white-collar work.

My fretful agonizing is interrupted by a deferential knock at the door. It's Visha, who's starting to get used to being my adjutant, and from the look on her face I smell trouble. I immediately abandon my less urgent thoughts and switch gears to focus on work.

"Captain, a message from the General Staff Office."

"Thanks. Do they need a response in a hurry?"

If it's some pointless errand, I want to take my time with it, if possible.

"Yes, ma'am. There's someone waiting for you."

"What?"

After taking a glance, I snatch up a pen and read the military telegram more closely.

It's from the General Staff. I'm being ordered to finish assembling my unit and deploy immediately to a base in the southeast. Top priority.

"Captain von Degurechaff? Is something the matter?"

"…It's too soon. It's still way too soon. Lieutenant, get the General Staff Office on the phone."

I order the uncertain second lieutenant to ring the General Staff. But at that moment, as if they expected me to do that, a high-ranking staff officer appears. No, they definitely knew, which is why they sent him from the General Staff Office to talk to a mere captain like me.

"That won't be necessary, Major von Degurechaff."

"Er, Colonel von Lergen. I didn't know you were here."

It's my acquaintance, Lieutenant Colonel von Lergen. He's sensible and a good soldier who is against sending children to the front lines. "Yes. Congratulations on your promotion, Major. I've come as an envoy. I expect you have a lot of questions."

The lieutenant colonel delivers this unofficial announcement as though it is already settled. I'm not unhappy to know I've been promoted, but I smell trouble. A high-ranking official would normally never come from the General Staff Office just to deliver the promotion papers for a simple battalion commander.

"…Thank you for your concern. Lieutenant, leave us."

"Yes, ma'am. Excuse me."

I immediately dismiss all third parties, including my adjutant. I want the room to be as private as possible when we get down to business. My promotion… I suspect the battalion would intuit what it means. To put it another way, the battalion has to get ready for combat. *Can I buy some time by saying the unit lacks discipline or hasn't gelled yet?*

"Okay, Colonel. What's going on here?"

After I completed initial formation of the unit at Central, the plan was deployment to a base in the southeast. I know that depending on the state of the war, there's a nonzero possibility of going north or west, but these orders are to immediately move to the southeast.

Standard operating procedure is to give at least six months for the creation of a unit. It's altogether unclear to me why they should think my unit would be ready so much sooner.

"You've got your forty-eight people. The brass considers the unit formed."

"Yes, it's 'formed,' but it isn't a unit yet."

Amateurs often fail to realize that finalizing the members and becoming a unit aren't the same thing. To make an effective fighting force, you have to take a certain amount of time to establish a chain of command and ensure everyone can work together; otherwise, it's only a unit in numerical terms. Politician-soldiers aside, this is the General Staff's job, so I would expect them to understand.

That only makes it all the more terrifying. I have to wonder what would make them feel they have to force this, when they understand how unrealistic it is.

"Troops, equipment, no problem. The General Staff is very pleased with how efficient you've been."

"Very funny, Colonel. We're practically a training battalion—we're still working on unit solidarity, practical training, and basic consensus among commanders."

"So you're saying your unit has some operational limitations?"

"Of course. I'd need at least half a year to bring them together."

It's a given, but turning an organization into an organism takes time. Getting everyone to know one another and building the requisite relationships demands at least six months. Even if that weren't a concern, these troops absolutely need remedial combat training.

"You completed initial training in just a month. The higher-ups think they can put your unit on the front lines tomorrow."

"May I inquire if they're out of their minds? A unit that has been formed and a unit that can fight are two completely different things."

Two fully manned units may look identical on paper, but one may be fresh out of basic, while the other has combat experience and all the supplies and rest they need. The difference would be enormous. To create a well-trained, coherent organization, time is essential.

"Even if training proceeds quickly after formation, it takes time to get troops disciplined. Everyone knows that."

"So we can't send them into battle the minute they're assembled? You know, the higher-ups only think they can do this because you're commanding."

That's no answer. It doesn't even make sense.

"They're more than welcome to send me into battle alone." I can say that because I know they won't do it. It's unthinkable to reassign a commander in the middle of creating a unit, so I don't hesitate to come on strong. "If they want the battalion to display its power in battle, that's a different matter, as I believe they well know."

It is absolutely ridiculous for them to treat what amounts to a bunch of fresh graduates like they can be instantly combat ready. It's as if they are admitting that not only can we not spare the time to train the unit but also that there are no usable veterans. In other words, the disease has been revealed as terminal.

"...Major. The Imperial Army is under a lot of pressure."

"So you're going to throw an unprepared mage battalion into combat?"

"Most of the Great Army's mages were drawn off to the west, so the north is in a precarious position."

Currently, most of our mages are deployed to the west, precisely because a large number of the Great Army's mages were transferred there. Still, more than a few remain in the other regional forces. The Entente Alliance is in its death throes, anyway. The Northern Army Group can easily handle it alone.

Which is precisely why I want to know what's so urgent in the southeast, far from the front lines. Accelerating our timetable just to stick us in the back seems as foolish as ruining a bottle of wine that would increase in value with age or failing to properly store cheese.

"That's why I don't understand, sir. Why the southeast?"

If they said the north needed reinforcements, I would understand it was because they were shorthanded. Things would be crystal clear. But now they're saying they're shorthanded, yet they're sending us in the opposite direction of the fighting. It doesn't make much sense to me.

"It's what the General Staff decided."

"May I ask why?"

"There are military secrets involved. Work on your combat capability in the southeast until you receive further orders."

So he's not going to explain the politics behind the decision. In that case, all I can do is guess, but it's probably a waste of time. I can only bear in mind the bottom line, which is that a unit under the direct control of General Staff has to be sent to the southeast for some reason.

"If it's combat capability you want, sir, I suggest you use a fully trained unit."

"I presume you're already above average."

"Colonel von Lergen, I feel compelled by the duties of my office to inform you that it is too soon to deploy this unit and that doing so could hinder their preparations to fight in a useful way."

My remark is also an attempt to probe. Any battalion commander worth their salt will naturally complain about being deprived of the necessary time to get their unit ready.

"Your warning is duly noted, but don't expect this decision to be overturned."

What I get back from him is a bureaucratic response. If the hard edge in his voice speaks to the higher-ups' resolve, it unquestionably indicates that the decision is set in stone.

"Understood, sir."

So I stand down. But they could have handled this with some paperwork or written orders. Why go so far as to send someone? I can't shake the question. I find the answer in a murmur from Colonel von Lergen, almost to himself, as he starts to pack up his belongings now that his work as an envoy is apparently done.

"Oh, take this as a word of advice from someone who has lived a little bit longer than you: Since you'll be going to the southeast anyway, why not take the time to learn Dacian?"

"Huh? Dacian, sir?"

"There's never anything to lose by learning a new language, especially for us soldiers."

That is true as far as it goes. But why Dacian specifically? There are two possibilities: Dacia is becoming either an ally or an enemy. If the Dacians are going to join us, we'll have to be able to communicate with them. And if they are going to fight us, it will be useful in gathering intelligence.

"If I can find the time, I'll try picking it up. Thank you for the advice, sir."

"Not at all. Congratulations again on your promotion, Battalion Commander von Degurechaff."

⟫⟫⟫   SEPTEMBER 24, UNIFIED YEAR 1924, RANSYLVANIA REGION,   ⟪⟪⟪
TURAO COUNTY, IMPERIAL ARMY FIELD MANEUVER AREA

Only a few days after the battalion is ordered to their new base, they undergo the inspection that will conclude the initial selection phase.

Due to the tense war situation, the deployment plan was bulldozed through, which pushed the inspection up. The high-ranking General Staff officers are concerned about unit discipline because of how hastily the members were thrown together, but their expectations are betrayed in the best possible way. That day, a sight they never could have imagined leaves them gaping in amazement.

"You numbskulls. Get your asses in gear and go higher!"

"It's only eight thousand feet! You wimps. Can't you hear me?"

For some time now, an even, emotionless voice has been coming over the radio. It's hard to believe, but it's the voice of a child—a little girl. The glow of her mana blinks ominously, showing her willingness to mercilessly shoot down anyone who dared to fly lower.

"You can't? Fine. Then die. Die right this minute. If you die, the resources we're wasting on you can go to your fellow soldiers."

If anyone dared to complain, they would be the target of a serious barrage formula. Anyone who lowered their altitude without either blacking out or using up their mana first would surely be shot out of the sky. It's an absurd pronouncement, and the mages don't expect her to follow through, but they soon learn that seeing is believing.

"Okay, be a sport and either die or go higher."

Today is another day that defies precedent.

The Republican Army mages can reach eight thousand, so we should aim for ten.

So murmurs Major von Degurechaff before ordering her unit to "immediately" ascend at full speed while the inspectors look on. Normally, trying to fight anywhere over six thousand feet is considered suicidal. But she nonchalantly orders her unit up to eight thousand.

It seems crazy, but she was serious when she said she would turn this band of inept soldiers into elites in just one month. She wasn't exaggerating. She did it. She whipped them till they bled, but they were elite.

"What do you think, Colonel von Lergen?"

When Lieutenant Colonel von Lergen had expressed his desire to inspect the 601st Formation Unit, Major von Degurechaff had agreed quite readily, as if to say it was no problem at all.

And indeed, there are no problems. At least, no one has died in training so far. And the mage battalion they see before them is, as promised, quite powerful.

"It's superb."

Truly, *superb* is all there was to say. Taking the troops to their absolute limits was a stroke of genius. She kept them hovering between life and death, squeezing every last drop of ability out of them.

The inspectors heard that her program involved dramatically increasing soldiers' capabilities via what amounted to fear of imminent death. And it certainly made sense that spending an entire month hounded by a simulated terror of the great beyond would lead to a jump in ability, though you couldn't help feeling bad for the tormented soldiers.

"How can they go above eight thousand without oxygen tanks?"

The technology officers in attendance are shocked for a different reason. Granted, this is training, but they make the approach to eight thousand so calmly. It has to be Major von Degurechaff. They wouldn't be surprised to see her flying at twelve thousand feet. But it is significant that she's able to get her troops to fly so high.

"Oh, it's quite simple." This confident answer comes from the military police officer who is their guide. He sounds like he's chatting over a cup of tea. "I heard they're continually using a formula that generates pure oxygen."

It takes a second for that to sink in. *Continually?* In other words, the formula is constantly used.

"Two perpetually active formulas...?"

"Yes. It seems that was the absolute minimum required of them."

The MP is not an engineer, so he doesn't realize how revolutionary that is in the field.

The engineers from the General Staff Office, however, are amazed. A furor breaks out among them, some even whispering that it's completely ridiculous. Yes. The simultaneous activation of multiple magical formulas is, in theory, possible.

The researchers have even performed some successful experiments. But the creation of a computation orb that allows for parallel sustained formulas that can also handle combat usage has proven difficult. Where in the world did she get such a thing?

"Where the hell did she get a computation orb that can put up with that kind of stress?"

It hasn't been officially supplied to the military yet. They don't know who made the prototype, but it's clear she has some serious connections. They can only marvel.

Well, she is an exceptionally gifted soldier. It wouldn't be a surprise if some arms manufacturer asked her to test out a new device. And indeed, that's what had happened.

"She commandeered the first of batch of Elinium Arms's mass-production model."

Oh, right—it's a bit anticlimactic. She did work in tech development there at one point. It must have been a connection from those days.

But Elinium Arms is full of secret projects. It wouldn't have been possible for her to get something from them without the implicit consent of the General Staff's Procurement Department or possibly even the Service Corps Division. Otherwise the MP probably would be fighting her to the death.

"I told you not to make your maneuvers too repetitive! Why don't you realize what easy targets you are?!"

The members of the battalion are struggling to maintain stable flight at eight thousand feet. Major von Degurechaff rises above them, still scoffing at them. Her breathtakingly fluid movements make everyone realize what it means to be a Named. Compared to the tortoise-slow trainees, Major von Degurechaff flies swift as a swallow.

"Very good. All that's left is combat."

"E-erratic evasive maneuvers! Now!"

"...I don't believe it. They can perform evasive maneuvers even while sustaining formulas in parallel?"

The exercise unfolding before them is basically just the battalion mages darting around. It looks as if they're playing a game of tag, and at first glance, you would wonder if it's possible to even be that pathetic.

But for someone with the right expertise, this is a parade of the incredible. They have already realized the stable activation of parallel formulas, which should have been technically impossible. A computation orb that can handle that *and* erratic evasive maneuvers—nearly the same thing as combat maneuvers—is like a dream.

But there's more. Several of the mages have proactively deployed optical decoys to evade enemy fire.

"They're making decoys, too!"

In other words, they have enough spare resources to create an optical decoy even during evasive action.

The decoys appear quite deceptive yet rapidly deployable. Several even seem to be taking autonomous action. Truly amazing performance. And all this from something that was standardized for mass production.

"Elinium's new model is beyond anything we imagined."

This has to be the next thing we adopt. No one would say otherwise when presented with this spectacle. At the very least, reliability isn't an issue; this unit is practically conducting the endurance test.

Cost is the only hurdle, but even that would decrease quite a bit once the orb was being mass produced.

"I want the documentation from Elinium Arms."

"I'll put in the request, Colonel."

Lergen leaves that to his adjutant and looks up to the trails in the sky. *Truly amazing aerial maneuvers.* The trails are so beautiful he could practically get lost in them. *Sometimes talent and humanity show up in inverse proportions, huh?* He's annoyed to find the thought, which reveals his own unkindness, prove his point.

"This is an excellent opportunity. Show the inspectors your worth."

"Major von Degurechaff, don't you think you're going a bit far?"

A basic doubt appears in his mind as she spurs her troops on over the radio. *They say she hates losses. If that's true, then this exercise is borderline. It's certainly too much in terms of cultivating people who can be used.*

"No, we're still well within accepted parameters. Please observe the results of allowing me to pick my people and purge them of their incompetence."

But her answer only deepens his doubt. Why? The ideas of "picking" and "purging" were exactly what she was talking about in her speech at the military academy. She had said, "It is our duty to defend the Imperial Army from the plague called incompetence." She isn't developing her people so much as abandoning those who aren't useful.

"People have limits. I heard half your candidates didn't make it."

Why?

"I was able to secure the numbers for an augmented battalion. I don't have any problems yet in terms of human resources."

"I see. Very well. Continue. Sorry to have bothered you."

Argh, damn it. So that's it. Yes, I see. Resources? Human resources? Is that what you call our soldiers?

Are soldiers just replaceable parts to you?

Now I understand what felt wrong. She's treating people like numbers. That's not so unusual among staffers, but she has unconsciously started counting people as resources. Well then, she's perfectly logical. She's calculating the most efficient use of what is available to her.

"It all makes sense now. Yes, you must have written it."

I was sure I had heard of total war and world war before. The source of it was right beside me. That's why all of this seemed so familiar.

The madness of numbers. The world has succumbed to insanity. Has everything truly gone crazy?

I picked a bad time to become a soldier. This war broke out in an era full of horrible people. If some shitty God even exists, I'm sure he's in league with the devil right now.

"Sheesh, I don't know if it's her who's crazy or the world."

He can't help but think the scene before him says it all. *How terrifying to see her true nature laid bare. She is a monster.*

The sighs from the General Staff members could be impressed or apprehensive, but their whisperings and ruminations die down in the face of a single report from the border.

"Emergency. An army-sized Dacian unit is violating the border. They appear to be heading for Herelmannstadt."

Dacia, army, border, violate. He doesn't want to think about it, but when the words line up, their meaning is hideously clear. The report that came from the border like a scream meant war—with yet another country.

"The inspection is suspended! Suspended! All troops, reassemble immediately. I say again, all troops, reassemble immediately!" The air was full of shouting commanders' voices.

"The inspection of the 203rd Aerial Mage Battalion is hereby suspended! Put me through to Border Command!"

Staffers are running around shouting into radios and telephones to be connected to this and get information about that. The proceedings are abandoned. Everyone is moving at top speed, not caring about the mud spattering their dress uniforms.

Those who don't have battle stations because they are there as observers head aimlessly back to the Command Post. Lieutenant Colonel von Lergen is among them. Even moving briskly, surrounded by the cacophony, he finds a chill running up his spine.

"World war. Could something so ridiculous..."

...*really happen?* he is about to say, when he is interrupted by Major von Degurechaff, who shows up at the Command Post a bit later.

"I absolutely agree, Colonel. Why should the Empire have to take on the entire world?" It seemed she arrived after her own subordinates simply because they had longer legs. As if irritated at her short stature, she stomps her booted feet and fairly spits in indignation, "Those stupid Dacians. I'm sure they're doing it for the sake of world or whatever. They're just dying for us to burn them to the ground. Who knew international cooperation could be so awful?"

She is angry at world war itself. She's furious and assuming that it's coming.

It is absolutely absurd, but Major Tanya von Degurechaff is indignant about the insane future she's envisioning, one in which the Empire will be up against the entire world.

"Fine. Come at us, you pigs. Or perhaps I should say—we'll give you a fight!"

O God... Is this...? Is this what you wanted?

(The Saga of Tanya the Evil, Volume 1: Deus lo Vult, Fin)

Appendixes

Interior & Exterior Line Strategies /
Mapped Outline of History

Attention!
Achtung!

Interior Lines

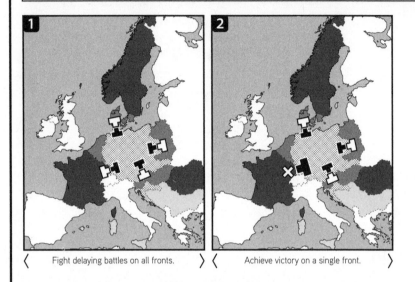

Fight delaying battles on all fronts. ⟩ ⟨ Achieve victory on a single front.

⟫⟫ The Imperial Army's Strategic Environment

The border situation compels the Empire to view every nearby country as a potential enemy.

The burden of garrisoning multiple fronts requires the dispersal of military forces, leading to each location being disadvantaged in terms of local combat strength.

For that reason, the Empire has based its national defense strategy on reorganizing its main force to be highly mobile so it can knock out each front in turn.

This is the so-called interior lines strategy.

⟫⟫ The Imperial Army's Interior Lines Strategy

(See the maps above.)

The plan is to achieve victory by overwhelming each enemy individually.

The Empire needs to secure overwhelming localized superiority and

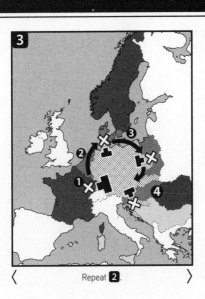

⟨ Repeat **2**. ⟩

while avoiding critical losses on every front.

The basic principle is to drive off the enemy by repeatedly winning that sort of battle.

The Keys to Interior Lines

The speed and punch the Imperial Army's main force packs.

The Empire will be victorious if it can rapidly take out the individually smaller enemies closing in from all directions before becoming completely surrounded.

If the Empire doesn't move fast enough, it will be defeated.

Exterior Lines

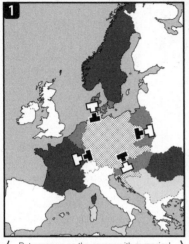

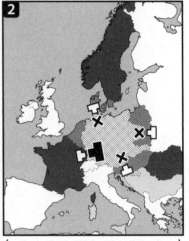

⟨ Put pressure on the enemy with numerical superiority on all fronts. ⟩ ⟨ Knock out regional defense forces before the Imperial Army's main force arrives to support them. ⟩

⟫⟫ The Strategic Environment of the Surrounding Countries

Since the Empire is too strong to take one-on-one, hostile nations aim to impose a multi-front war on it.

Due to the burden of manning on multiple fronts, the Empire has to stretch its forces thin. Since that means that each imperial position is disadvantaged in terms of combat strength, the other countries are aiming to speedily break through and knock out the Empire's defensive lines.

The overall goal is to win in each location before imperial reinforcements arrive. This is the so-called exterior lines strategy.

⟫⟫ The Exterior Lines Strategy of the Surrounding Countries

(See the maps above.)
The plan calls for pouring pressure on each front by outnumbering the Empire's forces.

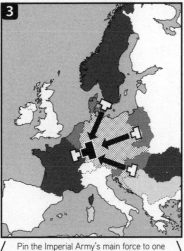

Pin the Imperial Army's main force to one front, then surround and annihilate it.

The goal is to take out the Empire's defensive units before their own units get taken out by the Empire's main force.

The decisive battle will utilize all remaining forces to surround and annihilate the enemy.

The Keys to Exterior Lines

The amount of time the Imperial Army can withstand continuous combat, as well as the surrounding countries' attack power.

If the surrounding countries can swiftly break the Empire's defensive lines, they will have the advantage.

Conversely, if the imperial forces can hold out, there is a large risk of their main unit rushing in to defeat the attacking units before allies can arrive from the other fronts.

Mapped Outline of History

Year 1

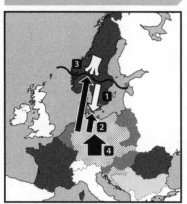

Year 1, Part 2

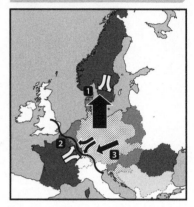

1 Entente Alliance forces begin their armed picnic.

2 Imperial Northern Army Group begins interception operations.

3 The Imperial Army advances north.

4 The Imperial Army General Staff begins general mobilization. They order their main force to execute an offensive aimed at destroying the Entente Alliance.

✓ Miscalculation on Both Sides

■ The Empire underestimated the political importance that the Entente Alliance placed on its military performance.

■ The Entente Alliance underestimated the possibility that the Empire would react to provocations with serious force.

Entente planners expected to receive concessions since it would be extremely precarious for the Empire to commit too heavily on any front.

1 The Imperial Army's main force advances north.

2 The Republican Army begins general mobilization and simultaneously launches an offensive at the border.

3 The Imperial Army's Western Army Group sustains losses in the early battles. What reinforcements that could be scraped together are deployed.

The Empire failed to understand the political reasons for the Entente Alliance to perform a cross-border attack (from the Alliance's point of view, "cross-border march") given their inferior military strength.

✓ The Imperial Army's Error

Not satisfied with crushing the Entente Alliance invasion, it aimed to take out the entire country with a major unplanned offensive.

Since the Empire's original defense plan assumed it could come under attack on any

Year 1, Part 3

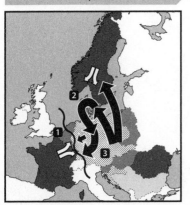

1 The Empire succeeds in delaying along the Rhine front, but the lines are invariably pushed back.

2 The General Staff orders the main army to shift positions.

3 With a few exceptions, redeployment begins. The main force of the Great Army arrives as support, which brings the fronts to a deadlock.

front, opinions were split on whether or not the military should capitalize on their momentary advantage, so they were indecisive. The idea of reducing the defensive burden to three fronts instead of four was just too tempting.

On the other hand, this action also caused the Republic to panic, fearing the exterior lines strategy might fall apart.

✓ Miscalculation on Both Sides

The Republic had no idea it would be unable to break through.

Year 2

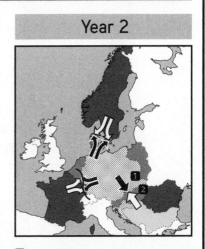

1 The 203rd Mage Battalion acquires the initial operational capabilities of the Type 97 orb.

2 The 203rd Mage Battalion is stationed near the eastern and southern lines. The Principality of Dacia mobilizes its forces.

As for the Empire, conducting the interior lines strategy with its main force out of the picture was completely impossible, and the original plan was progressing far slower than it needed to be.

Also, due to the dispersal and redeployment of its forces, overall combat strength was less than it would have been if they had acted according to the original plan, so the situation was a mess.

In the end, neither side could gain the upper hand, but neither could repulse the other, so the fighting became bogged down.

Afterword

Before I greet you, I, Carlo Zen, declare:

The publisher known as Enterbrain has most definitely got a screw loose.

The title *The Saga of Tanya the Evil*. All my religion, ideology, nationalism, etc., etc. nonsense. The whole time we were revising the manuscript they didn't ask for a single edit! How brave, am I right?

Unless this was all a bad joke, or I'm on *Candid Camera*, or there was some mistake, this book should be in your hands right now. Yes, if *The Saga of Tanya the Evil* isn't just a mass hallucination we share, then it must really exist.

And so, although I can still only wonder why, this book has gotten out and seen the light of day. I'd like to take this opportunity to thank the website where I started this novel, Arcadia (http://www.mai-net.net); the one who runs it, Mai; and all the users who left me so many comments.

And to everyone who was looking forward to this, I'm very sorry indeed to have kept you waiting. I do hope you will enjoy the modernized and repaired version of this heartful story. It's okay—it's Carlo Zen's *The Saga of Tanya the Evil*! The following warnings are for first-time readers, so if you're already familiar with this title, kindly skip ahead because it will be long and unnecessary.

*   *   *

Now then, first-timers. Greetings, this is Carlo Zen. It may be strange for the author to say something like this, but I wouldn't steer you wrong: This book is hard-core nerdy, so think very hard about whether you really want to read it.

First of all, this is a God, transsexual, transported-to-another-world novel with magic, and a ridiculously over-powered protagonist. I'll say this: I slapped the title on this thing as though I was feeling hungover, or like I'd just pulled an all-nighter, and they made it all huge and put it on the front of the book. If nobody stops us, we should probably start worrying about the future of Japan.

But this guy Carlo Zen, who writes the thing, is the worst kind of nobody. I mean, he'll coolly ask stuff like, "Why do original protagonists always succeed at stuff like domestic politics and managing national affairs?" And not only that, but if you leave him to his own devices, he'll start showing off, like, "Excuse me, have you read any books on development studies? Have you heard the latest about how a randomized controlled trial proved there is no such thing as a silver bullet?" Anyhow, he's just kind of obnoxious.

And he's incorrigibly argumentative and stubborn in this twisted way. Ahh, geez, it should already be self-evident that he's a good-for-nothing! Also this Carlo Zen suffers from a disease that makes him scoff at stuff like happy endings and the winning-is-everything mentality. It makes him adore delaying action and fighting withdrawals in the mud, losing battles, and the courage and solidarity of the international community.

If you only like dreams, hope, peace, and friendship; or you don't like it if the protagonist doesn't win; or you want a happy ending…you'll probably be better off, in an opportunity cost sense, if you skip this book.

Of course, it's true that it's a problem for me if the book doesn't sell…

And to you comrades who are like, "It's too late for us already!" and did me the favor of being tempted: Welcome to this side! We are wholeheartedly happy to have you!

October 2013 *Carlo Zen*